# A State of Treason

## By David Thomas Roberts

A State of Treason

Published in Texas by www.defiancepress.com

Printed in the USA

The Patriot Series© by David Thomas Roberts

For information about special discounts for bulk purchases or this author's availability for speaking engagements, contact sales@defiancepress.com or 888-315-9446.

Hardback ISBN#978-09905439-0-9
Paperback ISBN#978-0-9905439-1-6
eBook Epub ISBN#978-0-9905439-3-0
eBook Mobi ISBN#978-0-9905439-2-3
Also available in audio book format

Edited by Janet Musick
Cover Art by Radoslaw Krawczyk
Interior by Debbi Stocco
Distributed by Hillcrest Media Group

# ALSO BY DAVID THOMAS ROBERTS

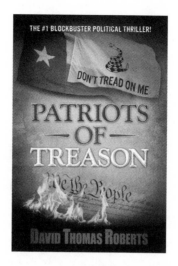

*"...so close to reality it's scary."*
~ Ken Mercer, Amazon® Reviews

*"...Wonderful read, could not put it down."*
~ J. Prejean, Amazon® Reviews

*"You will NOT be able to put this one down!"*
~ Mary Huls, Amazon® Reviews

*"If you are a fan of Tom Clancy or Dale Brown, you'll love this book."*
~ Shadow T, Amazon® Reviews

*"...masterful, fast-paced adventure that is hard to put down."*
~ P. Anthony, Amazon® Reviews

*"...had me on an edge the whole time I was reading his novel and could not put it down for one moment."*
~ R.A. "Pascual" Marquez, Amazon® Reviews

*"Fiction, but not!"*
~ Randy Councill, Amazon® Reviews

*"...better than excellent, I caution the reader to make sure you start this book when you have plenty of time."*
~ Marsha Randolph, Amazon® Reviews

*"Wow, what a ride!"*
~ Avexpert, Amazon® Reviews

# DEDICATION

This book is dedicated to James King III, Private William H. Fuller and Sergeant Thomas Nicholson.

*James King III* was a true American patriot and hero. In 1775, at the ripe old age of twenty, James picked up his musket and participated in the Battles of Lexington and Concord against the mighty British.

*William H. Fuller*, a private in Morgan's 51ˢᵗ Alabama Cavalry, Partisan Rangers, enlisted in the Confederate army with his own horse and fought under General Nathan Bedford Forrest, participating in battles at Fort Donelson, Murfreesboro, Shelbyville, Chickamauga, Maryville, Knoxville, Decatur and Jonesboro. He was one of the very few original survivors of this historic cavalry.

*Thomas Nicholson* landed at Utah Beach during World War II, advancing through France as a member of the 242ⁿᵈ Rainbow Infantry, participating in the Battle of the Bulge, and ultimately freeing the horrific death camp at Dachau. He was awarded the Bronze Star for heroically repairing vital communication lines under enemy fire throughout the worst night of fighting in the Battle of the Bulge.

James King III was my great, great, great, great grandfather. William Fuller was my great, great, great grandfather. Thomas Nicholson was my grandfather.

Defiance to tyranny is my most prized inheritance.

# FOREWORD

President Tyrell Johnson's administration was seemingly made of titanium coated with Teflon. There was no scandal too big, no corruption so sinister that it couldn't be spun to make Johnson appear brilliant. His attacks on the U.S. Constitution were couched in language that was designed to soothe or shame his political opponents, who could not muster enough support with the American people to have any effect.

The administration launched a surprise attack on Iran shortly before Johnson's re-election. It was the quintessential "October Surprise." It didn't matter that the president gave the order to attack a country without congressional approval; he didn't even consult congressional leaders, including those of his own party. Like the raid that killed a famous terrorist who was the most wanted man on the planet, Johnson's bold decisions just happened to work in his favor.

There were those who believed that, even had those events been miserable failures, they would have been spun through the most effective propaganda machine since 1930s Germany and come up smelling like roses. It happened with scandal after scandal in the Johnson White House.

On election night, when the president was celebrating his re-election victory at Lincoln Park in downtown Chicago, an assassin attempted to kill him. The assassination attempt threw the country into temporary chaos. Riots and looting broke out all over the country, especially in urban areas like Cleveland, Chicago, Detroit, Los Angeles, Newark, St. Louis and others.

As the president recovered from his gunshot wound, a full-scale conspiracy investigation was launched to determine the motives of the would-be assassin, who was killed by Secret Service agents during the attempt. When investigators found that Rashid Safly-Allah (also called Rash Sally), had ties, albeit not in the traditional sense, to local Tea Party groups in Texas, the administration and the Left saw their opportunity to discredit and destroy the Tea Party.

As the investigation deepened, the FBI learned the assassin had been motivated to act by Operation Python, the code name for the strike on Iranian nuclear facilities. The intense bombing killed Rash Sally's only living relative, his sister, who died in her own home at a site near a targeted facility.

A student at Southern Methodist University (SMU) in Dallas, Sally had been working on a master's thesis that centered on Tea Party attitudes toward Muslims. This fact, and the fact that Sally himself was a Muslim, was kept from the American people by the administration.

On specific instructions from the administration, especially the Department of Justice (DOJ), the Federal Bureau of Investigation (FBI) and the Bureau of Alcohol, Tobacco, Firearms and Explosives (ATF) began a systematic assault on the Tea Party under the guise of the National Defense Authorization Act (NDAA). Although the NDAA was approved by Congress, many civil rights and constitutional scholars decried its passage because it allowed the federal government to arrest anyone, including American citizens the administration could "link" to any terrorist group, without a bench warrant, Miranda rights, habeas corpus or due process. It even allowed for indefinite detention and "rendition" (the practice of shipping terror suspects outside U.S. boundaries to allow for torture).

Despite Sally's tenuous ties to Tea Party groups, the administration "justified" including the Tea Party with Al Qaeda, Hezbollah and the Taliban as "threats" to the United States. Under the direction of U.S. Attorney General Jamail Tibbs, the ATF raided Tea Party offices in several states, including local Tea Party organizers' offices and even their homes.

Chuck Dixon, a local businessman and Tea Party organizer in Houston, was arrested and detained at an unknown location after his wife and son were terrorized at their home by ATF and FBI operatives. The ATF destroyed the Dixons' home after a "Waco"-style raid, during which an armored vehicle punched holes in the structure to drag out a large gun safe. Dixon's best friend and fellow Tea Party patriot, Stan Mumford, was shot and killed by the ATF in front of his wife and kids on the street where they lived. Local news stations ran raw video footage of FBI agents striking elderly Tea Party volunteers in a raid on a Tea Party office in the Dallas area.

Much of the country, especially those on the Left, felt the heavy-handed actions used by the feds were warranted. However, public opinion in Texas and several southern and mountain-west states, traditionally conservative and opposed to many of the administration's actions, became increasingly alarmed. Many elected Democrats in those states were under extreme pressure from their constituents to voice their outrage in Congress.

Governor Brent Cooper finally had enough. A vocal opponent of the president and his administration, especially Atty. Gen. Tibbs, Cooper acted dramatically. Learning through local law enforcement that the ATF had secretly detained Dixon at Ellington Field Air Force Base near Houston, Cooper dispatched legendary Texas Ranger Pops Younger to rescue Dixon.

Younger, at seventy-some years of age, commanded the Texas Rangers. He was a law enforcement icon. His impressive six-foot-three frame came complete with handlebar mustache, Wrangler cowboy-cut denim jeans, snakeskin cowboy boots and a Stetson hat. He led a small group of Rangers to confront the ATF at Ellington Field. One ATF agent was wounded in the exchange, but there were no deaths, and Dixon was rescued. The daring raid made sensational news across the country.

Embarrassed at being outmaneuvered by "cowboys," the administration issued federal arrest warrants for Younger, Cooper, and other Texas officials.

Not to be outdone, Cooper and the Rangers successfully obtained arrest warrants from several Texas judges for the ATF unit at Ellington and for all FBI and ATF agents who conducted Tea Party raids throughout Texas. Younger and his Rangers led simultaneous flash raids on ATF and FBI offices in Houston and Dallas, arresting dozens of federal agents.

President Johnson was enraged. The entire country was riveted on the high-stakes drama that had Texas and the feds hurtling toward a dangerous confrontation.

Working on the attempted assassination investigation, DOJ attorney Tim Spilner became increasingly suspicious of the federal government's reporting of Rash Sally's motives. Spilner had been given top secret clearance to the files and data relating to the investigation, and it quickly became clear to him that a diabolical conspiracy and cover-up were occurring in the DOJ and the entire executive branch. He decided to take matters into his own hands. At great personal risk, he smuggled secret investigative documents to Texas Attorney General Jeff Weaver. On the same day that he sent a FedEx package to Weaver with the secret documents, Spilner and his wife were killed in a bizarre one-car accident on their way to dinner.

Meanwhile, the FedEx package sat on Weaver's desk for several days as more dramatic events began to unfold on the capitol grounds in Austin. Under direct orders from the administration, FBI, ATF, and units of the U.S. Army Rangers converged on the capitol building to arrest the Texas governor, lieutenant governor and attorney general, and to the Texas Department of Public Safety (DPS) to arrest Younger.

As the volatile confrontation grew, Gov. Cooper called out the Texas Militia and the Texas Guard, both under his direct control. As federal agents approached the capitol building to arrest the state officials, Texas Rangers stood their ground on the capitol steps. Texas Militia volunteers responded to an emergency message and flocked to the capitol grounds.

Tensions ran high as crowds at the capitol grew from a few hundred to several thousand. Return shots were fired across the street at the Texas Law Library. When the bullets stopped flying, eighteen Army Rangers, ATF and FBI agents lay dead in the street, with eleven more wounded. Details hit news agencies all over the world, causing them to break into regular programming to broadcast the drama evolving in Austin.

Explosions rocked downtown Austin as two Blackhawk helicopters the feds were to use to escort the Texas state officials to an undisclosed location were fired upon and destroyed by Texas Air National Guard Apache helicopters. Meanwhile, at Texas Rangers headquarters inside the DPS campus, a similar explosion destroyed a government Blackhawk. Pops Younger outsmarted the ATF and flanked the federal agents with volunteer Texas Militia, forcing the feds to surrender.

Shortly thereafter, an impromptu news conference was held inside the Texas capitol's famous rotunda while opposing troops were still in a stand-off. After the press was allowed to enter, the governor disclosed the newly discovered evidence provided by Spilner before his death. The country was rocked by the scandal. The lead FBI agent, Peter Hixson, seeing the evidence from Spilner, ordered the agents under his command to immediately stand down. The governor ordered them to surrender their weapons, which were placed in a pile on the capitol lawn, not far from a statue honoring Confederate cavalry heroes, Terry's Texas Rangers. News feeds broadcast the U.S. Army Rangers, and FBI and ATF agents surrendering their weapons, shocking the rest of the country.

With hundreds in custody, the governor agreed to allow any agents who signed a non-aggression agreement with Texas, including an agreement never to step foot in Texas again, to be transported by school buses to Austin's airport, where a C-130 transport landed to pick them up. The outrage of the Tea Party raids and armed incursion onto the Texas capitol grounds galvanized Texans. By the time the school buses were loaded early the next morning, thousands lined the route from downtown Austin to the airport, waving Lone Star flags, the infamous Gonzales Battle Flag with its famous single cannon and "Come and Take It" moniker, and the flag adopted by most of the Tea Party—the popular yellow Gadsden flag. Many shouted at the buses and some even threw rocks.

The governor called a special session of the legislature and demanded that impeachment proceedings be started in Congress over the conspiracy facts revealed from the Sally investigation documents. Unless Congress voted to start impeachment proceedings against Johnson, a non-binding resolution would be placed in the legislative session calling for a vote by Texans for Texas independence.

The administration, now adept at winning the propaganda wars and who also had the mainstream media doing its bidding, went into full demonization of Texas, its governor, the Tea Party, and the leak of top-secret information. Using practically all the political capital at their disposal, the administration and the Democrats completely defeated any chance of an impeachment vote, despite many southern Democrats voicing their support. The vote never made it out of committee.

Ironically, the Texas "story" had pushed the Sally investigation conspiracy and cover-up back into page two news, just like so many other Johnson administration scandals. None of the mainstream media types were keeping the story front and center. The ongoing news feeds now were about what to do with the Texas "problem." Many in the country were outraged at the eighteen deaths, the surrender of the feds, the ability of the Texas Guard to lock down U.S. military bases in Texas, and the humiliation of the school bus rides to the airport of federal agents and U.S. Army Rangers while onlookers jeered them.

The Texas Legislature convened and, as promised, put a resolution for Texas independence to a vote. The measure passed on the same day evidence was presented to news organizations that showed that Tim Spilner and his wife were killed in a car in which the accelerator and brakes had been tampered with.

Johnson was livid when the vote to secede from the Union passed with sixty-eight percent of Texans voting for secession. With cabinet approval, he decided that the insolence of the Texas Militia in taking over military bases throughout the state, and the incidents in Austin, deserved tough punishment.

He ordered federal troops to all major highway intersections, and restricted air travel to and from Texas. He also placed U.S. Navy ships in the Gulf of Mexico, with orders not to let any ships in or out.

Johnson issued orders to stop any federal payments to Texans, including Social Security, veteran's benefits and Medicaid, with the hope that Texas citizens would put pressure on the governor to surrender to federal authorities. The president stopped all banking transactions going into or coming out of Texas, isolating Texas banks particularly from access to the nation's banking system.

Not content with these drastic measures, Johnson ordered the Internal Revenue Service (IRS) to initiate actions against anyone in Texas with ties to Tea Party activism or organizations, including any who had donated to a Tea Party candidate.

The National Security Agency (NSA) and Department of Homeland Security (DHS) began intense investigations of phone records and emails to assist the IRS in identifying its targets.

President Johnson called a press conference hours after the independence vote. He was visibly indignant and agitated, even worse than when his assault weapons ban failed. The stakes, already high with mutual arrest warrants issued, reached fever pitch.

Accompanied by his entire cabinet, the president strode to the podium in the blue-carpeted East Room of the White House. He stared for several seconds into the cameras. He was a master at manipulating speaking opportunities, and this was high drama. Finally, he spoke, reading from teleprompters at each side of the podium.

"This vote is unconstitutional and it is illegal," the president proclaimed. "The state leadership of Texas continues to thumb its nose at the rule of law and the federal government. As I have stated previously, this is treasonous. The entire state of Texas, led by its state government, is in A STATE OF TREASON!"

# CHAPTER 1

*"The pursuit of Liberty is never convenient and often demands blood as the price to achieve it — and to keep it. Liberty is never permanent, for to believe in its permanence is most assuredly its ultimate destruction."*

~ David Thomas Roberts, Author

C huck Dixon crammed into the small rental sedan, barely able to get his knees under the steering wheel. After the events in Austin over the last ten days, he was fortunate to get a rental car at all. He couldn't remember when he'd last driven a subcompact.

The line leaving the parking lot was long; only one attendant booth was open. When Chuck finally reached the attendant, he rolled down his window and gave his driver's license and rental contract to the young man. The attendant looked at the contract, then compared it to Chuck's driver's license. His face lit up.

"Mr. Dixon, is that really you?"

"Uh—yes," Chuck replied hesitantly, unsure why the attendant was so excited.

"Oh, my God! I can't believe it's you! Mr. Dixon, we are all so proud of you. Oh, my gosh, wait 'til I tell my family. Wait…"

"Okay, thank you," Chuck said.

The attendant handed Chuck his license and the paperwork. Chuck slipped his license back into his billfold and put the forms in the glove compartment. As he reached for the button to roll the window up, the attendant shoved a piece of paper and a pen at him.

"Sir, could you please sign this for me?"

Nobody had ever asked Chuck for his autograph unless it was on a contract, loan document, check or some other important instrument. "Sure," he said, "what's your name?"

"Steven, sir."

"Okay, Steven, here you go." Chuck scribbled a note, and handed the paper back to the kid. It said, "Steven, God Bless Texas. Best regards. Chuck Dixon."

Steven read the inscription and blurted, "Sir, I'm so honored to meet you. I'm sorry about what happened to you and your house. I've never been prouder to be a Texan than I have been over the last few days. Again, thank you, sir!"

"Listen, Steven, we all have to pull together. We'll be fine, and so will Texas."

Steven lifted the gate, and Chuck drove off. As he did, he glanced back toward the gate to see Steven point to his car as he drove away as if to tell the next person in line at the booth he just met someone famous. Chuck smiled at Steven's exuberance.

As he tried to get comfortable in the small car, Chuck's thoughts turned to his wife Christy and son Colton.

The Dixons' house had been destroyed by the ATF raid when Chuck was taken into custody. As a result, Christy and Colton had been temporarily relocated to a remote and private Hill Country ranch.

After the climax of the tense stand-off in Austin, the family had been flown back to the Houston area by private jet, and Chuck knew his family was anxiously awaiting his arrival at a friend's home. He picked up his cell phone and called Christy.

"Hey, baby, I'm finally on the road."

"Chuck, are you sure that's safe?" she asked. "Why wouldn't you let the Rangers bring you back?"

"I need time to think and de-compress. I'll be fine."

"Sweetheart, I am so worried about them coming back for you." He heard her voice break.

"Babe, I think we chased them out of Texas for now," he laughed. But he knew, deep down, that this entire episode was far from over.

"When do you think you'll be here?"

"Probably around eight. The traffic leaving Austin is a little worse than I thought."

"Chuck, people are already here waiting for you."

He sighed. He was tired, somewhat frazzled and not looking forward to being around people again. He just wanted to get home and be with his family.

"Really? Damn! How did they find out?" Chuck thought where he was staying was to be kept quiet for now.

"I think Jane told one or two of the group and word just kind of spread," said Christy.

Jane was a member of the local Tea Party group Chuck and Stan Mumford had organized from scratch. The group had grown to a sizeable organization and was one of those that drew the attention of federal agents.

"Okay," he said, "but can you tell them I can only spend thirty minutes with them? Make up some excuse. I'll spend time with everyone as soon as I can, but tonight I want to be with you and Colton."

"We want to be with you, too, darlin'." He sensed the love in her voice, along with a wariness he knew came from the recent events. "I wish we had a home to go to."

"We will have, babe. We'll figure this out, I promise. Maybe the house can be repaired or rebuilt. Have you been back over there?"

"No, but some of the folks put tarps over the roof and other damaged areas to keep rain out," she told him. "They brought us clothes, including some for you. It's strange; news reporters are staking out the house and it has become something of a tourist attraction. A steady stream of cars passes by at all hours of the day. Chuck, there are hundreds of Texas flags in the front yard, placed there by complete strangers!"

"Wow! It's awesome that some of our friends thought enough to tarp the house."

"Well, you know what kind of people these are."

"Yes, I do."

"And Chuck, they know what kind of person you are."

Chuck tried to say something, but the weight of the last ten days was almost more than he could bear. He choked up as he tried to hold back tears.

"Okay, babe. I'll see you in a couple of hours."

He ended the call. As he drove, he mentally reviewed the events of the last few days, thinking about the cloud of uncertainty that hung over the immediate future.

A non-binding resolution had been passed for Texas to peacefully secede and once again become an independent republic, yet there was no conciliatory sign from either President Johnson or his administration. This administration had become the most effective in American history at managing its message to the public, manipulating the media, and swaying public opinion, even to the point of blatant lies and deception.

Just like the notorious gun-running scheme in Mexico, the administration seemed poised to completely dodge the criminal conspiracy in the Rash Sally investigation, despite indisputable evidence. There had been no federal investigation into Stan Mumford's murder, even with eyewitness accounts. Never in American history had an administration been this evil, Chuck thought.

"Why doesn't America care?" he said aloud without even realizing it.

Thinking back to the U.S. Constitution, he tried to remember if the Founders had created enough checks and balances to take on an executive branch that had become insidiously autonomous. When the executive branch controlled all levels of law enforcement, who could or would arrest the president or the attorney general if they acted criminally?

As the sun set, Chuck drove east into the darkness, wondering how the country got to this point. Would the evidence of the tampering of the vehicle that ultimately killed Tim Spilner and his wife turn public opinion? He was so deep in thought that he almost ran a red light going through one of the small towns on the route back to Houston.

As he came within blocks of his friend's expansive home, he spotted vehicles parked on both sides of the street as far as he could see. Lone Star flags lined the block, especially the dozens that adorned his friend's yard.

As he passed the mailbox, a man standing outside the friend's house recognized Chuck. He stepped out from the curb and waved Chuck down.

"Mr. Dixon, we have a parking spot just for you in the driveway. Go ahead and turn into the driveway and pull all the way up to the garage." Chuck recognized the guy from various Tea Party events but was embarrassed he couldn't recall his name.

"Thank you, son."

Chuck followed the instructions and drove up to the garage door. As he got out of the car, his slightly paunchy gut rubbed against the steering wheel, making it difficult to slide out. He promised himself that he'd lose some weight and never allow himself to get in this position again.

Once outside the vehicle, he reached for a small bag on the back seat, consisting mostly of toiletries that others had picked up for him. Since Chuck had been taken by the ATF from his home and imprisoned at Ellington Air Force Base near Houston, he'd had only one change of clothes that Gov. Cooper's staff picked up for him.

Before he could shut the car door, people streamed out the back door to greet him.

Christy ran up to Chuck and held onto him as if she would never let him go. He slipped his arms around her as they kissed, then he was almost knocked off his feet as Colton rushed up to him. As they stood there, arm in arm, it occurred to Chuck that he was going to do everything he could to prevent what happened to him from happening to anyone else.

As the small group of people escorted Chuck inside, a group of more than thirty people in the living room and kitchen spontaneously erupted into applause. Chuck didn't know what to make of it all, and he felt tears on his cheeks and in his eyes. He wiped them away, instinctively thinking that crying was a sign of weakness. Then it occurred to him that he'd never again think he couldn't cry. Life was too precious, his mother always told him, not to show honest sadness and grief or happiness and joy.

Chuck's gaze connected through the enthusiastic crowd with the diminutive wife of his best friend, Stan Mumford, who had been murdered by ATF agents during the raids on Tea Party organizers' headquarters and homes.

This was the first time Chuck had seen Sheila Mumford since that terrible day. Ignoring the rest of the well-wishers, Chuck went straight to Sheila. Almost apologetically, he took her into his arms for a long, comforting embrace. Nothing was said between them for several minutes, then Christy and Colton joined in for a group hug. Not only were Sheila and the Dixons crying softly, but the friends surrounding them broke down, too.

"Sheila, I am so, so sorry," Chuck whispered, his mouth close to her ear. "We all loved Stan. Are you okay? How about the kids?" He stepped back to peer down at her.

"It's hour by hour, day by day now, but we'll be all right soon," Sheila replied, wiping back tears.

"Stan was a hero to me," Chuck told her, "and I'm sure he's a hero to everyone in Texas. What can we do for you and the kids, Sheila?"

Deep inside, he felt responsible for Stan's death. Although Stan had originally introduced him to the Tea Party, it was Chuck's idea to organize their own chapter. Had Stan not gotten so involved at that level, he would undoubtedly be alive today, and Chuck knew it.

Chuck bent over to say something quietly in Sheila's ear, barely able to speak the words. "Sheila, I feel terrible that my involvement with Stan led to this. I'm sorry I didn't make his funeral. I don't really…"

"Shush." Sheila grasped Chuck's face with both hands, then put her forefinger over Chuck's lips.

"Now, you listen to me, Chuck Dixon. Stan absolutely believed in what you were both doing. He was his own man; you know that. I loved that about him. Don't feel guilty about what happened and don't apologize. This could just as easily have happened to you, and it nearly did. You understand me, Chuck?"

Chuck couldn't talk. He nodded as tears streamed down his face.

Just then, several others broke into the conversation with offers to provide any assistance Sheila needed. All the folks gathered at the house represented the core of the local Tea Party group Chuck and Stan had organized and led.

Chuck could tell the group was anxious for news. They were hungry for information and they kept him talking until nearly midnight. More than anything, they wanted to know what was likely to happen next.

"We appear to be at a dangerous stand-off," Chuck told them. "Federal troops are at the state borders and in the Gulf. The feds have put stops on banking and transfers of money. The worst thing is that Congress had no cojones; they couldn't get impeachment out of committee."

"And where does that leave us?" someone asked.

"President Johnson wants the governor for the raid that freed me and for the confrontation in Austin, even though it was started by the FBI and ATF. Unfortunately, the president now feels emboldened again because the Rash Sally conspiracy has taken a back seat to this crisis." Chuck paused. "The sense I got when I was with the governor was that this could get very dicey in a hurry. We all need to pray."

"Are we talking armed conflict?" asked another.

"Two months ago, I would have said that's not realistic but, after the stunts the feds pulled, I think anything is possible. We need to tighten up our communities, families and organizations. This could get very bumpy before it gets better."

"I'm frightened," murmured a middle-aged woman.

"I am, too," said Chuck. "But we better get smart. I need to get some sleep now, but we should meet tomorrow and start reorganizing. We have a lot of work to do to protect ourselves and our families going forward."

One of the men in the group stood up. "Texans have faced adversity before. Chuck is right; we need to pray. We need to reorganize from a political organization to a group of tightly connected and prepared citizens."

"Agreed," said Chuck. "It's time to circle the wagons for what might be the most stressful time in any of our lives. With God's help, we'll make it just fine."

# Chapter 2

*"All political power is inherent in the people, and all free governments are founded on their authority, and instituted for their benefit. The faith of the people of Texas stands pledged to the preservation of a republican form of government, and, subject to this limitation only, they have at all times the inalienable right to alter, reform or abolish their government in such manner as they may think expedient."*

*~ The Texas Constitution of 1876, Article 1, Section 1*

Gov. Brent Cooper sat in his deep leather chair behind a massive oak desk. The Seal of the Great State of Texas was intricately carved in the center, facing anyone who sat in front of the desk.

The governor was as massive as his desk. Tall, with salt-and-pepper hair, he still looked like he could put on a uniform and play tight end for his alma mater, Texas A&M. The governor invoked images of a conservative LBJ or even Sam Houston, who could command an entire room or any other venue with just his presence.

Gov. Cooper wore starched and creased Wrangler blue jeans, a pressed dress shirt and slightly western-style blazer that looked like he'd just stepped off the pages of American Cowboy magazine. If ever there was a modern-day image of the "Marlboro Man," he was it, without the mustache. Although the governor liked his hunting, whiskey and cigars, nobody in this room underestimated him. The governor's politics were usually of the sort where he would simply impose his will, rather than craft backroom compromises.

The governor had invited several people into his private office to figure out how to deal with the crisis. In attendance were the two U.S. Senators Kevin Simpson and Roberto Perez that Cooper had recalled from Washington, D.C., as well as several key members of the Texas Congressional delegation, including several Democrats. From state government were Lt. Gov. Gene Foster, Atty. Gen. Jeff Weaver, and several state senators and legislators who had shown they understood the situation both in Texas and in Washington. The commandant of the Texas Militia, the Texas Guard, the head of the Texas Department of Public Safety and several key lieutenant colonels stood at the back of the room.

The governor had also asked Rev. Mavis Scoffer and Clarence Cardinal Biggs to attend. Standing next to Cooper's chair was Pops Younger, commander of the Texas Rangers.

"Ladies and gentlemen, as you know, we have a growing crisis. I brought you here to get your input on a plan to diffuse this situation. Before I begin, may I ask Rev. Scoffer to bless this meeting?"

The black Baptist minister made his way to the front of the governor's desk, clutching a large weathered leather-bound bible and began, "Dear Jesus Christ, please heap your wisdom on the leaders of this great State of Texas as they put forward a plan to protect her citizens and to do the will of the Father. We ask the Holy Spirit to open their hearts and minds and lift them up to accomplish the great tasks that lay ahead of them. We ask this in our sweet, dear Jesus' name. Amen."

"Amen," came a chorus from the delegation.

Gov. Cooper rose. The room got eerily silent, so much so that one could hear the antique leather chair creak as he stood.

"Thank you, Rev. Scoffer."

The governor surveyed the entire room, looking at the contingent of Texas luminaries with his steel-blue eyes. Cooper was a hit with lady Texans, and many politicians credited his ability to draw a substantial Democratic vote was because of his popularity with women, driven by his rugged good looks, even though he was sixty-three years old. Whatever the reason, Cooper was one of the most admired and successful Texas governors of all time. Like many Texas governors before him, Cooper was a larger-than-life character.

"I have asked you here for what is likely one of the most important tasks of your lifetime. Texas is at a precipice. Texas has been here before. I likely needn't remind you of your Texas history. Today we have a new challenge," said Cooper. "It will be up to the people in this room to meet these challenges and lead Texas into a new day, whatever that may hold and whatever Texans decide. I would like to turn the floor over to Jeff Weaver for his assessment on where we stand."

Weaver was the antithesis of the governor. He was a University of Texas graduate who went on to Harvard Law School, although he would always joke that it was only because the University of Texas didn't have its own law school at the time. Always smartly dressed in a crisp suit, with his trademark State Seal of Texas cufflinks and Lucchese-handmade snakeskin boots, he looked like he could be as comfortable on Wall Street as he was in Austin. Raised in Port Lavaca, Texas on the Gulf, he was a good-looking man in his mid-forties with dark hair a little gray at the temples, and was a brilliant attorney and prosecutor.

Despite the natural rivalry of their two alma maters and the fact that each had little in common other than their love of Texas, they got along famously. Many would claim their friendship was born out of the same circumstances that drove many young men in battle to become great lifelong friends. Such friendships happen many times when men fight a common enemy and wind up in the same trenches with the same people. To Cooper and Weaver, the common enemy had become the current Johnson administration and the federal government.

"Folks, here's the situation as we see it," said Weaver. "First, we have federal troops blocking every major road and interstate leading out of the state. People with Texas drivers' licenses are allowed to return home, but that's about it. Texans trying to get to other parts of the country are allowed to leave. Any trucks with shipments of any kind are turned back and we have overflow situations at major interstate entries where trucks are sitting parked."

Weaver, reading off a clipboard, continued. "The railways are also shut down and the Navy is turning back ships trying to enter ports in Beaumont, Galveston, Houston, Corpus Christi and Brownsville. Certain ships have been allowed to leave because of official complaints registered with the State Department by the embassies of various countries."

He looked up over his glasses briefly to make sure everyone was paying attention, then continued. "The Federal Reserve has locked Texas-chartered banks out of the routing system. There's been a run on several banks, causing stability issues with at least one financial institution that had its reserves fall below acceptable limits, putting the bank in default failure when this crisis is over."

One of the congressmen attending stood up and said, "I am on the House Banking Committee, and I have been locked out of two closed door meetings."

"Did your fellow Republicans protest?" asked Cooper.

"No, Governor, as far as I know, they did not. I called two of them who told me the Republican leadership had threatened them and told them to follow orders. They apologized, but said their hands were tied."

The rumblings in the room grew louder because many could not suppress their anger.

Weaver continued his report. "Food stocks seem to be holding up and no crisis has been reported. There are some empty shelves and shortages reported; however, they have not been food staples. We don't anticipate any shortages in the near term. Many stores have instituted their own policies for limits on certain items when they run short. We are monitoring this closely. We don't anticipate the need for intervention by the State Department of Agriculture or any state agency at this time. We have some isolated reports of price gouging, but it's not widespread. We'll pursue any leads just as we do after a hurricane or other disaster. Any questions?" Weaver paused.

"What about medicines, vaccines and those types of items?" asked one of the congressional Democrats.

"If there are any areas of concern, this would be near the top of the list if this situation continues. Right now, our assessment of hospitals, pharmacies and doctors is that supplies are fine for about two more weeks before we start seeing sporadic shortages. If we have a major flu outbreak or other infectious diseases epidemic, this would be serious. Governor, I know you would like to comment on this."

Gov. Cooper stood up and took the huge Churchill-type cigar from his mouth. He had been chewing on it but had not lit it.

"At some point, we may consider a public statement on this issue. We all know how much President Johnson and Atty. Gen. Tibbs hate Texas," chuckled Cooper. "With all due respect to our esteemed Democratic friends, President Johnson is too much of a political animal to take the public relations hit from not allowing shipments of needed medicines into the state. He won't want to allow it, but I think we could create enough public pressure that he would. Hell, does he not want his beloved IRS and DHS employees in Texas to be able to get flu shots?"

Finally, some nervous laughter broke out among the group following the governor's comments, except for the sulking Democrats. Cooper sat back down in his overstuffed chair and put the cigar back in his mouth.

Weaver walked back to the front of the crowded room. "For those who have never met him, I would like to introduce Texas Ranger Pops Younger. He'll give us his assessment on the status of Texas law enforcement."

The energy level in the room, already high, took on a new excitement. Even in this small setting, those who had never met Younger wanted a better look. Those who were sitting in chairs adjusted them slightly or leaned one way or the other. People standing jostled a bit to see the living legend and probably the last of a dying breed.

Pops, as he had been known to three generations of Texans, had a natural flare for the dramatic, although those who knew him best knew it wasn't an act or intentional. The iconic lawman just had an air about him that drew people to him and frightened the hell out of criminals. The stories about this Ranger had grown over sixty years to almost mythical proportions.

Pops could put people under arrest just by looking at them. On at least three occasions, with multiple witnesses, Pops approached wanted fugitives who were armed, dangerous and knew, if they were ever arrested again, they would spend the rest of their lives in jail or worse, die by lethal injection. Although they pointed loaded weapons at Pops, they threw down their weapons as the Ranger stared them down. When he did speak, it was generally with few words and a look of invincibility hard to describe. Most in the room had never been in his presence. Nobody knew for sure how old Pops was. Even the governor didn't know how old Younger really was. Some speculated he was in his eighties.

It was hard to upstage the gregarious governor but, if anyone could, it was Pops. Most of the time, the Ranger was surprised at the attention he got. But, every now and then, he used his illustrious status to his advantage when it came to dealing with criminal elements or politicians he despised. Pops had an uncanny ability to get to the heart of the matter in a sentence or two, with simple homespun cowboy logic. Even the governor admired Pops and relished every opportunity he got to spend with him, which was typically on a south Texas quail hunt instead of inside an office filled with politicians and state bureaucrats.

Pops rose. His cowboy-cut Wrangler jeans, pearl snap western shirt, vintage silver Stetson, and black bull hide cowboy boots reflected his style. He rubbed his large bushy handlebar mustache, slightly tilted his hat and spit into his paper cup before he spoke. Those who knew Pops knew that, when he adjusted his hat, followed by a spit into his paper cup or on the ground, they were about to hear his common sense logic, or they were about to be made a fool.

Despite the crowd of twenty-some people in the room, each one felt Pops made direct eye contact with them individually with those piercing, Paul Newman blue eyes in the few seconds that he paused. Again, Pops' flare for the dramatic wasn't contrived or planned; it was just how his persona exuded from him.

In his unmistakable Texas drawl, he began. "The Rangers have been monitoring all local and state law enforcement departments. We have many that are happier than a pig in a poke that our people here in Austin are finally standing up to the damned carpetbaggers in D.C. However, we have some law enforcement officials who are openly trying to contact the feds and assist them with their intervention in our fine state. Most of these bastards are in the larger urban police departments in Houston, Dallas, and right here in Austin."

He paused, reaching for the Copenhagen smokeless tobacco in his back pocket. He took a pinch, and placed it between his cheek and gums in one effortless motion.

"One thing is as sure as the Texas sun rising tomorrow and, with the exception of just a few counties, the Texas sheriffs are with us. And, once again, it's the commie sheriffs in Dallas, Houston and several Rio Grande border counties that are the problem. That being said, we are in great shape with most Texas sheriffs and constables, with a few hold-outs in those same cities. Those folks are beholden to DHS and gladly take their money to help militarize their departments. They are essentially bought and paid for like a cheap Pecos River saloon whore."

"Mr. Younger," interrupted a young Hispanic Democratic congressman from a district that included south San Antonio, "are you calling the police chiefs in those cities communists? Don't you think we should try to solve this conflict instead of calling members of our law enforcement names?"

Pops stared fiercely at the congressman, then spit into his paper spit cup. Those who knew Pops knew what was coming, and were no doubt relishing the opportunity to see the Ranger handle his challenger. The room suddenly went eerily silent. Pops took three steps toward the congressman and stopped right in front of him. His eyes blazed right through the young man.

"Sonny, when is the last time you read our fine Constitution?"

"Well, Mr. Younger, I took an oath to uphold…."

"That's not what I asked you, son. I asked when was the last time you read it, or have you ever read it?"

The congressman squirmed under the Ranger's glare. "Mr. Younger, I would expect someone like you to have a little more respect toward a U.S. congressman elected by the good people of Texas."

"Son, a congressman who takes an oath of office to a Constitution he hasn't read or doesn't follow is as useless as nipples on a boar hog. Furthermore, either your constituents are as clueless as you are, or you have them fooled. But you ain't got me fooled. You're a damned socialist at best, but probably a communist!"

"I'm not a communist, Mr. Younger!"

"Did you vote for the Patriot Act? Did you vote for the National Defense Authorization Act? Did you vote for the assault weapons ban? Do you agree with wealth redistribution? If it walks like a duck, talks like a duck, and acts like a duck, it's a goddamn communist!"

The congressman glared at Gov. Cooper. "Sir, I don't have to sit here and take ridicule like that from anyone."

During this exchange, the governor took his time lighting his cigar, the slight smirk on his face indicating that he was enjoying the show. Eying the defiant congressman with something akin to disdain, he took a puff on the cigar and said, "Congressman, you have to understand that you are part of the problem, as is your party and, for that matter, so is the GOP establishment. Now I suggest that if you want to participate in averting the crisis we face with this administration and, as the junior member of the congressional delegation in this room, you sit down, shut up and watch how things are done by people in Texas who know how to get things done!"

The congressman's face flushed a dark red. "Sir, the federal government is going to come down on you so fast your head will spin. And I, for one, am going to enjoy the day we see you led away in handcuffs," retorted the congressman as he picked up his briefcase and made his way through the crowded room toward the door.

"Sonny, your assignment is to read that Constitution you took an oath to uphold," called Pops to the retreating back of the politician. He took another spit into his Dixie cup that was now about one quarter full of a mixture of brown tobacco juice and spit.

The few Texas Democrats who had been asked to participate in the meeting suddenly became more uneasy than they already were. Sensing their uneasiness as easy targets in the room, Cooper stood up.

"Ladies and gentlemen, I asked all of you here for input on how to protect Texas and Texans from any calamity. Now, it's true that we don't all agree on many issues, but it's time to come together to figure this out." He surveyed the room. "Does anyone else want to leave? If so, leave now," he said.

When no one responded, the governor continued. "Okay, let's hear from Maj. Gen. Rex Conroy with the Texas State Guard."

Maj. Gen. Conroy stepped to the front of the room with a manila folder that he began to pull papers from. Conroy was a decorated Vietnam War veteran and held command posts in the U.S. Army during Operation Desert Shield. He retired from active duty and became active in the State Guard, accepting his commission as commander from Gov. Cooper.

"We have a stand-off situation at various points on the state border, including I-35 at the Oklahoma state line, I-20 and I-10 at Louisiana and I-10 at El Paso. The location with the most tension seems to be at I-30 at Texarkana. There have been skirmishes at that location and others, but no exchange of gunfire since the original incident three days after the surrender in Austin."

Conroy continued. "The U.S. Air Force bases in Texas are still effectively shut down and are under my direct command as directed by Gov. Cooper. There are no federal flights in or out at the moment. However, some private aircraft have been able to operate.

"We have also locked down all border check points on the Mexican border. Interestingly, the U.S. Border Patrol has cooperated, and seems to have relaxed surveillance and enforcement activities.

"The administration still has U.S. Navy ships stationed in the Gulf strategically to intercept incoming and outgoing cargo ships and tankers. They are blockading ports at Brownsville, Corpus Christi, Galveston, Port Arthur and Beaumont, as well as the Houston Ship Channel entrance."

Conroy shuffled several pieces of paper as if looking for something. Finally, he glanced up and continued. "We have stationed Texas Guard and militia troops at key refineries where pipelines flow out of state," he said.

"We have worked with various oil companies and refineries per the governor to turn off those outgoing oil and gas pipelines to other states."

Gov. Cooper stood up and added, "We think it's a little comical that President Johnson has shut down tanker access. Those tankers take crude to other refineries on the Gulf Coast and other states for refinement to gasoline. It will be interesting to see the short- and long-term effects this has on gasoline prices and stockpiles nationally. OPEC will have this administration by the short hairs if this blockade continues. I would like to remind everyone not only of the vast oil reserves in Texas but, more important, is its refining capacity that is second to none. This will get painful for Johnson in a hurry. Continue on, Major General, and pardon me for interrupting."

"Yes, sir, no interruption at all. We have established rules of engagement with all Texas forces and they are defensive only. Do not engage unless we have been engaged."

"Do we expect them to engage?" asked Sen. Simpson.

"I have to prepare our troops as if they will," said Conroy, "but this may be more of a political question for the governor or attorney general."

Weaver stood. "I do not believe we will see any all-out assault of any kind. That would be messy for the administration."

Conroy nodded at Weaver, then continued his briefing. "What we do expect is some type of extraction attempt for the governor and other officials sitting in this room. This administration has a blood thirst for political theater when they think it will benefit its propaganda machine."

"The banking lockdown and halt of all federal payments and other actions by this administration are attempts to create internal pressure on state officials," said Cooper emphatically. "They are trying to make it hard on the average Texan, hoping our citizens will put pressure on state officials to cave."

The balding, twenty-eight-year-old incumbent Democratic Congressman Mario Pena from Laredo interrupted the governor to ask, "Sir, how bad does it have to get for Texas for you to consider turning yourself in to the Justice Department? Does our banking system have to come undone? Do food or medicine shortages have to get critically low? Does it have to result in bloodshed on the interstate?"

A little-known freshman state legislator, Mike Woods, from north of Houston, stood up. Woods had bucked the establishment good ole boy network in the legislature, introducing maverick legislation on everything from gun rights to nullification of federal laws, and had won the favor of Gov. Cooper and the Tea Party.

"Congressman Pena, there are no circumstances where our governor, our lieutenant governor or our attorney general can surrender. This administration hates Texas and everything it stands for. People around the world see Texas as the last hope for free enterprise, Christian values, capitalism and individual responsibility. I say to you and to everyone in this room, we have reached the point of no return."

Clearly caught up in the moment, Woods continued. "Everyone here sees the dysfunctional system we have in Washington. Hell, we have the president and his attorney general complicit in maybe the worst conspiracy in American history that includes the death of a federal whistleblower and his wife and the trampling of the constitutional rights of numerous Texans who just happen to be Tea Party activists. Yet we can't get Congress to invoke impeachment proceedings.

"So I say not only no, but hell, no! Under no circumstances does the governor, or anyone else for that matter, surrender to federal authorities! Governor, if you do that, Texas is over. It's as plain and simple as that."

Now the room's intensity went off the charts, with everyone talking at the same time, some so loud others had to yell to get their points across. Finally, the only one in the room who could quiet a crowd strode to the front of the governor's desk.

Without a word, Pops spit into his Dixie cup and looked at the arguments going on around him. One by one, he stared down each party involved in a sidebar discussion. When they noticed Pops staring at them, they immediately quit talking. As each small group got quiet, others noticed Pops and became silent themselves.

The Texas Rangers' motto is "One riot, one Ranger," emblazoned in history from the story of a Dallas sheriff who sent for the Rangers as a riot over an illegal prize fight broke out in town. When a Ranger showed up, the sheriff looked at him and asked incredulously, "There's only one Ranger?"

Ranger Captain W.J. McDonald shot back, "There's only one riot, isn't there?"

It was obvious Pops garnered the same type of respect the Rangers were famous for.

"Folks, neither this governor nor anyone else in this room ain't surrendering to nobody, but especially not to that federal attorney general.

Not while my boots still have dust from Texas dirt on them. Let's not forget that Texans voted the other day in favor of Texas independence. Now I'm not a damned politician like the rest of you fine folks," he said with just a smidgen of sarcasm, "but I can tell you that the average Texan does not want the governor or any of the rest of you hauled off by the feds. There's more than a few of you I wouldn't mind to run your hippie-thinkin' asses out of Texas, especially you folk that think left-handed but, at the end of the day, you're Texans."

"Pops is right," declared Weaver."

"We have the backing of the majority of Texans. I suggest we draw up a list of demands on this administration; otherwise, we'll be forced to take the next steps," said Gov. Cooper.

"I thought we already did that, asking for the impeachment vote," said Pena.

"May I remind you, sir, that I offered to surrender if the impeachment vote was carried forward. It never made it out of committee," said Cooper defiantly. "That was likely the only thing you good congressmen could have done that may have stopped the Independence referendum. Now the rest of the world knows we're serious, even if it was non-binding at that time. The situation has gotten much more serious and Texans recognize this."

"Sir, just how much do you expect Texans to suffer just because you won't turn yourself over to federal authorities?" asked Pena.

"Congressman, if the majority of Texans decide that is the best course, they'll let me know. I believe you saw the results of the referendum. I don't believe average Texans are of the same mind as you."

Congressman Pena knew his office was getting bombarded with phone calls, emails and social media posts that agreed with the governor. He offered ineffective arguments and little resistance. Packing up his computer and briefcase, he huffed out of the room.

Several of the Democrats who didn't agree with the governor left the meeting with Pena as a de facto show of non-support for the governor's position. The small group that remained represented the most loyal stalwarts of Gov. Cooper.

Of chief concern to Younger and Conroy was protecting the governor. Both were convinced the administration would try to remove him and other state officials from Texas in some manner to pursue charges against them for the disaster and embarrassment the administration suffered over the arrest of federal agents.

The group continued to discuss their options into the early morning hours of the next day, drafting demands to be made upon the administration and planning Texas' next move.

It was a critical time once again in the glorious history of Texas, and the governor wondered if Texans were up to the challenge. He couldn't help thinking about one of Sam Houston's most famous quotes, and he took some comfort in the belief that Texans at the core are defiant and resolute. He recalled Houston's famous words: "Texas has yet to learn submission to any oppression, come from what source it may."

# CHAPTER 3

*"Patriots have long memories."*

*~ Charlie Daniels*
*Country & Southern Rock Artist*
*American Patriot*

The White House situation room was abuzz with activity. Democratic operatives, the president's full cabinet and the military chief of staff were all in attendance, waiting on President Johnson and Atty. Gen. Tibbs.

Even the president's long-time political ally, Chicago Mayor Davian Kyler, was present, despite the fact that he didn't have clearance to be at such a high level meeting.

Vice President Doolittle and Treasury Secretary Benjamin Gould were in deep conversation when the president's press secretary, Ted Duncan, walked in.

"Ladies and gentlemen, the president will be here in about two minutes. Please take a seat so we can start as soon as he arrives," said Duncan. The president's second press secretary, who looked like the quintessential nerd with thick black rim glasses, Duncan was fiercely loyal to President Johnson despite the fact that the president regularly left him hanging out to dry with the press and often produced contradictory statements. Many times, the president or Chief of Staff Cliff Radford intentionally fed Duncan misinformation or failed to brief him in full, leaving him to fend for himself in regular White House press briefings.

Some were still standing in discussions as the president walked in with Secy. of State Annabelle Bartlett. Most who didn't know President Johnson well thought he was an affable and friendly guy who was the ultimate in *cool*. What they didn't know was that those close to him knew all too well that Johnson demanded certain protocol and respect. He alone had ushered the Democrats back into power and won re-election when economic numbers were dismal. Never had an American president won re-election when unemployment was over eight percent or gas prices were as high as they were.

Agitated that people still stood engaged in several private conversations, Johnson sat down and began talking immediately. At one point he was talking over Doolittle, which forced the president to pause and wait for the vice president and the treasury secretary to sit. The president's cold stare was enough to shut down any other conversations.

"Excuse me, Mr. President, I hadn't realized you arrived," said Doolittle. People didn't know how to take Doolittle. The continuous smirk on his face meant that one could never really tell if he was mocking the person he was talking to or if he was genuinely goofy. Part of this perception came from the vice president continually putting his foot in his mouth with gaffes only he seemed to be able to get away with.

Once Doolittle settled in his chair, the president began again.

"Ladies and gentlemen, let's dive right in. We have a serious situation in Texas. I have asked several folks to brief us on their areas of expertise with regard to Texas. I'll start with Defense Secy. Harry Brooks."

Everyone turned to look at Brooks at the opposite end of the large mahogany conference table. With his grey hair and beard, and spectacles, Brooks looked like a banker or a bookkeeper, definitely not like a high ranking member of President Johnson's cabinet.

Brooks was relatively new in the position, taking over after the resignation of the former defense secretary in the president's first term. Before Brooks could be appointed, he went through a brutal Senate confirmation hearing, especially blistering from Sen. Roberto Perez, the newly elected Tea Party candidate from Texas. The administration painted the senator as an "obstructionist," along with the rest of the Tea Party.

"We have positioned troops on all major roadways on Texas' state lines with New Mexico, Oklahoma, Arkansas and Louisiana. We are letting those with Texas drivers' licenses in but not out. We are not allowing any trucks, shipments, or private vehicles to enter the state unless they are residents. Truckers are required to drop their trailers at designated holding areas if they want to re-enter unless they prove they are empty."

Brooks had a slide presentation being shown on all the screens in the situation room, but never looked any further over his spectacles than to see the papers directly in front of him. The secretary didn't have much of a personality and delivered his report to the president and his staff in his usual dull monotone.

"It appears the governor has placed his Texas Guard and Texas Militia troops just opposite us at every location. In most cases, the troops can see each other but, except for two incidents in Texarkana, there have been no conflicts. In both of those incidents, shots were fired from both sides but nobody was injured and both sides stood down."

Brooks looked up over his spectacles again. "It is apparent that these guard and militia troops are there in case we decide to advance beyond the state lines."

"What about our military bases in Texas? What's the status there?" asked Johnson.

Brooks hesitated slightly because he knew the president was especially sensitive to this subject.

"Right now, all air bases in Texas are locked down. Texas has control of all aviation assets, traffic control towers, fuel and runways."

"Goddamn, Harry, how in hell is that possible?"

"Mr. President, we've discussed this. My predecessor had not envisioned this possibility. We were simply surprised and out-maneuvered. I don't know any other way to say it."

"How do we get them back?" Johnson demanded.

"Mr. President, it would take a special operations task force or full military intervention to take these bases back. Regardless of the political consequences, any Special Forces operations in Texas would be tedious and dangerous. Also, I think I should mention that Special Forces and command are heavily populated with Texans or those sympathetic to Texas."

"Harry, I want a military option on my desk in forty-eight hours to take these damned bases back. Am I clear?"

"Yes, sir," returned Brooks, motioning to a four-star general seated behind him. The general and several other uniformed officers left the room immediately.

Johnson had made his thoughts known to his entire cabinet when the Texas crisis escalated and the Texans captured the bases. He wondered how the most powerful military in the world could lose bases in its own country to part-time guardsmen and volunteer militia?

"Okay. Treasury Secy. Gould, you're up."

"Thank you, Mr. President," said Gould who, unlike Brooks, stood up to make his report. Gould was dressed in a dark blue twenty-five hundred dollar suit, and was a Columbia graduate like the president, although Gould didn't go to Harvard Law as the president did.

"We have essentially shut down any federal payments to Texas with the exception of federal government employees. We continue to pay all federal employees. We have ramped up IRS scrutiny on known Tea Party associates."

No one in the room seemed alarmed by Gould's last comment. If they were, they weren't about to bring it up to a full cabinet meeting because they had all demonized the Tea Party at one time or another.

"What about Social Security, Medicare and retired military benefits?" asked Secy. of State Bartlett.

Gould looked nervously at the president, then continued, "The intent of shutting down federal payments is to create pressure on Texas elected officials. People won't get their Social Security checks, their veterans' retirement benefits or income tax refunds. Only active duty military and current federal employees will receive any monies whatsoever in Texas. We have also halted all government payments to contractors or suppliers that we have identified as Texas-based or Texas entities."

Secy. of State Bartlett interrupted. "Mr. President, with all due respect, sir, I do worry about how the cessation of Social Security checks and veterans' retirement benefits will be viewed by Americans and your adversaries."

"Madam Secretary, obviously we have this concern as well, but we have weighed it against the alternatives and feel that Texans will place insurmountable pressure on Gov. Cooper to turn himself in. Additionally, we have started the political and public relations campaign to show that the governor could end his state's misery if he turned himself in," retorted Radford.

"Is it having any effect?" Bartlett asked.

"It's too early; so far, most of them are only a few days late in receiving checks, so the heat will start to turn up on Cooper in the coming days," answered Gould.

"What about their gold reserves?" asked Johnson.

"Mr. President, we have confiscated the gold and moved it to a secret government location. Again, this is intended to create more pressure on Texas state government."

"So what does that mean, given the current situation?" asked Bartlett.

Gould looked at the president, wondering if he wanted him to answer such a direct question. Johnson nodded affirmatively.

"Well, with Texas owning gold, that means the state has the means to trade with other countries if they can get goods into or out of Texas. They also have oil reserves. This is more of a concern long-term than short-term. According to Secy. Brooks, we have Texas blockaded so, even if they could trade, they wouldn't be able to get those goods into Texas."

What Gould did not bring up was what several in the room knew to be true: Texas had enough gold to start its own gold-based currency if the state were to go it alone as a result of this current or any future crisis. However, Texas would have to have the gold on hand, and the federal government had moved that gold to an undisclosed location.

"Next, let's hear from Secy. of State Bartlett," offered the president.

Secy. Bartlett got up to address the group. She wore a thin pink skirt and matching blouse that seemed to be right out of the fifties. Bartlett was in her sixties, probably thirty pounds overweight, with hair that always seemed slightly greasy at the roots. Even in the White House, some referred to her as Secretary "Frumpy." Up close and in person, she looked fifteen years older than she was. Bartlett always dressed in a manner that was unflattering, but she was an astute and ruthless politician. She remained popular in the Democratic Party, with many still clinging to the hope she might one day be the first female president. She and the president's relationship, however, bore the scars of past political battles.

"I have spoken with many of our allies," she said. "They are deeply concerned about this crisis, not so much the loss of life that occurred in Austin, but about the stability of the United States and how it affects the tenuous financial markets in Asia and Europe."

"That figures," sniped Gould.

"We have complaints at the UN and from Amnesty International about the tactics used with the Tea Party in Texas and other states. Those actions do not present this administration in a positive light on the international stage," continued Bartlett.

Johnson was extremely sensitive to criticism and typically lashed out at reporters, fellow politicians and the media for anyone questioning him or his administration. While Bartlett was speaking, it was obvious the president was working very hard to resist responding. He was visibly agitated as Bartlett continued her assessment.

"I do believe any further armed incursion into one of our states will de-stabilize global financial markets and risk condemnation from our allies and others," Bartlett said. Many in the room nodded, some almost subconsciously.

"Further, I think everyone should consider this. Shortly before this crisis began, we started to see the GOP start to unravel. Their leadership bickered among themselves and created a clear split that totally fractured the party. This crisis has the potential to galvanize the GOP once again. Are we missing an opportunity here, folks, simply because we want to arrest the Texas governor?"

"Now you wait just a goddamned minute," yelled Atty. Gen. Tibbs.

"Mr. Tibbs, you can respond when I'm done," shot back Bartlett.

"Madam Secretary..."

"Mr. Tibbs..." said Bartlett forcefully, surprising the attorney general with her substantial gravitas. He sat back down, causing Doolittle to sport his famous smirk again. Doolittle had always been jealous of the president's trust in Tibbs.

"If we do this correctly, the GOP may take twenty years to recover. Screw Texas. I'm not here to provide an opinion on how Justice played its hand with the Rash Sally investigation, but everyone would be naïve to think the tactics we used as a result of that investigation aren't part of the reason we are all sitting here," said Bartlett, looking around the room as if she were some matriarch or school principal scolding her underlings. She had the full attention of everyone in the room at this point. Tibbs, however, was fuming, and Johnson looked uncomfortable.

"Now, I'm not saying the Tea Party didn't deserve any of this," Bartlett continued. "They did. But make no mistake. You didn't eradicate them, Mr. Tibbs. You made them go underground temporarily and, when they rear their heads again, they could be potentially more impactful than they were previously."

Avery Smith, the trusted architect of the president's last two successful election campaigns, sat quietly for all the other presentations, but rose out of his chair after the last comment from Bartlett.

Smith was tall at 6'2," but he had a disheveled look with his balding head, bushy mustache, and a suit that always seemed wrinkled. His tie was never tied correctly nor was it ever straight, and it was not uncommon for him to have food stains on his button-down shirt or tie.

"Secy. Bartlett has a point," he interjected smoothly. "We have had the GOP on the run for a couple of years. I know we want Gov. Cooper's head on a stick, but think how this will play if we avert a larger crisis because of diplomacy."

"Avery, let me remind you that eighteen federal agents and U.S. Army troops are dead as a direct result of that cowboy's actions," interrupted Tibbs.

"Jamail, let's be frank. The GOP is in complete disarray. The fractures that began in the 2010 mid-term elections have morphed into political mutiny by many Republicans in the South and in Texas." Smith leaned forward, resting his chin on a thumb and his fingers, and continued in a silky, calm tone. "Let me also remind everyone that, just a few weeks ago, we were sweating out a possible impeachment hearing, and there are likely more repercussions possible in the Rash Sally investigation. So, sir, are you more interested in payback than in a diplomatic end to this crisis?" he asked.

Up to this point, the president had been in agreement. Gov. Cooper, the Texas attorney general, and Ranger Pops Younger had completely embarrassed the administration, the Justice Department, the U.S. Army, the FBI and the ATF.

"Avery, I see what you are saying. I'm not in total agreement on this without trying another option first, but go ahead," said the president.

He turned to look at Annabelle Bartlett. "I'll consider your option, Annabelle, but I'm not sold on it yet," he told her.

Smith looked around the room to gauge interest in this approach, then turned his gaze on Bartlett.

Being the cagey old politician Secy. Bartlett was, she recognized the plum Smith was offering. She could be the heroine who ended the crisis single-handedly with no shots being fired. And, with Johnson out of presidential terms, Bartlett was the odds-on favorite to be at or near the top of the next Democratic presidential ticket. She was already contemplating leaving her post to prepare for an all-out fundraising effort and political campaign launch fully three years before the next election.

Bartlett was also leery of the Rash Sally investigation. She wanted to leave the president's cabinet to avoid being tainted with one more large scandal that now seemed permanently affixed to this administration. She was very uncomfortable with the signs pointing to the suspicious deaths of Justice Department whistleblower Tim Spilner and his wife, which could come back to haunt the administration in an unprecedented manner if someone could prove that any federal agency had been involved in those deaths. The Johnson administration had been adept at sidestepping scandals, but she wasn't going to bet her potential presidential candidacy on averting a few more.

Like Johnson, Bartlett completely trusted Smith's political instincts, and she knew he was cracking the door open for her for this historic opportunity. She also knew Smith would expect the key role in her election campaign in return. That was how Smith operated.

"I would be honored to lead this contingent for you," Bartlett said, as she turned from Smith to Johnson.

"Let's figure out who would be the best political choices to join you in this effort if we go in that direction," added Smith.

Seemingly unconvinced, and knowing Bartlett's political ambitions when his second term was over, Johnson hesitated. It was very hard for him to let go of his hatred for Gov. Cooper. He relished the idea of the Texas governor being dragged out of his office in handcuffs for the entire world to see.

"I would like to have Bartlett, Tibbs, Brooks, Doolittle, Avery and Davian to remain. The rest of you are excused. You'll be briefed as appropriate. Let me remind everyone that any and all discussions in this room are top secret and cannot be discussed with your staff, spouses or anyone. Is that understood?" asked the president sternly.

"Yes, sir, Mr. President," responded those in the room, almost in unison.

It was not lost on those staying behind that any strategy on how to deal with the Texas crisis in the next meeting would likely be the most important decision in President Johnson's tenure as president.

As soon as everyone left the room, those asked to stay behind looked to the president.

"Before I make a decision on diplomacy or just sending in troops to arrest Cooper, I would like you to tell me how you see this going down and how long it would take," Johnson said to Bartlett.

"Mr. President, I believe the thing to do is to get a meeting with Cooper's underlings and find out if he will surrender or what it will take to normalize things from their perspective," said Bartlett.

"Are you friggin' serious?" yelled an enraged Tibbs.

"Hold on, hold on, Jamail," the president interjected, "let's see what her idea is first."

"Do we give a shit what Texas wants?" demanded Tibbs.

Bartlett was becoming even more irritated at Tibbs. Whenever she got agitated or nervous, it manifested in her neck and chest area and became red and almost rash-like in the same flushing manner as some people whose faces became red when they were angry or flustered. This was one of the principal reasons Bartlett wore frumpy, high-collar fashions. She wanted to be able to hide this tell-tale sign so as not to give away any hint of weakness—or to display a poker face when necessary—yet she now felt the all-too common flush as if it could be seen through her clothes.

"Mr. President," said Bartlett, "Texas has already started a publicity campaign to show the rest of the world the impact on ordinary citizens from the banking restrictions, the blockade and the stopping of federal payments. For the record, I want you to know I do not agree with the decision to suspend Social Security checks and veterans' benefits." Bartlett sent a piercing glance at the group. "What are we thinking here? Those decisions could backfire quickly—and I personally believe they will."

She looked around for a response. The first to offer one was Smith, who was the political sage primarily responsible for everyone in the room being in their current elected and appointed positions.

"Mr. President, I agree partially with Secy. Bartlett. I do believe that, over an extended period, these actions could be politically damaging. But," turning to Bartlett as he continued, "those damages could be outweighed by a swift conclusion. If we were successful in extracting and arresting Cooper, we believe the rest of the dominos would fall in line. The potential win politically from this action may outweigh the short-term consequences on military veterans or the elderly on Social Security."

"Avery, that is a very large gamble I would be extremely hesitant to take," Bartlett shot back.

"Where is this in polling?" asked Johnson

Bartlett couldn't help rolling her eyes. This president couldn't cross the street without polling data to confirm it was the right course. And then, he still got it wrong. "It's about where you'd expect, along party lines, Mr. President."

"Okay, but for how long?"

"I would expect more human interest stories about a starving elderly vet making national and global news before too long."

Johnson cringed.

"Sir, we would do this in a back-room manner. Nobody needs to know it happened or if it was successful. Let me see if we can resolve this crisis with negotiations," begged Bartlett.

"They won't live up to their end anyway. It's a waste of time," responded Tibbs.

"Atty. Gen. Tibbs, do you have any compassion for these folks who likely don't have enough money to buy food or their prescriptions?"

"Annabelle, don't act so damned morally superior to the rest of us! We all know your M.O. on this. You want to be the one who negotiates an end to this crisis and be the hero, simply for your own political aspirations," said Tibbs.

"Jamail, if I were you, I'd be more concerned with how the Spilners died in that car accident," retorted Bartlett.

"Okay, folks, relax!" Smith stood as if to stop the two cabinet members from coming to blows.

"Avery, let's you and I discuss this. I realize passions are high for everyone here. I'll make my decision and that will be what we do. Is that understood by everyone here?" asked the president.

Both Bartlett and Tibbs nodded. Gould, Doolittle and Kyler, who had just been spectators in the after-meeting, also nodded.

The thought that his impending decision on the actions to take regarding the Texas crisis would cement his place in history and could alter the American landscape forever was not lost on President Johnson.

It also wasn't lost on the key political players exiting the room.

# CHAPTER 4

*"A democratic government is the only one in which those who vote for a tax can escape the obligation to pay it."*

~ *Alexis de Tocqueville*
*French Political Philosopher*

It was four o'clock on a Tuesday afternoon when Cliff Radford walked into the Oval Office. As usual, the president had both feet propped up on the historic maple desk that had been used by presidents dating back to Teddy Roosevelt. It was obvious that Johnson couldn't care less about the historical significance of the desk.

The president had an obvious streak of defiance in him his entire life. This was likely deep-rooted, inspired by a father who was a devout socialist and believed America and most of the West were imperialistic colonial provocateurs. His mother was a practicing communist.

It was no wonder the president had little regard for any historic traditions surrounding the White House. About the only history the president endorsed was any history he could use or conveniently twist to propel his socialistic goals for America. It was common for Johnson to use quotes by Lincoln, FDR, Teddy Roosevelt or LBJ to his advantage; after all, those presidents were as responsible for a large *centralized* federal government taking root in America as all other administrations combined. In Johnson's mind, he could be *patriotic* in his socialist reformation of the country.

The president held his hand up to stop Radford from talking while he finished texting. He finally acknowledged his chief of staff by looking up.

"Cliff, what the hell? It's been more than forty-eight hours since I told Brooks to have a military option on my desk."

"Yes, sir, Mr. President. I just got off the phone with his staff and they are ready to present a plan to you in two hours."

"Damn, Cliff, are you serious? You know I have a political action fundraiser tonight. This was supposed to already be on my desk."

"Sir, the meeting tonight is at *your* option and *this* is obviously critical. Do you want them here afterward tonight?"

"No, not tonight. I believe we have some *whales* scheduled to stay in the Lincoln Bedroom tonight," commented the president, who referred to his major political donors in the same context Las Vegas casinos labeled large money gamblers. It wasn't unusual for Johnson to trade access to the White House for large political donations.

In his first term, these political exchanges were somewhat hidden. As his second term began, these trades became openly public, yet few complained that they violated election laws. The Democrats, in conjunction with the mainstream media, had become experts at demonizing anyone critical of Johnson's administration for anything as *racist*. Few in the GOP were willing to expend the political capital to take on the administration because they could not rely on political cover and backing from the GOP establishment.

Political correctness had become so prevalent that being called *racist*, whether true or not, was akin to or even worse than being branded a *terrorist*. Those who had been successfully branded with this moniker typically had their political careers damaged beyond repair.

President Johnson and his administration were operating in a vacuum successfully created by their propaganda machine and a willing lapdog media. The fact that impeachment proceedings never got out of committee, despite the apparent conspiracy, signaled to all that Johnson was untouchable. It wasn't the first time Johnson had seemed made of Teflon but, of all the scandals, the Sally investigation and Spilner deaths were the most serious.

"I can have them here at seven in the morning. Your schedule is clear until 11:30."

The president looked at Radford like he had lost his mind. Many prior presidents were in the Oval Office very early each day. Eisenhower and Reagan were known to start their days in the Oval Office before 6:00 a.m. It was well-known and understood by his staff that this president's schedule rarely started before 9:30 each morning.

"No, have them here at 10:00 a.m.," replied Johnson, who wasn't about to reschedule a $25,000 per plate dinner fundraising event where those in attendance would willingly slobber all over their narcissistic commander-in-chief.

"They will be there at 10:00 then, Mr. President."

The next morning, the Joint Chiefs, Radford, Kyler, Tibbs, Gould, McDermott and Smith assembled in the White House situation room, many of them arriving up to an hour before the appointed time.

Noticeably missing was Annabelle Bartlett, who kept a scheduled meeting with the president of Uganda, who was visiting New York City ahead of meetings at the United Nations. Bartlett could have moved her schedule, but did not want her political future to include answering questions about the possibility of further bloodshed in Texas if the president and his cabinet decided to launch some type of military action. She also abhorred the idea of stopping Social Security checks and veterans' benefits.

At the previous meeting, Bartlett had *purposely* gone on the record for favoring a diplomatic approach to end the crisis. She wanted no part of this one.

At 10:40 a.m., the president had still not made an appearance to the 10:00 meeting. This was another habit of this president, showing up late to his own meetings.

A few minutes later, Johnson walked into the meeting accompanied by Ted Duncan. Without any apology or explanation, the president asked for a cup of coffee and sat at the head of the large conference table.

"Okay, gentlemen, what's your plan?" he asked.

Secy. Brooks stood up and pulled over a presentation easel with numerous illustrations and maps sitting on it.

"Mr. President, to get straight to the point, our proposed plan is to cut the snake's head off, then take back the military bases. To do so, we have a plan to insert a DHS Tactical Assault team into Austin or wherever he may be to extract Gov. Cooper."

"Okay, but what about the other guys—the attorney general and that damned Texas Ranger?" asked Tibbs.

"Well, sir, we know from intelligence that they're moving each of them to a different location every day. The governor is not in the governor's mansion. They believe this type of operation by us is likely so they are taking appropriate precautions."

"How do we know where to extract him from?" asked the president.

"We still have law enforcement officials in Texas who are not in agreement with the current leadership. We're getting reliable intelligence where Cooper is being held, almost on a daily basis."

"Again, what about the others?" pressed Tibbs.

"Sir, in our plan, we extract Cooper, then secure the military bases. Cooper is the high-value target here. This will create confusion and will allow us to simultaneously take back the air bases."

"So you plan to swoop in and grab him, just like that?" asked Tibbs.

"No, sir, this won't be a cakewalk, but we expect the operation to have a high probability of success."

Brooks turned the floor over to DHS Director Sarah McDermott. McDermott, a former Democratic governor, had been a lightning rod for the GOP in her refusal to enforce immigration laws that eventually resulted in amnesty being granted to more than 15 million illegals in the first year after Johnson's re-election.

McDermott, a pudgy fifty-eight-year-old woman, was an outspoken lesbian activist with shortly cropped light brown hair with patches of gray. She never wore make-up or jewelry. Many Immigration and Customs Enforcement (ICE) officers who did not like her referred to her as Director "Butch." Adding fuel to that nickname, the director had not worn a dress a single day of her four years as director that anyone could remember.

"The intelligence for this operation is being coordinated through my office with local law enforcement not sympathetic to Cooper. We, in turn, are passing this information to the Joint Chiefs. We are in place for support but, make no mistake, this will be led by the Joint Chiefs' military choice for this operation."

"What are the risks?" asked Tibbs.

"Without going into every detail, the quantitative risk is that the raid is unsuccessful and we lose team members," replied five-star Gen. Miguel Herrera. The general had a distinguished career in the Marines and was now the first Hispanic chairman of the Joint Chiefs. Herrera was an unlikely choice to be chairman; however, Johnson wanted a Hispanic or other minority as his choice.

A competent officer and administrator, Herrera had only been elevated to five-star status for two years, supplanting many senior and seasoned officers as choice for chairman. And, although Herrera was a capable administrator, his actual combat experience was much lighter than his predecessors, even to some who reported directly to him. His appointment was perceived as a purely political appointment within the military because Johnson made no effort to hide the reasons for his choice.

The Johnson administration had successfully removed or replaced high-ranking military officials within each branch of service who did not agree with Johnson or whom administration officials believed did not advance the beliefs, goals and politics of the Johnson White House.

"Goddamn it, General, no disrespect intended, but the presidency is at stake here, too," blurted Avery Smith.

"This operation must not fail. It needs to be foolproof," added Johnson. "I mean, hell, if we can get Yasir Mahdi in Pakistan, extracting these cowboys out of Austin can't be that damned hard, can it?"

"Sir, the question comes in with engaging fellow Americans if that becomes necessary," replied Herrera.

"Gen. Herrera, these folks became criminals the minute they stepped on to Ellington Air Force Base to recover the Tea Party guy. They shot a federal agent. Then they killed eighteen in the Austin incident. They marched into federal office buildings and had the audacity to arrest ATF and FBI agents. Do you have a goddamned problem? Do your job!" ordered an angry Tibbs.

"Sir…"

"Sir, damn! I want you to make sure you remove anyone from this operation who is not sworn to it and who may have even an ounce of sympathy for Texas. Is that understood? There should not be a single Texan in your chain of command in this operation! I don't care one damned bit about how loyal you think they are," Tibbs said forcefully.

"Yes, sir," replied Gen. Herrera.

"Go on," said Johnson, looking a little bored, resting his chin in his hand.

"Our recommendation is a night operation capture of Gov. Cooper at one of the revolving holding locations they rotate him to every day," Herrera said. "We are not recommending extracting Pops Younger or any other state officials at this time. That is a multi-unit operation that increases the risks exponentially. Let's get the high-value target first."

"Who would lead this, Seal Team Six?" asked Tibbs.

"No, sir. We're recommending a highly skilled, professional DHS Tactical Assault team," answered Herrera.

"Why not Seal Team Six?" asked Johnson. "They got Yasir Mahdi."

Herrera paused for a second, seemingly hesitant to answer the question.

"Mr. President, Seal Team Six is predominately staffed by enlisted men and officers that hail from Texas," Herrera said almost apologetically.

The room went dead silent for a few uneasy seconds.

"Well, goddamn," said Johnson, turning to look off to the sky petulantly.

"Mr. President, the DHS Tactical Assault team is completely capable. Also, they will likely see this as a way to honor and avenge the deaths that occurred at the Austin state capitol," said Herrera.

All in the room looked to the president for his reaction.

"General, just so you understand the obvious, this mission cannot fail. Do you understand me, General?" Johnson leaned forward and repeated his question as he glared at his mission leader.

"Mr. President, as you are well aware, there are no guarantees in an operation like this. We have the best minds in the business on it," Herrera assured his commander-in-chief.

"Give me a probability of success percentage, Gen. Herrera."

The general rubbed his face, moved back in his chair a few inches, completely aware that his career depended on his answer.

"Eighty percent, Mr. President."

"Only *eighty* percent?"

"Sir, the Yasir Mahdi raid had a twenty-five percent chance of success."

"I'm fully aware of that, but that operation was in a foreign country!"

"Failure in this operation has more complex political ramifications," Tibbs said disdainfully, demonstrating his belief that the Joint Chiefs couldn't possibly understand the politics of the operation.

"Sir, you might be more comfortable if we shared the details of the operation," Herrera said.

"Well, isn't that what the American people pay you folks the big bucks for?" Johnson asked sarcastically. "I assume you designed this operation with the risks in mind. I trust you will be successful."

"But…"

"General, the president doesn't need the details," interrupted Brooks.

"Should Secy. Bartlett be briefed on Mexican cooperation in this operation?" Herrera sounded uncertain.

"Mexican cooperation?" repeated a confused president.

Secy. Brooks slammed his fist on the desk. "Damn it, General! We are not discussing every minute detail of this operation at this meeting. Is that understood?" Brooks spat out the last three words.

The president knew not to inquire further. Those at the upper echelon of the political food chain inside the White House knew exactly what Johnson was doing. He was protecting himself from knowing the details if the plan failed. It was called *plausible deniability*. In case of failure, the operation would have scapegoats. Johnson could claim not to have known the ultimate details if the plan went awry. He had an established backdoor to escape political harm in every scenario or attached to every major decision he made as president. His political operatives in the White House were the best ever assembled at providing their president with political cover from all angles.

"Is this operation ready to go?" asked Johnson.

"We would like to have twenty-four hours advance notice to go, but could operate on less. Anything less than four hours could be problematic," said Gen. Herrera. "Of course, it depends on identifying where Cooper is at the exact moment you give orders to launch."

"My orders will come through Secy. Brooks," said Johnson, "when and if they come." He leaned back in his chair, indicating he believed the discussion on the subject was complete.

"Yes, sir. May I ask everyone a question here?"

The president nodded.

"Is this a zero-sum operation?"

The president turned to Secy. Brooks with a slightly perplexed look on his face.

"Explain to the president, Gen. Herrera," ordered Brooks.

"Sir, are we to extract Cooper at all costs? This means we may have to take out certain folks who may be protecting him, such as state troopers, Texas Rangers and even U.S. military personnel operating under the Reserves or Texas State Guard."

President Johnson looked back at the general, then to the others in the room in disbelief.

"General, you are to follow your orders to extract Cooper for prosecution. Those protecting him are violating federal law. I expect you to treat those people as the criminals they are. I expect your operation to be one hundred percent successful. Do you understand?"

"Mr. President, just to be clear. There is a very high likelihood that we may have to neutralize those around Cooper in order to extract him successfully."

Looking at Brooks, but talking to Herrera, Johnson continued, "Am I not being clear here? Just get Cooper, no matter what it takes, Harry!"

"We understand. Do your job," Brooks said to Herrera, as if it were necessary to interpret Johnson's orders.

The general knew he was never going to get the president to authorize the zero-sum possibility. That decision ultimately would be left up to others in the chain of command

The meeting adjourned with Brooks and Herrera to decide on a timeline and further plans for the operation. Johnson didn't trust the entire cabinet to keep a launch date secret.

The president left without any small talk; he had a 12:45 p.m. tee time set with Democratic operatives, followed by a major fundraiser.

# CHAPTER 5

*"Guard with jealous attention the public liberty. Suspect everyone who approaches that jewel. Unfortunately, nothing will preserve it but downright force. Whenever you give up that force, you are inevitably ruined."*

~ *Patrick Henry*
*American Revolution Hero & Founding Father*
*Ardent Supporter of States' Rights (Federalism)*

Annabelle Bartlett knew President Johnson couldn't help himself. She admired and loathed the man at the same time. She admired his unmatched political prowess but didn't like his methods when he used all his weapons, including playing the race card on her during the primary process. Johnson, a political unknown outside his home state, had sprung out of nowhere to snatch the Democratic nomination from her. Despite the fact that the GOP offered up a candidate who didn't energize the GOP, Johnson's meteoric ascension was historic in American politics.

The primary campaign was especially brutal, but Johnson's camp found the political sweet spot against her by tagging Bartlett a soft-core *racist*. The model used to destroy her in the campaign was so successful that Johnson's operatives continued to use it to exert their political will on Congress, political foes and even those in Johnson's own party when he needed a certain outcome. Bartlett was his first political foe where this strategy actually worked, and it worked well enough to win Johnson's nomination over an established candidate like Bartlett.

Johnson nominated Bartlett for secretary of state to help close the ranks of his party, eyeing his re-election campaign in a matter of days after his initial election. Avery Smith managed the campaign like a world class chess master, positioning Johnson for ultimate success.

Even after her appointment, there always existed an uneasy form of détente between Johnson and Bartlett. They used each other for their individual political gains. With Johnson limited to two terms, Bartlett was in a perfect position to become the first female president after Johnson stepped down.

Unfortunately for Bartlett, she had been taken to task in the media and polling over an embassy that was overrun in Africa, where a high-ranking embassy officer and several staff were killed by Muslim extremists. Staff at the outpost had begged for additional security, and Bartlett's State Department did not respond quickly enough to provide military assistance. State appeared dysfunctional and inept. In Senate hearings, Bartlett was combative, evasive and appeared haggard. She knew she needed to turn public opinion back in her favor, and the Texas crisis looked like a prime opportunity.

Johnson had hung Bartlett out to dry on several occasions, especially on the African embassy affair. Bartlett never forgot. Her plan was to resign to work full-time on her election campaign after the first year of Johnson's second term, and the Texas crisis provided a unique opening she couldn't resist. Her political handlers were wary of any Johnson administration stigma that might attach to her from the Rash Sally investigation and the suspicious events surrounding the deaths of Tim Spilner and his wife.

Bartlett contacted senior Texas Republican Sen. Kevin Simpson through Under Secy. of State Marjorie Callum for a secret meeting. Callum had reached out to the senator discreetly to gauge his temperature for a negotiation of the Texas crisis.

This was a calculated move Bartlett knew could backfire. The meeting was entirely her idea, and the administration wasn't consulted. She had not been given a green light. Being a complete control freak who detested anyone who didn't follow protocols and the chain of command, Johnson would be enraged if he found out the Bartlett meeting was happening without his knowledge.

Bartlett and her staff had an initial meeting with Sen. Simpson at the home of a Simpson staffer outside the Beltway.

Simpson was a tall, fair-skinned former prosecutor who always seemed a little stiff when he spoke publicly. He had recently become a vociferous opponent of the president. Still, he was identified as a moderate senator by many Texas voters, especially compared to the newly elected firebrand and Tea Party favorite, Sen. Roberto Perez. Perez had become something of a media darling overnight and was surprisingly effective in his first few months in office with his brazen style for confronting administration officials in various hearings.

Simpson had been rendered irrelevant since Perez's upset win in the primary against a much better-funded establishment state Republican. Perez went on to trounce his Democratic challenger in the general election.

Now, the "Texas" problem was Simpson's chance to steal the spotlight back, not only in Texas, but nationally. He had his own political aspirations for the GOP nomination.

Both Simpson and Bartlett knew that, if they brokered a peaceful end to the "Texas Crisis," their political capital would shoot through the roof. They also knew that it was important to operate incognito for now from the president and the governor.

Bartlett, Callum and three staffers arrived for the meeting at a home in Arlington, Virginia shortly after dark. Bartlett traveled in an unmarked black Suburban with heavily tinted windows, driven by one of her trusted staff. When Bartlett arrived, they pulled into the long driveway and honked once. An automatic garage door opened to an empty bay. The driver carefully parked the huge SUV that barely fit without the garage door hitting the rear of the vehicle. Secrecy was paramount and no one was taking a chance of being seen.

Eight minutes later, Sen. Simpson arrived in a similar vehicle, pulling into a second empty garage bay. Inside, they all made their introductions and pleasantries, but it was clear this was Bartlett's show.

"Thanks for coming, everyone," she said. "As you know, this Texas crisis continues to expand and could be headed for the precipice. I am here of my own accord, without administration approval. I want all of you to know that. I know the political risk involved for Sen. Simpson and want you to know I appreciate your confidence."

"Thank you, Madame Secretary, for arranging this meeting. I also thank you for taking the same risks. If I'm not mistaken, our goal here is to try to establish a framework for a peaceful resolution to this crisis." Simpson sounded as if he were making a major speech from the Senate floor.

"Senator, my suggestion is to start with what we both believe each side has as the major outcome of the current crisis. I'll begin with the administration. Johnson simply wants Cooper's head on a plate. He'll take the attorney general and lieutenant governor, too, and the cowboy," Bartlett stated, referring to Pops Younger. "President Johnson was thoroughly embarrassed by the events in Austin. He was livid over the Ellington Air Force Base raid, the shutdown of air bases, and the fact that there are still federal agents under arrest and being indicted for crimes for following federal orders. And, of course, there are the deaths."

"Secy. Bartlett, those are all reasonable assertions that do not surprise me. The major issues for Gov. Cooper are the detention of citizens, raids on homes, confiscation of Texans' guns; lack of due process, and the incursion into Austin of federal agents and U.S. Army troops. Now we have what amounts to a blockade and the assault on the Texas banking system. What can we do to reconcile the issues?" asked Simpson.

During this exchange, it was apparent that both staffs were instructed to remain tight-lipped. Bartlett and Simpson had to restrain themselves from expressing their opinions on the crisis, with diametrically opposed views of their individual versions of the facts. They were clearly on opposite ends of the crisis and the debate. But, being the political animals they were, they were both seeking a larger outcome, and not necessarily for the good of the country nor Texas.

"Senator, let me make a proposal to start this off and you tell me if it will sell in Austin," said Bartlett.

"Okay, Madame Secretary, I appreciate you taking the initiative," answered Simpson.

"I would propose Justice drop all federal charges against Cooper and state officials. In return, Texas releases all prisoners who refused to sign non-intervention agreements in Austin after their arrests and, of course, a release of the federal agents arrested in the Ellington raid."

"Seems reasonable," said the silver-haired Simpson, resting his elbows on the table. "In return, troops on the border are pulled back, banking transactions return to normal and the blockade in the Gulf ends," added Simpson.

Bartlett thought for a moment, then said, "I think that could work, but I can tell you this. Johnson wants and has to have some kind of skin on the wall."

"Like what?"

"Some kind of apology, admittance of a mistake, something…"

"Wow, Madame Secretary, you obviously don't know our governor."

"But you do know the president. He has to perceive this as a *win* in some fashion."

"Ha, never let a good crisis go to waste…"

"Don't go there, Senator. His words, not mine."

"I would need to know exactly what form this contrition by Cooper would be, obviously."

"Let's put our heads together. I need your insight on what your governor would agree to."

What Bartlett apparently wasn't clued in about was that, like Johnson and Bartlett's political relationship, Simpson and Gov. Cooper were not that fond of each other, either. They also had an uneasy co-existence.

"I can tell you," said Simpson, "if Cooper thought it would end the crisis, he would already have turned himself in to federal authorities. He doesn't, so he hasn't."

The room fell silent for a few uneasy moments before Simpson continued. "The key here is what the president wants from Cooper for his act of contrition. He's not going to get much, if anything at all, from Cooper. Cooper is a straight-forward kind of guy. Isn't it possible to end the crisis without anyone *winning*?"

"Senator," Bartlett said, "you know the president. Every move he makes is politically motivated. He has to be perceived as the winner. Now, whether it becomes patently obvious that he is or the press spins it that way, doesn't make much difference to him."

Bartlett hesitated slightly before expanding on her proposal. "We propose the state of Texas pay $1 million each to the eighteen victims who died in Austin, to be paid to the victims' families."

Despite his disagreements with Gov. Cooper, Simpson was incensed by Bartlett's proposal. Using every ounce of civility he could muster, he replied, "Madam Secretary, I can assure you the people of Texas do not consider those eighteen folks *victims* by any stretch of the imagination. Also, there is the death of Mumford, the Tea Party guy."

Bartlett sighed, then sat back into her chair. "Senator, you know Johnson. It will be difficult, if not impossible, to convince him this is better than your governor doing the perp walk in handcuffs. But it will give him skin on the wall and possibly end the crisis."

"I don't see it, Madam Secretary," Simpson retorted.

"If not that, please offer something up. Otherwise, it will appear that a sitting U.S. president bowed to a governor in a crisis. Maybe your team can come up with another offer?"

"Give me a chance to run this by Cooper. Make no mistake; he's a shrewd politician but, despite my differences with him, I do believe he has Texas' best interests in his heart."

"Let's meet again in twenty-four hours. Can we all meet here or should we move the meeting?" asked Bartlett.

"Let's move it to another location," suggested Callum.

After agreeing to a new location, the group exited the suburban home, quietly and furtively, leaving the same way they'd arrived, secretly.

# CHAPTER 6

*"Democracy... while it lasts is more bloody than either aristocracy or monarchy. Remember, democracy never lasts long. It soon wastes, exhausts, and murders itself. There is never a democracy that did not commit suicide."*

*~ John Adams*
*Signer of the Declaration of Independence*
*2nd U.S. President*

C huck Dixon had been at the center of the storm during the federal assault on the state capitol, but he was anxious to hear how the feds' actions were affecting day-to-day life in Texas, his business, his employees and his friends.

As he drove the rental car to his business in Houston early that morning, he heard a news conference from Washington, D.C. indicating that the Federal Reserve had confiscated Texas' $2 billion in gold that the feds held for the state. The Fed indicated it was a *cautionary* step due to the current instability in Texas. "That's going to be another incentive toward secession," Chuck muttered.

At his office in Houston, he immediately met with his entire staff. His managers informed him that his information technology business had ground to a halt. New customer contracts that were to be completed with out-of-state clients were put on hold. Cash flow had been reduced to a trickle, as the only clients paying were in-state customers who happened to bank at state-chartered banks.

Additionally, the IRS had frozen all of the company's banking accounts, causing every employee's last paychecks to bounce. The day after the Austin incident, the IRS again showed up at Chuck's business to confiscate records. Despite the fact that no search warrant was produced, the agents conducted their raid, using sheer terror by showing up with dozens of federal agents wearing bullet-proof vests and flourishing assault weapons. Chuck's employees, caught completely by surprise, offered no resistance.

Most of the employees remained, despite the raid and the fact that most had no money. They believed in Chuck and his ability to figure out a solution.

Although federal workers continued to get paid, many local police, fire and emergency crews operated without pay. There was a rising resentment against federal employees. Texans, in general, who were by nature distrustful of Washington, D.C., were incensed that federal employees were still being paid, yet benefits Texans had earned were not.

There was a run on several national banks in Texas that immediately adopted Greek-like emergency banking standards, limiting customer withdrawals to no more than five hundred dollars per day.

What began as sporadic shortages of certain items now became full-fledged runs on supplies similar to what Texans and Gulf Coast residents had seen on a limited basis in advance of a large hurricane. This scenario always occurred when an intense rush on supplies, such as bottled water, gasoline, generators, diesel fuel, milk, eggs, batteries, candles and other staples outran the ability of the normal supply chain to keep store shelves stocked. For Texas, these goods were still available in-state and could sustain citizens for months, but the ability to replace it as fast as it was hoarded was a challenge. Many stores in urban areas began to limit customer purchases on certain items.

Riots at grocery stores over food shortages had already broken out in the Parkdale Heights area of south Dallas, not far from the Cotton Bowl, and in the Fifth Ward in Houston. The shortages were isolated, but Texas was sitting on a tinder box in large urban areas if the shortages lingered and became worse.

The Fed had also stopped federal firearms dealers in Texas from conducting background checks for gun purchases in Texas. Gun dealers were in a quandary. Texans were rushing to purchase weapons at a pace even faster than when the administration was pushing its assault weapons ban. The ATF let the dealers know they would be prosecuted if they sold weapons without the check, and now the system was unavailable to them.

Firearms dealers knew the Independence referendum was non-binding and the chances they would still be under ATF scrutiny after the crisis subsided was likely. Other than private gun transactions, which had recently become illegal without government paperwork and a federal background check, guns could not be purchased in Texas for the first time in her rich, gun-loving history.

President Johnson's order to shut down points of presence (POPs) for major internet providers serving Texas was partly effective but not nearly as effective as hoped. Many Texas-based telecommunications companies had disaster recovery plans that re-routed communications and had the ability to bypass the POPs the president ordered suspended from typical suppliers such as AT&T and Verizon.

To completely cut Texas off from the Internet, Johnson would have to take down the entire U.S. telecommunications network and satellites that provided back-up and remote Internet access. If Texans were lucky enough to use a Texas Internet provider and not a national telecom company, those customers likely still had Internet service, but it was slow and service was sporadic. President Johnson's effort to isolate Texas' communication to the outside world was only partially effective.

The administration actions to isolate Texas began to have national implications. Texas shut off all oil, gasoline and natural gas pipelines out of the state, and the blockade in the Gulf of Mexico halted tanker shipments coming out of Houston, Beaumont and Corpus Christi. Texas had the largest refining capacity in the United States, and turning off this supply of energy produced a dramatic and immediate impact. The European Union was also feeling the pinch of the reduced refining capacity and continued to put pressure on the Johnson administration to end the crisis.

It was February, when much of the northeast depended on natural gas and fuel oil. Prices for fuel oil skyrocketed 200 percent to reach all-time highs within days of the Austin skirmish. Gasoline was now over $7.00 per gallon in California and the northeast. Food prices nationwide, especially beef and chicken, also shot upward, as Texas was a prime provider of both.

Texas was fortunate to be the only state with its own electrical grid. Without direct federal military intervention, there wasn't anything the Johnson administration could do to jeopardize the grid, outside of direct military strikes.

Texas, with the fourteenth largest economy in the world if measured as a country, was intertwined with the global economy on a scale that even President Johnson and his administration underestimated.

Shortly after his own assessment of Texas affairs, Chuck sat down with almost twenty of his leaders from the *Spring Creek Tea Party* he and Stan Mumford had set up years before. In the past, a meeting like this would have drawn over two hundred folks. Now, however, people were scared to participate for fear of becoming targets of the IRS or federal agents. They knew Big Brother could monitor all their communications, whether email, cell phone or land line.

"Folks, we have to reorganize like never before," Chuck said sternly.

"Okay, Chuck, we know you know what's going on in Austin. Can't you fill us in?" asked one member.

"I'm not so much in the *know* as you think. I was there for all the fireworks, but I know the wheels are turning there and in DC. I can't predict the outcome, and I'm certain they can't either."

He paused. "How are your families set for food?" he asked.

"Most of us are okay, as we were storing food anyway," answered Lansford.

"How many still have Internet?"

About half the group raised their hands.

"Do any of you have short-wave radios?"

Two raised their hands.

"Ammunition?"

The entire group now had a collective look of concern.

"Do you know something we should know?" asked Lansford.

"I'm talking about being prepared for any and all circumstances. I'm not saying armed conflict is coming or is unavoidable, but we would be stupid not to be prepared, for our families' sake. How are your ammunition supplies?"

Almost to a man, they agreed they had lots of ammunition, but nobody was satisfied that it was enough. They all wanted more, but ammunition was in very short supply due to the administration's previous actions and the government purposely buying up supply.

"Let's compare notes to see who has what and if it makes sense to trade ammo or weapons to maximize your arsenals. For instance, if you have a .223 but no ammo and your buddy has 10,000 rounds but doesn't have a .223, you can trade to maximize firepower." The group then went into a thirty-five minute discussion about who had what weapons and ammo, and several agreements to trade were made.

There was general concern among a few that this topic was even discussed. It was apparent to the group that Chuck had gone through some sort of transformation. Having his home raided and destroyed by federal agents with military gear and a tank without a warrant, being removed from his wife and child, having his best friend shot and killed by federal agents in front of his family, and being held at a secret location without due process can do that to a person. Being rescued by Texas Rangers compensated somewhat for the imprisonment part but, on balance, it was not nearly enough.

"Due to the circumstances we find ourselves in, I am hereby declaring that we are officially transforming into a Minuteman group. We want to establish a core organizational message you can take back to your neighborhoods to prepare for anything. Contact your local sheriffs to find out their positions on our current crisis. We need the sheriffs, but only if they are like-minded."

"Chuck, you always said we were a peaceful political grassroots organization. Are we now converting to a *militia*?" asked an elderly man.

"I think we can all agree the political process is broken. What we become in the future is dependent on the federal government's actions forward. As a political organization, we were denied our Constitutional rights. They even shot and killed my best friend and a great friend to many of you in Stan Mumford."

"I'm not sure about all of this," said a man Chuck recognized from some of the early meetings of the group. "The minute we reorganize into a militia, won't we become a target?"

"Are you serious?" asked Chuck.

"We were a target before any of this," yelled an incredulous Lansford. "Hell, the administration pinned the assassination attempt on the Tea Party when they knew damned good and well it was carried out by a Muslim extremist! Chuck was dragged out of his home and had to watch it being destroyed. They raided our homes. They killed Stan. What the hell are you talking about? Jesus…" The man that asked the question dropped his head, realizing any attempt to argue his point would be pathetic. They were right. He knew it. They knew it. The decision he and the others had to make was to acknowledge the fact that the political process they had attempted to fix with the Tea Party was unfixable.

"Let's make a list of preparedness notes to distribute to the entire group. It's entirely possible this thing gets worse before it gets better. I don't see Cooper capitulating to the feds, but I may be wrong. I hope not, but I don't think so," Chuck said.

"What happens if the crisis passes?" asked another of the group.

"Then we will go back to being a Tea Party, a political grassroots constitutional organization in the same form. Let's hope that's what happens." Chuck jammed his hands into his jeans pockets. "But let me assure everyone of something. The Independence referendum passed by a 68 percent to 32 percent margin. We are like-minded here with most Texans. The simple fact is that most other Texans and even those in other states are coming to the same conclusion; it likely isn't fixable."

"A lot would have to happen to turn the tide. Over 50 percent of the country is on some kind of government dole. We just granted amnesty to fifteen million illegal aliens. We all know how they vote. President Johnson has dictated gun control in Texas through executive order. The Republican Party is in shambles and completely ineffective at the top. Every day that goes by, we have less in common with our fellow Americans. Even the Supreme Court doesn't know how to interpret the Constitution. We have become a godless society. Should I continue?" asked Lansford.

"Let's all pray," said Chuck.

Men removed hats and caps, and they all bowed their heads.

"Dear Heavenly Father," Chuck prayed fervently, "we ask that you protect our families and all Texans in this time of crisis. We ask that you impart your wisdom to our state leaders so they follow the path that honors your will. I also ask that you shine your light and wisdom on this president and his administration that they diffuse this crisis. We ask this in your holy name, Jesus Christ, our Lord and Savior. Amen."

"Amen."

# CHAPTER 7

*"You may have to fight a battle more than once to win it."*

~ *Margaret Thatcher*
*Former Prime Minister of Great Britain*
*& Conservative Party Leader*

T exas Gov. Cooper stood at the podium in the famous rotunda of the Texas state capitol building. He was flanked at the podium by Atty. Gen. Weaver, Lt. Gov. Foster, and U.S. Sen. Perez. Standing off in the background were Pops Younger and five other Texas Rangers.

On the walls of each floor of the rotunda were portraits of former governors and past presidents of the Republic of Texas. It was an appropriate setting for what would be a historical event.

Approximately one hundred fifty reporters and members of the press had gathered in the rotunda area for a press conference. Approximately two hundred more were not granted access and were left to broadcast from the north or south steps of the building. Satellite news vans and trucks took all parking for blocks near the center of downtown Austin. The intrigue generated by the crisis created a media frenzy not seen in modern times. The drama was being played out on the daily news in every country that had access to news feeds.

"Ladies and gentlemen, thank you for coming," said Cooper. "This morning we learned the Federal Reserve has confiscated Texas gold that was formerly stored in Federal Reserve facilities. This represents more than two billion dollars in gold reserves at today's prices owned by the people of Texas."

Looking sternly into the cameras as if he were speaking directly to President Johnson, Cooper cautioned, "Let me state emphatically that the gold confiscated by this government and the Federal Reserve belongs to Texans. It does not belong to the U.S. government. We hereby demand that this gold be returned to Texas. This is a direct violation of the Tenth Amendment. This administration continues to operate outside the limits of our Constitution and this is one more blatant example of outrageous overreach. Texans won't stand for it. I won't stand for it."

During the next pause, dozens of reporters started yelling questions at the governor.

"Hold on, hold on. We'll try to get to some of your questions." Cooper held both hands up as if to stop a car approaching an intersection.

"Please allow me to continue. Please!" insisted Cooper. As the noise stepped down several notches, he continued. "This is more proof that this president has no desire to diffuse this crisis. In fact, this only escalates tensions. We can also report that there have been more military sorties over Texas airspace. These are dangerous and provocative acts by this administration."

The press seemed about to explode with questions. Murmurs going through the audience were unsettling. To the press in attendance, the stakes were going up and the crisis would not easily be averted.

"Let me state again for the record and for the entire world to see. This administration and this Congress are the only ones who can dispel this situation. We have no other agenda. I will read to all of you what Texas expects for relations to return to normal."

Cooper pulled out a sheet of paper, then turned and handed it to Atty. Gen. Weaver. Weaver stepped to the podium.

"Here are the steps the federal government must take to normalize relations with the state of Texas," stated Weaver, reading directly from the paper. "First, the Justice Department must drop all charges against state officials, including Gov. Cooper, the lieutenant governor, all state officials and the Texas Rangers, for recovering Texas citizens detained without due process and for the events initiated by the Johnson administration that resulted in the deaths of eighteen federal agents and members of the U.S. Army Rangers."

Looking up from the paper briefly, Weaver went on. "Next, the Federal Reserve must return all Texas gold illegally seized and allow it to be shipped back to Texas for safe storing.

"Congress must appoint an independent prosecutor and commission to investigate the Rash Sally assassination task force. It's become *blatantly* obvious that the Tea Party had no part in the assassination attempt," Weaver added sternly.

"Next, Congress shall appoint a separate independent prosecutor to investigate the suspicious deaths of Stan Mumford and federal whistleblower Tim Spilner and his wife.

"This administration must remove the limitations on banking transactions, restore Internet points-of-presence, remove troops at our borders and end the naval blockade in the Gulf. Additionally, the IRS must stand down and immediately cease and desist punitive actions against Texan citizens solely because of their political affiliations."

Looking extremely agitated with his next point, Weaver stated, "This administration has taken the cowardly action of withholding Social Security benefits from those who have paid into it their entire lives, simply because they live in Texas. This administration has stopped unemployment checks for those who have paid into unemployment insurance. And, most cowardly of all, this administration has refused to pay those who have served this country in the military by withholding VA benefits and retirement checks of those veterans. The benefits earned by Texans must be restored immediately."

Weaver moved away as Cooper stepped back to the podium.

"Once these actions are completed by the administration, and not one minute before they comply one hundred percent, we will turn control of the military bases back to the federal government. Additionally, we will pardon those under arrest for various crimes committed against Texas and her citizens by members of the FBI, ATF and U.S. military for actions at Ellington Field, raids on Tea Party offices and members' residences and the assault here in Austin just a few weeks ago, with the exception of any charges brought for the murder of Stan Mumford."

Cooper finished his demands and then looked to members of the press to take questions. Many were yelling questions at him already.

"Governor, will you allow the feds to take you into custody to avert this crisis and help Texans restore their Social Security benefits?" asked a female reporter from the New York Times.

"No, I just read to you what Texas wants me to do."

"Governor, are you saying that, if the administration tells you this is what it will take to settle this crisis, that you will allow Texans to continue to have their Social Security and veterans benefits suspended because you don't want to be arrested?" she asked as a follow-up question.

Cooper said firmly. "Ma'am, I just read to you our terms for normalization of relations with this administration. Nothing more, nothing less. Texans paid into those systems with the guarantee by the good faith and credit of the United States that they would get certain benefits in return. Whether this government reneges on its responsibilities to people who have faithfully served in the military or who have trusted in Social Security, has absolutely nothing to do with this administration's desire to arrest me on fabricated charges. Pay these people, Mr. President. Do the right thing!" Cooper stated emphatically.

"Governor, will you turn yourself in?" the reporter persisted.

Cooper turned around and looked at his staff in disbelief.

"Next question."

"Sir, you mentioned sorties being flown over Texas by U.S. military. Can you expand on that?" asked another reporter.

"I can't be specific for security reasons; however, I will tell you that this administration has authorized provocative flights over Texas by B-2 stealth bombers and by B-52s. Also, they have launched several fighter aircraft from a carrier in the Gulf that has skirted our shoreline."

"Do you believe these are meant to intimidate or are they responses to your administration taking over U.S. military bases?"

"Both," said Cooper stoically.

"What right do you have to take over U.S. military bases?" asked a reporter from MSNBC.

"Our takeover of those bases was in response to an armed incursion by federal troops into a sovereign Texas."

"You mean Texas, a state in the union?"

"No, I mean a sovereign Texas. The fact that we are a state at this current point in our history does not mean this administration can trample the U.S. Constitution and trample our sovereignty."

"Are you going to argue that the Supremacy Clause in the Constitution does not give the federal government jurisdiction over Texas when certain laws between the state and federal government conflict?" pressed the MSNBC reporter.

"Son, are you going to sit there and tell me that the Supremacy Clause gives this administration the power to hold Texans without due process?

To invade their homes? To violate their right of privacy? I believe you need to go back and read the Bill of Rights, son. Next question."

"What will you do, Governor, if the administration sends in troops?" asked a reporter normally stationed in Washington, D.C.

"That would be a grave mistake and miscalculation," Cooper said patiently.

"Are you saying Texas would respond militarily?"

"I'm not going to state our options, but I can tell you all options are on the table."

"So you would respond militarily?"

"Ma'am," said Cooper. "I'm not going to offer conjecture nor am I going to state our intent in that event. I will state that I sincerely hope this administration does not elect to take up arms again against its own citizens as they did a few weeks ago in Austin."

From a CBS reporter, "Governor, why does Texas want its gold back? Is it to have a gold-backed currency in the event Texas secedes?"

"We want our gold back because it belongs to Texas. Period. Next question."

"It's obvious the administration is trying to put the squeeze on Texas with blockades, federal payment suspensions, road closures and Internet interruptions. How long can you go before conditions get so bad for Texans that you must consider surrendering for the good of your citizens?"

"That's obviously the president's intent. We'll make that decision when Texans tell me that's what they want me to do. Right now, they are overwhelmingly in favor of the stance we have taken. If you need evidence of that, look at the recent Independence referendum where 68 percent voted in favor."

"Well, sir, that was a non-binding resolution before these sanctions were in place," said the reporter. "If these were to go on for six or eight weeks or longer, don't you think that support would fade?"

"I think you would need to ask your average Texan that question. Texans are a fairly resolute bunch and have been throughout our history. They feel like they have been wronged by this administration and that the government has essentially abandoned the U.S. Constitution. If they want me to take another course, they will tell me."

Another of the media asked, "Do you have anything you would like to say to President Johnson?"

"No, but I do have something to say to the U.S. Congress and that is to do your damned job," barked the governor. "You have an executive branch that is out of control. Appoint independent prosecutors and let's get this resolved."

"You have nothing to say to the president directly?" the reporter persisted, failing to notice the governor's change of temper.

"Okay, yes, since you insist," Cooper said. "Mr. President, spend some quiet time reading the United States Constitution. Then, after you have read it, give it to your staff to read and have someone administer a test on it to you and your administration."

"Governor, are you mocking the president of the United States?"

"No, but he's mocking our founding fathers with his actions."

"Will you pursue secession if this isn't resolved?"

Cooper stared down the questioner. "I can't answer that at this time. Our preference would be for this president to take the actions we outlined."

"But 68 percent of Texans voted for secession in the resolution referendum, right?"

"I'm aware of that. Texans are mad right now. I dare say that, if this crisis continues, that 68 percent number will grow."

"So you're saying Texas could be headed toward secession if the administration does not back off?"

"No, I'm saying all options are on the table."

"Including secession?"

"That would be up to Texans," said the governor.

"Wouldn't that also be up to the United States?"

"I'm not going to get into that argument with you."

"But, sir, don't you believe the rest of the U.S. has any say in the matter of Texas deciding to secede?"

"Ma'am, what I do know is that we have sent blood and treasure to all corners of the globe to spread democracy, to help countries win their independence from dictators and tyranny," Cooper said wearily. "Wouldn't it be a little hypocritical for any American to deny a state *its* independence if its population wanted it?"

"Wasn't that issue settled in 1860?"

"No, the Civil War started in 1860. Different time in history, different circumstances."

"But the Supreme Court ruled in Texas vs. White...."

"Ma'am, there are constitutional scholars who can argue the validity of that court case until the cows come home. I will say that ruling was made with a full re-constructionist court appointed by President Lincoln. I'll leave it to you and the scholars to make your own interpretations."

Another reporter shouted, "But that's the Supreme Court and their rulings are final!"

"Oh, really?" Cooper grinned at the reporter. "I guess you're not familiar with the Dred Scott decision. The Supreme Court is not infallible, sir. It took the Thirteenth Amendment to fix that Supreme Court decision." Cooper was referring to the court decision that blacks could not be citizens, fixed only by the amendment that ended slavery.

"Folks, that's all I have for today. Thank you for coming. God bless Texas."

# CHAPTER 8

*"The marvel of all history is the patience with which men and women submit to burdens unnecessarily laid upon them by their governments."*

*~ George Washington*
*American Revolution Hero, Founding Father*
*1st President of the United States*

Gene Foster's cell phone rang shortly after eight a.m. He glanced at it, then picked it up immediately when he saw it was from Sen. Simpson.

"Good morning, Senator," he said.

"Hello, Lieutenant Governor."

"Senator, we missed you at our meeting here a few days ago."

"Gene, I've had a meeting with Secy. Bartlett and I have some interesting proposals to share with the governor."

"From the administration?"

Simpson paused. "Well, yes, but not directly. Bartlett thinks she can broker an end to the crisis. I need to float some ideas by the governor."

"I'm sure the governor will be interested in hearing what you have to say. When did you talk to Bartlett?"

"I've had two meetings with her."

"Well, Senator, I trust you presented our positions clearly."

"I believe I did. Can we tee up a call with the governor?"

"Give me a few minutes to put together a secure call. I'll call you back after I've reached the governor to give you the access information."

Thirty minutes later, the governor, senator, lieutenant governor, and attorney general were on a secure conference bridge.

"Governor, thank you for jumping on this call on short notice. I'll get right to the point. Bartlett has reached out to me to help broker a solution to the situation."

"No offense, Senator, but why you and why now?" asked Foster

"I really don't know, except that I'm accessible," said Simpson, who had returned to Washington after the meeting with Cooper and other congressmen at the capitol in Austin.

"Okay, Simpson, what's the proposal?" Cooper asked sharply. The governor had a penchant for getting directly to the point and purposely didn't address Simpson by his title.

"Here it is," said the senator. "Release the incarcerated federal agents, restore the military bases to federal control and turn the oil and gas pipelines back on. In return, they will drop any charges against you, state officials and Pops Younger, and they'll restore all banking, Internet, roads and shipping."

A few moments of silence followed the senator's proposal.

"That's it? What about the IRS?" asked Cooper. "That simple?"

"Secy. Bartlett claims there is no IRS targeting," replied Simpson.

"She's a wily old dog, Senator. Surely she knows better. That has to be on the table as well."

"I believe it can be, Governor."

"And what do I tell Stan Mumford's widow?"

Another few moments of silence.

"Governor, that's a tough question but we are talking about the overall good of Texas."

"Senator, I don't think we release those under indictment for his murder. I think that is a non-starter."

Clearly frustrated, Simpson continued, "Governor, I know that sucks. But again, look at those who will suffer over the loss of Social Security benefits. What about the blockade? What if necessary medicines become unavailable?"

"Senator, you don't have to lecture me about what is in the best interests of Texas. The problem with this so-called solution is it only puts a temporary Band Aid on the issue. This administration will still flout the Constitution. I need some type of commitment that Congress is going to act on the criminal actions of this administration. I suggest you go confer with your fellow senators and congressmen and get a special prosecutor appointed for Mumford's death, the Spilner couple, and the entire Rash Sally investigation."

"Governor, that will take time and you know it. Do you really have that much time? Does Texas have that much time?" asked the exasperated senator.

"The problem, as everyone on this call knows full well is that, even if we avert this crisis, this administration will continue to punish Texas and will continue to shred the Constitution. So, the question is, do we draw a line in the sand now, or regroup?"

"Governor, let's meet and get back to the senator after we discuss this internally," suggested Foster.

"Senator," said the governor, "let us talk among ourselves. Let's get back on this same conference bridge at noon today. That gives us a little over two hours to decide how to move forward."

"Thank you, Governor."

"I have one question."

"Yes, sir?"

"Is this an official administration offer or is this Bartlett on her own?"

"Sir, the secretary has indicated she can get the administration to agree to these terms."

"So this is not an *official* offer from Johnson?"

"Officially, no, sir."

"Why not?"

"Governor, this is just not how this president operates. As you know, Tibbs wants to tack your hide on the wall, and he carries a lot of weight with the president."

"Too much weight," Cooper retorted.

"I understand, sir. Bartlett is motivated by her own agenda, as I'm sure is obvious at this juncture."

"Well, Simpson, this would be a nice feather in your cap, too, if successful," Cooper said half-sarcastically just to test Simpson's reaction.

"Governor, my motivation is solely in the best interests of Texas. For those on the call, let me remind everyone that Bartlett came to me."

"Oh, I'm sure that's not lost on anyone here," said Foster.

"Gene, let's figure out how to pull everyone together," said the governor as he closed the conference call.

Ten minutes later, the same participants, including Maj. Gen. Rex Conroy and minus Sen. Simpson, were on another secure conference bridge.

"Okay, what does everyone think? Is it genuine?" asked Foster.

"First of all, in good conscience, no matter what is decided here today, I want input from Pops and I want to talk to Mumford's widow," Cooper said.

"I'll see if we can get Pops on the call. Be back shortly," said Foster.

The governor for the most part made small talk as it took a few minutes to run Pops down and get him to call into the conference bridge.

"Younger here," he drawled.

"Pops, welcome to the call. We received an interesting call from Simpson this morning."

"Is that turd still in D.C. or has he decided to come back?" Pops asked in what was obviously a rhetorical question.

Over the next twenty minutes, the group went through the offer from Bartlett.

"Well, Pops, you know I value your instincts. What are your thoughts?"

"They'll renege," Pops said flatly.

"In what way?" asked Cooper.

"Sir, I wouldn't trust them damned carpetbaggers to unscrew a longneck beer the right way. There's a catch somewhere. There always is."

"We have an obligation to try to settle this peacefully. I've always said I would allow myself to be arrested if that's what it took."

"Governor, you know that wouldn't solve anything and it could make things worse. We appreciate your willingness to be a martyr in this, but Texans know this isn't the answer. In fact, they are vehemently opposed to having their governor arrested after an armed incursion into the state by the feds," said Weaver calmly.

"Gentlemen, I'm willing to go down this road if everyone agrees this is the right course but, again, allow me to speak to Mrs. Mumford before I let those who shot her husband walk. I also want to speak to Chuck Dixon."

"Absolutely, Governor," agreed Foster.

"Understandable," said Weaver.

"Please do, Governor. That would make us all feel better about this deal," said Sen. Perez.

After the call ended, the governor's staff placed a call to Chuck Dixon for a thirty-minute discussion. Next, Cooper called Sheila Mumford and, although not on the phone with her as long as he was with Dixon, Gov. Cooper had to wipe tears away when he finished.

The governor turned to Foster. "Gene, let's make this deal. I don't trust that Johnson or Tibbs will live up to it, but we have to give it one more chance."

"Well, nobody in Texas trusts Johnson or Tibbs. What if they get the bases back and then pull some stunt or renege on the deal?" asked Foster.

"Texas can only stand so much, Gene. If that happens, I think our path is clearer than one might have ever imagined."

"Let's pray this fixes the immediate situation, but we both know the feds are on an unsustainable path and dragging Texas down with them."

"A battle for another day, Gene, I hope…."

"Amen, Governor."

The next day was Sunday. After attending an early church service and a short private meeting with its pastor, Gov. Cooper called Sen. Simpson to give him the okay to negotiate with Secy. of State Bartlett with terms Texas was willing to accept.

"Senator, I agree to all terms; however, I have one demand of my own."

"And what would that be?" Simpson said somewhat reluctantly.

"I demand that a special and independent prosecutor be named by Congress to pursue the Rash Sally conspiracy and cover-up, the Spilner deaths and the Mumford shooting," stated the governor.

Simpson objected. "Look, Governor," he said, "we both know Texas doesn't have enough time for Congress to get its act together, but I promise to deliver the terms to the secretary of state as dictated."

Cooper was taking a calculated gamble that pressure was also mounting on Johnson from other sources. The price of gasoline hit the ozone. The Dow Jones had lost 24 percent of its value since the crisis began. Other nations were feeling the pinch from Texas' refining capacity being offline. Allies were critical of the Johnson administration for sending troops into Texas.

The national leadership of the GOP was critical of Johnson as expected, but was also leaning heavily on the Texas congressional delegation to end the stand-off by influencing the governor. The GOP had long since abandoned trying to reach Cooper and knew they had zero credibility with him. The governor had despised Republican leadership for years and had made his criticism very public.

Adding to the grief Johnson was feeling, a big northeaster hit the New England area and fuel oil prices were at record highs. Although the banking transaction shut-down was impacting Texans, it also rocked the financial markets. Large corporations who had operations in Texas were predicting huge losses.

On CNBC, the host of Squawk Box condemned the administration, mocking Johnson for thinking he could unilaterally shut down the fourteenth largest economy in the world.

"Positioning troops on their borders? Blockading ports? Shutting down bank transactions? Suspending payments legitimately owed to seniors and veterans? Interrupting telecommunications?" he questioned. "If this was a country, this would be tantamount to declaring war!

"Texas has now shut off the spigot on oil, gasoline, aviation fuel and fuel oil to rest of the country. For those of you ticked at Texas, what did you expect?" he said. "If I'm Texas, I say we aren't going to take it anymore!"

# CHAPTER 9

*"The best argument against democracy is a five-minute conversation with the average voter."*

~ *Sir Winston Churchill*
*Prime Minister of Britain during WWII*
*Author (Nobel Prize Winner), Historian and Hero*

I n Texarkana, where Interstate 30 crosses the state line between Texas and Arkansas, several incidents were reported between federal troops stationed just over the blockade at the border and Texas State Guard forces stationed at the visitors' center at the expansive Texas Welcome Center just over the state line on the incoming side. Shots had been fired sporadically with no particular intent and mostly by civilians, but no injuries were reported.

Both sides of the Texas crisis pointed to this location as an indication of the tinder box effect that existed. Despite two prior incidents, troops from both sides occasionally tested each other by driving their vehicles close to the others' encampments and hurling insults at each other.

A local CBS affiliate in Texarkana ran a story of Winona Mae, an elderly African-American widow living on a small Social Security check. It had been more than a month since she'd gotten her check. Winona Mae had not taken her blood pressure medication for more than two weeks. Her daughter, who lived in Baltimore, was denied entry at the I-30 checkpoints by federal troops because she wasn't a Texas resident.

For two days she pleaded to enter and each time she was denied. On the third day, Winona suffered a stroke at her home. She died before an ambulance could get her to the hospital. Her daughter managed to sneak into Texas via a route she wouldn't disclose to the reporter. She was livid. She blamed her mother's death on President Johnson.

"Why would the president shut off Social Security to the elderly? She lived in Texas her entire life! What was she going to do, move because the president doesn't like what Texas is doing? This president is responsible for my mother's death!" Winona's daughter was inconsolable.

The segment ran the night before. At noon on Sunday, more than forty pick-up trucks barreled down the wrong way of the shutdown frontage road on I-30 on the inbound side headed to the Texas Welcome Center. Hanging out of the trucks were dozens of men with shotguns, deer rifles, axes, broom handles and anything else they could find to inflict injury. Their horns blared and their lights flashed. Most had the Lone Star flag flying from the backs of their trucks and all the men were black.

Lt. Col. Luther Donaldson was sitting with several other officers of the Texas State Guard in the main building of the Welcome Center eating lunch when a junior officer ran inside.

"Sirs, we have a situation!" he screamed.

Everyone jumped up and ran outside just as the noise hit the Welcome Center. Most of the State Guard had brought weapons ready, not sure if these were friends or foes.

"Hold your damned fire!" yelled a lieutenant.

A man about forty, wearing denim overalls and holding a deer rifle, jumped out of a nearly rusted-out old Ford pick-up. He kept the weapon pointed up in the air.

"We're here for payback for Winona Mae. We are going to open that damned interstate ourselves. Are you going to help us or are you going to sit on your asses?"

Lt. Col. Donaldson walked up to the man. The State Guard was obviously somewhat nervous of the aggressive display of weapons being waved and thrust into the air from the men in the trucks.

"What is your name, sir?" asked Lt. Col. Donaldson.

"Elijah Jefferson, but mostly I'm known as Bo."

"Bo, I'm Lt. Col. Donaldson. This is my unit here, and I'm directly responsible to Gov. Cooper for this checkpoint."

"Nice to meet you, Colonel. Now, we aim to open that interstate. Are you going to help us?"

Reports of this convoy of trucks had already made their way to the U.S. Army outpost less than a mile from Donaldson's camp. The commander ordered an armed drone launched to observe at a minimum, but to be ready to strike if the convoy appeared to be a threat.

"Bo, I can't let you do that, sir."

"These folks don't want anything like what just happened to Winona Mae to happen again," Bo shouted. "We're gonna make sure it don't."

"Bo, let me explain. If you launch that convoy of trucks and head toward that state line, two things are going to happen. The first is you and your men are going to be cut to shreds. Those troops are full-blown U.S. Army troops with advanced weaponry. I see your guys with shotguns, axes and shovels. They will certainly die. Secondly, the interstate will not get opened," Donaldson reasoned.

"Why won't you join us?"

"I take my orders from the governor, Bo."

"Well, get him on the line!"

"Okay, Bo. If I let you talk directly with the governor, will you have your men stand down? Will you tell them to surrender their weapons and calm down?"

Bo was in no way expecting to be in a position to talk to Gov. Cooper. This tactic taken by the lieutenant colonel was completely disarming, and was a blind attempt to disarm the mob.

"Okay, well, I guess. But call him now."

"Get your men to stand down, and you and me will go into the Welcome Center and make that call," the officer said measuredly.

Bo yelled back at his friends to put their weapons down for now. "I'm going to talk to the governor!"

There were about fifty steps between the two forces and the Visitors' Welcome Center.

The group had taken about ten steps when shots began ringing out from the back of several pick-up trucks.

"What the hell?" yelled the lieutenant colonel.

Within seconds, the unmistakable noise of automatic and semi-automatic heavy caliber weapons started drowning out the sounds of the shotguns and deer rifles. "We're under attack!" Bo yelled.

Over the pine trees just beyond the frontage road, a drone was turning directly toward the Welcome Center. Two semi-automatic .50-caliber guns, mounted on tripods surrounded by sandbags, were operated by two men positioned at the center's entry. The Texas State Guard knew these drones could be fully weaponized, and some started running for cover immediately.

Texas State Guard troops yelled at the contingent of civilians in their trucks to take cover. Men were running everywhere to get cover, including under the trucks and behind trees.

The drone banked sharply to the left, turning directly into the path of the .50-caliber guns. To the men on the ground, that drone took a menacing position, as if it were coming in to launch some type of attack. They'd have to take it out.

The Guard troops were effective at hitting the drone. Sparks flew with each impact, and the drone started to break up in mid-air less than five hundred feet from the ground.

Suddenly, the left wing of the drone broke free, cartwheeling to the ground as the drone crashed onto the asphalt of the eastbound lane of Interstate 30 and erupted into a small explosion.

As soon as the shooting at the drone started, the Army troops a mile away heard the gunfire. The alarm sounded for battle stations.

A similar alarm sounded at the Welcome Center for the State Guard. A few minutes of chaos followed the crash of the drone, with officers shouting orders, equipment being moved and troops scrambling into pre-determined positions.

Two news helicopters were stationed in Texarkana to monitor the roadblock. They immediately launched after receiving a tip about the convoy of pick-up trucks traveling down the interstate. They got the entire event on film before Lt. Col. Donaldson ordered them to leave the vicinity because they could get shot down by mistake.

Before the confusion, chaos, and shots subsided, several civilians jumped into the cabs of the two pick-up trucks, accompanied by several others who leapt into the beds of both trucks. The trucks rambled across the lawn of the Welcome Center headed for the frontage road.

"Wait! Stop them, dammit!" yelled the colonel.

It was too late. The two trucks hit the asphalt, tires spinning and white smoke rising from the asphalt.

There was no traffic on the inbound side of I-30 headed east. The occasional cars let through the roadblock were few and far between.

The two trucks got side by side, flashers flashing, lights on, and Texas flags flying. Men stood in the back with guns pointed forward.

The U.S. Army outpost commander received word over his radio that the drone was shot down and destroyed. Then word came that two vehicles were coming directly toward them at a high rate of speed.

Warning shots were fired across the front of the two trucks. A loudspeaker blared, warning the men inside to turn around.

"Sir, do we shoot?" an infantryman asked his squad leader.

"Dammit," the squad leader yelled. "If they get to five hundred yards, take out the tires and engines!" At five hundred yards, the two trucks hadn't slowed down. If they saw the warning flares that were shot at them, they didn't flinch or slow down.

"Sir, we have four vehicles behind them mounted with .50-calibers, also traveling at a high rate of speed coming this way."

"What the hell is going on?"

"500 yards, sir!"

"Fire! Fire! Fire now!"

Two .50-caliber and three .30-caliber machine guns began the blat, blat, blat as their empty shells were discharged all over the ground, smoke emitting from the used cartridges.

Within a few seconds, one of the trucks swerved wildly to the right, clipping the front quarter of the second truck. Both trucks began a death roll in unison, tossing their riders and the cab occupants out as if they were rag dolls. Both trucks were traveling more than eighty miles per hour at impact.

The Army gunners tried to render the trucks inoperable by taking out tires and radiators but, inexplicably, the machine guns were still shooting, finally stopping when the trucks stopped rolling. One truck rolled over six times before coming to a fiery stop. The second truck rolled four times before stopping, landing completely upside down.

"Stand down! Stop firing! Stand down!" yelled an officer.

A thousand yards behind, the four vehicles that had left the Welcome Center to try to intercept and stop the pick-up trucks rolled to a slow stop in shock. Bodies were strewn all over the highway and in the grassy median.

"Colonel, they took 'em out! Oh, my God!" the sergeant in the lead Hummer screamed into the radio.

"Shit! Any survivors?" yelled Donaldson.

"Sir, I need to get closer to tell."

"Do not advance. Let's get them on the radio."

The Texas Guard at the Welcome Center was able to establish phone communications with the Army outpost. After explaining the first trucks were being driven by civilians who were not under any supervision from the Guard, the Texans were cleared to give aid to the victims in the trucks after the Guard commander dispatched two of the follow-up vehicles to assist. Civilian ambulances were called in; meanwhile, precious minutes were ticking away. If anyone had survived the carnage on the interstate, it was a miracle.

"Sir, we have nine casualties, but we haven't determined how many survived."

"Lieutenant, ambulances have been dispatched. Report back on any survivors ASAP!"

"Roger that."

When the two Hummers pulled up to the site of the carnage, four State Guardsmen spread out to tend to the men who had been ejected and strewn about.

"I've got one breathing here!"

"This one's still alive!" shouted another about forty yards away.

"This one, too, but he's trapped under the truck!"

At the U.S. Army blockade, all troops moved forward to the temporary concrete emplacements on the interstate that were typically used to protect American assets such as embassies and checkpoints where terrorism was likely.

Lt. Col. Donaldson reached the U.S. Army commander in charge on the other side.

"This is Lt. Col. Donaldson with the Texas State Guard. Am I speaking to the U.S. Army commander on I-35?"

"This is Maj. Rippert."

"Rippert, those two trucks were lone rangers. We tried to stop them but were unsuccessful. We have four civilian ambulances en route. I'm asking you to allow them to recover the injured."

"We will not engage; however, I will warn you that any further attempt like that to test our checkpoint will meet the same fate."

"Rippert, I'm not calling you to argue with you. If I have your word no shots will be fired, we will recover the civilian casualties."

"Sir, you have thirty minutes. You already have two fully armed guard vehicles within five hundred yards of the checkpoint. If they have not retreated in that time frame, they will be engaged."

As Donaldson hung up, he turned to two of his aides. "That goddamn son of a bitch! If we wanted his checkpoint, we could have it."

The EMT staff arrived to find five men dead and four still alive. One of the truck drivers was pinned in his truck as it lay on its roof. Despite the efforts of the State Guard and the EMTs, they could not extract the driver, who was clinging to life.

"Sir, this is Cullen. We can't extract one driver from the truck."

"Sergeant, you have zero minus thirteen minutes to get him out," snapped the colonel, looking at his watch.

Sgt. Cullen understood the clock was ticking on the life of the injured driver, but had no clue of the deadline imposed by Maj. Rippert. He didn't have time to think it through.

Two ambulances left the scene with the other three injured. The dead were still lying on the interstate and the grassy median, strewn about as all efforts were being applied to free the last driver. They needed the Jaws of Life.

"Sir, the EMTs have called for the Jaws of Life from the Texarkana Fire Department."

Donaldson looked at his watch.

"Damn! Raise the major on the radio."

"Rippert here."

"Major, the EMTs have dispatched the Jaws of Life from the downtown Texarkana Fire Department. They won't get there by your thirty-minute deadline."

"Sir, you have four minutes to pull back your troops. You can leave the EMTs there. The State Guard vehicles and troops must pull back."

The colonel took his finger off the mic, his face red with anger.

"Sergeant, pull back. Leave the EMTs for the rescue effort."

"But, sir, these folks need help."

"Sergeant, the U.S. Army will begin engaging you in zero minus four minutes if you do not pull back."

"What? We are recovering the injured!"

"Sergeant, pull back now."

"Guys, I'm being ordered to pull back. Our Army friends over there do not want us to assist. They have threatened to fire on us."

The EMTs still struggling to administer first aid to the trapped driver paused. They looked at the sergeant, then back at the Army checkpoint in disbelief. Two of them started yelling in that direction.

The two news helicopters were capturing the entire event live as every network broke into live programming to stream this new crisis.

"They won't fire on civilians."

"Bullshit! That's why we're here," claimed one EMT.

"These guys intended to open that checkpoint, fellas. Ya'll are tending to the injured."

"I don't trust them," yelled another, holding the IV they had started on the unconscious driver from an awkward position lying on his back with one arm stuck inside the small opening between the roof of the truck and the pavement.

"I'm sorry. We're under direct orders. Saddle up!" the sergeant yelled to the other State Guardsmen.

They piled into the two Hummers. Instead of turning around to take the most direct route back to the Welcome Center, the sergeant gave other orders.

"Circle in front of the trucks. Let's give them a message!"

The two Hummers pulled around in a wide circle in front of the two trucks. Pulling around slowly, the troops stood on the Hummers and hung out the windows, shooting the finger at the U.S. Army troops, cussing at them while one waved a damaged Lone Star flag picked from the carnage of the trucks.

The Welcome Center was over a mile from the scene and the men from Texas were unable to see events as they unfolded. Officers and enlisted men gathered around two television sets streaming the scene on two different networks.

The troops stationed at the Welcome Center burst into cheers and wild celebration as the cameras zoomed into the two Hummers with the State Guard personnel hurling insults at their checkpoint counterparts.

"Bastards! Let me take out those two Hummers, Major!" yelled the Army infantryman who was manning one of the .50-caliber machine guns.

"Stand down! Hold your fire!" yelled Maj. Rippert.

Both President Johnson and Gov. Cooper received updates within minutes of the trucks being blown off the interstate.

Now the entire world was watching to see if the incident was going to be the spark that ignited an already tense stand-off between the federal government and the defiant state of Texas.

The president was monitoring the event from the Oval Office with Tibbs and Radford, interrupting a pre-scheduled meeting between the three of them. The close-up video of the Texas troops shooting fingers and yelling at the U.S. Army deployed at the checkpoint was about all Tibbs could take.

"Bastards! Mr. President, are we going to negotiate with these imbeciles? Let's just take them out," shouted the agitated attorney general.

CNN and other news outlets reported that federal troops would not let the State Guard render aid to the civilians and were forced to retreat or risk being shot at. The driver died before the Jaws of Life could arrive.

The Winona Mae story and the civilian deaths continued to add fodder to the building resentment by Texans. The mocking display by the Texan troops also agitated those in the administration camp.

Even the talking heads at MSNBC were questioning the logic of shutting off Social Security payments to the elderly in Texas. The death of Winona Mae was a huge public relations nightmare for the administration, aided by the fact that it touched off enough anger from a group in the local black community to strike out to open the interstate on their own, embarrassing the Left and Democrats who had been backing the administration on how it dealt with the Texas crisis up to that point.

Leaders from all over the globe were calling for calm from the administration. Human rights groups were condemning both the shut-off of entitlement payments but also questioned the need for Army troops to annihilate the pick-up trucks and their inhabitants. The administration kept making the case that the trucks were a threat to the checkpoint troops, but the trucks never opened fire.

The administration that used its internal polling more than any administration in U.S. history was stung by the fact that the president's approval rating was plummeting again.

"Mr. President, over time this entitlement shut-off will become a problem. It's not having the effect we intended. I believe we will feel the brunt of public pressure on this issue before the governor does," said Radford.

"Well, let's revisit this. Pull everyone together for another strategy session. My patience is over. It's time to end this thing."

"Goddamn right, Mr. President. I've been saying this for weeks now," agreed Tibbs.

"I'll pull everyone together right away, sir," said Radford.

# CHAPTER 10

*"Government, even in its best state, is but a necessary evil; in its worst state, an intolerable one."*

~ *Thomas Paine*
*Author and American Revolution Hero*
*Published "Common Sense,"*
*Sparking the American Revolution*

Two days after the Texarkana incident, Tea Party activist Mitch Lansford arranged a meeting with Chuck Dixon and the sheriffs of three local counties. These sheriffs had taken a newly popular pledge not to follow any unconstitutional orders, especially those related to the Second Amendment.

The three sheriffs were excited to get the opportunity to meet Chuck and to get some inside information on what was going on in Austin and the governor's office.

After the normal pleasantries, the small group of five sat down in the back room of a local hamburger joint in Old Town Spring. Spring, a suburb of Houston, was a small railroad stop twenty miles north of Houston that had a small hotel that included a brothel, saloon and café in the late 1800s. The area had grown over the years to include small antique shops, boutiques, eateries, crafts and festivals.

"I'm glad all of us could make it. First, what is everyone thinking on the events of the last two days?" asked Lansford.

"I'm not sure the Army had a choice. Those trucks were headed for them at high speeds with guns. You wouldn't let them get right on top of you," said Sheriff Alvarez.

"I can tell you this; President Johnson is the vindictive type. The beating he's taking in the press is going to be vented on Texas somehow, some way," added Sheriff Preston.

They all looked at Chuck, realizing nobody had heard his opinion, and his was the one they wanted to hear.

"My sense is the governor is not going to give in. I believe he is the kind of man who would go ahead and turn himself over to federal authorities if he was convinced this would solve our issues with the federal government."

"That's good to hear," remarked Sheriff Alvarez.

"That being said, this administration continues to get embarrassed over events like the other day. For the life of me, I have to ask: how is it that Congress and the people in the rest of the country aren't pressing for impeachment? I mean, the Sally investigation, the Spilner deaths? What does it take?" asked Lansford.

"Gentlemen, I believe we have reached the crossroads. It's not fixable. The Constitution is not relevant anymore to the federal government. Heck, how many times have we heard that it was written by old, rich white men who had slaves and that it's not relevant anymore?" answered Chuck.

"Well, the country is divided; that's for sure. I think many are sitting on the sidelines, especially in the South, who are waiting to see how this plays out with us," said Sheriff Reeves, meaning how Texans would handle the crisis.

"Are you men getting any orders from administration officials?" asked Chuck.

"We get daily communiques from the Justice and Treasury Departments, FBI, ATF and DHS. Even a few from the IRS."

"What's contained in those orders?" asked Chuck

"Well, I get daily reminders that the background check system is disabled for gun purchase approvals in Texas," answered Sheriff Preston. Sheriffs Alvarez and Reeves answered affirmatively that they were receiving the same.

"And that any gun purchases during this *cooling-off* period would be prosecuted under federal laws," affirmed Alvarez.

For the next hour, the five discussed the next steps each sheriff was taking locally to protect his citizens from federal overreach, especially from DHS, the IRS, and the effects of the NDAA, which the administration used to detain Chuck and attack local Tea Party organizations.

While the waitress was refilling their pitcher of iced tea, a tall gentleman walked through the door. Lansford had told the group there might be one more joining them, but he was en route from Beaumont. Apparently recognizing Lansford, the man walked right up to the table.

"Mitch, how ya doin'?"

"Gentlemen, this is Zach Turner, president of Free Texas Now," introduced Lansford.

Everyone at the table knew who Zach Turner was. For years, Turner led a small but fast-growing organization that promoted and campaigned for Texas independence peacefully. Turner was a Texas history expert, self-taught constitutionalist, small business owner, and had been politically active since he ran for mayor (and lost) of his local community when he was only nineteen years old.

Upon meeting Turner, Chuck stood. "It's about time we met. For years I didn't agree with your positions, thinking this federal problem was fixable." He held out his hand.

Turner grasped Chuck's hand and shook it. "Well, we all have to come to that realization eventually," he chuckled. "Some of us just may have come to that conclusion a little sooner than others."

"As you now probably know and agree, the Tea Party was likely our last hope to save the Constitution," stated Dixon.

It was obvious these two men had great respect for one another as they continued to stand while their hands remained in a handshake clasp as if they were the only ones in the room.

"I don't hold that against you, Chuck. You were doing what you thought was right. Many of our leadership and members were once Tea Party patriots, too."

As they sat down, Turner told the group the history of the organization, its peaceful attempts for years to get an Independence referendum through the state legislature and the many other obstacles Free Texas had endured in its eighteen-year history. Chuck went on to congratulate Turner for the non-binding Independence resolution referendum that was put before state voters immediately following the showdown at the state capital.

"The governor already had a model for this resolution, thanks to Zach," Chuck said. "Sir, your repeated efforts to get this on the ballot paid off, although you probably never dreamed it would be under these circumstances."

"No, I sure didn't, but I am definitely not surprised by these events."

"I really didn't know much about your group until after Johnson's first election," Sheriff Reeves said.

"Well, let's just put it this way. This cake has been baking for a long, long time; his election just lit the candles!" stated Turner to a chorus of chuckles from around the table.

Turner continued to bring everyone up to date on the growth of Free Texas. "We have more than a million members, which has spiked since the events of the last several months. Before the feds interrupted Internet services, we were adding a couple of hundred members a day. We've re-tooled because of it and we are almost back to that rate. These folks plop down hard-earned money, albeit not a lot of money, but money just the same, just to join."

"Your group is well organized, if I'm not mistaken, with county coordinators in every one of the two hundred fifty-four Texas counties?" asked Lansford.

"Yes, that's correct."

"Your organization is much larger than my local and regional Tea Party chapters," Chuck returned.

"Gentlemen, you asked me or, I should say, Mitch asked me to come here today. I assume I don't need to make the case for Texas independence at this juncture with you fine folks?"

"No, sir, we're right here with you. Late to the party, but here nonetheless," admitted Chuck.

For the next two hours, one of the most significant Tea Party organizers in Texas, who had been illegally terrorized and detained, only to be rescued by the Texas Rangers, laid out detailed plans to merge organizational forces with the longest-standing Texas independence movement since 1836, and three county sheriffs who represented dozens who had taken an oath of office to defend both the U.S. and Texas Constitutions.

Texas and the federal government were two trains speeding toward each other on the same track. The impasse stakes were escalating as unique and different pressures were being applied to both sides.

Would Secy. of State Bartlett and Sen. Simpson be able to intervene in what was sure to be a calamity that could tear the American fabric into pieces?

# CHAPTER 11

*"The right of a nation to kill a tyrant in case of necessity can no more
be doubted than to hang a robber, or kill a flea."*

*~ John Adams*
*Signer of the Declaration of Independence*
*2nd U.S. President*

Seventy-five miles west of Austin, deep in the heart of the Texas hill
country, Gov. Cooper, Lt. Gov. Foster and various members of their
staffs and families, along with Texas Rangers' Cmdr. Pops Younger and
Texas Guard Cmdr. Rex Conroy, were being sheltered at the Swingin' T
Ranch.

The officials and their staffs were housed randomly and rotated between
four large Texas ranches every several days in case federal authorities made
another attempt to arrest them. Very few people were in the inner circle that
knew how, where and when the governor was moved.

The ranch, owned by a Midland oil man, spread over eight thousand
acres and two counties. It was approximately eighteen miles north of Llano,
Texas on a two-lane farm-to-market road. The main house and guest houses
were a full two miles from the main gate.

The Swingin' T was a *working* ranch in typical Texas fashion. The
owner had more than two hundred head of registered Longhorns, and some
individual bulls valued in seven figures. To many well-heeled Texas ranchers,
raising registered Longhorns was as prestigious as raising thoroughbred
racing horses, and this rancher was one of the world's foremost breeders of
the revered breed. He also owned more than twelve hundred head of Black
Angus and there were seventeen oil- and gas-producing wells on the property.

Like most Texas ranches of this size, the Swingin' T was used to entertain clients in high-end whitetail deer and exotics hunts. The lodge was geared for entertainment purposes, adorned with head mounts of trophy deer, exotics and a huge shoulder-mounted Texas Longhorn over an impressive Austin limestone fireplace. The mounted burnt orange and white Longhorn's rack stretched eighty-two inches across from tip to tip, with the famous up-and-out twist at the end.

The length of a Longhorn's horns, its mass, and the degree of its famous up-and-out twist had a large impact on its value. Longhorns were no longer prized for traditional cattle breeders, as it is virtually impossible to fatten a longhorn as is done with other cattle to increase their weight for the cattle auction markets. Longhorns are a feisty breed, surviving on little grass, resistant to disease, and able to be driven on one thousand-mile cattle drives. They are a symbol of the Old West and a proud Texas tradition.

The governor dispatched Pops Younger to Texarkana immediately upon learning of the incident at the Texarkana checkpoint. Pops was also scheduled to visit several checkpoint locations under orders from the governor. Maj. Gen. Conroy begged the governor to let him go with Pops, but Cooper wanted him to stay put for planning purposes and to keep a centralized command structure over the Guard, state troopers, Texas Rangers, the air wing and the Texas Militia. Both Pops and Conroy reported directly to the governor, but there was no doubt that Pops had become Cooper's most trusted advisor since the crisis started.

The governor sat in the expansive rustic lodge at the Swingin' T on an overstuffed burnt-orange leather-and-cowhide chair. Cooper loved the lodge; he smelled the leather and cigars the second he stepped into the open room. Hanging from the ceiling, which was thirty-two feet high, was a huge elk horn chandelier.

The governor always had a big cigar after supper and tonight was no different. Several of his staff joined him to discuss the day's events and Pops' report from Texarkana.

The staff had notepads and laptops opened while in deep discussions when an aide's cell phone rang. She got up from the group so as not to disturb the conversation and to try to get better wireless reception. Wireless coverage at the ranch was so weak that the owner had to have wireless repeaters installed in three locations on the ranch to improve reception, but the steel roof of the buildings still hampered reception. A few minutes later, the aide returned to the group.

"Excuse me, Governor. That was Sen. Simpson's chief of staff." All of them immediately stopped what they were doing.

"Both the senator and Secy. Bartlett can meet you tomorrow. They apparently have a proposal to end the crisis to present to you. They will meet wherever you designate."

"How do we do that?" asked another staff member, knowing that, if the governor risked leaving Texas, he could be arrested the minute he crossed any state line.

"They will come to us," the aide added.

"I want a conference call immediately with all of us and Pops," said the governor, looking directly at Maj. Gen. Conroy.

Ten minutes later, the governor was connected on a conference call with Pops Younger and Maj. Gen. Conroy. In the meantime, the senator's office called back to inform the governor's staff that the administration had approved the senator's travel on a private jet from Washington, D.C. to Austin, meaning there would be no encumbrance at the border or with his air travel.

"Gentlemen, it seems that Sen. Simpson and Secy. Bartlett are coming to visit us."

"Johnson is allowing Bartlett to come?" asked Pops.

"Excuse me, sir," interrupted the staff member, "Simpson's people are saying Bartlett is coming without the administration's knowledge!"

"On the same aircraft?" asked Cooper.

"The plot thickens," remarked Foster.

"We are not to give them your location, Governor," said Conroy.

"Absolutely not!" repeated Pops.

"If they fly into Austin, we can send another aircraft to pick them up to bring them out here, or we can arrange ground transportation. They are *not* to know where the governor is being housed. Is that clear to everyone?" demanded Conroy.

"So you think we should do this meeting out here?" asked Cooper.

"Absolutely, sir. I agree one hundred percent; however, it will be the end of your stay here as soon as they leave. You will have to be moved ahead of schedule," said Pops.

"Damn, I like this place! Okay, let's get it arranged, folks," agreed Cooper. He turned back to the staff person who'd taken the first call. "Are there any preset conditions?" he asked.

"Yes, sir. They want the meeting to be completely off the record. The administration knows Simpson is coming, and they really don't care about him, but we are not to leak any information about Bartlett coming. If that gets out, the meeting is off and her camp will categorically deny it."

"That's very interesting," mused Cooper, "but, knowing the political hack Bartlett is, that makes sense. If she wants to be the hero, that's fine; let's do it. If it ends the crisis, fine. But, if we cut a deal with them, it essentially guarantees her the Democratic nomination. It's almost worth it just to see her trump Johnson and Tibbs."

Just after dark the next evening, a black SUV pulled into a private charter hangar in Washington, D.C. The large hangar doors closed behind the vehicle. Sen. Simpson was already on the Citation jet with two of his senior staff members. After several cell phone communications between the plane and the vehicle, and once all doors of the hangar were secured, Annabelle Bartlett and two of her staff exited the vehicle and scurried up the steps into the jet. Shortly after 9:00 p.m. EST, the Citation took off from Dulles Airport to Austin, Texas.

The traffic in the skies over Texas had come to a complete halt as the federal government had shut down FAA tower operations at all sites in Texas by turning off the FAA's computer systems to Texas airports. The state had taken over limited air traffic control duties within the state from military bases and volunteers at private airports.

The U.S. military was closely monitoring flights near Texas airspace as no flights had been allowed in or out, except for a few air ambulance emergencies. The military knew about this flight request from the State Department, but had no idea Bartlett was on it. The manifest only listed the senator and his staff and no other names. Johnson's administration knew nothing of this individual flight. This was the first flight allowed into Texas since the crisis erupted at the state capitol.

During the flight to Austin, Bartlett, Simpson and their staffs fine-tuned their proposal for Gov. Cooper. The entire contingent was confident and almost gleeful. While not admitting it to each other, they both figured they would go down in history as manufacturing the negotiations that led to the end of the most serious crisis in American history since 1860, Pearl Harbor and 9-11.

Meanwhile, Gov. Cooper and his staff worked in the main lodge until 11:00 p.m. to finalize what they would and would not agree to.

The Citation carrying Simpson and Bartlett landed in Austin at 12:10 a.m. Two limousines waited in a hanger at another private jet facility at the Austin airport. The same drill performed at Dulles Airport occurred in reverse; the jet went into the hangar where the limos were waiting. The huge door closed, then the occupants of the jet transferred quickly into the darkened-window vehicles and sped off to different destinations.

At 7:00 a.m., the limos would again pick them up separately by pulling into a private garage facility to remain completely hidden. A state-owned helicopter would be waiting to pick them up at a pre-determined location on a private ranch forty minutes west of Austin. Unbeknown to them, the chopper would then take them on a thirty-minute flight to the Swingin' T for a 9:00 a.m. meeting, followed by more meetings throughout the day if necessary.

Shortly before midnight, and within minutes of the Citation landing in Austin, Jamail Tibbs had just fallen asleep when he received a call on his cell phone from a source within the State Department. Only those close to Tibbs that he trusted got access to his personal cell phone number.

"This better be goddamn good," mumbled a sleepy but irritated Tibbs as he got out of bed to move to another room so he wouldn't awaken his wife. He pressed the cell phone to his ear.

"What?" blurted an incredulous Tibbs. "Say that again? Are you friggin' serious?"

Tibbs listened for the next two minutes, not saying a thing.

"Yes, I'm here. What the hell! This changes *everything*!"

Tibbs was now pacing back and forth in his office. As he listened, he strode into the family room.

"Is this information reliable? It's going straight to the president of the United States. If any of this is factually incorrect, it's your ass! Do you understand me?"

Tibbs shoved the phone down into a pocket of his robe and sat on the brick hearth of his fireplace, pondering his next move.

"Holy crap," he thought. "Now I can finally get that bastard! I've got that damned cowboy!" A wide smile lit up his face as he dialed a special number to reach the president.

# CHAPTER 12

*"They that can give up essential liberty to purchase a little temporary safety deserve neither liberty nor safety."*

*~ Benjamin Franklin*
*Signer of the Declaration of Independence &*
*the U.S. Constitution*
*Author, Historian, Philosopher & Inventor*

At 2:45 a.m., three Blackhawk U-60 helicopters lifted off the pavement at the tiny airport in Piedras Negras, Mexico. The airport was a few short miles from the Rio Grande River across the border from Eagle Pass, Texas. *Operation Santa Anna* was underway.

The local airport had been cordoned off two hours earlier with Mexican federales. The black night and moonless sky made the black helicopters extremely hard to detect. There were no running lights on the choppers. The faint lights of the two hangars at the airport barely illuminated the insignia of a small American flag on the tail and the blue seal of Homeland Security on each of the cargo bay doors.

The choppers headed out together toward the southwest but, upon clearing the populated areas of the border town, they banked hard to the right, headed in a northwesterly direction. The choppers lowered to three hundred feet, then to one hundred fifty feet as they cleared the Rio Grande and the United States border, traveling at one hundred seventy-three miles per hour just north of Eagle Pass.

This area of Texas is about as remote as it gets, with gently rolling plains of Texas brush country full of small mesquite trees, cactus, and scrub yaupon trees. Despite the harshness of the brush country, it's a favorite of hunters who travel there during hunting season from around the world, as the area boasts trophy whitetail deer, quail, javelina, rattlesnakes and dozens of other species native only to the area. In this part of Texas, nothing grows that doesn't have a thorn, needle, thistle, or pricker, which makes it remarkable that abundant wildlife thrives in south Texas. For a clandestine route, you couldn't ask for a less populated scenario to launch a Special Forces-type operation.

The Blackhawks sped over the Rio Grande River into Texas, cruising barely above the scrub oaks and mesquite trees. In a little more than an hour, the fully armed Blackhawks would be approaching Llano, Texas and the Swingin' T Ranch.

Two of the three choppers carried eleven DHS tactical assault troops each. The third chopper had only five additional troops. Although the Blackhawks were designed to carry eleven troops each, the third chopper was light of troops on purpose so it could *pick up* additional passengers. The Blackhawks were outfitted prior to the operation with the same stealth-plating technology that was used to hide the choppers from radar in the Seal Team Six raid into Pakistan to kill the most famous terrorist of modern times.

The choppers hugged the horizon as they sped along in the dark. Radar stations along the border, already operating on a skeleton-crew basis or not at all, did not pick up the choppers, nor did the closest fully functional radar stations at Lackland Air Force Base and the commercial airport one hundred forty miles to the northeast in San Antonio.

Two more fully equipped Blackhawk U-60 DHS choppers, in reserve and for recovery efforts if needed, sat ready at the Ciudad Acuna, Mexico airport. DHS had dubbed this reserve operation *Prickly Pear*. Ciudad Acuna was also on the Rio Grande directly across the river from the Del Rio, Texas airport fifty-five miles west of Piedras Negras. Sixty miles from Llano, the lead chopper banked west, the second banked hard to the east, while the third continued north on the original flight path, still undetected. Despite the low flight path, both Blackhawk and Apache helicopters are hard to detect at night, as enemy forces in Iraq and Afghanistan learned the hard way. They are even harder to hear until they are right on top of their targets, or past them. Enemy forces in Iraq and Pakistan always noted that, many times, choppers were right on top of them before they heard them.

Maj. Gen. Conroy's decision to keep state officials in this remote area of Texas was partly based on how difficult it would be to find and reach the various ranches, even if the feds knew where the governor was hidden. It was just far enough from the Gulf of Mexico to make any extraction attempt unfeasible because there was too much ground to cover.

Nobody would have thought seriously that Mexico would have granted use of its airspace and airports to launch such a mission. Mexico has a long history of protecting its sovereignty from the U.S. military and rarely conducts joint operations for any reason.

The choppers triangulated their position vectors to converge on the main compound of the Swingin' T, coming from three separate directions and ready to deliver hell from above.

Four Texas Rangers were posted at various locations on the property, along with six state troopers.

In the main lodge's master bedroom, Gov. Cooper and his wife Lyndsey had just fallen asleep in a massive king-sized, four-poster bed made from hand-hewn mesquite.

Lt. Gov. Foster and his wife were asleep in a separate guest house, as was Atty. Gen. Weaver. The remainder of the staff was spread out in various bunk houses and guest cottages near the main lodge. Maj. Gen. Conroy was in a guest cottage approximately one hundred yards from the main lodge.

The lone entrance to the Swingin' T, just off the two-lane state highway, had a small temporary plywood guardhouse erected just behind the massive limestone entrance. Typical of a large Texas ranch, the entrance was impressive and had double electric gates adorned with metal art of the ranch's insignia, cactus, and whitetail deer.

Inside the guardhouse, a Texas Ranger and a state trooper kept vigil with a thermos and two coffee cups. Not a single vehicle had driven by on the remote road since before midnight. The small talk and coffee thermos kept the two occupied with an occasional radio check-in with the command post at the main lodge.

A short radio burst from the lead chopper broke radio silence among the three Blackhawks for the first time.

"*Santa Anna One*, operation confirmed. We are a go."

"Roger, Anna Two, we are a go," replied the Blackhawk converging from the west.

"Roger, Anna Three, we are a go," radioed the Blackhawk converging from the east.

Suddenly, blat, blat, blat, blat, blat echoed the .30-caliber rotating Gatling-style machine guns as the lead chopper approached the guard shack from a quarter mile away. With two short bursts of the dual guns, the guard and state trooper, who had just been talking about high school football, were obliterated in a combination of splintering wood, shards of glass, and blood.

The main lodge had been set up as a command post, and Texas Ranger Colby Smith, in charge of the Swingin' T command while Pops Younger was gone, walked into the main lodge used as a command post to relieve a state trooper monitoring radios used by Rangers and state troopers on the range. The main entrance off the state highway was two miles away down the partially paved asphalt-and-caliche ranch roads.

Suddenly, Colby stopped and cupped his ear as if to listen to coyotes in the distance. But this wasn't coyotes. In the rolling south Texas hills, sound carries a long way, especially gunshots.

"Radio the shack!" yelled Smith to the trooper at the command desk. Smith grabbed his holster and a fully automatic standard government issue Colt AR-15 he had just leaned up against wall. He scrambled outside into the courtyard. He couldn't believe his eyes as he grabbed his radio.

"Wake everyone!" he yelled. "We are under attack!"

Ranger Smith barely finished speaking into his radio when the .30-caliber burst from the second chopper coming from the east hit him. It caught the Ranger on his left side, ripping off his left shoulder and arm, slamming him to the ground, blood spurting two feet in all directions. He was dead within seconds.

Troopers and Rangers ran out of the buildings they were sleeping in as ropes dropped from a chopper and DHS troops quickly rappelled to the ground. The Blackhawk hovered fifty feet over the terrace of the main lodge, throwing a thick blanket of dust in every direction.

A hunting jeep with two Rangers making its way from a guest cottage three hundred yards from the main lodge never saw the third Blackhawk approaching from the north behind them.

Blat, blat, blat, blat, blat, blat.

The jeep veered hard, hit a mesquite tree and flipped twice before it burst into flames. The Blackhawk's M134 Gatling-style rotating six-barrel machine guns were relentless, never backing off from the trigger as the jeep and occupants were strafed with 7.62 mm. tracer rounds until the occupants were neutralized.

The governor and his wife woke suddenly into a nightmare of chaos from the noise of the first rounds that took out Ranger Smith.

"Lyndsey, get in the closet!" Cooper yelled.

"Oh, my God. Brent?"

"Get in the closet!" he repeated forcefully.

Gunfire erupted all over the lodge area as the second chopper's DHS troops rappelled to the ground in front of the main house. The screaming of the wounded could be heard over the gunfire and even over the sound of the M134s positioned over the compound to provide air cover to the troops on the ground. Even when the .30-caliber guns weren't firing, there was no mistaking the sound of the Gatling-style rotation.

The federal troops entered the main house next to the lodge and cleared all resistance, leaving two troopers and a Texas Ranger dead on the floor in pools of their own blood and with grotesque wounds from multiple gunshots. The Ranger was slumped over the leather chair the governor had sat in just hours before.

Cooper noticed his wife approaching the bedroom door. He moved to keep her in the master bedroom closet.

"Brent, I thought they were coming to work out a deal!" Lyndsey said. Her eyes, wide with fear, were full of unshed tears.

"Sweetheart, just stay in here," Cooper pleaded. "They aren't after you."

"Don't go out there, Brent, please!"

"Lyndsey, the governor of Texas ain't hiding in a damned closet!" retorted Cooper.

Just then the bedroom door flew open as senior Texas State Trooper Kelly Armbrister rushed in to protect the governor. Armbrister only had time to get a weapon, with no time to go back to his room and recover his bullet-proof vest. Not sure who had just come into the darkened bedroom, Gov. Cooper looked down to chamber a shell in his pearl-handled Colt 1911 that had been given to him as a gift from the NRA.

"Governor, both of you come with me! We have to get out of here!" the trooper yelled.

Recognizing Armbrister's voice, Cooper turned to pull his wife from the closet. Simultaneously, two shots ripped through the jacket with the yellow state trooper letters on the back, then exited Armbrister's chest as he was shot by the two approaching federal assault troops, splattering blood over both the governor and his wife.

The governor immediately raised his pistol, emptying his clip into one of the intruders who fell forward as Cooper's shots tore through him. Despite the heavily armored bullet-proof vest worn by the government assault troops, two of the governor's shots shredded the unprotected neck of the agent.

In an instant, the second agent reacted by firing his assault rifle into the darkness of the bedroom from the direction of the Colt's flash. The assault troops all wore night vision goggles, but the multiple flashes from the barrel of the pistol temporarily blinded the man as he flipped up his goggles to return fire from behind the door frame.

The agent's first round hit the governor right below his left rib cage, penetrating completely through his body, entering Lyndsey's chest as she knelt behind him.

"Oh, Brent! Oh, no," she screamed.

The second burst of shots hit the governor in the face, chest and lower abdomen, knocking him backward into Lyndsey. He fell across his wife, dying instantly. She lay on the floor, bleeding profusely, with her husband lying on top of her. She coughed blood as she tried to speak, trying to hold her husband's face as she lay dying. In a scene reminiscent of Jackie Kennedy during JFK's assassination, the governor's wife appeared to be trying to scoop up the blood pouring from the governor's mouth and put it back in, oblivious to her own mortal wounds. With a deep gasp, Lyndsey died. .

The gunfire throughout the compound fell silent as the choppers finally landed. The moans of the wounded and the screams of the female guests on the ranch were horrific. The lopsided gun battle lasted less than five minutes, but the carnage from the raid was appalling. Bloodied bodies were strewn all over the main lodge, terrace and outbuildings.

"Find the governor!" ordered the blackened-faced operation commander over the radio. "Look in all buildings, all bedrooms!"

"He should be in the main house or the lodge!" yelled another of the assault team.

The federal troops who weren't wounded or killed went room to room in each building to find the governor and his staff, intent on bringing them all to federal justice.

"Oh, crap, sir! Oh, no!" came a horrified voice over the radio. "He's in here, sir! He's in the main house. The governor has been shot!"

"Damn it. Get medical in there right now!"

"Sir... he's dead!"

The *Santa Anna* operation commander and two DHS agents stepped into the doorway of the master bedroom, literally walking over the agent sitting next to the bedroom door. The agent rocked back and forth next to the body of the agent killed by the governor and the state trooper.

Taking off his helmet and night goggles, the commander reached down to take the pulse of the governor and his wife.

"What the hell happened?" He directed the question to the agent in the hallway.

"Sir, there was a firefight in here. I returned fire. He killed Jameson." The federal agent pointed to the Colt 1911 held loosely in the governor's grip.

"Did you not identify?" demanded the commander.

"Sir, we didn't have a chance... It happened so quickly," said the agent in a dejected tone, never raising his head to make eye contact.

"This is *very bad,* gentlemen. This is *really* bad," the commander growled.

"Take pictures and then get Jameson's body out of here! Send Holmes in here to bag these two," ordered the commander, looking disgustedly at the bloodied bodies of the Texas governor and first lady. "God damn him for causing this!" He stepped back into the hall and left the scene.

In the main courtyard on the terrace, the DHS forces were gathering the remaining state government officials, their spouses and staffs to determine who they had, who was missing and who was going to be transported in the choppers. They were being held at gunpoint. The wounded were being moved into the main lodge. Three federal agents had been killed, including the one shot by the governor. Two other agents were seriously wounded.

"Where's the governor?" demanded Weaver. Nobody answered him.

"Where's Foster?" asked Foster's senior staff person.

"Just shut the hell up!" yelled a federal agent, pointing his weapon at Weaver's head. Weaver stared the agent down, showing no fear.

It was chaotic. Women were crying, and federal agents were yelling insults at staff members and others gathered in the courtyard. The agents made no attempt to remove any of the Texans' bodies, only those of dead agents.

The agents searched each state employee for radios and cell phones. They then scoured the entire compound for any cell phones left in the guest houses, main lodge and house. Comfortable that all cell phones had been recovered, the commander got on his radio.

"*Prickly Pear One,* this is *Santa Anna One.* Commence recovery immediately. All is clear."

Within minutes, *Prickly Pear One* and *Prickly Pear Two* lifted off from Ciudad Acuna Airport and sped off to follow the same flight path to the Swingin' T.

Four F-15 fighter jets immediately lifted off the decks of the USS Harry S. Truman aircraft carrier positioned one hundred miles from Brownsville, Texas in the Gulf of Mexico to ensure the safe return of the Blackhawks.

"Where the hell are Gov. Cooper and Lt. Gov. Foster? Where is Maj. Gen. Conroy?" asked Weaver again.

"Bring him over here," barked the commander.

Weaver was led over to a separate area of the terrace away from the others being held at gunpoint.

"Are you Weaver?" asked the commander.

"Yes, I am, but where is the governor?"

"Mr. Weaver, it gives me great pleasure to tell you that you are under arrest by your federal government as an accessory to the murder of eighteen federal agents and U.S. Army troops in Austin. Cuff and shackle him."

"Oh, Jesus. What the hell is wrong with you people? Where is the governor?" demanded Weaver, his glare showing his disgust for what he saw around him.

The commander hesitated for a few seconds as he looked off into the distant Texas night. Then he turned back, looking at Weaver with emotionless eyes.

"Your governor chose to engage our troops. It was a fatal decision. As with any other criminal or enemy, our troops returned fire. Both the governor and his wife are dead," the commander stated.

"Oh, my God! You didn't have to shoot them! Oh, Jesus! Who ordered this killing? We were to negotiate an end to this crisis tomorrow! Who ordered this raid? Who, dammit? Are you sure he's dead?" Weaver yelled at the commander as veins popped out from his neck.

"The governor brought this on himself. All this was unnecessary if you damned cowboys had turned yourselves in. Personally, I have no remorse for any of you. You killed eighteen Americans in Austin. I have three more dead in that lodge, one of them killed by Cooper. He got what he had coming. The governor's wife appears to be collateral damage."

Weaver stared at the federal agent coldly.

"Are you serious? I want to see the bodies right now!" demanded Weaver.

"Pipe down, counselor. You're just going to have to take my word for it."

"Where is the lieutenant governor?"

"Your lieutenant governor and his wife have sustained injuries. He has been wounded in the leg. We don't know the extent of the injuries to his wife; however, they are both being readied for transport."

"Dear God...."

Weaver sat quietly for a brief moment, then continued, "So tomorrow's meeting was a ruse. It was obviously set up to get us to let our guard down so you could come out here like thieves in the night and take out Johnson's political enemies by murdering the governor and his wife!"

"I don't know a damned thing about any meeting," retorted the commander. "We were exercising a legal warrant under federal orders. Your men here were armed. Austin wasn't happening all over again. Not with *my* men. We did what we had to do. We returned fire when fired upon."

"Of course, you don't know about Bartlett coming here. That was obviously never going to happen."

"Secy. of State Bartlett was coming here? I seriously doubt that," said the commander realizing that, if it was true, it was possible the bloodshed at the Swingin' T may have been premature or unwarranted.

"Apparently not. Johnson and Tibbs wanted Gov. Cooper and they got him. They killed him. They killed his wife," continued the angry and shaken Weaver. "You and your boss in D.C. are sneaky bastards, I'll give you that."

The commander strode close enough to Weaver to deliver a stinging slap to his face. "I don't give a rat's ass about Texas and neither do my men! We had a job to do. The governor would be alive right now if he hadn't fired on our men!"

Weaver's face flushed bright red. "Don't think for one second Texas will *forget* this! Texans don't forget attacks on our sovereignty! I promise you they won't forget the feds murdering our governor and his wife!"

"Put him in the chopper!" yelled the commander to his underlings. "I'm already tired of his whining."

The stunned Texas officials, their spouses and staff sat quietly on a cedar bench in the terrace at gunpoint for the next few minutes. The silence was broken only by the radio communications from the commander to the USS Harry S. Truman in the Gulf.

"*Santa Anna* command, this is *Santa Anna One*. Eight minutes to lift-off," radioed the pilot.

Weaver looked at the commander. "*Santa Anna*? Are you friggin' serious? You boys sure know how to escalate things, don't you? Wait until Texans hear what this operation was called to invade Texas and kill their well-liked governor!"

The commander looked at Weaver with no expression. He knew little of Texas history and Weaver's comments didn't resonate. He was clueless that the Mexican dictator, General Antonio Lopez de Santa Anna, had nullified the Mexican Constitution of 1824. That led to the Texas Revolution, and it was Santa Anna's troops who killed all one hundred eighty-nine men at the Alamo.

"Reap the coming whirlwind, commander. Reap the whirlwind," said Weaver.

"Gag him now," the commander said tersely.

# CHAPTER 13

*"True patriotism sometimes requires of men to act exactly contrary, at one period, to that which it does at another, and the motive which impels them the desire to do right is precisely the same."*

~ *General Robert E. Lee*
*Commander of the Confederate Army*
*Son of an American Revolution Hero*
*West Point Graduate & Widely Regarded Military Tactician*

B y 4:40 a.m., the two reserve Blackhawks from Ciudad Acuna arrived at the Swingin' T. The first assault Blackhawk, *Santa Anna One*, loaded with two wounded agents, a shackled Weaver and the injured lieutenant governor and his wife had taken off thirty minutes before *Prickly Pear One* and *Two* arrived at the ranch. Instead of heading back to one of the two border town airports where the operation originated, *Santa Anna One* took a direct path to the USS Harry S. Truman. Included in the cargo bay were black body bags containing the bodies of the governor and his wife, along with the three dead federal agents.

The aircraft carrier had a full medical staff and facilities onboard and was waiting to treat the wounded. Two of the four fully-armed F-15 fighter jets that were already airborne over the Gulf after the governor was found crossed over Baffin Bay near South Padre Island, headed on a direct path to San Antonio. These two fighters had a defined mission planned in the event *Santa Anna* suffered casualties. Nobody on the Joint Chiefs expected to suffer casualties in the operation but, like any good military plan, they were prepared in case.

The USS Truman was nearly at full power, steaming from one hundred fifty miles from land toward the Gulf Coast. Every mile the carrier could put behind it would be one less mile the Blackhawk had to travel to deliver the wounded to treatment facilities and lessened the chance that the Blackhawk or F-15s might encounter Texas State Guard aircraft en route.

Now that *Santa Anna One* was en route, the F-15s were ordered to fulfill their specific missions. The fighters were locked on targets in San Antonio, Brownsville, Corpus Christi and the reserve Naval Air Station at Beeville, Texas.

The Joint Chiefs had determined, in planning Operation *Santa Anna* that, if the mission resulted in casualties, any Blackhawks with wounded or prime targets would be re-routed to the most direct path to the carrier.

The most advanced aircraft used by the Texas State Guard were F-16s, which were generally outclassed in air-to-air combat scenarios by the more powerful U.S. F-15s. The F-15s had a maximum speed of 1,875 miles per hour, three hundred miles faster per hour than the Texas F-16s. The F-15s had some air-to-air tactical advantages, including two engines versus one and two pilots versus one. U.S. military planners knew that any hastily prepared radar might pick up the Blackhawks and the F-15s, and were fully prepared to engage if necessary.

The stealth skin attached to *Santa Anna One*, *Two* and *Three* was most effective at very low altitudes and slower speeds designed to sneak in *under* radar. This chopper had a single purpose: to get its cargo to the Truman as fast as possible. The F-15s would provide air cover if needed.

At the Swingin' T, federal agents loaded the remaining choppers with confiscated cell phones, laptops, notebooks, briefcases and papers they found from Texas officials. The four choppers took off simultaneously from the courtyard of the Swingin' T. Staffers and family left behind scrambled to get clear of the swirling rocks and dust caused by the rotors.

The remaining staff, still unaware of the governor's whereabouts, dashed into the main lodge to see if the governor was still there. They had not heard what the operation commander told Weaver when he was separated from the group being held at gunpoint in the courtyard. The survivors rushed into the master bedroom, and came upon a pool of blood in the entry and a larger pool of blood just off the right corner of the bed on the knotted pine hardwood floor. Blood spatter was also on the French doors out to the courtyard, along with a mirror, and a door frame and wall in the entry way. It was obvious there had been a battle in this room, but whose blood was this? Were the governor and his wife okay? Lt. Gov. Foster's chief of staff, Rory Kendall, a young dark-haired thirty-two year-old, took charge.

"Try all the phones. It looks like they cut them all. Does anyone have a cell phone? Did they miss anyone's cell phone?"

Some ran back to their guest cottages to see if the federal agents had gotten theirs.

"Look! They destroyed the cell repeaters," yelled one of the staffers from inside the telephone closet. Kendall went and found that all the phone equipment had been ripped off the walls and bashed on the floor.

"Somebody has to get word to Pops! Did anyone call Pops?" Kendall asked, knowing Pops would know what to do next. During the quick strike and chaos caused by the DHS assault troops, nobody left alive at the Swingin' T had a chance to, or even thought about, sending a message to Pops.

At 4:49 a.m. in San Antonio, Lackland Air Force Base's radar alarms went off as their systems picked up the two incoming F-15s just as they crossed the Gulf Coast. Radar stations across Texas at military and civilian airports were manned by skeleton crews as air traffic over Texas had been reduced to a trickle since the crisis began. Federal air traffic control workers were ordered to stay home by the FAA and access to the national air traffic support system was made unavailable by executive order. This left the civilian airports without air traffic control, but some larger airports still had radar and the Texas State Guard air wing staff was able to get Lackland's control up and running.

The nature and intent of the two radar blips of very fast moving jets left the Texas Guard confused and questioning the veracity of the original interpretation of the jets' radar signatures. Precious minutes were lost while State Guard command tried to decide if this was any kind of imminent threat. Traveling at thirty-one miles per minute, the F-15s needed less than ten minutes to reach San Antonio two hundred ninety-two miles from the USS Truman.

A U.S. F-15 Eagle closed on the Brownsville airport, banked sharply to the southeast, then let loose two air-to-surface Maverick missiles that struck and destroyed the air traffic control tower. Fortunately, the tower was not staffed in the early morning hours; if it had been, there would have been more casualties.

In Corpus Christi two minutes later, the control tower and radar facilities on the airport property were destroyed in the same manner by an F-15. This was not the case in Corpus Christi, which was still allowing some limited private aircraft to take off and land. Two civilian volunteer controllers in the tower were killed instantly.

At the Naval Air Reserve Station in Beeville, Texas, just south of Corpus Christi, the dormant base was just brought back to life as a result of the crisis in Austin. The outdated control tower and two State Guard helicopters sitting on the tarmac were completely destroyed by Maverick missiles from the third F-15.

Thirty-five miles from San Antonio, radar indicated that three F-15s had peeled off in different directions, but four new images appeared. That could only mean one thing. One of the radar blips was on a route tracking directly to Lackland Air Force in San Antonio.

Suddenly, one radar blip turned to five.

The F-15 had launched AMRAAM long-range missiles, satellite-guided and "beyond visual" of the pilots, and they were deadly accurate. Two Texas Guard F-16s blasted down the Lackland runway, their thrusters glowing bright orange in the near-dawn sky. Two more were being readied when the first two missiles hit the control tower, exploding the top off the tower as it fell.

The tower had just become fully manned when the first alarms went off. Nine souls died in the explosion and the collapse of the tower. Two more missiles hit the tarmac where two F-16s were being scrambled, and the jets erupted into giant fireballs that could be seen more than ten miles around the San Antonio area by anyone who might have been awake that early in the morning.

Within seconds of the first launch, the F-15 turned back north and launched two Mavericks that struck the San Antonio commercial airport control tower.

There was no time to alert the airport by the Lackland control tower before it was destroyed, and the four volunteers in the San Antonio airport tower never knew what hit them as missiles slammed into the concrete tower, throwing large chunks of concrete hundreds of feet into the air with many of them crashing into empty adjacent terminals.

If the U.S. military thought it had just rendered south Texas' airspace completely blind to Texas state military forces, they may have been over-confident. They knew towers in Laredo and Del Rio were not likely manned at night because of the lack of air traffic. Even so, those radar towers only had a one hundred fifty-mile radar footprint.

*Santa Anna One* was informed it had a clear path to the Truman.

The Joint Chiefs had planned *Operation Santa Anna* to be a covert *snare-and-snatch* mission to bring Texas state officials to federal justice. When the *Santa Anna* Blackhawks radioed that they were taking incoming fire at the Swingin' T and had federal casualties, command figured the Texas Guard would scramble fighters and engage the Blackhawks. It was assumed by operational command that their cover was now blown. The admiral in charge on the Truman made the judgment call to protect the Blackhawks by striking radar installations and F-16s where they sat.

Lackland radar in San Antonio was blinded, but command had quickly established rudimentary communications with civilian radar towers at Laredo and Del Rio airports. General chaos ensued at Lackland with fire crews attempting to douse the fires and recover survivors.

If the feds had taken out Laredo and Del Rio, and crippled key cell towers, they could have rendered themselves invisible. The limited radar facilities were of little concern at night as they were unmanned. The Johnson administration had been convinced by military planners that strikes on radar facilities in Laredo and Del Rio were probably unnecessary. The Joint Chiefs had presented the operation to President Johnson as having an eighty-five percent chance of success without casualties.

State Guard command at Lackland was furiously trying to reach the governor while barking out orders to fire control crews as fires on one of the damaged aircraft were perilously close to jet fuel storage tanks. Unable to reach the governor or lieutenant governor, they tried and were able to reach Texas Ranger Cmdr. Pops Younger. Communications could not be established with Texas Militia headquarters in Austin or various other air wing sites that kept aircraft on standby.

"We've been attacked, we have multiple casualties, and we've got a damned mess here, sir! We can't reach the governor! I can't reach Maj. Gen.

Conroy! The fighters that hit us appear to be headed out to the Gulf. Two of our F-16s didn't make it off the tarmac. Our tower is down!"

"Damn Yankee sons of bitches!" responded Pops. "We can't reach the governor either. One of my Rangers got a cell phone message from the governor's staff, but it was unintelligible. That was about 3:30 a.m. We haven't been able to reach the local command at his hideout location in the hill country. I'm worried they hit there, too. There must be a mole somewhere that disclosed the governor's location. I've just dispatched the Apaches in Austin and the Texas Militia to aid immediately."

"Sir, where is the governor?"

"I can't say over the phone."

"Yes, sir. I can't reach my chain of command. Are you able to give me orders, sir?"

"Blow 'em out of the sky if you can find 'em!"

"Sir, I've got Del Rio reporting four aircraft moving relatively slowly— must be choppers, moving south toward Eagle Pass at very low altitude. Are those ours?"

"No. Damn!"

"I also have the F-16s reporting a chopper moving southeast towards Brownsville shadowed by two U.S. F-15s."

"What the hell is going on?" said a frustrated Pops.

"I need orders, sir."

"Send one F-16 to intercept the choppers headed to Eagle Pass. Send the other one to find out where that chopper is headed to near Brownsville."

"Sir, I just got handed a note saying shrimpers radioed in that they have spotted an aircraft carrier fifteen miles offshore about sixty miles due south of Corpus Christi."

"I'm afraid that one may have the governor! The chopper is headed to that carrier. I don't know what the hell the other four are doing. See if the pilots can make radio contact. I'll stay on the line. Tell them to ask what their purpose is and who is onboard. Do not authorize anyone to fire on any of those choppers. One of them is likely to have the governor or other state officials onboard."

"Geez, sir, do you think they captured him?"

"We don't know for sure, but they're sure making a mad dash to get outta Texas!"

For the next ten minutes, the pilots of the two F-16s were in radio contact with the chain of command at Lackland. They had not made radio contact with the choppers but were gaining on them quickly.

"Son, I've got an unknown call coming in. I have to take any calls on this line. Stay on the line."

"Yes, sir."

It was now after six a.m. and daylight was breaking through. The ranch hands, maids and cooks that normally stayed at the Swingin' T had been moved to local hotels with their families because the heads of state government took all the available guest cottages and bunkhouses on the ranch. A small group of Hispanic ladies came to the ranch every morning at 6:00 a.m. to deliver breakfast to lodge guests.

The occupants of two vans carrying containers of scrambled eggs, refried beans and tortillas saw smoke coming from the ranch entrance and from the ranch when they were more than sixteen miles away over the rolling Texas hills as daylight broke.

When they pulled up to the ranch entrance, they saw that the limestone entrance was in rubble and the guard shack was splintered like shredded toothpicks, still smoldering. They immediately called the sheriff's office in Llano and turned around to head back to town.

"This is Younger," Pops answered his cell phone.

"Pops, this is Sheriff Porter from Llano County."

"Joe, what the hell is going on out there? I can't reach anyone!" Pops said.

"We just received a call from the ranch's breakfast crew that smoke is coming from the ranch, and the guard shack and entrance are leveled. They were pretty hysterical," said Porter. "I am en route with all my crew. I should reach the ranch in less than twenty minutes. We are driving over a hundred to get there."

"That's not good," Pops said, "not good at all. Damn. Please hurry, Sheriff. I've got two Apaches coming that way from Austin. Don't shoot at 'em, Joe. The bad guys are beating a path to the Gulf and to the Mexican border by air."

"Roger that, Pops."

The next fifteen minutes created one of the most excruciating waits of Pops' entire life. Finally the call came in.

"Pops, we're here," said Sheriff Porter. "I don't have good news. They've got the governor. There are casualties. I've got dead troopers. Sir, all four of your Rangers here are dead. We've got hysterical staff members, and there's blood everywhere, including in the governor's bedroom. We have several injuries but nobody seems to be seriously wounded. We dispatched ambulances when we headed this way," said the distraught sheriff.

"Sweet Jesus… is there anyone there from the governor's staff that is coherent enough you can put on the line?" asked Pops.

"Pops, they just found Maj. Gen. Conroy. He is lying by his bed in one of the guesthouses with a single gunshot wound to the forehead."

"Mother… I should have stayed there!"

The sheriff handed the phone to Lt. Gov. Foster's chief of staff.

"Kendall here."

"Rory, this is Younger. What the hell happened?"

"Pops, they hit us a few hours ago while we were sleeping. There was no warning. They came in helicopters, and they weren't here to negotiate. Foster and his wife were wounded. They have them and Weaver."

"Where's Gov. Cooper, Rory?"

"Pops, I don't know. Nobody that's left here saw him during or after the raid, but his bedroom has blood all over it. They must have hustled him and Lyndsey into the first chopper without us seeing them. It was chaotic here. I've asked everyone and nobody saw them."

"Did all the choppers leave at the same time?"

"No, one left with their wounded first. I know for a fact they had the Fosters on that chopper, but I can't say the governor was on the same one."

"Think hard, Kendall!" implored Pops.

"Two more choppers arrived as they rounded us all up. They took everything—phones, papers, laptops, briefcases, guns—everything. That's why we couldn't call anyone."

"How long were they there after the first chopper lifted off? Think, Kendall! This is critical!"

"At least twenty minutes, Pops. I saw them all take off. They didn't have any of our staff on those four choppers. I'm sure of that."

"Rory, are you absolutely sure?"

"No doubt about it, Pops."

"Okay, Rory, thanks. The sheriff and deputies are there to assist. We have two Apaches close to the ranch. Let everyone know they're ours because everyone there understandably might have some trepidation seeing another couple of choppers coming over the ranch."

"What are we going to do, Pops?"

"I've got to get back to the folks at Lackland. Godspeed, Kendall. If anyone finds anything out about the governor, call me immediately!"

When Pops cleared the line, his call went back to the line holding with Lackland's commander

"Younger here. Okay, listen carefully. That chopper headed to the Gulf likely has the governor, lieutenant governor, their wives and Weaver. Do not engage that chopper. Do you understand?"

"Roger, Pops. They will only tail, but they have to stay far enough back to be free of the F-15 air-to-air missiles—at least seventy-five miles but probably more. Those birds are protecting that chopper. What's the order for the pilot heading to the four southbound choppers? He'll be on them very, very soon."

A few uneasy seconds of silence followed.

"Sir, what are my instructions to the pilot?" the commander asked again.

"Blow them the hell out of the sky!" Pops said in his patented Texas drawl.

"Engage? Is that affirmative?"

"*I said blow them out of the sky!*" yelled Pops.

"Sir, I'm not sure if he will be able to intercept and engage them before they hit Mexican airspace, if that is their escape plan."

"Colonel, I don't care if that pilot has to follow those choppers to the end of hell. *Take 'em out now*! Do you understand?"

"Roger that, sir."

# CHAPTER 14

*"The more corrupt the state, the more numerous the laws."*

*~ Cornelius Tacitus (55-117 AD)*
*Roman Senator*

Twenty-nine year-old Texas Air National Guard pilot Lt. Cmdr. Danny Hendrix asked the colonel twice to repeat his orders. Hendrix was a reserve pilot who had gone through the Texas A&M Corps of Cadets, followed by U.S. Navy flight training, then decided not to re-up for active duty and had just moved into the reserves. The young man had never flown a single minute of actual combat.

Loaded with six "beyond visual" Sparrow air-to-air radar-guided missiles, the Texas F-16 Falcon was fully capable of taking the Blackhawks out from 75 miles away.

Radar on the Blackhawks picked up the streaking Texas F-16, causing the flight operation commander to order a maneuver for the choppers to spread out to make it more difficult for the F-16 to target. The Blackhawks changed to four different headings.

The Blackhawks were inviting targets for the F-16 Falcon air-to-air missiles. Primarily used for ground assault operations and rescue, Blackhawks aren't equipped with long-range missiles. These four had two Stinger-mounted missile launchers onboard, but their range was in the hundreds of yards to approximately three miles—certainly no match for the F-16. Stingers are typically shoulder-mounted as they are small and have limited range, but these had been fitted to Blackhawks for Iraq.

Hendrix's F-16 was nicknamed *"Yellow Rose"* and was painted with a sexy, long dark-haired Hispanic woman with a low-cut flowered hacienda dress hiked up on her thighs and cowboy boots. The female image clung to a long-stemmed yellow rose like it was a strip bar stage pole. The image was just below the canopy on both sides of the fuselage.

The F-16 locked onto the first two targets as the young lieutenant commander radioed Lackland once more.

"Locked on targets. Confirm orders," radioed Hendrix nervously. For a split second, his mind wandered. After all his training, his first combat mission was over his Texas homeland.

"Engage, engage, engage," radioed the reply from Lackland. The Blackhawks' electronic systems, sensing the F-16 radar lock, began sounding alarms inside the cockpit. The openness of the interior of the choppers allowed anyone close enough to witness the panic that had suddenly engulfed the cockpit.

In a very few choreographed seconds, the radar-guided Sparrow missile was released. It dropped a few feet from the right wing of the *Yellow Rose*, fired its initial burner stage, then sped forward quickly at Mach 3 speed.

"Locked on target one. Releasing for target two."

"Incoming missile!!! Incoming! Fire off chaff!" screamed the co-pilot of *Santa Anna Three,* referring to aluminum pieces fired from the rear to throw off radar-guided missiles.

"No change of missile's course! Not working, sir!" yelled the co-pilot.

"More chaff! Chaff off!" responded the Blackhawk's captain.

In their panic, the Blackhawk pilots shot off the chaff too soon to distract radar guidance of the missile. "Two miles and gaining!"

Six-and-a-half miles from the Rio Grande, the Sparrow slammed into *Santa Anna Three* traveling one thousand feet in the air. The explosion and fireball lit up the new dawn sky for miles as hundreds of glowing pieces of the chopper cartwheeled to the ground like an Independence Day fireworks show. Twenty-seven seconds later, the second Blackhawk, *Santa Anna Four,* was demolished in the same manner.

"Target one down!!! Target two down!!" radioed Hendrix, too hyped on adrenaline to realize he had just instantly killed more than twenty people with two pushes of a button from his cockpit.

The pilots of the two other Blackhawks heard the radio communications just before the missiles hit.

"*Santa Anna Command*, two Blackhawks down. I repeat, Two Blackhawks down!" shouted the pilot from *Santa Anna Two*.

"Drop altitude to three hundred feet. Get over Mexican airspace, Commander!" yelled radio control from the carrier.

"Roger, command, we are now over Mexican airspace, proceeding to hen house."

"Command, this is *Santa Anna Five*, confirming we are also over Mexican airspace and five miles from hen house."

"Roger, *Five*, proceed as planned."

Hendrix had no time to dwell on what just happened as his advanced training had taken over like muscle memory. He banked the *Yellow Rose* sharply to the east, pulling several Gs.

"Confirm orders, sir. Two more bogeys on radar but they just crossed Mexican airspace."

"Lt. Cmdr. Hendrix, this is Lackland command. You are to follow those choppers and take them out. Do you understand?"

"Sir, confirm they are in Mexico. You want me to engage in Mexico? Please confirm."

"That is a roger, son! Engage until you have eliminated. I repeat, engage until you have eliminated!" ordered the agitated commander.

Hendrix took a deep breath. "Engage until downed. Confirmed. Roger."

The Mexican air force had been put on alert when permission was granted to the Johnson administration to allow the Blackhawks to operate freely in Mexican airspace for Operation Santa Anna. The ranking air force generals vehemently disagreed with the order from the Mexican El Presidente to allow the operation to take place. The generals talked among themselves in the twenty-four hours leading up to Operation Santa Anna, wondering what deal El Presidente had made with Johnson to allow such a breach of Mexican sovereignty. Surely, some special deal was made, and the generals' distrust of El Presidente only added to the drama.

The F-16 was still streaking toward Mexico in hot pursuit of the two choppers that just cleared Texas airspace. Apparently, that got the Mexican air force sufficiently concerned that they immediately scrambled three F-5 jets. The control tower at Piedras Negras continued to attempt to radio the F-16 in English. "This is a warning. Do not enter Mexican sovereign airspace," came the order in broken English.

"Sir, I'm getting radio communications from Mexico warning me not to enter their airspace. Please confirm orders."

"Hendrix, Mexico obviously assisted in this raid. Texans have been killed. We just learned Maj. Gen. Conroy was one of them. Your orders stand. Engage."

"Roger. Engage if necessary over Mexican airspace. Do I respond to the Mexican radio messages?"

"Hendrix, tell them whatever the hell you want—but down those damned choppers!" yelled the Lackland commander.

"Roger."

*Santa Anna Five* had cleared the Rio Grande and was now only two minutes from the Mexican border town airport. The *Yellow Rose* had just crossed the Rio Grande and was gaining on the chopper quickly.

"One chopper is off radar. It must have landed. I will engage airborne chopper but it's approaching populated area," the pilot radioed.

"Confirm. Engage."

"Fire. Missile away."

The pilots onboard *Santa Anna Five* had mistakenly figured they were out of harm's way upon entering Mexican airspace.

"Incoming! Crap, he's still on us!"

That was the last radio transmission from the Blackhawk as the missile struck with the same effect as the previous missile but, with the chopper only a few hundred feet above the ground, there was not enough altitude for the grandiose fireworks display. The chopper burst into a fireball, dropping like a lead balloon on fire. It crashed on a Mexican federal highway just a mile short of the airport.

"Target down! Target down! One left, but he must be on the ground!"

"Go find him! He's got to be at the airport! Take him out if you can minimize collateral damage!"

"There he is! He's on the ground! Rotors are still turning!"

"Take him out, Hendrix!" came the orders.

With the chopper on the ground, Hendrix had to switch armament. He was now too close to the chopper for a Sparrow to be effective and he had no way to contain collateral damage to civilians.

"Switching to cannons," he radioed.

The *Yellow Rose* banked hard to the right and dove toward the airport and the Blackhawk with its rotors slowing. Hendrix flipped his cannons to the fire position. As he dove in less than three hundred feet from the tarmac, the Vulcan six-barrel Gatling-style cannons lit up the Blackhawk with tracer rounds. In less than fifteen seconds, the chopper was strafed with over two hundred rounds and burst into flames. As Hendrix pulled up, the fuel tanks on the Blackhawk exploded, creating a fireball mushroom explosion shooting up into the new morning Mexican sky.

All of the federal agents managed to get out of the Blackhawk before the chopper was strafed.

"*Rose,* Del Rio indicating you've got three Mexican bogeys with a heading of three five zero traveling at Mach I. Divert now to heading of zero six zero, range thirty-one miles. Get out of Mexico, son," radioed Lackland command urgently.

The Mexican F-5s that had been scrambled from Monterrey as a result of the *Yellow Rose's* engagement of the Blackhawks, were older Northrup Falcon models no longer used by American military but, if he got within their outdated missiles' range (twenty-two miles), they could be lethal. The Falcons carried four air-to-air missiles each, so the *Rose* would need to outrun them or launch its Sparrows from a greater range outside twenty-two miles.

Since the *Rose* only had three air-to-air missiles left, there was no room for error and best just to get out of Dodge. Surely, the F-5 Falcons wouldn't pursue Hendrix into Texas air space, still considered U.S. air space by Washington, D.C. and Mexico.

# CHAPTER 15

*"Collectivism holds that the individual has no rights, that his life and work belong to the group (to society, to the tribe, the state, the nation) and that group may sacrifice him at its own whim to its own interests. The only way to implement a doctrine of that kind is by means of brute force—and statism has always been the political corollary of collectivism."*

*~ Ayn Rand (1905-1982)*
*Playwright & Author of "Atlas Shrugged"*

Hendrix had all three Mexican bogeys now tracking on his radar. "Lackland, clear of the Rio Grande," he radioed to command.

"Del Rio indicates bogeys have not changed heading or speed and are ten miles from border. Keep your head up, *Rose*. Do not engage unless they cross into Texas airspace or unless they engage."

"Roger, command."

Hendrix watched radar intensely as the three F-5s never slowed, racing across the Texas-Mexico border. It's one thing to be chasing down slower Blackhawks fleeing in the opposite direction. It's quite another to potentially conduct air-to-air combat outnumbered three to one.

"U.S. pilot, this is the Mexican air force. We hereby command you to return to Mexican airspace, land your aircraft at Piedras Negras, and surrender for your incursion and crimes in Mexico!" ordered a Mexican pilot in barely intelligible English.

"U.S. pilot, do you copy? Do you copy?"

"This is Lt. Cmdr. Danny Hendrix of the Texas Air Guard. This ain't no U.S. fighter."

"Señor, if you do not change your heading and return immediately, you will be shot down."

"Señor, I ain't going nowhere, but you are! "

Hendrix pulled the stick back swiftly to the southwest as he banked hard, heading directly in the direction of the incoming Mexican F-5s, almost blacking out from the g-force generated.

"Very wise decision, Señor pilot. Adjust to heading cero dos cuatro (zero two four)."

"Like hell, amigo! You have exactly fifteen seconds to change your heading back to where you came from!" answered Hendrix.

"Mexican air force pilots, you are in Texas airspace. Return to Mexico now!" commanded the radio voice from Lackland.

"Hendrix—missiles launched!" shrieked Lackland.

"Roger, command. Permission to down these aircraft!"

"Permission granted, *Rose*! Del Rio indicates Mexican missiles at twenty-eight miles but gaining quickly. Take evasive actions now!"

The *Rose* was speeding toward the incoming missiles at Mach 1.6 while the three Mexican air-to-air missiles were closing the gap quickly at over Mach 2. Hendrix only had seconds, not minutes, to evade the missiles.

Lackland command had a decision to make and only seconds to make it. The other Texas F-16, tailing the Blackhawk to the Truman, was almost to the Gulf. Precious minutes would be lost waiting for that aircraft to aid Hendrix.

"*Rose*, we are turning *Cochise* to your heading immediately."

"I've got 'em, Lackland! These Mexican birds are going to be Texas *toast*!"

Hendrix pulled the *Rose* into a steep climb and then began taking evasive actions that strained the structural limits of the multi-million dollar aircraft and the pilot's consciousness from the strain of g-forces as the three incoming missiles closed quickly.

"Chaff away. Chaff away."

At Lackland, command sat at the speaker phone set up on a folding table to communicate with both Del Rio and Laredo air traffic controls. It was obvious the commander was irritated at dealing with civilian controllers, but he was doing a good job keeping his cool so as not to excite the tower's staff members who were now calling in details on a highly fluid air-to-air combat situation. Their assistance would be critical to keep Lt. Cmdr. Hendrix alive.

The first missile hit the chaff and exploded less than two hundred yards away, rocking the *Rose* but not causing any damage. The second missile was diverted by the explosion and lost radar contact with Hendrix's F-16.

"*Rose*, report status," said the commander, anxiously trying to triangulate radar interpretations coming from both towers on the speakerphone. Everyone seemed to be talking at the same time. Two blips were off the radar, but Del Rio couldn't determine if it was Hendrix.

Released a little more than ten seconds behind the other two missiles, the third missile was locked on the *Rose*. Hendrix was fully aware he was not out of danger.

"Chaff released. Locked onto targets. Fire. Missiles away."

Hendrix had managed to get a radar lock on two of the Mexican Falcons sixteen miles away even as he was taking evasive actions to avoid the third Mexican missile. Lackland let out a brief and temporary sigh of relief to hear Hendricks on the radio.

Unable to shake the third missile and out of chaff, Hendricks resorted to classic extreme maneuvers to avoid impact. The F-16 was throwing radar jamming signals out as he went into a steep dive and roll. Suddenly the missile was on the *Rose* and clipped the rear tail stabilizer as it exploded a few milliseconds later only feet from the aircraft.

The young pilot's cockpit lit up with flashing red lights and alarms.

"I'm hit. I'm hit!" screamed Hendrix.

"Eject, son—eject!" yelled the Lackland commander.

"Losing altitude! Rear stabilizer damage! Pitching badly!"

For a few seconds it was lost on everyone listening to Hendrix that the three Mexican Falcons were still bearing down on the *Rose*.

"Lt. Cmdr. Hendricks, Del Rio reporting six missiles away on direct heading. Eject now, son! Eject now!"

The *Rose* was a sitting duck now. Hendrix turned his attention to the incoming aircraft, one of which he still had a radar lock on.

"Focus. Fire the remaining missiles, then eject!" he said to himself, trying to remain calm as his training again kicked in.

"Missile away! Second missile away!"

"Eject, lieutenant commander, that's an order!" roared the Lackland commander.

"Gig 'em!" yelled Hendrix as he pulled the ejection lever, a reference to his alma mater.

Nothing had prepared him for the sheer violence of the ejection. Even though various training exercises in the Navy tried to simulate what actually occurs in a fighter aircraft ejection, nothing came close. The rockets under the pilot's seat exploded, shooting him through the glass canopy and hurling him end over end like a just-kicked football.

Hendrix lost consciousness in the air. U.S. Navy studies used to believe the violent collision with the canopy knocked pilots unconscious, but a growing faction believes it's the body's auto defense mechanism in such a traumatic situation, in much the same way people lose consciousness when falling from great heights long before they ever hit the ground.

Briefly regaining consciousness and now separated from the seat as he flew through the air, Hendrix felt a sharp pain in his left shoulder as the parachute opened and suddenly jerked him upward as it caught air. Hendrix didn't know it at the time, but his shoulder had been separated during the ejection through the fighter aircraft canopy.

Through the pain, Hendricks looked up into the cloudless sky. The extreme stress of the last few minutes was surreal as he floated in the beautiful Texas morning sky. He saw the *Rose* twisting and tumbling toward the ground, then exploding as she was hit by two Mexican missiles on her way down.

In another instant, he heard an explosion and looked south to see a huge fireball in the sky. Then he noticed another fireball already heading to the south Texas ground.

Two of the three Mexican Falcons could not outrun or outmaneuver the Sidewinders Hendrix released from the *Rose* in her final seconds as he tried to manage the damaged aircraft.

"*Rose, Rose, Rose!* Do you copy?" yelled the Lackland commander. "What's radar show? Del Rio? Laredo? I need info NOW!"

"Sir, we have one aircraft heading south on a heading of two four two, speed nine hundred thirteen. It appears to be one of the Mexican fighters," replied Del Rio control.

"Damn it! Hopefully Hendrix ejected. What is the nearest town?"

"We lost all three of those four aircraft just south of Brackettville."

"Get fire and rescue moving out of Del Rio!"

"Roger, commander."

"I need coordinates on the second Texas fighter!"

"His heading is three four five traveling at fourteen hundred miles an hour. He's burning up the Texas sky to get there!" responded a controller in Del Rio.

"*Cochise*, this is Lackland command. State your heading."

"Lackland, this is Cmdr. Parsons with a heading of three four zero. Mexican bogey on radar. Trying to reach before leaving Texas airspace. I need orders, sir."

Cmdr. Delton "Tex" Parsons was a decorated F-15 pilot with over four dozen combat missions, including shooting down five Russian-made MIG Iraqi fighters, becoming the second-most decorated U.S. pilot in Desert Storm.

Parsons heard the radio chatter and knew his fellow pilot Hendrix had been shot down. He was bursting at the seams to get this last Mexican bogey.

The Lackland commander looked at the fifteen-something officers who had gathered in the small communications room that had been made into a makeshift situation room.

"Gentlemen, now in addition to our little problem with the feds," he told them, "we've got ourselves a genuine international incident going on here. Damn it."

Picking up the mic slowly and bringing it to his mouth, the commander barked orders to Parsons.

"Get him before he gets out of Texas, commander. But, if you can't, track him down wherever he goes and shoot his ass out of the sky!"

"Roger that. My pleasure, sir. I'll follow him to hell and put him there myself if I have to!"

The *Cochise*, a much faster aircraft than the Mexican Falcon, closed on the Falcon quickly. At fifty miles away, Parsons released two advanced AM-RAAM missiles.

"Missiles away!"

"Stay on him, Commander!"

At a speed of Mach 4, the missiles closed the distance quickly.

The Mexican Falcon tried desperately to avoid the missiles, successfully avoiding the first one. But the second one pierced the left wing, separating it from the fuselage. Without exploding, the Falcon began a grotesque cartwheel to the ground. Seconds later, it slammed into the ground and exploded into a mushroomed fireball. The aircraft fell less than one hundred yards short of the Rio Grande on the Texas side, across the river from the border town of El Moral, Mexico.

The small situation room erupted in applause and jubilation, but the commander stayed calm, still grasping the radio mic.

"I need someone to call the Mexican consulate in San Antonio now!" he said, turning to a junior officer. "We need to calm the situation before it gets worse."

"Cmdr. Parsons, congratulations. Change heading to three five four and see if you can aid Del Rio recovery of Hendrix," the commander said. "Keep an eye on radar. The Mexicans may launch more aircraft."

Over the next few minutes, the commander was on a local phone call with the Mexican consulate office in San Antonio. The consulate was surprised by the actions of the last few hours and refused to believe Mexico was involved in the DHS raid on the Swingin' T.

"Two more fighters scrambled from Monterrey, commander!" said the controller from Del Rio.

"Cmdr. Parsons, more bogeys on the way."

"Roger that, Lackland. They haven't hit my radar yet."

"*Cochise*, change course to one seven five. Mexico has scrambled two more fighters. We need you to be prepared to meet them at the border. Del Rio emergency will find Lt. Cmdr. Hendrix."

"Roger that," responded the unflappable pilot.

The Lackland commander hung up the mic to get back on the phone with the Mexican consulate. Meanwhile, the Mexican fighter jets were on a direct collision course with Parsons. For the next ten minutes, the commander negotiated with the consulate to end the newly created crisis.

The two Mexican Falcons came into Parsons' radar. "I've got two bogeys on radar with a heading of three five zero. I can paint them right *now*!" said Parsons, referring to the fact that the *Cochise* could lock on its targets from a further distance than the Mexican Falcons.

At the Lackland makeshift situation room, a heated discussion ensued while the commander was still on the phone with the consulate. Many wanted Parsons to take the Mexican Falcons down before he got inside their missile range.

The commander slammed down the phone.

"The consulate had no luck with its air force and apparently they can't reach El Presidente! Sounds like President Johnson. Nowhere to be found when critical decisions need to be made."

He picked up the mic.

"Cmdr. Parsons, reverse heading to one two zero. We are not going to escalate an already bad situation. They think you're going to cross their airspace again."

"Roger. Changing course to one two zero."

For the next six minutes, Del Rio and Laredo air traffic control tracked the incoming F-5s.

"This is Del Rio control. This message is a warning to the two Mexican fighter jets on a heading of zero one five. Do not cross into Texas airspace. Do you read me?"

Both towers in Laredo and Del Rio attempted to get the Mexican air force pilots to respond, to no avail.

"Lackland, this is Del Rio control. The incoming fighters are sixteen miles from the border and have not changed course or altered speed. We will continue to issue warnings."

"We just received word that Hendrix has been spotted and recovered! He's okay. He has a separated shoulder and is banged up, but he'll be fine!" said the commander, after hanging up a different cell phone as the room broke into applause again.

"Sir, the last Blackhawk made landing on the Truman. The F-15s are still in the Gulf. They don't appear to want any part of this fight," claimed a junior officer who came running in from another room.

"Where's the Truman now?"

"Speeding off on a northeasterly course."

"Who is tracking the F-15s?" asked the commander.

"Ellington Field in Houston."

"I want to be notified immediately if they change course."

"Ellington and Mabry want to know if they should scramble fighters. It seems the chain of command has broken down. They can't reach Maj. Gen. Conroy or any state officials."

"I don't want to tell them the major general has been killed yet. Tell them to keep their fighters grounded but ready to scramble."

"Yes, sir."

"Sir, this is Del Rio. The two fighters have crossed over. They're in Texas airspace, sir!"

"Damn!" exclaimed the commander as he slammed his fist on the table.

"Permission to change course, sir," requested Cmdr. Parsons.

"Permission granted. Commander, do not let them encroach inside the radar window for their missiles. Take them out as soon as you have radar lock."

"Affirmative. Roger that, Lackland."

"Get the damned consulate on the phone again! What the hell are they doing?" the commander screamed at nobody in particular.

Cmdr. Parsons changed course to intercept the incoming Mexican Falcons. The very second the *Cochise* got within one hundred five miles, he could paint them with radar and send his advanced AM-RAAM missiles to greet the incoming Mexican Falcons.

"Lackland, I have targets in range. Request permission to lock on radar."

"Permission granted. Do not fire. I repeat, do not fire your missiles," was the command sent by Lackland.

"Roger, lock only."

Cmdr. Parsons locked onto the two Mexican fighters. He knew alarms were going off in the enemy planes, and their pilots would be near panic. They had to know their only hope was to get Parsons inside their radar because his missiles had much greater range. Of course, they had another choice, and he wondered if they would take it.

The Del Rio tower started chatting immediately.

"Lackland, the Mexicans have just reversed course. They are bugging out!"

Again, the room at Lackland erupted.

"Commander, turn on your afterburners and escort our Mexican visitors the hell outta here!"

"My pleasure, Lackland."

"Continue to paint them, Commander. If they flinch for one second, lock radar or change course other than returning to Mexico, smoke 'em!"

With a one hundred fifty mile advantage, the *Cochise* was gaining on the Mexican jets fast, but Parsons wanted to stay outside their missile range. When the pilots got within ten miles of the Rio Grande, Parsons couldn't help himself.

"Adios, my friends. Wish you could have stayed longer!" Parsons sent out over his radio as he switched to the commercial airline frequency to make sure anyone on the channel could hear.

When the planes crossed over into Mexican airspace, the *Cochise* was only minutes behind them and gaining fast.

"United States fighter pilot, this is the Mexican air force. Do *not* cross into sovereign Mexico airspace."

"Piedras tower. This is not a U.S. fighter. This is *Cochise*, a Republic of Texas fighter!"

When Parsons reached the Rio Grande, he lowered altitude and headed straight for the Piedras Negras airport.

"Lackland, *Cochise* is in Mexican airspace!"

"Cmdr. Parsons! What the…"

"Still tracking those fighters, sir!"

"Commander, return to Texas airspace with a heading of three five eight."

"Roger, change course to three five eight."

As Cmdr. Parsons changed course, he took the liberty to lower his altitude even further to two hundred feet. The control tower at Piedras Negras suddenly panicked, thinking the fighter might easily strafe the airport.

Before much of anything could be done at the small Mexican airport other than general panic, the *Cochise* screamed over the control tower as Parsons dipped a wing and hit the afterburners, rattling the entire small airport terminal, hangars and tower. Parsons couldn't help but key his mic.

"*Remember the Alamo*, amigos. *Remember the Alamo!*"

# CHAPTER 16

*"Why is patriotism thought to be blind loyalty to the government and the politicians who run it, rather than loyalty to the principles of liberty and support for the people? Real patriotism is a willingness to challenge the government when it's wrong."*

~ *Former Texas Congressman Ron Paul*

Secy. of State Bartlett and Sen. Simpson, with two staff members each, had just lifted off in their helicopter from a private residence thirty miles west of Austin. They were en route to the scheduled morning meeting with Gov. Cooper at the Swingin' T Ranch when the helicopter pilot got a message from the Texas Air National Guard.

The co-pilot turned and yelled back to the occupants, "Senator, we just received a message to hold our pattern and not proceed as there is some type of air-to-air conflict going on near our destination."

Neither the senator nor the secretary knew exactly *where* they were headed to meet Gov. Cooper.

"This doesn't sound good," yelled Simpson to Bartlett over the roaring of the helicopter engines and rotors.

"No, it doesn't," she replied.

Both began to look at their smart phones to see if any messages had come through to them that may give a hint about what was happening.

"I have an urgent message from Justice!" said Bartlett. "I'm told to call Tibbs' office immediately and not meet with Gov. Cooper!"

"Oh, crap," bellowed her chief of staff.

"Tibbs knows?" Simpson was stunned.

Bartlett stared off into the Austin sky, contemplating her next move. Somehow her cover was blown, but could she still make this meeting happen and negotiate some type of end to the crisis? Then panic struck.

"Tibbs did something! Air-to-air conflict? Are you serious? This has the attorney general's signature all over it. They must have found out about our meeting and the governor's location!"

"Geez, let me see what the pilot knows," said a worried Simpson.

He unbuckled from his seat and took a few steps up into the cockpit area to speak to the pilots. The pilots gave him a headset as he knelt behind them.

"I need to know what's going on. Who are you guys taking your orders from?"

"Sir, we were in contact with Lackland Air Force Base in San Antonio originally, but we were switched to Texas Rangers command."

"Under Pops Younger?"

"Yes, sir."

"Can you radio back and get Younger on the radio? Let him know it's Sen. Simpson."

"Yes, sir," said the co-pilot.

A few minutes passed while the pilots tried to reach Ranger command. Meanwhile, the helicopter was holding a twenty-mile circling pattern over the west Austin hills.

"Senator, we have Ranger command on radio!" called the pilot.

The senator shuffled back to the front of the chopper and again knelt behind the pilots as he put the headset back on.

"This is Sen. Simpson. Who's on the line with me?"

"Senator, this is Younger."

"Pops, good to hear your voice. What the hell is going on out here? We were scheduled to meet with the governor this morning. I have Secy. of State Bartlett on board with me."

"Senator, in the early hours, the ranch where the governor, lieutenant governor and other state officials were being housed was attacked by federal agents of some kind, probably DHS and ATF, using DHS Blackhawk helicopters. I don't know yet where they came from or how they got in undetected."

"What? Oh, my God!" shrieked Simpson

"At a minimum, the governor has been taken," said Younger. "We have casualties on the ranch. This morning there have been air attacks on radar and control tower facilities in San Antonio, Brownsville and Corpus Christi. There have been air-to-air combat scenarios over south Texas and somehow they include operations by Mexican air force combat fighters over Texas air space. There's an aircraft carrier off South Padre Island. We have a real crap storm going on, Senator."

The senator turned to look at Bartlett while he was talking to Pops. She could tell by his expression something was terribly wrong.

"We don't believe there are any more U.S. or Mexican fighters in the air near the area," said Pops with obvious disgust. "I suggest your pilot take you to the ranch so Bartlett can see firsthand what ya'lls Yankee buddies in Washington just did."

"How far away are we?" Simpson asked.

"Less than an hour," interrupted the pilot.

"Take us right now. Any more news on Cooper?" asked the senator.

"Senator, you better tell your people that they are going to see some damned horrific images at the ranch. I want you to make sure Bartlett and her staff witness *everything*. Hell, take pictures for the whole world to see!"

"Will do, Pops. Who's in charge out there right now?"

"The sheriff of Llano County. I'll let them know you are still coming."

Secy. Bartlett tried mightily to figure out what was going on from the little bit she could hear of the senator's conversation. She could barely hear the radio over the engine noise, but not enough of it to prepare for what she was about to hear.

"They attacked the ranch! There are casualties and the governor is missing!"

"Damn, it had to be Tibbs!" exclaimed Bartlett. "He had to know we were meeting. The timing is not a coincidence."

"Nothing with this administration is a coincidence," retorted the senator.

"I want to go to this ranch," Bartlett said.

"Oh, you're going, Madam Secretary. We are headed directly there now."

"What else should I know? Where's the governor?" asked Bartlett. The four staff members were hanging on every word they could hear over the rotors and engine.

"Apparently, either Special Ops or DHS launched an early morning raid this morning with Blackhawks."

"Oh, my…" was all Bartlett could get out before Simpson continued.

"He said fighter jets struck civilian airports in San Antonio, Brownsville, Corpus Christi and air bases like Lackland and Beeville. What I'm unclear about is that he mentioned something about fighters from the Mexican air force."

"Mexican fighters? I don't understand."

"Neither do I."

As the helicopter changed course to the Swingin' T, the staff members began texting the state department and the senator's office back in Washington for news of the morning's events.

It was difficult to hear on the noisy helicopter. Since operation *Prism* was made public and revealed NSA's ability to listen, track, record and catalog all cell phone calls made by Americans, most administration cabinet members had switched to satellite or encrypted phones for sensitive communications. Secy. Bartlett had a separate satellite phone but wasn't able to establish a link over the Texas hill country to call her office.

News was sketchy at best, but reports came across their cell phones. Bartlett's chief of staff handed the secretary her smartphone opened to a CNN app.

"Feds Conduct Raid on Texas State Government Officials! Casualties Reported!"

"This is *not* good. Not good at all," said Bartlett, shaking her head.

"How did Tibbs find out about this meeting, Anna?" asked Simpson suspiciously.

"You're assuming he found out," said Bartlett. "We don't know for sure yet that he knew."

"Oh, come on, Madam Secretary! Even you know better."

"If you are asking if I tipped them off or if anyone on my staff did, then you just back up, senator. I had a lot to gain by a successful negotiation down here, just as did you."

Bartlett was visibly angry at the suggestion. Simpson knew the old political war horse could verbally devour him easily.

"What about your staff, senator?" quipped Bartlett, looking directly at Simpson's chief of staff."

"Okay, okay, truce here. My mistake. I agree we both wanted a negotiated settlement."

The pilot flipped his intercom switch on and announced they were just a few miles from the Swingin' T.

All the occupants strained against their seatbelts to look out the windows.

"Look, there's smoke coming up in several places! Looks like something is on fire," yelled one of the staff members.

The helicopter made several passes around the main lodge as they reached the sheriff's department by radio. On the ground, they were greeted by various law enforcement personnel, including state troopers and Texas Militia.

"Senator and Madam Secretary, I'm Sheriff Porter. All the remaining state officials and staff were loaded up and sent elsewhere. We have crime scene investigators here, as well as some Rangers, state troopers and Texas Militia. Over there is the coroner. We have a damned mess."

"There are fatalities? Who are they?" asked Simpson.

"Maj. Gen. Conroy was killed, as well as several state troopers and four Texas Rangers. We lost some damned good men, Senator."

"And news of the governor?" said a hopeful Simpson.

The heavy-set buzz-haired sheriff looked at the ground for what seemed like an eternity.

"Follow me," he replied, speaking to the entire contingent as he began walking to the main lodge. Sen. Simpson and Secy. Bartlett were visibly shaken as they walked through the carnage.

"Here is where the governor and his wife were sleeping."

"Oh, my God," said Bartlett, putting her palm over her mouth and nose, "look at the blood!"

"Christ!" exclaimed Simpson.

"A federal agent and state trooper were both shot and killed in this room; we know that for a fact. So whose blood is whose is anyone's guess," said the sheriff as he looked at several Texas Rangers in the room doing what amounted to a crime scene investigation.

"It appears, however, there are two blood areas," said Porter, pointing to blood spatter on the wall next to the end of the bed and on the floor, and then pointing to the entrance to the bedroom where the other blood stains were concentrated.

"Nobody saw them take the governor? What about bodies? Did anyone see them load bodies into the choppers?" asked Simpson as he looked for any clue or sign of the governor's fate.

"Nope. Whatever happened to the governor, they made damned sure it would leave us guessing," answered Porter.

As they walked the compound to tour the rest of the crime area,

Bartlett's chief of staff handed the secretary her smartphone, again opened to the MSNBC website.

**"Mexican President Reports Texas Air Guard Violated Mexican Air Space and Downed Several Mexican Fighters. Mexican Military Mobilizing Along Texas Border!"**

"What the hell is going on?" muttered Bartlett. "I need a briefing as soon as possible from the White House. Get Washington on the phone now!" she screamed to her staff.

# CHAPTER 17

*"Communism possesses a language which every people can understand—its elements are hunger, envy and death."*

~ *Heinrich Hein (1797-1856)*
*German Poet & Writer*

*S anta Anna One* maneuvered into a landing pattern in eighteen-knot winds as it prepared to land on the USS Harry S. Truman in the Gulf of Mexico. The massive carrier was pitching slowly in moderate seas as the stealth-skinned Blackhawk came to rest on the deck.

Dozens of crewmen and officers lingered on the deck to maneuver the chopper once the rotors stopped turning. The airmen had orders to immediately position the chopper on the elevator deck; the chopper's occupants were ordered to remain onboard. The Blackhawk was to be lowered two deck levels before the pilot, crew and others could get off. Deck level three was ordered to be empty with the exception of crew and officers who had security clearances.

Command did not want anyone to see who got off the chopper, whether it was Texas state officials in custody or body bags. Per Adm. Victor Beacham, only a small percentage of the Truman's crew knew the Blackhawk's mission or why the carrier was in the Gulf of Mexico.

The Blackhawk drew quite a crowd when it landed as very few people outside of special operations had ever seen the stealth skin on the chopper, made famous in the raid that netted the most famous terrorist in the world. The scuttlebutt had already started among the sailors, trying to guess why a stealth Blackhawk was operating in the Texas Gulf Coast instead of its normal Persian Gulf and Indian Ocean venues. Adding to the mystery were a number of fighter jets in the air circling the carrier. The fact that the occupants did not exit the chopper only heightened speculation.

Adm. Beacham was already on the third deck waiting for the Blackhawk as it slowly descended from the flight deck. Joining him in the wait were six men in suits and other officers from the Truman. The *suits* included four men from the FBI and two from DHS. Naval corpsmen and surgeons were standing by with gurneys and medical equipment to attend to the wounded.

The elevator deck locked into place with a loud clank as it settled onto the third deck. The crew and occupants began climbing out of the cargo bay, first with the two wounded agents who were immediately loaded onto gurneys. They each had an IV, started onboard during the flight from the Swingin' T by crew members who were also trained in emergency EMT procedures.

Next, Lt. Gov. Foster and his wife were helped out of the craft. Foster also had an IV started, and it was obvious he had suffered a wound to the thigh. He looked gaunt and weak, and it was apparent that he had lost a lot of blood. Although not wounded, his wife could barely walk, no doubt stunned by the trauma of it all and noticeably shaken by her husband's worsening condition.

Texas Atty. Gen. Jeff Weaver was accompanied on both arms by DHS forces in full combat gear. His hair was disheveled, and he still wore just his boxer shorts and a t-shirt, a result of the sudden raid on the Swingin' T. Weaver was slightly bent over with handcuffs on his wrists, attached to a chain that went around his waist and connected to shackles on his ankles. The shackles were so tight that he could only take baby steps as he inched toward the edge of the Blackhawk cargo bay.

Weaver looked up to see the contingent of officers and suits staring at him from twenty feet away, and he recognized the ranking naval officer.

"Admiral, if this was *your* operation, you should be ashamed! Texas won't forget, I can guaran-damn-tee you that! What happened this morning was criminal!"

"Shut him the hell up!" yelled back one of the *suits*.

The two commandos holding Weaver by the arms forced him to the ground, face down, with a knee in his back. Another stepped over and gagged him. At that point, Weaver started resisting, prompting one of his captors to start kicking the Texas attorney general in the ribs.

"Stop that!" snapped the admiral.

"Excuse me, Adm. Beacham, but he's got it coming!" replied the *suit*.

"You won't treat a prisoner on *my* ship like that!" said the red-faced admiral.

"This turd is a prisoner of the U.S. Department of Justice," said the *suit*.

"Son, if you touch that prisoner one more time, I will have my sailors strap you to the catapult on the flight deck and launch your ass into the Gulf of Mexico and you can swim back to Washington, D.C.!"

Two chief petty officers moved toward the offending *suit*, who took two steps back, raising both hands slightly to indicate he was finished beating on Weaver.

Adm. Beacham next ordered most of the remaining sailors off the deck. The *suits* walked over to the chopper and turned to make sure there was no unnecessary crew still on the elevator deck.

"Get everyone the hell out of here!" yelled one of the suited men to the admiral.

Adm. Beacham wasn't used to someone barking orders at him, especially in front of his staff and worse, from a civilian. "Son, this is my ship. If you attempt to issue an order to me or any of my officers from this point forward, you will spend the night in the brig down below. Is that understood?"

"Okay, Admiral. I get it. Can you please make sure non-essential personnel are cleared?"

"The officers and seamen that remain on this deck have the clearance to be here. Now let's get on with this."

The admiral and the suits anxiously waited for the operation commander to bring out Gov. Cooper. The commander had indicated, through coded transmissions, that they had gotten Cooper. The suits were especially anxious to see the governor in shackles. The governor's true condition wasn't relayed to the carrier command while in flight in order to keep radio silence and to keep the status of the mission and the occupants and their status secret.

When the crew began offloading the black body bags of the four dead federal agents, the mood changed slightly until the body bags had been carried into an adjoining room and the door closed behind the gurneys.

Everyone now stepped closer to the Blackhawk as the operation commander of *Santa Anna One* jumped down out of the cargo bay. The admiral did not like the look on his face.

One of the *suits* blurted out immediately, "Bring the bastard out. I want to see the criminal that killed my brother agents."

"Here you go…" said the flight commander as two of the crew members pulled out another black body bag.

"Oh, my God. You can't be serious!" exclaimed Adm. Beacham.

"He brought it on himself, sir."

"You boys were supposed to arrest him, not kill him!"

Just then another body bag was brought to the edge of the cargo bay.

"Who the hell is that?" barked the admiral.

The commander looked away for a brief second. "The governor's wife, sir."

"Instead of capturing him, we killed him and his wife? Are you serious?" asked the admiral in disbelief.

*Operation Santa Anna* was the admiral's mission. The Joint Chiefs had chosen him and the Truman to carry it out, although he had objected to the name given the operation by DHS. Even though federal agents conducted the raid, the coordination and operation were his responsibility. The admiral knew in that instant his naval career was over.

"Who else knows this?" asked another *suit*.

"Just the crew. We were able to contain the rest at the ranch and keep them separate. I seriously doubt anyone knows they are dead, but I cannot guarantee that, sir," answered the operation commander.

The admiral continued to rub his chin in deep thought. "There might be some in Washington that will be happy about this. But I can certainly tell you this… You just killed the duly elected sitting governor of the state of Texas and his wife. No matter how it happened, this is a bad, bad scenario," he lamented.

"Sir, there was a firefight in his bedroom. One of the body bags contained a dead federal agent who was shot and killed by the governor himself."

"Then it was justified. Whatever happened, he had it coming for what happened in Austin," retorted one of the *suits*.

"Gentlemen, he was killed in his *bedroom* as a result of this operation. I can tell you this for sure; any chance this administration had to win over the hearts and minds of ordinary Texans just went out the window. To them, the federal government has just murdered a popular Texas icon and his wife."

"Well, screw 'em. Like I said, he had it coming. There are dead federal agents' blood on his hands for what happened in Austin. I'm certainly not shedding any tears," said the same *suit*.

"I want those two bodies treated with the utmost respect and the same respect you gave those others in that room. This man was a duly elected governor. You will not defile their bodies or treat them any differently than the others while their remains are on my ship. Is that understood by everyone?" asked the admiral.

"Aye, aye."

"Yes, sir."

The admiral was visibly shaken. His senior officers had never seen him in such a state of shock and uncertainty. He was a rock, always a beacon of confidence and assuredness to his staff and sailors on ship. He paced aimlessly, looking down at the deck floor while rubbing his chin and the back of his neck.

The corpsmen then began the task of loading the remains of the governor and his wife onto gurneys to the refrigerated room where the other remains were placed.

"Gentlemen, I need my senior officers and the commander in my quarters. We have a satellite debriefing with the Joint Chiefs in fifteen minutes."

As Adm. Beacham walked back through the interior maze of the carrier, he was in deep thought and oblivious to anyone around him, failing to acknowledge the salutes of numerous sailors he passed on his way to his quarters. He stepped into his quarters, shut the door behind him and sat down in his overstuffed leather chair.

Adm. Beacham, an Annapolis graduate and forty-two year naval officer, was highly decorated and well respected. He sat in his chair and lit up a cigar. He had lost his wife of thirty-seven years thirteen months ago. He missed her greatly. He always felt guilty that he wasn't at her side when she died from cancer much faster than doctors had predicted.

The admiral was at the helm of the Truman in the Indian Ocean steaming home, and had been assured by her doctors that his wife was in remission. The admiral was not going to miss the opportunity for the Truman to be part of Operation Python, in which sorties from his flight deck contributed to the destruction of Iran's nuclear capabilities. The guilt ate at him twenty-four hours a day.

This entire mission, from the time the Joint Chiefs and Atty. Gen. Tibbs laid it out until they pulled the governor's body bag from the Blackhawk, was surreal. Like any good officer, he accepted his orders, but he never liked it.

Launching a secret special ops mission into one of the United States' sovereign states to capture a sitting governor and having him and his wife turn up dead as a result of the operation under his watch was something the admiral could have never imagined. As an astute student of U.S. military history, he was ashamed his name would forever be attached to this debacle. He was sure this would launch the country into a dangerous spiral from which it might not recover.

He reached around his desk and pulled out his military issue .45-caliber Colt pistol, originally issued to him as a new ensign toward the end of the Vietnam War. He picked up the picture of his wife that sat on his desk and laid the pistol in his lap, stroking the image of his wife through the glass of the frame.

Near the door of Adm. Beacham's officer quarters, the executive officer and other senior officers of the ship waited outside in the narrow steel hallway. The *suits* were not far behind, all gathering to conduct the satellite video conference link-up with Tibbs and the Joint Chiefs to debrief them on *Operation Santa Anna*. Suddenly, a loud bang echoed through the hull of the ship, coming directly from the admiral's quarters.

"Admiral, Admiral, are you okay in there?" yelled the XO.

No answer came.

"Admiral! We're coming in! Break the door, now!" he ordered.

Two junior officers began kicking the door; finally the latch seemed to partially break. Another kick and the door flew open.

"Oh, no, oh, no!" shouted the XO.

*Operation Santa Anna* had just claimed another victim.

The admiral slouched in his leather chair, covered in blood still oozing from his mouth. He had put the Colt .45 into his mouth and pulled the trigger. Blood was still running down the chair onto the floor. Momentary chaos broke out in his quarters and the hallway as the XO and others tried unsuccessfully to revive the admiral.

In the meantime, Atty. Gen. Tibbs and the Joint Chiefs sat impatiently in the situation room at the Pentagon, along with the secretaries of DHS and Defense and the directors of the FBI, NSA and ATF. The Truman was already ten minutes late for the designated satellite video conference call link-up.

"What the hell is wrong with your people?" yelled Tibbs at the Joint Chiefs and then turning his gaze upon Secy. of Defense Brooks.

"We are in touch with the Truman. Apparently, something has happened to cause a delay," said a confused fleet admiral.

"Well, I don't appreciate being kept waiting. Make something happen now, General!" barked Tibbs.

"Sir, that's *Admiral...*" said Secy. Brooks.

"General, Admiral, Sergeant, I don't really give a damn. I want to be debriefed. I want to know if they have that damned cowboy governor and I want to know NOW!"

# CHAPTER 18

*"I wouldn't go to war again as I have done to protect some lousy investment bankers. There are only two things we should fight for. One is the defense of our homes and the other is the Bill of Rights. War for any other reason is simply a racket."*

~ *Major General Smedley Butler (1881-1940)*
*Most Decorated U.S. Marine in History*
*Author of "War is a Racket"*

B y 10:30 a.m., stories were breaking over news outlets all over the world that something significant had happened in Texas, but details were sketchy at best. Although it was several hours after the raid that began very early that morning, few details were available, leading many mainstream news media pundits to speculate on the facts, including wildly exaggerated stories with no factual basis.

The most accurate reporting of the situation on the ground was coming from local Texas television and radio. They were first to the scenes at the control towers hit by the fighter jets in San Antonio, Corpus Christi and Brownsville. The local media was having difficulty tying in the Mexican air force with the unfolding events. But the world was finding out that something huge had happened in Texas that morning involving the United States federal government and Texas.

The claims made by the Mexican president two hours earlier heightened the speculation, and local TV and amateur video footage from the wreckage of the Blackhawks, Mexican Falcons and the Texas F-16s confirmed something serious had occurred.

Beat reporters at the Pentagon and the White House were pressing for statements, but were told a statement would be made later in the day.

Then the dam broke.

Local San Antonio television station KSAT was beamed into the national network as a reporter broadcast live from the Swingin' T Ranch near Llano.

"We are here at the sprawling Swingin' T Ranch near Llano in the Texas hill country where Texas Gov. Brent Cooper and his staff were staying last night. According to Llano County Sheriff Joe Porter, federal agents conducted a raid on the ranch at approximately four a.m. to arrest the governor and numerous other state officials. There appears to have been a firefight between Texas Rangers, state troopers and agents from several federal agencies such as DHS, the FBI and the ATF."

The young female reporter had to take a deep breath because she was talking so fast.

"The sheriff has reported there have been casualties, including fatalities. We have not been able to confirm any specifics on the casualties. We are, however, able to report that Gov. Cooper and Lt. Gov. Foster and both of their wives are missing and assumed to have been arrested by federal agents. There have been unsubstantiated reports that the lieutenant governor is wounded, but we have not been told the extent of his injuries. We have been attempting to have officials on the scene come on live camera, but they have indicated there will be a coordinated news conference sometime later because the situation here at the Swingin' T Ranch is very fluid at this particular moment."

The excited reporter had to take another deep breath. She was breaking the story of most reporters' lifetimes. Even her cameraman had trouble keeping the camera on her as she moved excitedly about.

"Once again, this is Rebecca Marlin reporting near Llano, Texas. There has been a federal raid on a private ranch here in the hill country of Texas by the feds to capture and arrest the governor of Texas and other state officials. Casualties have been reported, including a number of unknown fatalities. We are told the governor and his wife are missing, presumably arrested and taken elsewhere by helicopter. We are also told the Texas lieutenant governor has been wounded. Both he and his wife were also reportedly taken by federal agents in helicopters."

The cameraman swung the camera off the news reporter and scanned the entrance to the Swingin' T, which was still smoldering and smoking from the attack. The Llano sheriff's department was keeping onlookers and the reporter's news van about two hundred feet from the entrance.

"Also, there are reports of some type of Mexican air force conflict with Texas Air National Guard fighters. We don't know if these two events are related; however, the president of Mexico has announced some type of armed conflict with Texas aircraft. Texas shrimpers reported they spotted a U.S. Navy carrier near South Padre Island on the Texas Gulf Coast."

The reporter's brunette hair kept sweeping across her face in the constant wind. She had to brush it aside constantly, but she stayed calm and unflappable in the awkward situation. "Reports are coming in about some types of bombings or strikes on airports in San Antonio, Corpus Christi and Brownsville," she stated, "and we have received damage reports from Lackland Air Force Base in San Antonio and the Naval Air Station near Beeville. We don't know at this time who conducted those bombings and if the Mexican air force is involved. I will turn this back to New York for live coverage. This is Rebecca Marlin, reporting for KSAT live from the Swingin' T Ranch in the Texas hill country."

This live report was the first news to the world confirming that the Texas crisis had just entered a new and extremely dangerous phase. Immediately, news organizations began churning, with announcements, claims, demands and prognostications coming from all sides. For every call to remain calm and wait for the facts of what had occurred, there were those already speculating what should be done to the Texas governor. Some parts of the country actually began celebrating the apparent capture of the brash governor. In Times Square, the marquee streamed across the screen indicating the feds had captured the Texas governor.

Texans throughout the world were outraged. A federal raid into Texas to capture their very popular governor? U.S. government military strikes on civilian Texas airports? How could that be? How was that possible?

Any Texans who were on the fence about the current crisis with the administration were about to be shoved off, one way or another.

What had begun as a general disdain by the average Texan for federal involvement in Texas' affairs had grown to a level of outrage already heightened over the unconstitutional actions of the administration.

Now the Swingin' T was about to become a modern-day *Alamo*…

# CHAPTER 19

*"The provision in the Constitution granting the right to all persons to bear arms is a limitation upon the power of the Legislature to enact any law to the contrary. The exercise of a right guaranteed by the Constitution cannot be made subject to the will of the sheriff."*

*~ The People vs. Zerillo (1922)*
*Joseph Zerillo was arrested for carrying a pistol without a permit from the local sheriff, and the decision was overturned by the Michigan Supreme Court*

The Johnson administration cabinet members assembled in the Pentagon operations center were becoming anxious. They had received word that something tragic had occurred on the USS Truman, but had not gotten any definitive communications from the ship in nearly twenty minutes.

Atty. Gen. Tibbs was especially frustrated as he awaited news of the capture of his prize—the Texas governor.

"Try them again," he ordered.

"USS Truman, this is Fleet Adm. Cummings."

"Admiral, this is Capt. Roger Abner. I am the executive officer. I regret to inform you that Adm. Beacham took his own life in his quarters just before our scheduled link-up."

"Captain, please repeat," said the fleet admiral.

"Sir, the admiral shot himself in his quarters. He is dead."

"Why the hell would he do that?" demanded Tibbs.

"He did not leave a note. I'm sure some of you know he lost his wife about a year ago, and he was visibly shaken by the news today regarding *Operation Santa Anna*."

"What news?" shouted Tibbs. "What the hell is going on? Where is Gov. Cooper? Did they get that damned Texas Ranger?"

"Sir, we lost four federal agents in the raid and we have two wounded."

"Dear God," gasped Secy. of Defense Brooks.

"Where is Cooper?" repeated Tibbs, irritation apparent in his voice.

The captain paused for a few uneasy seconds, then continued. "I regret to inform everyone that Gov. Cooper was killed in the raid."

"Repeat that, Captain," requested Adm. Cummings urgently, hoping he misunderstood.

At that very moment, some sitting in the operations center stood up while others pulled closer to the huge round mahogany conference table.

"Gov. Cooper engaged our agents. We know he is responsible for at least one federal agent's death based on eyewitness accounts. He was killed in the firefight."

"Oh, geez… Are you serious? This is confirmed?" interrupted Brooks as he rubbed his hands through his hair nervously.

"Yes, sir, he is in a body bag in the refrigerated morgue aboard the ship and was positively identified."

"Damn, people, we have serious problems now. Who is going to inform the president?" asked McDermott.

Tibbs sank back in his chair. The thought of the Texas governor being dead meant nothing to him, but his opportunity to have Cooper do the classic perp walk in handcuffs in front of the worldwide news media was gone. His mind raced on how to manufacture some type of win for himself and the administration.

"What about the Ranger?" Tibbs asked.

"We have no word on him, sir. We believe he wasn't at the ranch," replied Capt. Abner.

Multiple conversations erupted in the operations center while several tried to calm the group and settle them back down to a formal meeting process.

"Can we please have silence, people?" asked Adm. Cummings. "The captain has indicated he has more news. Capt. Abner, please continue."

"I regret to inform you that Gov. Cooper's wife was *also* a fatality in the raid."

"That's just great! This just keeps getting better and better!" declared McDermott sarcastically.

Again, a mild form of chaos broke out in the room with cabinet officials pointing fingers at each other and separate individual arguments breaking out. Tibbs sat with chin in hand, deep in thought, seemingly unaffected by the eruption of tempers around him. "Captain, we need your other assessments. Status of the other state officials with arrest warrants?" Tibbs asked loudly over the conversations of others.

"Lt. Gov. Foster was captured; however, he is wounded and in critical condition from loss of blood. His wife was captured with him and, although she's in shock, she is not wounded," Abner reported.

"We have reports that the Texas State Guard commander, Maj. Gen. Rex Conroy, was also a fatality, but his body was not brought to the Truman. Of the five Blackhawks involved in the operation, it appears four were shot down. We do not have reports of casualties at this time," Abner said in a monotone voice. "We also know that at least two of these Blackhawks were shot down over Mexican air space; one had just landed and was sitting on the tarmac at a Mexican airport. We believe the Texas Air National Guard was able to scramble two F-16s from Lackland Air Force Base in San Antonio. Lackland was hit extensively, but they still managed to get two birds off. One of their F16s was shot down by the Mexican air force."

"I thought you geniuses knocked out control towers and radar in Texas. How in the hell did four Blackhawks get shot down?" screamed Tibbs, who was back in his angry tone.

"Mr. Attorney General, we did incapacitate the towers and hit the runways but, unfortunately, two fighters got off the ground," replied Capt. Abner. "What we are unclear on is the downing of the Mexican fighters. It looks like they were over Texas air space."

"So they launched *two* fighters who downed *four* choppers, plus however many Mexican fighters?" asked an astonished McDermott.

"We are told one of the pilots was a highly decorated Desert Storm veteran now flying for the Texas Air Wing," said the captain.

"Well, we now have an international incident as the cherry on top of this damned Texas mess," said the NSA director.

"Please provide more information on the ranch and the raid," said McDermott.

"We do not know the exact number of wounded or fatalities regarding the personnel at the ranch," said the captain.

"Well, we are getting news reports from some little rookie sweetheart reporter out of a San Antonio news station and it doesn't look good," remarked Tibbs. "Sarah, our orders were clear. Extract these certain individuals as if they were armed and dangerous. It's clear they were exactly that."

Suddenly, Tibbs' chief of staff walked into the room.

"Sir, the president wants an immediate update. The news cycle is in hyper-drive over this. Did we get Cooper?"

"Tell him I'll have one for him in ten minutes," replied Tibbs.

"The media isn't reporting Cooper's death. Who else knows, Capt. Abner?" McDermott asked.

"The operations commander has indicated he believes they got Cooper, Foster, and Weaver on the lead chopper while they had the rest of the group on the ground at the Texas ranch separated," said the officer. "Other than the agents on the ground, we do not believe anyone outside of the operation has any first-hand knowledge."

"This operation remains top secret, captain. Let your folks know that I will prosecute anyone who leaks any part of this operation outside the chain of command," ordered Tibbs.

As was typical of Tibbs, he drew no distinction regarding Constitutional authority. Although he may have had prosecutable authority over the federal agents, he had none over the military. As usual, nobody questioned his authority.

Nobody wanted to cross the man closest to President Johnson, who was known to be politically vindictive and who seemed to be as Teflon-coated as the president. Just like President Johnson, Tibbs survived scandal after scandal, helped by a Congress that seemed to be spineless, evidenced by the failure to appoint a special prosecutor to investigate the Rash Sally conspiracy and the mysterious death of a Justice Department whistleblower despite overwhelming evidence.

Joint Chiefs Chairman Gen. Herrera sat quietly while the cabinet was debriefed, a growing sickening feeling in his stomach. He had opposed this operation, but to voice his opposition to the president would have spelled the end of his career.

He was keenly aware that part of his rise to such a highly regarded position was principally due to the culling out of members of the Joint Chiefs who didn't always agree with the president. Part of the culling process was directly asking military leaders their thoughts on taking military actions against American citizens. The president and his minions in the cabinet subtly but clearly drew the distinction of loyalties to Johnson's administration or to the Constitution.

"Do we have news of Secy. Bartlett?" asked Tibbs.

"The news media is reporting she is onsite at the ranch in Texas," answered Tibbs' chief of staff.

"That figures," Tibbs whispered to his aide. "I want to know any and all comments she makes to any news outlet while she's down there! She needs to stand down until we brief the president. Have someone get in touch with her. We need her expert political analysis to settle down the Mexicans," Tibbs added sarcastically.

"Ladies and gentlemen, sooner or later Texans will know their governor was killed. What preparations should we be making militarily in anticipation of this news breaking?" asked Gen. Herrera.

"I'll dictate *when* that news is released; nobody is to say a damned thing until the president has been briefed and we make an official statement from the White House. Is that clear?" snarled Tibbs.

"I understand, sir. I'm asking what military preparations we should be making."

"What, you think Texas is going to launch some type of counter-attack?" laughed McDermott.

"Well, ma'am, I think we should consider all options."

"We just cut the head of the snake off. They will be in disarray for quite a while. We should just go ahead and go in and get the rest of the traitors, including that cantankerous old Texas Ranger," answered Tibbs. "We still have Capt. Abner on the line from the Truman. I suggest we adjourn so I can brief the president. The Joint Chiefs here can instruct the captain's next steps. And I want those remains brought to D.C. Is that understood?" declared Tibbs loudly.

It was not lost on Gen. Herrera that he had just conducted the first military action against an American state since Lincoln ordered troops to march on the South in 1860. He knew all too well that resulted in the bloodiest conflict in American history. He also believed the administration was underestimating the resolve Texans would have when they knew their governor had died at the hands of federal agents on Texas soil.

The partisan political divisions that had stymied Congress and created deep-rooted resentment of Americans against Americans on a regional, political and racial basis was very real and growing, especially since the Sally assassination attempt.

America, already as divided as it had been since the Civil War, was boiling below the surface. Any significant event could be the crack that could precipitate another bloody civil calamity.

# CHAPTER 20

*"Decency, security, and liberty alike demand that government officials shall be subjected to the same rules of conduct that are commands to the citizen.... If the government becomes a lawbreaker, it breeds contempt for law; it invites every man to become a law unto himself; it invites anarchy."*

*~ Supreme Court Justice Louis Brandeis (1856-1941)*
*First Jewish Supreme Court Judge*

Chuck Dixon's phone rang at 6:17 a.m. the morning of the raid. He had just gotten out of the shower and his phone was lying next to the sink where he started to shave. He answered.

"Chuck, this is Mitch. Something has happened in San Antonio!"

"What are you hearing?" asked Chuck, putting down the razor.

"The San Antonio airport and Lackland have been bombed!"

"Holy crap! What the heck is going on?"

"I've been flipping channels trying to find out more but news is all over the place. There's news of downed aircraft and now I just heard Corpus Christi and Brownsville airports were also attacked!" said Mitch.

"They had to be coming after the governor. What did they hit?" asked Chuck.

"Apparently, the air traffic control towers and radar facilities. They even hit Lackland and took out some Air Wing fighters. I'm getting some firsthand reports from some Tea Party folks in north San Antonio."

"Sounds like they are trying to take out radar facilities for a raid or an attack of some kind. Did they hit Austin?" Chuck said.

"No, apparently Austin wasn't touched."

"Time to go *nocturnal*," suggested Chuck.

"Okay, let's do it."

*Nocturnal* was the code word that various Tea Party and militia patriot groups throughout Texas had adopted when imminent danger from the feds was identified. The security leaks from the NSA had exposed the fact that the NSA, along with numerous other agencies such as the FBI, ATF and CIA had complete access to American citizens' emails, text messages and phone calls. The ability to communicate without the potential of government eavesdropping was now nearly impossible. To make matters worse, if a citizen or group was classified in any way as an enemy of the administration, the feds used the NDAA and the Patriot Act to violate Americans' constitutionally protected right to privacy and undue searches and seizures.

Chuck and millions of others had always wondered how Congress and the rest of American citizens could be so blasé about allowing such a blatant transgression of constitutional privacy rights. The government's argument that this level of intrusion into citizens' privacy was necessary for security and protection from terrorists was now either the majority opinion of most Americans at worst, or was simply representative of total apathy. Thomas Jefferson and the founding fathers would surely be rolling over in their graves, he thought.

Going *nocturnal* for these groups was a strategy for making it more difficult for the government to track communications. Part of this strategy was for individuals to open a new email account for each message they wanted to send, then creating a draft message and leaving it in the draft box. The recipient, who would know the new email login information, would log in and read the draft message, then delete it. The message never got sent.

Although the CIA and other agencies knew of this tactic, it was much harder to track without actually penetrating users' computers. Simple netbook computers were commonly used and only turned on long enough to log in and draft the message. When not in use, the computers were turned off. Government forensic tactics could recover strokes, but they had to have the computer to recreate the key strokes. By the time the feds could acquire a Tea Party computer, the message would be outdated.

Users were encouraged to "jump computers," meaning to use different public computer sources to go *nocturnal* in case someone suspected their personal computer, laptop or smart phone were being closely monitored.

Chuck got in his truck and drove to a nearby Internet cafe, opened a new Yahoo account and typed this draft message:

*"Nocturnal* **in effect! Feds move on Texas. Airports in Corpus Christi, San Antonio and Brownsville attacked. Report to your local militia leaders. Do NOT use normal mode of communications. Status of Gov. Cooper unknown. Level 4 (out of 5) Warning. Orders to follow. Stay alert."**

In the previous meeting with Sheriffs Alvarez, Reeves and Preston weeks before, Chuck and Mitch had set up a simplified communications system wherein various county leaders would get a coded number via text or by phone call. This coded message would determine what new email account, login and password to use. They had a pre-determined list of one hundred email platforms to access. Once the draft messages were opened, the recipient would set up a completely new email account and replicate the message in draft form only and leave it until the next person came and erased it, passing it along in an entirely different email account.

All the county leaders had purchased prepaid cell phones in fictitious names. Chuck broadcast a coded text message to his more than two hundred county leaders with the code "57349." Facebook and Twitter were also used to communicate simple coded messages. Those recipients would then know there was an important message coming to them from militia leadership. The various organizations in Texas statewide had done three dry runs with this communication technique and, by the third try, the message had gotten through to all two hundred fifty-four county coordinators within three hours by using this simple methodology.

Knowing the feds could essentially shut down the Internet and disable cell towers, the groups set up a combination of other communication techniques including ham radio, low-frequency radio transmissions and messengers whose job was to carry messages to the next county by whatever means necessary—by car, boat, train, foot or even horseback. Along with this communications network, there were a set of coded pre-determined messages and orders. For instance, message code 97A45T was an order to disable certain communications towers in a particular county, while message code 74D73U was an order to disable a particular bridge over the Brazos River in Washington County by any means available.

Chuck left the Internet café and headed to a pre-determined meeting spot in a rice field thirty-eight miles southwest of Houston. Within fifteen minutes, six other vehicles parked near Chuck's pick-up truck at a huge field with one entry, surrounded by levees on three sides.

"Pay attention, folks, I suspect things will be heating up very quickly. The word I'm getting is that they may have gotten the governor. We need to be ready to mobilize in an instant. I trust everyone has prepared. We don't know what the feds' next steps might be, but we all know we and our families are targets," said Chuck grimly.

"What I can't figure out is how Mexico comes into play in this," said Mitch.

"We have all kinds of communications coming in from the hill country and south Texas. There seems to be some confusion in Austin, as my contacts in the governor's office aren't replying to me right now," said Chuck.

"I pray what has happened this morning isn't what we think it is. If the feds were stupid enough to take this kind of action inside Texas, all holy hell is going to break out," said one of men as he looked down at the ground, kicking some dirt around with his Tony Lama cowboy boots.

"Get back to your families and stay tuned. This could get ugly in a hurry," said Chuck forcefully.

As the small group split up and got back in their vehicles, none of them had a clue that the governor of Texas and his wife had been shot and killed by the federal government just a few hours earlier.

# CHAPTER 21

*"These things I believe: That government should butt out. That freedom is our most precious commodity and if we are not eternally vigilant, government will take it all away. That individual freedom demands individual responsibility. That government is not a necessary good but an unavoidable evil. That the executive branch has grown too strong, the judicial branch too arrogant and the legislative branch too stupid. That political parties have become close to meaningless. That government should work to insure the rights of the individual, not plot to take them away. That government should provide for the national defense and work to insure domestic tranquility. That foreign trade should be fair rather than free. That America should be wary of foreign entanglements. That the tree of liberty needs to be watered from time to time with the blood of patriots and tyrants. That guns do more than protect us from criminals; more importantly, they protect us from the ongoing threat of government. That states are the bulwark of our freedom. That states should have the right to secede from the Union. That once a year we should hang someone in government as an example to his fellows."*

*~ Lyn Nofziger (1924-2006)*
*Political Consultant & Author*
*Press Secretary for Governor Reagan*
*White House Advisor to Richard Nixon*

The situation room in the west wing of the White House was abuzz with anticipation and the stress was palpable. President Johnson's most trusted advisors were gathered for a briefing on the operation that had created a media firestorm worldwide for the last several hours.

Secy. Bartlett had been summoned to Washington immediately, but none of the State Department staff had been able to reach her since her first-hand visit to the devastation at the Swingin' T.

It was now noon on the day of the raid and speculation on the whereabouts of the Texas governor was feeding wild speculation. Congressional leaders now demanded that the president brief them on what exactly happened in Texas earlier that morning. While everyone waited for President Johnson, they anxiously watched the big screen monitors on the walls of the situation room, which were tuned to a hastily called press conference being held in Austin.

The television satellite trucks and news vans again filled the streets in the blocks surrounding the Texas capitol, awaiting a major news conference that had been called by freshman Sen. Roberto Perez and Texas Speaker of the House Alvin "Smitty" Brahman.

Pops Younger was also expected to attend the news conference but was late arriving because he had traveled earlier by private plane from Texarkana to Llano to survey the situation on the ground at the Swingin' T. The news conference had been delayed as everyone awaited his arrival and his debriefing to numerous state officials in Austin.

As news cameras panned the sprawling grounds of the Texas capitol, people streamed in from every gate to find out what had happened that morning. For many Texans, a Sunday morning was time for church, and many came straight from church, dressed in their Sunday best. Television reporters had just interviewed a local Methodist preacher who adjourned his church service early, said a prayer for Texas, and then encouraged his entire congregation to walk the few blocks to the capitol grounds in downtown Austin to support the governor.

Sen. Perez stepped to the podium on the south steps of the capitol entrance. The crowd of reporters shouted questions at him. It took several minutes for the crowd to settle down long enough for the senator to speak.

"At approximately three a.m. this morning, the United States federal government, on orders from President Johnson and Atty. Gen. Jamail Tibbs, launched an unprecedented raid into a sovereign state to kidnap various Texas state officials, including Gov. Brent Cooper. United States military aircraft bombed civilian airports in San Antonio, Corpus Christi and Brownsville. Lackland Air Force Base in San Antonio and the Naval Air Station in Beeville were also hit in a Pearl Harbor-style, unannounced attack.

We have numerous casualties at each airport; three deaths of civilian airport staff have been reported in San Antonio."

The large crowd seemed dazed by what they just heard but remained silent as they waited for more.

"This operation involved DHS and various other federal agencies, according to eyewitness reports. These assault-style troops used stealth Blackhawk military choppers to raid a private ranch near Llano, Texas where Texas officials were meeting over several days. These reckless and unconstitutional actions resulted in the deaths of four Texas Rangers and two Texas state troopers. Also killed was Maj. Gen. Rex Conroy of the Texas Guard. Our prayers go out to the families of those who were needlessly killed in this raid."

Perez paused and looked out at the crowd for what seemed like a long time, but it was probably only a few seconds. "These federal agents were essentially assault troops that came onto the ranch firing weapons first. There was no effort made to announce themselves before engaging the Texas Rangers and state troopers. Any attempt by this administration to say anything different is a flat-out lie. At this time, we do not know the fate of several Texas officials, including Texas Gov. Brent Cooper and his wife Lyndsey, Lt. Gov. Gene Foster and his wife, and Texas Atty. Gen. Jeff Weaver. These officials were taken against their wills by DHS. The state of Texas and Texans worldwide demand an answer from this administration on the whereabouts of our state officials and to allow access to them, wherever they are being held."

Suddenly, angry obscenities began coming from the audience on the capitol lawn toward the president and the feds. Texans in the crowd looked angry as they shouted and waved fists. The senator had to raise his hands to quiet the crowd.

"Many of you saw the president of Mexico this morning announce that Texas Air Wing fighters had violated Mexican airspace. What he failed to mention is that there are at least two Mexican air force fighter jets still smoldering on the ground in south Texas, shot down by the Texas Air National Guard. We do know the Mexicans were involved in or assisted in this raid, but to what extent is unclear at this time. If the Mexican government was involved in this unjustified and illegal act, they should expect consequences from Texas."

Reporters began yelling questions again, and the uproar of the assembled crowd that had grown to almost one thousand was getting angrier by the minute.

Flanked by Speaker Brahman, Pops Younger and many state legislators and various staff members of the missing state officials, the senator was getting somewhat nervous about the tenor of the crowd and subconsciously decided to cut his remarks short.

"This administration has declared war on the state of Texas, and we expect Congress to convene and act immediately. We call on the immediate assembly of Congress to address this unprovoked and illegal armed action against fellow citizens. Ladies and gentlemen, fellow Texans and fellow Americans—we have a full-blown constitutional crisis on our hands. If congressional leaders and America do not rein in this administration, this dangerous crisis will continue to escalate."

The crowd was almost uncontrollable. The anger on the faces of the common folks coming across television sets all over the world was readily evident. Sen. Perez stepped aside as Speaker Brahman stepped to the podium. What the Speaker did not realize, absent the governor and lieutenant governor, was that the Texas Constitution called for him to be the next in line in the event they were unable to perform their duties for any reason.

"This president, this attorney general and the entire administration is a collection of lawless misfits that have now endangered our constitutional republic," said Speaker Brahman. "This administration launched *air strikes* on commercial *civilian* airports in three Texas cities.

"As the Speaker of the House in the Texas Legislature and on behalf of all Texans, we demand access to the governor and lieutenant governor, their wives and Texas Atty. Gen. Jeff Weaver immediately!"

The crowd was becoming more agitated by the minute. State troopers and Austin police stood by, hesitant to engage the crowd for fear it might instigate a full-blown riot.

Back in the White House situation room, President Johnson had still not arrived, nor had Tibbs. Most in the room watching the broadcast had a certain uneasiness. Some thought the administration might have underestimated the effect the raid would have.

"Killing civilians? That's going to rock some poll numbers," said Tibbs' chief of staff, shaking his head.

"Maybe in Texas, but poll numbers in California, New York and Illinois will go up," laughed a senior staff member with DHS.

A large section of the crowd on the Texas capitol lawn began moving south through the streets of downtown Austin, led by a few who seemed to be organizing the march.

The cameras moved to the J.J. Pickle Federal Building just a few blocks from the capitol building. Suddenly, the crowd turned more angry, throwing anything they could find—rocks, bottles, dirt, sticks—at anything they viewed as a symbol of the federal government. As the crowd grew larger, the level of violence ramped up; now windows were being shattered as some of those objects slammed into them.

Another reporter for a local news station broke in and reported the same type of scene at the large Internal Revenue Service Processing Center south of downtown. At the site itself, live video showed a small but vocal and angry crowd in front of the building. There were no picket signs or posters. It was fairly clear to anyone that the crowd was reacting spontaneously. There were likely few in the demonstration that went to bed the night before thinking they would be picketing the IRS offices by noon the next day.

Even the downtown post office was not immune; however, the downtown crowds were more physical, throwing bottles, cans and trash at the building. Many people hurling rocks and other items were still in their church clothes.

# CHAPTER 22

*"Since March 9, 1933, the United States has been in a state of declared national emergency.... Under the powers delegated by these statutes, the President may: seize property; organize and control the means of production; seize commodities; assign military forces abroad; institute martial law; seize and control all transportation and communication; regulate the operation of private enterprise; restrict travel; and, in a plethora of particular ways, control the lives of all American citizens."*

*~ U.S. Senate Report on Presidential Executive Orders*
*93rd Congress (1973-1975)*

The mood in the White House situation room suddenly changed. "The president is on his way down," announced a staff member as he stuck his head in the room. The president had just played a round of golf earlier that morning and was not to be bothered until the 12:30 lunch debriefing.

Johnson strolled into the room, looking unusually relaxed and at ease. "Well, ladies and gentlemen, where's my prisoner?"

The president sat down at the large mahogany table and scanned the other attendees. The others in the room, who waited for Johnson to sit, uncomfortably sat down and pulled close to the table.

Atty. Gen. Tibbs began. "Mr. President, the raid was successful; however, the Texans did put up resistance and there are fatalities on both sides."

"Where's the governor? Just please tell me we got him," Johnson demanded.

"Well, we got him all right. The governor engaged our agents, Mr. President, and he was *killed*. He also killed one of our agents."

Had anyone else told the president this news, the rest of the cabinet assembled in the situation room would likely have seen some hesitation or remorse for how the operation went down. Not Tibbs.

"Are you telling me the governor of Texas is dead?" said the president as his body language became upright and stiff.

"Yes, sir, Mr. President, but we have captured the Texas attorney general."

"Mr. President, during the operation, the Texans engaged our agents and there was a firefight," stated Joint Chiefs Gen. Herrera.

"Okay, I'm listening…"

"We lost three agents on the ground, sir. But we also have fatalities from downed choppers. Fatalities in the operation also included Maj. Gen. Rex Conroy of the Texas Guard. We have the lieutenant governor, who has been wounded and is in critical condition, aboard the USS Harry S. Truman. His wife was also captured and is unhurt. We also have captured Weaver, the Texas attorney general."

"These deaths were justifiable? How many men did we lose?" asked the president.

Tibbs interrupted. "Yes, sir. They engaged our agents."

"Sir, unfortunately, the wife of the governor was also killed. It was unavoidable and apparently occurred in the governor's firefight with our agents," said Gen. Herrera remorsefully.

"Damn. We killed his wife?" asked the president incredulously.

"It was the governor's fault, sir. This is what our operational command has informed us," replied Tibbs.

The president sat in his chair rubbing his chin. He looked like he had aged twenty-five years since his initial inauguration, although it had only been five years. The president who came into office in his mid-forties fit, hip and cool, now was almost fully gray with deepening wrinkles that indicated the stress of his office.

"Who knows?" asked the president.

"Nobody outside this room and the officers on the Truman," said Defense Secy. Brooks.

"We have been monitoring the news coming out of Texas. They know he was taken, but they don't know about his death or his wife's," said Tibbs.

The president turned to Avery Smith. "Avery, what impact will these deaths have?" Johnson asked.

Smith sat there, deep in thought for a few seconds as he took in what had just been revealed to President Johnson.

"Well, we definitely have to structure our response that the deaths were unavoidable and caused by the actions of the governor. We were there serving legal federal warrants. We need to focus on the deaths of the agents caused by the Texans and the Texans need to be portrayed as *outlaws* and, sometimes, when lawful personnel are chasing criminals, there can be unfortunate collateral casualties," Smith responded. "We will focus on the administration taking decisive action, noting that no one is above federal law, not even a sitting governor."

"Okay, I like that approach. I sure would have liked to have news coverage of him in shackles, just like our esteemed attorney general here," chuckled the president, along with others at the table.

"We will make sure we use the Texas attorney general for that purpose," said Tibbs.

"The damned Mexicans added complications," said Brooks.

"Sir, two Texas jet fighters were scrambled despite our efforts to contain any threat by air. We hit radar installations, including air traffic control towers, but they got two birds off and they wreaked havoc on the operation once it was in the recovery phase," said the general. "One of their fighters took down two Blackhawks and then pursued the third into Mexico, shooting it down. The fourth Blackhawk, also chased into Mexico air space, was destroyed on a Mexican airport tarmac."

"They knew we had prisoners on the last chopper that landed on the Truman; that's the only reason they weren't all shot down," added Brooks.

"How many dead?" asked Smith.

"We don't know. We assume, because of how they went down, that nobody survived. There were no casualties at the Mexican airport, but Mexico scrambled fighters that chased one of the Texas fighters back to Texas. Those Mexican fighters were also taken out but, unfortunately, they were shot down in Texas," said the general.

"How many Mexican fighters were shot down?" asked the president.

"There were four, sir," replied General Herrera.

"Let me see if I've got this straight," said an increasingly agitated president. "Two Texas fighters shot down four American Blackhawks and four Mexican fighter jets? Is my math correct?"

"Well, technically, three choppers. One was already on the ground. Yes, sir."

"Did we shoot down the Texas fighters?" asked the president.

"Yes, sir, we got one of them. Well, actually, the Mexicans got one of them."

"Well, thank God for that!" said the president sarcastically. He looked around the table for a brief period, then asked, "Where the hell is Bartlett?"

"She's not back yet, sir."

The president feigned no knowledge of Bartlett being in Texas. Tibbs had called the president shortly after he found out Bartlett was trying to broker a settlement to the crisis. The attorney general could never give the green light to this operation without presidential approval, but Smith had taught the president well, always providing an escape hatch to any scandal by properly insulating the president through plausible deniability.

"Well, she can deal with El Presidente when she returns. Has anyone told him to shut his damned mouth yet? We won't live up to our end of the deal if he complicates things," Johnson said.

"We have reached out to him this morning unsuccessfully so far," said another cabinet member.

"We'll let Bartlett handle this, but Avery, we need to coordinate our response with Mexico."

"Yes, sir, that's the plan. It appears he has some serious political pressure being exerted on him due to the incursion by Texas into Mexican airspace. If you recall, the Mexicans were very hesitant to provide rights to their airports, and apparently El Presidente acted without the full knowledge of his military. He has a tough situation to deal with at home, but don't think he won't hang us out to dry if it helps him politically."

"Well, you folks know where his vulnerabilities are. I expect that you will use all tools available to bring him under control so we avoid any political backlash," the president said firmly, looking directly at CIA Director Zachary Hamlin.

"We will persuade him to shut the hell up," said Hamlin.

"I want him locked down before tonight's statement. Is that understood?" asked the president.

"Fully," responded Hamlin.

The president appeared bored in the discussion of the Mexicans. "How did the governor die?" He was genuinely interested in the details of how Gov. Cooper was killed.

"The operation was a surprise raid and, when the agents got to Cooper's bedroom, he opened fire on them, killing one. Unfortunately, our agents returned fire, and Cooper's wife was either hit by the agents' return fire or some rounds penetrated the governor fully and struck her. We're not sure of the forensics, but they are trying to determine this on the Truman as we speak," said Herrera.

"How is it that this news is not generally known?" Johnson questioned.

"Operation command on the ground kept it contained to that bedroom while others were moved to other parts of the ranch. The bodies were loaded into choppers out of sight of the others at the compound."

"That's a good job of keeping things contained, General. I assume we all agree this action was unavoidable and justifiable?" The president surveyed the entire cabinet assembled in the situation room.

"Of course. Yes, sir. Without a doubt," came responses from the officials in the room.

"Avery, I assume we have to be very careful how this is announced and, more important, how it is portrayed to the press."

"Absolutely, Mr. President. Critical. The response has to be crafted carefully, with a lot of thought, but done quickly," answered Smith.

"I want any and all responses to be coordinated with Avery, ladies and gentlemen, is that understood?"

"Sir, since this was effectively a DHS operation, I suggest any announcement takes place from that perspective," said McDermott.

"I'm sorry, Sarah, but I respectfully disagree. This is a major announcement and needs to be made from the White House," commented Smith.

"Press conference?" asked the president.

"No, sir. This should be a nationally televised statement from the Oval Office. No questions. We want to control the message here."

"Makes sense," said the president.

"When do we do this? How long before the world knows he's dead?" asked Tibbs.

"I think we need to pull in some of the Democrats on the Hill and brief them. A prime time statement tonight makes sense unless you folks tell me the world has a way to find out about this before the president delivers the message," said Smith.

"It has to be our guys only," said the president, not particularly referring to his party but only to the *most trusted* in his party. "Do we have a sense of how the country will react to this?"

"We will craft the message carefully," said Smith. "Most of the polling in the areas that mean anything to us (meaning outside of traditional Red States and the South) has been favorable on how the Texas crisis has been handled. I wouldn't expect that would change. I suggest we prepare a preliminary statement and leak some pics of the Texas attorney general in shackles, and we can prepare a preliminary statement."

The president and his administration had complete confidence in Smith. He was an expert at containing political damage, single-handedly exerting extreme political pressure on congressional members to keep the president out of any potential impeachment hearings as a result of the Sally investigation.

Smith had an aura of invincibility and had managed to surround the president with the same invisible force field. He had unfettered access to the NSA and CIA, and access to all the personal files of Congress, their phone records, emails and website activities, including those of their families and staff.

Only a handful of congressional leaders were "untouchable," meaning Smith couldn't find any *dirt* on them or anyone close to them. But he didn't need them all, just enough of them and he had them, and they knew it.

# CHAPTER 23

*"People who object to weapons aren't abolishing violence, they're begging for rule by brute force, when the biggest, strongest animals among men were always automatically 'right.' Guns ended that, and social democracy is a hollow farce without an armed populace to make it work."*

~ *L. Neil Smith*
*Author, Political Activist & Libertarian*

The White House issued the following press release to all news wires: *"Early this morning, the Department of Homeland Security, along with the FBI and ATF, under the direction of the Joint Chiefs of Staff and the Justice Department, attempted to serve federal arrest warrants for various state officials in Texas, including Gov. Brent Cooper, in a remote area southwest of Austin, Texas.*

*"During the attempt to arrest these state officials, three federal agents were killed. There were also casualties reported at the site of the arrests. We know that a number of Blackhawk helicopters involved in this operation were shot down. We do not know at this time the number of casualties involved with those aircraft at this time. Also, our good friend and neighbor Mexico lost several jet aircraft while attempting to assist Homeland Security helicopters that were under attack by Texas jet fighters. Mexico has reported that Texas fighters bombed a border town airport.*

*"Several Texas officials were successfully apprehended in the raid. The president will make a statement to the nation live at 9:00 p.m. Eastern time tonight from the Oval Office."*

The statement from the White House only stoked the media firestorm, as they had been on a feeding frenzy of sorts since the news broke that something *big* had happened in Texas and the state's governor was missing.

California, Illinois and New York news outlets offered live coverage of protestors burning the Lone Star Flag and other iconic symbols of Texas, protesting more deaths of federal agents, supposedly at the hands of Texans. The mainstream media continued to portray Texas as the problem, affixing blame to state leaders for the continuing crisis. Opinion polls that popped up online during the day showed an unfavorable opinion of Texas and its leaders of almost three to one.

Congressional members from both parties wasted no time in condemning the bloodshed, but few condemned the administration. World leaders in general criticized the raid, with the exception of countries like China and Russia, who had experienced uprisings from states like Chechnya that tried to break away from Russia as an independent state. Leaders in France and other countries wanted to convene an emergency meeting of the United Nations Security Council. The fact that Mexico somehow became involved posed an imminent threat to regional stability, according to some of the permanent members of the Council.

While news reports during the day began to put a face to the names of the officers killed at the Swingin' T and the civilians killed in the airport bombings, the mindset of average Texans, already simmering over the escalation of events that began with the Tea Party raids, began to boil.

Station network affiliates in Houston, Dallas, Ft. Worth, Austin, San Antonio, Corpus Christi, Lubbock and Amarillo were streaming live feeds of growing crowds of protestors at federal buildings from post offices to federal courthouses. Crowds were especially large at various IRS offices across the state.

Protestors waved the Gonzales Battle Flag, the infamous "Come and Take It" flag where the Mexican government demanded that the small town of Gonzales give up the cannon they used to ward off Comanche Indian attacks. The town dared one hundred dragoons from the despot Santa Anna to try to take it. The town's militia turned back the dragoons and the Texas Revolution was on.

There were also plenty of Lone Star flags, along with handmade posters that displayed Texans' sentiments such as *"Feds, Get Out!"* *"Impeach Johnson!"* *"Arrest Tibbs,"* as well as many with simply *"Secede!"*

Texas politicians from across the state, even many Democrats, demanded access to the governor. CNN was first to flash images of Texas Atty. Gen. Weaver in full shackles being led from a helicopter to a waiting black van, then again when he was taken into the Justice Department building in Washington, D.C.

The fact that the administration didn't comment on the status of the governor only fed the anticipation of the presidential news conference. CNN reported several top congressional leaders were summoned to the White House, but not a single senator or representative from the GOP.

CNN attempted to interview several as they left a two-hour meeting at the White House. CNN couldn't hide the angst on the faces of the leaders coming out of the meeting. Whatever news or debriefing they received was obviously weighing heavily on them as they departed in their darkened-window vehicles, most not willing to make any statement.

The CNN news crew cornered a senator from California in the capitol hallway when he arrived back at his office. He made a very brief statement from his office door. As with most politicians, he couldn't help himself.

"These are trying times for America. I won't get into any details about the somber events that occurred early this morning in Texas. It's a shame that federal agents lost their lives simply carrying out their duty serving arrest warrants in *Operation Santa Anna*. I ask we all support our president and remember those families in your prayers. Thank you."

"*Operation Santa Anna*? Did he really say that?" asked a Houston television news station reporter.

News that the operation to arrest Texas officials inside their own state was dubbed *Operation Santa Anna* spread like a west Texas wildfire. Even state Democratic Party leaders began to publicly question the wisdom of naming a federal quasi-military operation into Texas after the hated tyrannical Mexican president responsible for the deaths at their beloved Alamo.

For anyone who has lived in Texas longer than ten minutes, naming a federal incursion into the state after Santa Anna was a horrific slap in the face to all Texans.

For an administration that was the most skilled in shaping messages in the history of presidential politics, this was a public relations disaster. The administration had been advised that naming the operation after Santa Anna would gain sympathy from Texas Hispanics against the governor. This backfired. The only Hispanics that would favor any reference to Santa Anna would be illegal aliens from Mexico.

By 7:00 p.m., crowds located at federal buildings and IRS offices across the state were substantial. Local TV affiliates were setting up makeshift outdoor TV screens so the crowds could see the president's live statement.

The crowds included Texans of all ages from all walks of life. A fifty-something-year-old woman, accompanied by her nineteen-year-old daughter, was interviewed live in San Antonio on the steps of the federal courthouse.

"Tell us why you are here with your daughter," said the television reporter.

"We are here to support our governor. We want to protest the federal government's actions. The president bombed our airport. Why does he hate Texas so much? We aren't going to take this anymore," she said.

"If you were talking to the president right now, what would you say to him?"

"Return Gov. Cooper and leave Texas alone!"

A member of the White House staff knocked on the door of the Oval Office, interrupting the meeting the president was having with his speechwriters and Avery Smith, handing Smith a folded note.

Smith opened the note while all stopped their conversations.

"What's it say, Avery?" asked the president.

"Texas Lt. Gov. Foster has just *died* from the wounds he sustained during the raid," said a grim Smith.

# CHAPTER 24

*"But you must remember, my fellow citizens, that eternal vigilance by the people is the price of liberty, and that you must pay the price if you wish to secure the blessing."*

*~ Andrew Jackson (Old Hickory)*
*7th U.S. President & War Hero*

The television commentator remarked that the crowds out in the streets all over Texas were large and getting larger, eagerly anticipating the president's statement. Mostly peaceful, the crowds were still boisterous and loud. ABC News reported that numerous "anti-Texas" rallies were being held in San Francisco, Detroit, Chicago and Washington, D.C. to support the president.

In Texas, local and state police were told to monitor the crowds but not to engage or incite them. Pops Younger had issued communiques to all state law enforcement jurisdictions to stand down, although urban police chiefs indicated they were not under any particular inclination to follow orders from the famous Texas Ranger.

A 9:02 p.m., the broadcast from the Oval Office began. There still had been no indication of the whereabouts of the Texas governor.

Dressed in a black suit, white shirt and red tie, President Johnson stared at the camera with his teleprompters at the ready on both sides of the camera.

"My fellow Americans, as you know, tensions have existed between the state government leaders of Texas and the federal government for some time now. Federal arrest warrants were issued for certain individuals who were responsible for the deaths of eighteen federal agents in Austin several months ago.

"These state officials thumbed their noses at federal law, refusing to turn themselves in and engaging in the illegal retaliatory arrests of federal law enforcement officials based in Texas. These officials were also responsible for ordering the confiscation of federal property such as military bases that are owned by *all* Americans.

"Secy. of State Bartlett, as well as congressional leaders, have tried unsuccessfully to broker a settlement of the tensions that exist between this state and Washington, D.C. to no avail.

"Despite attempts to get the Texas governor and others in his administration to turn themselves in, Gov. Cooper refused to cooperate.

"Because of this and because of the escalation of incidents such as the tragedy in Texarkana, my administration and congressional leaders made the decision to lead an operation into Texas to arrest those responsible and to exercise federal warrants issued legally by federal judges.

"We identified that most of these officials were in hiding at a private ranch of one of the governor's chief political donors. Under the direction of the Justice Department and in cooperation with DHS, the FBI, the ATF and the Joint Chiefs of Staff, a unit of federal agents led the execution of the warrants in central Texas very early this morning."

The president paused, and took a deep breath. Looking seriously into the cameras, he continued. "When federal agents arrived at the compound, they were fired upon by members of the governor's staff and security forces in place at the ranch, resulting in the deaths of three federal agents. Our hearts and prayers go out to the families of these brave men, who were simply doing their jobs."

Taking another deep breath, the president looked out of place, even nervous, for his next statement.

"Unfortunately, Texas Gov. Brent Cooper decided to engage the federal agents who were legally serving a federal arrest warrant. In the exchange of gunfire, the governor shot and killed one of the agents. In the ensuing exchange with our agents, I am sad to report that the governor was killed, along with his wife."

The president shuffled the papers on his desk, although it was clear he wasn't using them for notes.

"This is a very sad and unfortunate event. But make no mistake; it is a tragedy brought on by the governor himself. Also, Lt. Gov. Gene Foster was wounded and was brought in for medical treatment but has since passed away at a hospital. Texas Atty. Gen. Jeff Weaver was arrested and is unhurt, and he will be arraigned by a federal judge tomorrow morning.

"Among the fatalities were sixteen brave federal agents and pilots shot down in unarmed Blackhawk helicopters by jet fighters under control of the Texas Militia. In defending themselves against Texas fighters, U.S. Naval fighter jets were forced to engage, resulting in several civilian deaths in San Antonio and damage to several other airports.

"I want to thank the Mexican government and the Mexican air force for attempting to assist the unarmed Blackhawks. Four Mexican fighter jets were also lost. Their pilots perished in defense of those helicopters, including a Mexican fighter downed by Texas fighters on sovereign Mexico soil."

Changing his demeanor from sorrow to indignation as quickly as a chameleon changes colors, the president continued. "Now it is time for the remaining leadership of the Texas state government who have outstanding federal warrants to surrender to federal authorities so Texas and Americans everywhere can begin the healing process. I call on all Texans to demand this from their leaders. The bloodshed over the last few months is directly attributable to Gov. Cooper and the state leadership of Texas, and the loss of life is directly attributable to their actions.

"I have instructed Secy. Bartlett to arrange a summit with the state leadership of Texas to avoid further bloodshed.

"I want the American people to know that the decision to launch this operation into Texas was not taken lightly. America is a land of laws and, whether it is a common criminal or a state official who flaunts our laws, it is my job as chief law enforcement officer to enforce those laws.

"There is no one person, not one elected official, not one state government, that is above federal law. It is time to put this crisis and this tragedy behind us. For that I ask for your support, your prayers and your patience.

"God Bless America."

# CHAPTER 25

*"A standing army, however necessary it may be at some times, is always dangerous to the liberties of the people. Such power should be watched with a jealous eye."*

~ *Samuel Adams (1722-1803)*
*Founding Father*
*American Revolution Patriot*

A deafening roar started like a jet engine; it began as a slow guttural rumble and grew to a decibel level that shook buildings. The crowd reaction to the president's speech started like a chain reaction in Houston, Austin, Dallas, Ft. Worth, Amarillo, Lubbock and San Antonio. There were even sizable crowds in Corpus Christi, College Station, Nacogdoches and Texarkana.

It took a few minutes for the word to spread through the masses of gathered Texans as not everyone had access to the hastily erected big screen televisions and news crews. But spread it did, like spontaneous combustion. Thousands upon thousands of Texans who were on the streets when the president's Oval Office address started never heard a word from the president past "...*the governor was killed, along with his wife.*"

To most, the federal government and this administration had just killed the most popular Texas governor in modern times. Even worse, his wife, the first lady of Texas who was loved by all, was also dead at the hands of the feds.

The initial chaos started in Houston. Windows in the Mickey Leland Federal Building were shattered as over 25,000 protestors converged on the building. Within minutes, the building was ablaze. Protestors prevented the fire department from getting within four blocks of the building. Then the crowd marched to the federal courthouse and, within minutes, that structure was subjected to the same treatment.

Without any organized coordination, a huge crowd in Austin descended on the large IRS processing center complex and began a methodical destruction, first on the ground floor windows, then setting the complex on fire.

This same scene played out in every major Texas city. If a building had "federal" in its name, it was destroyed—Department of Agriculture, U.S. Attorney's offices, even post offices.

Clashes with local police departments who tried in vain to stop the crowds quickly died down as the urban police chiefs were forced to draw back several blocks and let the protestors do their thing.

Reporting remotely and live from the scene in downtown Houston, reporter Sylvia Gomez stated, "The protestors have destroyed two buildings but, amazingly, they are not looting, and they are not destroying local businesses! All the focus and energy is on big government buildings! Anything that represents the federal government is a target."

On Fox News, a panel that had been assembled to analyze and debate the president's speech were in shock.

"Folks, look at these live shots! These aren't hooligans! These aren't thugs! These are everyday Texans who are mad as hell! This reaction was spontaneous. It was obvious local authorities weren't prepared for this news and definitely not for this type of reaction!"

One of the panel experts added, "Wow, this looks like the demonstrations in Cairo, Egypt, except there's no fighting among the protesters. They are taking out their anger on symbols of the U.S. government!"

At the White House the president, who was still in the midst of congratulatory pats on the back for his brilliant speech, was shuffled down to the White House situation room by Avery Smith.

Without saying a word, the president's face said it all. It was a "Holy crap, what the hell is going on?" look after he walked in and saw all the feeds coming in on multiple screens. What was a congratulatory mood on the president's brilliant speech appeared to have ignited the crisis that was unfolding before his eyes, and the eyes of the world.

Stunned, everyone in the rooms watched the screens without speaking for at least two minutes.

"They're destroying government property!" remarked a staffer.

"Avery, did you anticipate this type of reaction?" asked a worried president in a low tone not meant for the entire room to hear.

"Well, I sure didn't plan for the fact that we would kill their governor and his wife in their damned bedroom, Mr. President," replied Smith, in his typical sarcastic style.

Smith quietly scanned several monitors. "*Texas is enraged*," he said, stating the obvious to the shocked president.

# Chapter 26

*"The liberties of a people never were, nor ever will be, secure, when the transactions of their rulers may be concealed from them."*

~ *Patrick Henry*
*American Revolution Hero & Founding Father*
*Ardent Supporter of States' Rights (Federalism)*

At 10:00 p.m., news stations broadcast a message live from Austin at the Texas capitol. Flanked by scores of elected state representatives and senators, Texas lawman and legend Pops Younger stepped to the podium alongside Speaker of the House Brahman.

Brahman took a step back to allow Younger to speak first.

The steely blue-eyed Younger stepped up to the podium wearing a black leather western-style holster with an ivory handled .45-caliber revolver on his right hip. The Rangers' famous five-pointed star badge encased in a circle was visible on his shirt. His iconic wide handlebar mustache made the outfit complete. If ever there was a throw-back to the 1800s in living color, it was Pops Younger, commander of the Texas Rangers.

"Ladies and gentlemen of Texas, the United States government, and this administration in particular, has *declared war* on Texas," said Younger in a direct and solemn tone.

"My very good friends," Younger paused to gather himself, "your Gov. Cooper and his wife Lyndsey were *murdered* by federal agents in the bedroom where the couple slept, unaware that they would soon be dispatched by federal agents. Lt. Gov. Foster was also murdered, dying from wounds suffered in the same attack. Maj. Gen. Rex Conroy was killed execution-style in his bedroom. Four Texas Rangers and a state trooper were killed. These were good family men, loyal to the governor and to the people of Texas.

"It is a testament of the failure of Americans and this Congress to rein in and impeach a criminal president and to arrest his attorney general. The governor of Texas was killed—*our* governor. There will be consequences, I can guaran-damn tee you."

Nobody had ever seen Pops Younger emotional. He looked down at the floor for a long few seconds before raising his head to continue.

"The feds hold Texas Atty. Gen. Jeff Weaver and the lieutenant governor's wife. We demand their safe return and immediate access to them."

People in the small crowd gathered inside the capitol building began screaming for the return of Jeff Weaver and Mrs. Foster, hurling insults at President Johnson and his administration.

"The federal government launched a military raid, with the aid of Mexico, into a sovereign state—*our* state. This administration chose to name this illegal raid *Operation Santa Anna*."

Again, the small crowd allowed into the press conference was yelling at anyone who would listen.

Looking at a woman who had been yelling, Younger said, "Yes, ma'am, Santa Anna. That's right. I guess it goes without saying that the tyrant we have now is not much different than the tyrant we threw off in 1836."

Younger looked back at the crowd and reporters, tilted his hat slightly and continued. "We are here tonight, along with all these folks behind me, to swear in Mr. Brahman as the next Texas governor. As Speaker of the House, he is next in line after the governor and lieutenant governor to be governor. Here in Texas, we follow our Constitution. The Texas Legislature chaplain, Hon. Rev. Scoffer, will swear the speaker in."

Rev. Scoffer moved to the podium where Speaker Brahman waited. "Do you swear to uphold and defend the Texas Constitution, so help you God?" asked Rev. Scoffer after Brahman held up his right hand, his left hand resting on a bible held by Younger.

"I do, with the help of God," answered Brahman.

There was no clapping or celebrating from those in attendance. Newly sworn-in Gov. Brahman stepped to the podium.

"Fellow Texans, we live in troubled times. We are literally under attack from our federal government. These latest actions against a sovereign state are unprecedented and uncalled for. I have called an emergency session of the Texas Legislature to begin tomorrow morning at 10:00 a.m. I am officially recalling all Texas elected officials who are in Washington, D.C. in any capacity. I hereby demand, on behalf of Texans, that any further military operations or actions by DHS, the FBI, NSA, CIA or ATF in Texas be halted immediately."

The crowd started clapping and raising a commotion. Gov. Brahman lifted his hands to quiet the crowd.

"I call on the leadership from both parties, as well as the governors and state legislatures across America, to condemn this unlawful action by the Johnson administration."

Again, the new governor had to wait for the crowd noise to subside.

"I have also notified the Mexican Consulate that a meeting needs to be held no later than tomorrow afternoon to explain their participation in this unlawful raid that resulted in the assassination of our governor, his lovely wife, the lieutenant governor, Maj. Gen. Conroy, state troopers and Texas Rangers. In the meantime, the Texas Rangers under Pops Younger have directed all border crossings, in conjunction with local sheriffs on the Mexican border, be officially closed until further notice."

The governor looked like he was about to adjourn, but the press corps shouted out questions frantically.

"Sir, how can you close the Mexican border when that is the job of the Border Patrol?" asked a female reporter.

"I'll let Ranger Younger answer that for you."

Not expecting to speak again, Pops had already snuck a pinch of tobacco in his mouth. He strode purposely to the podium with an obvious dip of Copenhagen in his cheek. "The Border Patrol, under DHS, has been *relieved* of duty in Texas. For that matter, all federal law enforcement agencies in Texas are relieved of duty in Texas."

"What if they don't cooperate?" she pressed.

"Well, ma'am, they forfeited the right to operate in Texas when they killed our governor," he replied.

"But what if they don't?" she demanded persistently.

Younger was obviously irritated by the young reporter who asked questions that, in his mind, should be obvious. "Ma'am, I would say Texans are rather pissed off at this time. When you swat a hornet's nest, ma'am, your best bet is to get the hell away from it."

"Will you meet with the president?" asked another reporter.

Brahman stepped up to the podium. "We will consider it, but that offer has not been made by this administration."

"When a government recalls its ambassadors, isn't that a prelude to war in most cases?" asked another.

"Well, we don't have ambassadors to speak of, only elected officials. I felt it necessary for all of Texas' leadership to get on the same page as quickly as possible."

"What about the destruction of government property going on right now?" asked a CNN reporter.

"I can definitely understand Texans' outrage in general. Their very popular governor and his wife were just killed this morning. We aren't condoning or encouraging the actions on federal buildings, but I understand the frustration of all Texans."

"Have law enforcement agencies been told to stand down regarding the protests that have resulted in the destruction of government and IRS offices?" followed up the same reporter.

"I'll let Pops Younger answer that question." The governor stepped back as Pops again stepped forward.

"We have been in contact with numerous city police and sheriff departments. The crowds have been large, and this happened so quickly that there wasn't much they could do. These folks are very angry. When you have crowds of thirty or forty thousand and a few hundred police officers, there is a limit to what they can do. Since the protests have been solely focused on federal government buildings and not on businesses or other individuals, most have decided to let it run its course."

"You mean they are just standing by doing nothing?" asked a reporter from NBC.

"Son, this president is responsible for the murder of the Texas governor. How do *you* expect Texans to react? What would you have us do?"

"So you condone the violence?" the reporter pressed.

News cameras caught several state legislators standing behind Pops shaking their heads, as if they thought, "Here we go. They are about to have Pops Younger in their faces...."

"I'm a lawman, junior. It *matters* to these folks that their governor and his lovely first lady were murdered!" Younger said with authority. "They ain't like the rest of the country, who are more concerned about a three-day vacation and the latest flavor at Starbucks. If Texans are out there protesting, it's because they're pissed off."

"Yes, but sir, Texans work at these places. We have reports the IRS Processing Center in Austin was completely destroyed."

With a slight smirk, Pops drawled, "Well, I'm sure a lot of Texans would tell you there's a special place in hell reserved for all IRS employees, past and present."

The reporter had no idea how or what to say to Younger at that point.

"How will Texas act if the United States government or military takes further steps in Texas?" asked a St. Louis Post Dispatch reporter.

"Appropriately and *disproportionally!*" replied Pops.

Knowing that Pops did not have a single ounce of political correctness in his bones, Brahman stepped back to the podium. "Nobody wants this to escalate any further, but make no mistake. On behalf of those standing behind me here, we will not continue to tolerate these unlawful attacks of any kind on Texas by this administration. I hereby ask all military and law enforcement, wherever you may be, to consider the constitutional basis in which you follow any orders by this president, especially when it comes to any actions against fellow citizens in Texas."

"What is your opinion of several countries calling for an emergency meeting of the United Nations Security Council?" asked a New York Times reporter.

"I'm glad they recognize that a crisis exists. I am, however, skeptical of their ability to rein in this president. They haven't been able to do it in other countries, failing to stop his drone attacks and direct military actions taken during his administration without the consent of Congress."

"Sir, the United States flag still flies over the capitol building tonight. Do you have any thoughts on that?" asked a Fox News reporter.

"It's up to this president and, ultimately, the citizens of Texas to determine whether it stays there."

# CHAPTER 27

*"Those who begin coercive elimination of dissent soon find themselves exterminating dissenters. Compulsory unification of opinion achieves only a unanimity at the graveyard."*

~ *Justice Robert H. Jackson (1892-1945)*
*Associate Justice, U.S. Supreme Court*

C huck and Christy Dixon were getting tired of constantly being on the move. Never sure if the feds were still after him, there was no denying that a federal arrest warrant for Chuck was still out there. They had mostly moved from house to house, being put up by Tea Party friends.

Chuck tried to keep his business afloat after the events surrounding his rescue by Texas Rangers at Ellington Air Force Base. The IRS had locked down and frozen both his personal and business bank accounts. The last payroll checks that went out to twenty-eight employees bounced, as the IRS had even levied the payroll account. Chuck tearfully told his employees they needed to do whatever was necessary to support their families, as the federal government had obviously targeted him. Even his tax attorney and CPA claimed the IRS's actions were unprecedented in their long tax careers. Chuck was simply on the administration's *enemy list*.

As traumatic as the events had been over the last few months, Christy felt like she and Chuck had grown closer. Being persecuted by your federal government causes you to close ranks, determine who your real friends are, and rely on each other. For the most part, they stayed in a friend's one-bedroom apartment above a garage in the Houston suburbs. Colton slept on a sleeper sofa. He couldn't attend school for obvious reasons, so Christy was homeschooling him.

They all sat in the small apartment and watched the president's speech from the Oval Office.

"Liar!" Chuck exclaimed.

"I know, honey, but stay calm," Christy said with a calmness she didn't have.

"Damn, Christy, they killed the governor and his wife!"

"Oh, my God!" shrieked Christy.

"We knew they had him, but they didn't have to kill him. Poor Lyndsey."

"Chuck, that could have been us!" said Christy.

The governor had tried to talk Chuck and Christy into staying at the Swingin' T with them. It was common knowledge that there was a federal warrant out for Chuck. He had become a hero of sorts to many Texans, and the governor liked to chat him up about current events. Both of the Dixons had known Lyndsey, the governor's wife of forty years.

"This is so sad," Christy said, tears streaming down her face.

"The stakes just went way up, baby. This is not good. This is likely to get much worse before it gets better." Chuck pulled her closer to him in a spontaneous message of protection and love. "Johnson and Tibbs aren't going to be content with killing just them. They're going to want to punish Texas for the Blackhawks, for everything. He's making a statement. The sad thing is that most of the country is falling for it. If there wasn't proof before that America as we know it is lost, this is sure it."

"What's going to happen next?" she asked.

"Wait a sec; there's a press conference in Austin!"

They both watched as news coverage switched to Austin for the swearing in of Speaker Brahman as governor.

"Gosh, you gotta love Pops!" said Christy.

"Everybody loves Pops. I have a feeling things might have turned out a little different had Pops been at the Swingin' T," he replied. "I was told this was only the second night he wasn't with the governor at that ranch. Knowing him, he feels responsible."

Chuck began putting on his blue jeans and boots.

"Where are you going?" Christy asked.

"I have to meet up with Mitch, the sheriffs and some of the county coordinators tonight, then we have a 7:00 a.m. meeting. I just got a coded text message," he said, referring to his temporary pre-paid cell phone.

"Honey, please be careful. I'm scared to death of what's going to happen."

"You're safe here for now. We will likely need to change locations in the next couple of days. We've been here too long already," he told her.

"But I'm worried about you. You are a trophy to them. I'm not sure who would be higher on their list—you or Pops?"

"Definitely Pops!" he chuckled.

"Seriously, I…" Christy started to say, but she got quiet as Chuck pulled her closer, put a finger gently over her lips, then kissed her passionately.

"I love you, baby, and I will be careful, but stay locked and loaded here," he said, referring to a .38-caliber revolver given to them for protection by a fellow Tea Party member.

Chuck eased his pick-up truck past the gate of the remote rice field west of Houston where he regularly met with fellow Tea Party organizers.

Within twenty minutes, there were nearly thirty pick-up trucks parked along the south levee of the rice field. Sheriff Reeves, Mitch Lansford and Chuck stood on the tailgate of a truck to address the small gathering.

Sheriff Reeves addressed the group first. "We all knew the Johnson administration was capable of this. The question is, what happens now? We have been preparing for months for this kind of scenario. You need to make sure your contingency plans are in place, your food stocks are good to go, and your weapons are functional. We can't predict what this nut job has in store for us, but we would all be wise to expect the worst."

"Every time I think this administration and government can't surprise me anymore, they pull a stunt worse than the previous one. My God, they killed the governor and his wife! Ladies and gentlemen, this is going to get worse before it gets better. The good news is that Texans are waking up in large numbers, as you saw yesterday and today. Our ranks will swell as we get the word out—neighbor to neighbor," said Chuck.

"What's their next move, Chuck?" asked someone from the group.

"I don't see how they restore their sense of order without some type of military action, especially if the destruction of federal property continues. Johnson has totally lost control of the situation. I mean, what statesman in Washington has the clout to negotiate an end to this? There ain't one," replied Chuck.

"We are headed to Austin after this meeting to meet with the legislature," said the sheriff.

"What is the status of the rest of law enforcement in Texas? Are they with us?" asked another member of the group.

"Many are. Some are not. I can tell you the urban police departments are generally not sympathetic. They are mostly Democrats but, as you know with these folks, party loyalty comes before the Constitution. I believe this latest disaster will shake some out of their party loyalty," said the sheriff.

Mitch Lansford hadn't said anything to the group yet, deferring to Chuck and Sheriff Reeves. Chuck felt Mitch was ready to say something. He glanced at Mitch standing on the truck's tailgate in blue jeans and a Texas Longhorns t-shirt. In his mid-forties, Mitch looked younger. He certainly didn't look the part of a leader who led hundreds of Tea Party followers, but he was an organizational genius. He was the key cog in bringing together hundreds of Tea Party organizations across all two hundred fifty-four counties in Texas and was instrumental in the rudimentary emergency communications network set up to foil the feds' NSA-style eavesdropping.

"Folks," Mitch said, "the message everyone here should be taking back to their families, churches and organizations is that we are at the *precipice*, in my humble opinion. Either Texas or the federal government is going to blink, and it will set history forward for the next one hundred years.

"Personally, this is our line in-the-sand moment. We either stand for what we know is right on behalf of our kids and grandchildren, or we have lost Texas, possibly forever. Texans are mad. If Texas falls in line politically with most of the country, it is over. I have a duty to them. I have a duty to Texas. Let's not let the deaths at the Swingin' T be forgotten. If they can kill our governor, they wouldn't think twice about killing *you*, or *you* or *your families*!" he said convincingly as he pointed to individuals standing in the dirt surrounding the pick-up.

"Will anyone outside of Texas stand up to them, or are we alone?" asked another.

"I think we need to assume we are alone," Chuck said. "If other states were going to intervene, they would have put pressure on their representatives to impeach. There is a lot of sympathy for us out there, but who knows how it will manifest itself if the feds try more drastic measures?"

"What do you think the legislature will do tomorrow?" asked the same group member.

"Nobody knows at this point." Chuck shrugged.

"There damn well better be a secession bill on the agenda!" yelled a large man standing furthest from the three men on the tailgate.

"I expect that to be introduced. Politicians who were afraid to step out on this issue before will be hard pressed not to at least have it as an option. But let me warn everyone again. If an Independence bill comes up for a vote and passes, expect actions by Johnson and Tibbs to be stepped up considerably, both in level of force and how fast their reaction will be. God bless ya'll, and God bless Texas," shouted Chuck as he climbed down off the tailgate.

"Texas!" shouted one.

"Texas!" came another.

The entire group spontaneously raised their hands into fists and yelled, "Texas!"

# CHAPTER 28

*"A patriot must always be ready to defend his country against his government."*

~ *Edward Paul Abbey (1927-1989)*
*American Author*

P resident Johnson sat in the White House situation room the next morning with Anna Bartlett, Avery Smith, Jamail Tibbs and the directors of DHS, the FBI, NSA, CIA and Gen. Herrera. At 11:00 the night before, the president asked his staff not to wake him. He had been getting updates from his staff about the surge on government facilities in Texas.

The president finally awoke to the news that the Federal Reserve buildings in Dallas and Houston were surrounded by protesters. These facilities were heavily protected during normal times. The protesters had not been able to get close enough to either building to inflict any damage, but the crowds were growing.

Five minutes before the meeting was to start, Johnson's chief of staff informed him the Dow had plummeted twelve hundred points in the first few minutes of opening. Financial markets hate uncertainty, but they hate instability more. The Texas crisis was rocking financial markets across the globe. Oil, which was already at all-time highs due to the shut-down of oil exports to refineries outside Texas and the president's quasi-embargo on Texas ports, shot up another nine dollars per barrel in early commodities trading.

"As of 0900 Eastern Time this morning, Mr. President, it appears the IRS Processing Center in Austin is a total loss, completely gutted. Almost every major IRS office in Texas is badly damaged or destroyed. Six federal courthouses are heavily damaged, with two still burning. A total of thirty-seven other federal buildings are heavily damaged. The list includes offices of Homeland Security, Social Security Administration, even Department of Agriculture buildings in rural areas," stated Sarah McDermott in her normal matter-of-fact tone.

"So much for cutting the head off the snake," said Smith, sarcastically referring to Atty. Gen. Tibbs' theory that, if Gov. Cooper was arrested and somehow Texas was left leaderless, the federal government could bring the Texas crisis under control.

"Well, it was never the plan to *kill* the son of a bitch," retorted Tibbs, who secretly couldn't care less that the governor was dead.

"Go to that feed up there!" yelled the president, pointing to one of the many TV screens streaming live coverage from multiple news channels.

A San Antonio news station was at Breckenridge Hospital interviewing a new Texas hero, Lt. Cmdr. Danny Hendrix, as he lay in bed with a maroon Texas Aggie ball cap on.

Standing next to his bed was another new Texas hero and fellow Texas Air Guard pilot, Cmdr. "Tex" Parsons. Hendrix had a broken collarbone and separated shoulder, but he was all smiles as the reporter interviewed them both. Hospital personnel crowded next to the bed to get in pictures with both men. There was even a crowd outside the room in the hallway as more staff and even some patients clamored for pictures and autographs with the two handsome pilots. Both recounted the episode from forty-eight hours prior.

"Is there *anything* we can do to a Texan where the rest of Texas doesn't make a damned hero of him? Tell me. Anything?" asked Smith disgustedly.

"I don't know how we could have screwed this up any worse," commented Secy. Bartlett.

"Well, what the hell were you doing there without the president's blessing anyway?" Tibbs demanded in an accusatory tone.

"Tibbs, this cluster you-know-what has your fingerprints all over it. Now the president and the rest of us have to figure out how to salvage what could have been a peaceful and workable solution," retorted Bartlett, shaking her finger in Tibbs' face.

Tibbs was incredulous. "You know, you could have been at that damned ranch when we hit them. That could be you in a body bag instead of the cowboy," Tibbs shouted, standing up and returning her finger with a clenched fist.

"I'm not stupid, Tibbs. This crisis has been going on for months, and the day that I finally get a meeting set to negotiate an end to this, you launch this poorly planned strike. Did you even for one minute examine the possibility that you would kill him? Well, did you?" she yelled back, her sarcastic glance ripping over Tibbs and Herrera.

"I want to know why she is not forced to resign," Tibbs lashed out at the president impetuously. "Going to Texas on her own, without your knowledge, is insubordination at a minimum, and maybe treasonous!"

"Jamail, how many of your messes does the president have to clean up? Between the ridiculous gun-running scheme in Mexico to the Sally investigation, and now this?" She fixed the attorney general with a piercing look, and he slipped back into his chair as if trying to get some shade from her blazing eyes.

"Okay, this isn't getting us anywhere," said the president, a slight smile lingering on his lips as if he almost enjoyed the banter between the two political appointees for a few minutes before he stopped it.

"Jamail, is Texas the enemy? Don't we have to be in a war to aid an enemy?" continued Bartlett, referring to Tibbs' remark about treason.

"Hell, yes, they're the enemy. Look at what they just did to government property!"

"And have we declared war on one of our states?" she asked.

"It sure looks like they declared war on us! Read the damned damage reports!" shrieked Tibbs.

"Okay, enough!" The president's voice showed he was serious about bringing the shouting match to an end.

Ignoring the president, Bartlett replied, "You killed their governor, Jamail! He was popular. Hell, you killed his wife! Was there a contingency plan in place for this?"

"Madam Secretary," began Gen. Herrera, looking down at the table as if not wanting to look directly into her eyes, "I don't think anyone planned on the contingency that the governor himself might shoot at and kill a federal agent during this operation."

"The guy was a poster child for the NRA. Are you serious? How many videos do you have of him hunting, of him shooting at a gun range, of him walking around all over Texas with a gun holstered at his side?" reasoned Bartlett.

"We thought the element of surprise..." tried the general. Bartlett interrupted.

"Yeah, he surprised you! You dropped into his bedroom and he began shooting. I think any male in Texas would do the same damned thing. Is there a man, woman or child in that state who doesn't own a gun?"

"Look, everyone, we have to come to consensus here on how we move forward. The financial markets are reeling over this..." said Smith before he also was interrupted.

"Oh, great, look at this!" yelled Tibbs.

On another live feed was the newly sworn-in Texas governor speaking at a joint session of the Texas Senate and Legislature in Austin.

"...we hereby demand the return of the remains of Gov. Cooper and his wife, as well as those of Lt. Gov. Foster. We demand access to Mrs. Foster and to Texas Atty. Gen. Jeff Weaver."

"Mr. President, I've never lived in Texas, but I can tell you this," Secy. Bartlett said. "If you want to take some steam off this situation, I suggest you announce the return of the remains. I don't know why we would want to hold their remains, but what little I do know about Texans is, if you keep the governor and his wife's remains, it will only ratchet up the intensity of this thing," she reasoned.

"It could get more intense?" laughed Tibbs. "We aren't done with forensics and the autopsies."

"Wait until Texans hear the federal government is poking and prodding the remains of Texas' first lady," said an exasperated Bartlett.

"Do I have to remind you this is a criminal investigation?" asked Tibbs.

"I think Anna has a point," said Smith.

"I think I know where you are going with this, Avery, and I like it," said the president.

"Let's let Anna escort the bodies back to Texas. She can then meet with the new governor and see if we can reach a settlement. If Secy. Bartlett makes a joint statement with the governor and state leadership, maybe we can calm the situation," suggested Smith.

Bartlett was all smiles with this suggestion, as this would put her in the role she initially sought—the peacemaker that is above the fray. This would be a perfect lead-in to her presidential campaign.

"What if that doesn't work?" asked Tibbs.

Looking to Smith, the president asked, "What's the downside, Avery?

What if the governor won't meet? What if all negotiations fail?"

"If Anna is escorting the remains back and we make this a dignified scenario, I can't see them not meeting with her. They want their governor back; Anna is bringing him to them. It's beautiful!"

"I'm asking again, what if this doesn't work? What if a week later, or a month later, we still have these problems?" pressed Tibbs.

"There's no doubt the violence against government facilities cannot go unchecked. There's also no doubt that they cannot continue to hold our military bases. Anna, part of your job at this meeting will be to offer a peaceful resolution; however, we need to be unequivocal about what our actions could or would be if Texas remains in *a state of treason*," instructed the president.

"And if that doesn't work?" asked Tibbs again.

"Then they will suffer the consequences. I'm tired of this situation. I'm ready for it to be over. If they won't end it, I will, by whatever means necessary. We look incompetent to the rest of the world that we can't even control one state," said the president.

# CHAPTER 29

*"The tree of liberty could not grow were it not watered with the blood of tyrants."*

~ *Bertrand Barere de Vieuzac (1755-1841)*
*Journalist, Politician and a Leader of the French Revolution*

The Mexican president, interviewed by CBS News, admitted that the administration contacted them about using their air space and their airports to launch the raid on the Swingin' T. In his interview, El Presidente would not admit to any special deal with the Johnson administration for allowing the raid to be staged from Mexico. Nobody believed him.

When asked about the Texas Air National Guard downing Mexican fighters, he simply stated that the Texans had stolen advanced technology from the United States that enabled the two pilots to wreak havoc on the Mexican air force. The president also said he was helping his neighbor as any good neighbor would.

When the reporter asked if Texas wasn't also his neighbor, he stated, "They used to be a good neighbor also, but their efforts to discriminate against Mexicans should not be forgotten."

Without going into great detail, El Presidente mentioned efforts by Texas to require voter ID and to fight President Johnson's gun control executive orders. He pointed out that these two orders were examples of discrimination against Mexican nationals and were non-supportive of El Presidente's war against the Mexican drug cartels.

To add further insult, the CBS News reporter asked him specifically about the naming of *Operation Santa Anna*.

"Sir, could you understand why Texas might be sensitive to a military operation launched from Mexico under that name that ultimately resulted in the death of their governor?" asked the reporter.

"It's regrettable the governor lost his life. From what I have learned, it appears he caused his own death and that of his wife. Regarding Santa Anna, he was a great Mexican hero, so I don't know why this would have added any additional grief to an already sad situation," he replied in a broken Spanish accent.

"Was that name a suggestion from you? From the Mexican military?" asked the host.

"No, we did not name the operation, but are honored they chose to name such an important mission after Generalissimo Antonio López de Santa Anna."

It was lost on the average American why naming the operation after the last dictator to march into Texas, resulting in the deaths of one hundred eighty-nine Texians at the Alamo, added incredible insult to the fact their governor had been killed in the *Santa Anna* operation.

"Who in hell chose to name the operation after Santa Anna?" asked Smith.

"DHS," said Tibbs.

"Does anyone in this room know the historical significance of this?" asked an exasperated Smith.

"Folks, you're sure making my task difficult," commented Bartlett.

It was clear most of the White House staff and cabinet members in the situation room did not fully understand the significance of using the *Santa Anna* moniker as the operational tag. Smith was unsure if the president even knew.

"Okay, quick history lesson. Santa Anna declared militias illegal in Mexico. Then he suspended their legislative body and revoked their constitution. This is why Texas rebelled. Santa Anna was merciless and bloodthirsty, executing all those who opposed him. He was the commander of the Mexican forces at the Alamo. He also shot over three hundred captured Texas troops at Goliad. He was and is reviled in Texas history."

McDermott sank in her chair. "I guess we should have vetted the name of the operation. I'll take responsibility for that," she said.

Ignoring that significant responsibility statement, Johnson continued.

"General, I want a contingency plan drawn up by the Joint Chiefs in the event our little plan with the secretary goes awry," said the president.

"Yes, sir. I need to know what the end game is for additional operations by the military regarding Texas," answered Gen. Herrera, looking at Defense Secy. Brooks and then back to the president.

"In order for Texas to fall back into line, we need a swift and significant impact. We need to set a precedent for this type of behavior. If Anna is not successful, it will be time to step on their necks until they succumb. If we have to replace every elected official and declare martial law, we will do it," said the president forcefully.

"Let me remind everyone that Texas has more citizens with guns than any other state, and it's not even close," stated McDermott.

"Well, we'll see if a damned deer rifle stands up to a damned M-1 Abrams tank rolling down a Houston city street," sneered Tibbs.

"Surely you're not so naïve as to think deer rifles are the only weapons in the average Texan's closet?" asked Smith.

"Need I remind everyone that most firearms dealers started ignoring the president's executive orders regarding halting the federal firearms background check system?" asked ATF Director Barnaby Adamson.

"If I'm not mistaken, sir, you turned off the federal firearm background check system to Texas purchases. They just simply continued on their own. They have always ignored the U.N. Small Arms Treaty. Hell, it's actually more convenient for them now and, to make it worse, you don't know what they're buying or who's buying them!" Bartlett insisted.

"Anna, I hate to put this kind of pressure on you, but you see the magnitude of the stakes at hand. This could get much uglier than it's already been. All of us need to pledge our support and any resources you need to calm this situation," reasoned Smith.

"My only request is you restrict our esteemed attorney general from any actions that would inflame the situation," Bartlett wisecracked.

"You have my personal assurance of no surprises," assured President Johnson, cutting off Tibbs before he could respond.

"Anna, you have three days. Jamail, you have twelve hours starting now to wrap up any forensics or autopsies," ordered the president as he looked at his watch.

"Can I bring the Fosters and Weaver back to Texas with me? That would go a long way," asked Bartlett as Tibbs fumed.

The president looked at Smith for his political insight, ignoring Tibbs and the fact that the lieutenant governor and attorney general were being held under federal arrest warrants.

"If Anna thinks returning them to Texas gives her enhanced leverage, I say what the hell," answered Smith.

"Are you serious?" exclaimed Tibbs.

"What about setting bond and letting them bond out? That way, they are still under indictment and aren't set completely free," Smith proposed.

"I like that idea. It's decided. Get a judge to set bond and let them make bond. Jamail, if we need to go get them again, we will simply do it. If Anna is successful, the federal justice system in Texas will be functional again. Then you can crucify them to your heart's content," said the president with finality as he stood, indicating the meeting was over.

Anna Bartlett had three days to resolve the Texas crisis, or else.

# CHAPTER 30

*"Governments rest on the consent of the governed, and that it is the right of the people to alter or abolish them whenever they become destructive of the ends for which they were established."*

~ *Jefferson Davis (1807-1889)*
*West Point Graduate*
*Mexican-American War Hero*
*Secretary of War (Franklin Pierce Administration)*
*President of the Confederate States of America 1861-1865*

News organizations throughout the world were especially harsh on the Johnson administration for launching the raid into Texas that killed the Texas governor and his wife, but the mainstream media continued their unabashed support of the administration and continued to demonize Texas and its leadership.

The newly sworn-in governor was contacted directly by Secy. of State Bartlett about returning the remains of Gov. Cooper, his wife Lyndsey, and Lt. Gov. Gene Foster. Mrs. Foster would be released, and Bartlett also indicated that Weaver would be arraigned in federal court and would be allowed to make bail. Bartlett would escort the bodies back herself and requested a meeting with the governor, to which the governor agreed.

Bartlett set up a hastily arranged news conference from the State Department offices indicating she would be making the trip in person to offer a peaceful resolution to the crisis and to attend the funeral for the governor. Just as she had hoped, the news cycle began touting Bartlett as the only logical statesperson that could broker a settlement. The news analysts on MSNBC and others touted her credentials and how a settlement to the crisis only heightened Bartlett's lock on the Democratic Party's likely presidential nomination.

In Austin, Gov. Brahman ordered all state offices closed for a day of mourning for the slain Texas leaders. The entire state government was shut down on a Thursday for the event that was being carried live worldwide.

The huge C-130 military transport carrying Bartlett banked toward the southwest, then circled Bergstrom Airport making its final approach to the southwest runway. Four Texas Air Wing F-16s, led by Cmdr. Parsons, had escorted the huge military cargo plane as it crossed over the Louisiana state line into Texas airspace.

The plane touched down on the Austin airport runway, smoke coming from the tires, at 9:32 a.m. Waiting on the tarmac were hundreds of Texas dignitaries, including many in the legislature and public officials from around the state. Chuck, Christy, and Colton Dixon were among them; they had gotten a special invitation from Pops Younger.

In the terminals and lining the fences along the airport were thousands of Texans. It seemed as if everyone in attendance had a Texas flag. For the most part, the huge crowds were silent and reverent.

The C-130 came to a stop as all waited for the propellers to stop turning. Slowly, the massive cargo door began to lower. Once the door touched the ground, eight U.S. Marines in full dress uniforms began slowly bearing a coffin covered in a United States flag down the ramp door.

At the bottom of the ramp stood dozens of Texas State troopers, Texas Guard troops and Texas Rangers. The plan was to turn over the remains to the Texas officials, who would load them into three hearses standing by. Four hearses were just outside the airport fence with the remains of Maj. Gen. Conroy and the Texas Rangers and troopers who were killed at the Swingin' T. A large procession of mourners would accompany the remains from the airport to the state capitol building. All were to be eulogized at the capitol building and then were to lie in state for three days with burial of all on Sunday.

Walking in between two rows of state troopers were Gov. Brahman and Texas Rangers Cmdr. Pops Younger, who met the first coffin at the bottom of the C-130 ramp.

The Marines slowly brought down the first coffin, containing Texas First Lady Lyndsey Cooper. Each U.S. flag-draped coffin was transferred to the Texas contingent of full-dress troopers, Rangers and Texas military.

The last coffin brought down the ramp was that of Gov. Cooper. Television cameras taking shots of the crowd showed many Texans openly weeping as the last coffin made its way to the end of the ramp with the slow cadence of the Marines. Cameras also caught various disturbances in the crowd as people began shouting incomprehensibly at the procession on the tarmac. None of the television hosts could make out what was causing the random yelling and anger by hundreds in the crowds, but it was clear something was agitating many in attendance.

Once the governor's coffin was transferred to the Texas pallbearers, Secy. Bartlett and several of her staff followed, along with newly freed Texas Atty. Gen. Jeff Weaver. Bartlett was received politely but coldly, as opposed to the hugs and warm handshakes given Weaver as he stepped back onto Texas soil.

The hearses pulled around the plane in a row and troopers opened the rear doors for the coffins. Several dignitaries looked around as the disturbances grew louder, but nobody seemed to understand the commotion... at first. News analysts were clearly clueless as to what was driving the previously reverent onlookers to begin shouting toward the ceremony on the tarmac.

Suddenly, Weaver stalked over to the governor's coffin and ripped off the U.S. flag draped over it to the shock of the Marines standing at attention. Weaver crumpled the U.S flag and threw it back on the C-130 ramp.

"Screw that flag! It's a disgrace to have that flag on these coffins!" Weaver yelled at the Marines.

Two of the Marines began to move toward Weaver before Pops stepped in front of both of them.

"Boys, you're in Texas. I suggest you back the hell up," said Pops quietly as many in the crowd finally realized what had happened and began cheering wildly.

"Sir, I will not allow that flag to be disrespected," answered a Marine.

"Son, I will allow you to go to the other coffins and kindly remove those flags from these Texas heroes. Now git to it!" commanded Pops.

The Marines hastily walked over to the other coffins and carefully removed the flags, folded them and carried them back up the ramp of the C-130. Secy. Bartlett was stunned, but stood motionless without saying a word.

Two Texas Rangers reached into the waiting hearses and distributed folded Lone Star flags to other Rangers who carefully draped the coffins with them. The crowd began clapping and cheering as if a Texas high school Friday night football touchdown was just scored.

The mainstream television news reporters and commentators went ballistic, calling Weaver and all the other Texans classless traitors, ripping into them for removing the Stars and Stripes from the coffins.

In the White House situation room, a large crowd of staff and cabinet members joined the president to watch the event.

"Damn them! I hope they don't take the settlement!" yelled Tibbs.

The mood in the situation room went from curiosity to anger. President Johnson got up out of the chair he had just sat in to view the event. Before leaving the room, he said, "It will be a miracle if Bartlett can end this peacefully."

"Don't worry, Mr. President. When they pull these kinds of stunts, it just makes them look crazy to the rest of the world," Avery Smith replied as he and the President walked out of the situation room together.

"The rest of America that doesn't hate them surely will now," laughed Tibbs.

# CHAPTER 31

*"If you think we are free today, you know nothing about tyranny and even less about freedom."*

~ David Boaz, Radio Show Host
Spirit of '76 — Voice of Warning

The funeral procession moved slowly toward downtown Austin with hundreds of thousands of Texans lining the streets. The crowds stood silent in reverence for the hearses as they passed by slowly but, as soon as they passed, the crowds got louder and louder. This created an effect similar to the "wave" at a football game as people rose when the hearses passed near them.

Secy. Bartlett rode in a Suburban behind the procession by herself with her small security detail. The Lone Star flags and the famous Gonzales Battle flags with the "Come and Take It" slogan were waved by thousands of Texans along the route.

At the capitol building, where the bodies were to lie in state for three days, the crowds had been growing all morning. News reporters were interviewing Texans who had camped out all night to get first in line to view the deceased governor, his wife, the lieutenant governor, and the others who lost their lives at the Swingin' T.

The Stetson-clad pallbearers, all Texas Rangers, carried each Lone Star flag-draped coffin into the picturesque rotunda of the Texas capitol building to lie in state, joining several coffins already there containing the troopers and Rangers killed at the Swingin' T.

On Sunday, the coffins were to be moved to various funeral sites across

Austin and other cities. The only public funeral scheduled was for the governor and his wife. The new governor called a special session of the Texas Legislature the following Monday.

Across televisions and the Internet streamed images of hundreds of thousands of Texans spilling over the twenty-two acres that make up the capitol grounds.

"There's no doubt Texans loved their governor!" stated a Fox News analyst.

"Well, how much of this display is support for the governor as opposed to a show of defiance against the federal government?" asked a liberal columnist on the Fox News panel.

"I suppose some of both. Okay, there's Secy. of State Bartlett's vehicle pulling up now. She's getting out. She appears to be the only dignitary to come out of that vehicle. It looks like the Texas leadership let her ride in the procession without any Texas dignitaries. Let's listen in and see how the crowd reacts," said the host.

As Bartlett exited the vehicle, the booing started and steadily picked up momentum.

"Get the hell out of Texas!" came a shout from one of the mourners in the crowd, picked up clearly by Fox.

"Not much of a warm welcome. Did we expect this?" asked the news host.

"She's just another symbol of the federal government to Texans who, despite whatever facts anyone chooses to debate, killed their governor," answered another analyst on the panel.

As the secretary passed by, the crowds were mostly respectful as she made her way through the rotunda, then out the other side of the capitol to be whisked away by two Secret Service agents and several troopers.

Regrets and condolences poured into news organizations from leaders from all over the world, including some that were critical of the administration.

TV coverage began filming the procession and noted the elected officials and dignitaries who passed by the coffins, including Chuck Dixon with his wife and son. Pops Younger filed through with the Dixons and the team that rescued Chuck from the grasp of the ATF at Ellington Air Force Base, which was a symbol of federal overreach for most Texans. Each of the Rangers carried their Stetsons in their hands by their sides as they filed by the flag-draped caskets. The world finally got a glimpse of the rough-hewn Texas icon as Pops put his hand on the governor's casket and said a few soft-spoken words. Try as they would, the press couldn't make out what Pops was saying.

Slowly, two lines formed on both the north and south sides of the capitol building as Texans began to enter the rotunda to pay their last respects. Volunteers were asked to gather the flags and flagpoles that many carried so they could enter without them. Those with concealed carry permits had a special line to enter that moved faster than the rest. Unlike any other state, Texas allowed concealed-carry permit holders to enter their capitol building with weapons.

MSNBC picked up shots of concealed-carry holders showing their weapons to DPS officers as they went through metal detectors. The panel covering the day's events used the backdrop as proof of how different Texas was from the rest of the country. Two analysts even went so far as to say that, if Texas were to separate from the U.S., it would be no big loss.

The news quickly shifted to the meeting of Gov. Brahman and Secy. Bartlett, and the impending special session of the Texas Legislature just days away.

Secy. Bartlett was to meet the governor at the governor's mansion at 7:00 p.m. that evening. The next few days could be as pivotal to Texas as the fateful days of March in 1836 in the early days of the Republic.

# CHAPTER 32

*"How bad do things have to get before you do something? Do they have to take away all your property? Do they have to license every activity that you want to engage in? Do they have to start throwing you on cattle cars before you say, "Now wait a minute, I don't think this is a good idea." How long is it going to be before you finally resist and say, "No, I will not comply. Period!" Ask yourself now because sooner or later you are going to come to that line, and when they cross it, you're going to say, well now cross this line; okay now cross that line; okay now cross this line. Pretty soon you're in a corner. Sooner or later you've got to stand your ground whether anybody else does or not. That is what liberty is all about."*

> *~ Michael Badnarik*
> *2004 Libertarian Presidential Candidate*
> *Software Engineer & Talk Show Host*

Secy. of State Bartlett arrived at the charming Texas governor's mansion promptly at 7:00 p.m. in a small two-car procession escorted by state troopers. As she exited the vehicle, she was informed that only one of her security agents from the Secret Service would be allowed to enter, which clearly agitated the agents.

As Bartlett was led into the mansion, she was struck by the magnificent beauty of the Greek Revival-style architecture and the Victorian-era manner in which the mansion was decorated. She was led into a large parlor with ornate couches and window treatments. Hanging on the wall were various paintings of early Texas heroes, including Sam Houston and Stephen F. Austin.

Texas' First Lady Lyndsey Cooper had her stamp on the mansion, helping to restore the historic structure to capture the grand style used when it was built in 1856.

"Madam Secretary, the governor will be here shortly. He does not reside here yet, as you are probably aware, because the mansion still has the personal effects of Gov. Cooper. Gov. Brahman was held up some at the capitol with events surrounding the procession and all," said a staff member.

"I understand," she answered.

Fifteen minutes later, the governor arrived with several other staff members, including Atty. Gen. Weaver, Sen. Perez, several key legislators, and Pops Younger. Noticeably absent and not invited by the governor was senior Texas Sen. Simpson, which was noticed immediately by Bartlett.

She ignored the absence of Simpson, and got on with her task. "Gentlemen, I will get down to business right away. The president wants to end this stand-off. He allowed me to escort Mr. Weaver and the remains of the governor and his wife as a goodwill gesture. I know you have many differences of opinion with this administration, but this crisis needs to end before there is more bloodshed."

"Madam Secretary, I'm sure you had something to do with the return of the governor and the release of Mr. Weaver here and, for whatever you had to do to make this happen, we appreciate it," answered the governor.

"Governor, that being said, you need to know that there are forces within the administration that have no qualms about letting this escalate. I likely don't need to explain to you who might be in that frame of mind."

"Oh, we have a fairly good idea," Brahman replied confidently.

"Well then, you must know that the path taken so far is unsustainable and could lead to a chaotic situation in Texas," she warned.

"Do you have a specific proposal, Madam Secretary, or were you just sent here to threaten us again?" asked Sen. Perez.

Bartlett ignored Perez's comment. "First, the administration is prepared to drop all criminal arrest warrants and to drop charges against Mr. Weaver," she stated, looking directly at Weaver.

"That's a good place to start. What else?" asked the governor.

"In return, you will give control of the military bases back to the U.S. military and re-open the oil pipelines and refineries to U.S. distribution. You will also agree to coordinate state and local law enforcement with Homeland

Security to allow us to protect federal property such as the IRS offices and other government buildings, including a significant presence of agents at these facilities."

"You want us to allow the same people that killed our governor back into our state to stand watch over government properties? That will surely sit well with Texans," said the governor sarcastically.

Bartlett did not hesitate for one second "Yes, but only if you can't provide the protection required."

"Well, that's a helluva an offer," retorted Weaver. "How could we refuse? Is there anything else, because we haven't heard a word about our grievances with this administration and Washington?"

"And, finally, you are to re-open the Mexican border and to re-submit to the national background check system for gun purchases. The administration also wants any gun transactions conducted over the last few months using your own system to be re-run through the national database."

"And for all of these wonderful concessions, what does Texas get in return?" asked the governor politely.

"Once the administration is convinced you are taking the steps necessary to return to normalcy, they will return all banking transactions back to the Federal Reserve system and restart federal payments to Texas citizens, including any back pay that may be owed to Social Security recipients and veterans. We will also re-open air traffic to and from Texas and the Gulf blockade will be removed."

"Is that it? Are there any more conditions?" asked the governor.

Bartlett paused, knowing this last condition was maybe the most difficult one to present.

"President Johnson wants a formal apology from Texas state government, preferably from its governor," Bartlett stated without a hint of hesitation for asking for this final condition.

There was a noticeable change in body language with the Texans, and the governor stood up and walked over to one of the three fireplaces in the room. He opened a small cigar humidor on the mantle.

"You know, Gov. Cooper always invited me to have a cigar or two when we were together, so I'm sure he wouldn't mind under these special conditions if I grabbed one," said Brahman as he took one out and started to lightly chew on one end.

"Madam Secretary, I'm just a country boy who grew up on a small ranch right outside of La Grange. You know, the La Grange made famous by the ZZ Top song?"

Bartlett nodded affirmatively, not clear where Brahman was going.

Brahman took a few steps, still chewing on the cigar as he looked back at the Texas contingent sitting on Victorian couches and chairs with a few standing. He knew they were chomping at the bit to respond to the demands sent by Johnson and presented by Bartlett.

"Ma'am, I've called a special session of the Texas Legislature beginning tomorrow morning. Although I was duly elected to my previous position, I was not elected *governor*. Need I remind you that the *only* reason I carry this title today is because the federal government killed our governor and lieutenant governor. As foreign as this may sound to someone coming from Washington, D.C., any decision of this magnitude regarding the acceptance of any of these terms you presented requires the input of the people of Texas through their elected representatives, or maybe even by direct vote themselves," stated Brahman.

"Governor, I appreciate your position; however, it is time for someone to act. The process you discussed could take weeks. President Johnson and especially the attorney general will not allow a prolonged debate while federal government property is destroyed and you have pipelines shut down," answered Bartlett sharply.

"Ha, so much for this administration's reliance on green energy," quipped a legislator.

Bartlett's face turned grim, and the red blush she hated when she was stressed flowed up her neck and face. She continued, "Sir, your folks here are suffering. They have no banking and no federal payments."

"And we also don't have a functioning IRS! Most Texans would likely take that trade!" the same legislator snapped back.

"Madam Secretary, we appreciate your efforts, but Texas will have some of its own demands. I'm not prepared to tell you what those demands are today. For starters, I would imagine that impeachment hearings would have to take place in Congress, but I'm not going to stand here and speak for all Texans," Brahman said matter-of-factly.

Bartlett sensed that the opportunity for her to negotiate the "grand bargain" she had hoped for was slipping from her grasp.

Brahman continued, "We have a governor, lieutenant governor and first lady to bury on Sunday. We also have some fine individuals, state troopers and Texas Rangers, to lay to rest. Texas will turn its full attention to this crisis on Monday, but only after the funerals," said Brahman.

"Governor, I cannot commit to you that this administration will allow a protracted resolution."

"What the hell does that mean? Is that a threat?" asked Weaver.

"Instead of me speaking for everyone here, let's let my fellow Texans chime in," said Brahman, looking at Sen. Perez.

"I never heard any offer of an apology from the administration on these unnecessary deaths," said Sen. Perez.

"The administration is prepared to offer *regrets*," said Bartlett flatly.

"Well, that's mighty fine of them!" retorted Perez.

"Short of impeachment hearings being approved by Congress, I really don't know how offering regrets would satisfy my constituents," declared one of the state legislators from west Texas.

"The people of Texas will not forget that the federal government launched a military raid into a sovereign state, staged it from a foreign country, named it after Santa Anna no less, that ultimately killed our governor and lieutenant governor. I'm not sure how they will reconcile that. I'm not even sure how I reconcile that! Then, for you to sit there with a straight face and ask for a Texas apology as a condition to normalize relations is exactly what separates you people from Texans. I for one would be embarrassed to carry that offer to my people and ask them to support it, and I can tell you and everyone sitting here today that I won't," said another legislator forcefully.

Standing in the background during the entire meeting, leaning on another fireplace, was Ranger Younger. Nobody had asked him his opinion, but most knew Pops would have one and it was never politically correct. Knowing that Pops carried a lot of influence in the capitol, Bartlett decided to address him directly.

"Mr. Younger, I'm happy to finally get to meet you. As a law enforcement professional, I'm sure you have some of the same concerns about further bloodshed. Do you have any thoughts I can take back to Washington with me to relay to the president?" asked Bartlett in an almost-condescending manner. She didn't intend it that way, but she just couldn't help herself.

Pops grabbed his spit cup sitting on the mantle and spit into it. He never answered a question without contemplating it first.

"Ma'am, no offense, but why isn't your boss here himself delivering these terms? He sent a *woman* to negotiate his way out of this?"

Some in the room squirmed slightly. Bartlett kept an emotionless and straight face.

"Ain't it your job to negotiate treaties and such with foreign countries?"

"Well, yes, sir, that is one of my duties," Bartlett replied

"The president already thinks of us as some foreign country," stated Pops.

Looking confused, Bartlett asked, "How so, Mr. Younger?"

"He invaded us like a foreign country, blockaded us like a foreign country, and sent his secretary of state to negotiate a peace treaty." He paused to spit into the cup again. "Heck, we may as well go ahead and be a foreign country!"

The room broke into some nervous laughter, as not all were convinced Bartlett really knew what Pops was stating. Bartlett was of the mindset of most Americans and politicians that the notion of a state once again becoming independent was preposterous.

Sensing that Pops had no real political skills and thus not taking him seriously, Bartlett turned back to Gov. Brahman. "Governor, I will take back the message that you need a few days. I will tell you, however, that it is my opinion that this president will act swiftly and decisively if this drags on, and the crisis will continue in a manner that will present very few options," warned Bartlett.

"We will act in Texas' time frame, Madam Secretary, whatever that may end up being," answered Brahman.

Disappointed, Bartlett got up to shake hands with everyone before leaving; however, Pops made no attempt to dispatch Bartlett with any warm farewells. As the group slowly exited the large foyer beyond the grand staircase, Bartlett made a point to walk over to Pops to say something quietly to him as she held out her hand.

"Sir, I would hope that you would use your incredible influence with these men to help me broker a peaceful resolution to this situation. Is there any private message you would like for me to deliver to the president?" she half-whispered.

After shaking hands with Bartlett, Pops didn't let go of her hand. With those famous and penetrating blue eyes, Pops got closer to Bartlett, literally in her personal space, making Bartlett extremely and noticeably uncomfortable. It was enough for the Secret Service agent to take a small step toward them.

Pops leaned in to her and said quietly, "When an apology is presented and it's genuine, I can forgive, but I never forget. Your president killed my friends, ma'am, just as if he had pulled the trigger in each death himself. Texas won't forget. My guess is they won't forgive either."

# CHAPTER 33

*"Never give in. Never, never, never, never, in nothing great or small, large or petty, never give in except to convictions of honor and good sense. Never yield to force; never yield to the apparently overwhelming might of the enemy."*

~ *Sir Winston Churchill*
*Prime Minister of Great Britain during WWII*
*Author (Nobel Prize Winner), Historian & Hero*

M ost worldwide news organizations carried the governor's funeral live Sunday morning. The crowd that surrounded the capitol building and the funeral procession route was estimated at over 400,000 people.

The president, his staff and cabinet, watched the funeral broadcast from the situation room. The president had been briefed by Bartlett late Saturday evening on her return from Texas. They had scheduled a follow-up meeting for 3:00 p.m. on Sunday after the funeral; however, most of the scheduled attendees came into the White House early to watch the funeral with the president.

In what had become an all-too familiar scene to the president's administration, the funeral procession route to the Texas State Cemetery just east of downtown was filled with thousands of Texans holding Texas flags.

Reporting on the Texas State Cemetery, MSNBC noted that thirteen Texas governors were interred there, along with sixteen Texas Rangers, nine Confederate generals, two thousand Confederate soldiers, fifteen signers of the Texas Declaration of Independence—but only one Union soldier. Union soldiers had been buried there, but were later removed to Fort Sam Houston, a U.S. Army base in San Antonio.

MSNBC failed to mention that the Union soldiers were moved at the direction of the federal government to Fort Sam Houston. The tone of the reporting would lead one to mistakenly believe that Texas had removed the Union soldiers simply because they didn't want them there. The network did a piece on the lone remaining Union soldier, attempting to further stoke the growing wedge between Texas and the rest of the country.

"Not one American flag. Not one," said Tibbs flatly, referring to the crowds and the funeral procession.

"Jamail, you've been to Texas. Even in normal times, that state flies its state flag on everything from a muffler shop to day care centers," Smith said with just a hint of sarcasm.

"Immense pride, gentlemen. What other state has the story of the Alamo?" asked Secy. Bartlett.

"It almost reeks of some kind of perverted nationalism. Something you would see in the Chechnya Republic," responded Tibbs.

"Or Scotland," added Smith.

"There are a couple of similarities. Texas was once its own republic but, more importantly, both Chechnya and Scotland, like Texas, are also fiercely independent. We all know Chechnya broke away from Russia and there is an active movement by Scotland to break from the United Kingdom," said Bartlett.

CNN was first to report several Texas state representatives and at least three state senators were introducing bills in the state legislature on Monday for a binding statewide referendum on separation from the United States. Although CNN talking heads were quick to dismiss the notion, the situation room seemed to get tense instantly.

"Mr. President, this is exactly what we discussed yesterday," said Bartlett as she turned her swiveled chair toward the president.

"I know our meeting is not for thirty minutes," said Johnson, "but let's go ahead and kick this off by moving to the Cabinet Room. I think most everyone is here already." The entire cabinet, staff and the Joint Chiefs moved out of the situation room into the Cabinet Room that overlooked the White House rose garden. The president sat in his chair, which traditionally is taller than all the other chairs at the historic mahogany table.

"I've asked Secy. Bartlett to highlight the points made to her by the new Texas governor. Anna, will you proceed please?" asked the president.

"Thank you, Mr. President. I will get straight to the point, ladies and gentlemen. I believe the Texas government is ready to work this out, but there are factions within state leadership who continue to push for other solutions that are not in their or our best interests," reported Bartlett.

She glanced around the room. "First, they demanded an apology from the federal government over the deaths at the Texas ranch."

"That's doable," said Smith.

"Are you serious?" asked Tibbs.

"There are apologies, and then there are regrets," came the reply from Smith.

"They know the difference, Avery. They even brought that up," stated Bartlett.

"What else?" asked the president.

"They want an impeachment hearing."

"That's never going to happen," retorted Smith.

"Well, we all know that. Also, I think all of you should know that there is serious, real and growing interest into some type of independence movement. Call it secession, separation or whatever you want, but I can tell you the majority of the people pulling the ears of those in power are attempting to convince others that this course of action is viable," said Bartlett.

"That can't and never will happen. So, if this referendum makes it through the legislature and then passes due to the emotions of the moment, what happens next?" asked the president.

"It gets uglier than it is now," proclaimed Smith.

Tibbs was eagerly waiting for his chance for input, tempered somewhat by the fact that Operation Santa Anna was a disaster politically.

"They will continue to flirt with this idea that somehow they are different, that they can destroy government buildings and defy this administration. The elephant in the room is that each one of you knows that it is going to take military intervention on a large scale to bring them in line," Tibbs snorted. "We know we aren't going through any damned impeachment hearing. They know it, too. Let's just stop kidding ourselves. We have been dancing around the edges of this problem for months. Now we let them get the idea in their heads that some stupid referendum in Texas is somehow binding on us? Geez. Let's just put an end to this nonsense once and for all," said an exasperated Tibbs.

Bartlett interjected, "I do think an apology would go a long way.

Obviously an impeachment hearing would be up to Congress and not to the executive branch. We would just get Avery to work his usual magic and defeat it before it gets any traction."

Smith stood up, walked around the table and then turned to Bartlett. "We would definitely defeat it. But there are other political ramifications that are detrimental to the party and the agenda for the remaining term of the president. All of his key legislation going forward would be imperiled."

"As opposed to an all-out war with Texas?" replied Bartlett.

"This is just crazy!" Tibbs continued forcefully. "We cut the head off the snake but it continues to stay alive and bite us. My recommendation is to put a permanent end to this nonsense. Declare martial law, invalidate the entire state legislature and leadership, and go back and take over the military bases. This is exactly what Abraham Lincoln would do!"

"Avery, is there any benefit to waiting to see if this referendum gets out of their state legislature?" asked the president. "I am having a hard time believing that it could and, even so, that it would pass with the voters. I think a heavy political campaign in Texas could defeat this effort rather easily," said the president.

"Mr. President, with all due respect, your popularity in Texas is at an all-time low. Jamail is the most hated man in Texas, but you're not far behind and the results of the raid on the ranch are horrific. If we stand pat on the stand we have currently taken, I would not be surprised for Texas to be emboldened by this vote coming on the heels of burying their governor and first lady," replied Bartlett, who took any opportunity she could to try to enlighten other cabinet members about her opinion of Tibbs.

"Honestly," she continued, "and I know this stings—the best thing you could do is release the people responsible for the raid. Now, Jamail, I know you feel like this is a personal attack; however, those Texas folks had blood in their eyes. I really don't think a cleverly worded non-apology is going to work."

"You're entitled to your opinion, Madam Secretary," replied Tibbs quietly but confidently.

Tibbs was convinced that, outside of Smith, the president's personal political strategist, that he himself was both trusted and protected by the president. Despite the fact that the president had a chief of staff, most insiders knew that Smith and Tibbs always had his ear.

No matter what scandal seemed to emanate from Tibbs' office in Justice, the president never seemed too concerned nor did he take definitive action that would be typical of other presidents. This fact led to two chief of staff resignations in his cabinet in just over five years.

What Bartlett could not possibly know is how much fallout the president would have with a forced resignation of Tibbs. Tibbs knew way too many secrets in the White House. Bartlett was previously a political enemy and the president never forgot the dirty campaign in the primary. Johnson never fully trusted Bartlett. The cabinet spent the next hour discussing all options, except specific military actions. A possible resignation of Tibbs was never openly discussed.

The president scheduled another cabinet meeting for Tuesday morning, following the first day of the Texas legislative session, called by the new governor before the funeral services. In the meantime, Tibbs went back to his office with plans of his own to ratchet up the intensity of the crisis. From his cell phone, he called to schedule a meeting of his own with embattled DHS director Sarah McDermott.

"Sarah, is Border Patrol still on stand-down on the Texas border?"

"Yes, status quo. Texas has the border closed. In order to avoid confrontation, we have not challenged Texas on the borders," she replied.

"That's about to change, Sarah. We are about to let your federal border agents do their jobs once again."

# CHAPTER 34

*"The Internal Revenue Service is everything the so-called tax protesters said it was: nonresponsive, unable to withstand scrutiny, tyrannical, and oblivious to the rule of law and the U.S. Constitution."*

~ *Joseph Bannister*
*Former Special Agent*
*IRS Criminal Investigation Division*
*IRS Whistleblower*

Ten Border Patrol vehicles, including an armored personnel carrier, pulled into parking at the United States Customs office located next to the bridge that crossed the Rio Grande at Laredo, Texas.

Since the crisis that unfolded at the Swingin' T and the military aircraft dogfights over south Texas, the governor had dispatched Texas Guard troops to major border crossings with Mexico, supplemented by local sheriffs' and constables' deputies from surrounding counties. Mexican citizens were allowed to cross into Nuevo Laredo, but they were turned back if they could not prove they resided in Texas.

This move was detrimental to the local economies on both sides of the border. For multi-generational Hispanics, the Mexican air raid and the Santa Anna operation reinforced their support for their Texas heritage during the crisis. That was not necessarily true for the younger "Dreamers" who had been smuggled in illegally or who had been born of illegal aliens on Texas soil. For those, support remained with the federal government that had granted them amnesty despite their prior illegal and undocumented status. Many of the border patrol agents working for the federal government were Hispanic dreamers who had gotten jobs with the federal government.

The Texas Guard and sheriffs' deputies who manned the checkpoint numbered about twenty at any one time; however, when the Border Patrol vehicles pulled into the checkpoint, there were only fourteen on duty.

A Border Patrol agent looking like a man with a mission exited the first vehicle and strode to the office. "Gentlemen, my name is Lt. Col. Carranza. We are here to relieve you of duty at this station by orders of the Department of Homeland Security," Carranza said.

The ranking officer of the Texas Guard, Col. "Shep" Davis, stood up from his desk and approached Carranza, who was standing on the other side of a counter at the entrance, flanked by ten of his agents.

"Sir, we are here by orders of the governor of Texas. We do not report to you nor to DHS," responded Davis firmly. "We will not abandon this post, nor will we re-open this checkpoint. I suggest you and your boys scurry back out of here."

Davis motioned to one of his staff. "Call Austin right now, then call Lackland." Davis wanted to make sure the Border Patrol contingent knew he could call in air support from San Antonio if needed.

"Gentlemen, this is federal property you are occupying," barked Carranza. "My orders are to relieve you of this command and to resume operations as a functioning Customs and Border Patrol station, including re-opening the bridge."

At this point, Davis could finally see how many agents were outside. He was easily outnumbered three to one. The Border Patrol agents were in full para-military gear.

When the call came into the governor's mansion, Gov. Brahman was meeting with several state senators and Pops Younger. An aide came in with the news. After learning of Davis' situation, Pops immediately got on the phone to Brownsville, Del Rio and El Paso to find out if this was a coordinated effort by DHS.

"Pops, do we have another fed operation being launched in Texas?" asked the governor, abruptly changing the subject of the meeting.

"Governor, Brownsville and Del Rio are quiet but we haven't gotten confirmation from El Paso. We are checking with other smaller entry points. So far, Laredo is the only one, but more could be on their way. The duty officer in Laredo is asking for orders. He's outnumbered, sir, and has been caught by surprise."

"Damn, here we go again," snapped Brahman. "I don't want any more bloodshed, but I also don't want to give in to the feds. Pops, get the major general in here from the Texas Guard. Tell the duty officer to stall if possible but, if he can't, tell him to retreat for now, but take all his communications gear with him. Do not leave anything behind."

Pops moved to the next room to contact the new commanding officer of the Texas Guard who had taken over for Maj. Gen, Conroy.

Meanwhile, at the Laredo checkpoint, Carranza was growing impatient.

"Sir, you're outnumbered. Nobody wants this to escalate, but my orders are to take this government installation immediately," said Carranza.

"I'm waiting for orders from Austin."

"My orders don't include you having to get permission from Austin to vacate the premises. I'll give you ten minutes, sir, before I give orders for my people to take this building and the bridge, by force if necessary."

"You do what you have to do. My folks aren't budging from this site without orders from Austin." Davis was nervous. "Why don't ya'll just wait outside until Austin calls me back."

"No, sir, this is a federal facility. We'll just stay right here," replied Carranza as the agents behind him adjusted their M-16s to a ready position but kept them pointed upward.

A few nervous minutes ensued where neither side spoke a word. Finally, a lieutenant came up to the colonel. "Sir, Austin is on phone."

"Excuse me. I'm going to take this call in my office."

"You go right ahead, sir, and then be ready to vacate the building," Carranza persisted.

Carranza, a career Border Patrol agent, moved from Coahuila, Mexico to Zapata, Texas with his family when he was eight years old. He remembered his apprehension during the night crossing near Langtry, Texas. Ironically, Carranza's career involved monitoring the border his family crossed illegally many years before. He earned his citizenship under the first amnesty program by President Reagan.

Known by his peers as extremely lenient toward Mexican illegals during his career, he rose through the ranks at unprecedented speed during the Johnson administration. Although criticized heavily by the Border Patrol Union, Carranza was a darling of the administration and DHS. Now in his late forties, Carranza was heavy-set and dark-complected with jet-black hair, cropped closely because he had noticed just recently that he had gray hair at the temples.

Carranza was a pawn used by the administration every time the right had congressional committee hearings. The agent was their antidote for criticism by the right regarding the administration's lack of enforcement of existing immigration laws. Carranza was used in four congressional committees and had even been invited to the White House.

Pops Younger hung up the hastily prepared conference call. The Texas Guard commander and Pops called Col. Davis in Laredo.

"We have assessed the situation, Colonel and, as much as we regret to tell you this, you need to stand down. You are outnumbered. Take all the communications equipment with you. Do not leave anything behind. We will allow them to take custody of the checkpoint for now."

"With all due respect, sir," Davis said emphatically, "we can hold them off. I do not want to surrender this post to federal agents."

"Colonel, we understand. This is a direct order."

"But, sir…

"Colonel, this is Younger with the Texas Rangers."

"It's an honor to talk to you, sir. I'm sure you understand my men don't want to be the first Texas Guard to surrender to federal agents in this crisis."

"Colonel, let me assure you, it's temporary. If I have anything to do with this going forward, those bastards will be out of there in the next forty-eight hours."

"Sir, can I promise my men that they can be part of the take-back of this facility?"

"Colonel, if we implement a plan to retake this, you will be part of it, I assure you."

"Thank you, sir. I will give the orders."

Col. Davis instructed his officers to remove all communications equipment, then walked out of his office to the counter where Carranza and his agents stood impatiently.

"Lieutenant, Austin has ordered us to vacate the premises for now. We will be gathering our things, so you need to allow us about ten minutes."

"It's lieutenant colonel, sir," barked Carranza, noting the intentional faux pas by Davis.

"Pardon me," Davis replied sarcastically.

"You don't need ten minutes to vacate, sir; just walk on outta here. If it was up to me, every one of you would be arrested on federal charges of terrorism," said Carranza.

Davis laughed sneeringly. "Terrorists? I wonder how many times you have let terrorists cross this border? Border patrol, my ass."

Carranza's face turned beet-red but, before he could say another word, Davis moved right across the counter from him. They were literally face to face with the small counter between them.

"If you want to have a firefight over allowing a few minutes for my men to gather their belongings and those that belong to the state of Texas, then so be it, lieutenant colonel!" said Davis, picking up a twelve-gauge short barrel riot shotgun.

A few seconds passed where neither officer said a thing, only stared at each other. Carranza sized up Davis' intent as genuine and was the first to blink. The Border Patrol agent broke Davis' stare and looked down at his watch.

"All right, sir, I'll compromise. You have five minutes."

The Border Patrol agents had already begun taking down the barricades and pylons at the mid-point of the International Bridge. Although the bridge was considered the main bridge to connect the two border towns, three other bridges that connected Nuevo Laredo with Laredo remained closed and under the control of the Texas Guard.

The Mexican federales had gathered on their side of the bridge. It was obvious that they had been tipped off to aid the Border Patrol in a showdown and would likely participate if a firefight broke out.

As the Texas Guard and sheriffs' deputies filed out of the building, words were exchanged between them and the Border Patrol.

"If you people are Texans, you should be ashamed," said a sheriff's deputy from Frio County to the agents as he walked by them.

"And you folks are treasonous and should be hung," replied one agent. "Your day of reckoning is coming."

Davis was the last one to walk out. Before he crossed the doorway, he turned to Carranza, "*Lieutenant*, don't get too comfortable here. We'll be back."

# CHAPTER 35

*"Pity the poor, wretched, timid soul, too faint hearted to resist his oppressors. He sings the songs of the damned, 'I cannot resist, I have too much to lose, they might take my property or confiscate my earnings, what would my family do, how would they survive?' He hides behind pretended family responsibility, failing to see that the most glorious legacy that we can bequeath to our posterity is liberty!"*

*~ W. Vaughn Ellsworth*
*American Author*
*IRS Protestor*

Atty. Gen. Tibbs and DHS Director Sarah McDermott got the word that the Border Patrol had successfully taken the checkpoint at Laredo without a struggle. Within minutes, they were on the telephone to each other.

"Damn, Sarah. That was too easy. I'll check with the president, but we should make plans to recover all Texas checkpoints on the Mexican border. Looks like they won't put up a fight. This may be the first step in forcing them to normalize again."

"Yes, that's good news. We have some dedicated Border Patrol agents," McDermott said. "I'm proud of them. Let's get with the president as soon as possible to give him the good news in person!"

Less than twenty-four hours after Col. Davis surrendered the Laredo checkpoint, he received a coded message to report to the Texas DPS office in Laredo, along with units of the 1st Regiment of the Texas State Guard, known as the "Alamo Guard."

Almost two hundred members of the Alamo Guard were assembled at dawn, standing at full attention and in combat gear. Col. Davis walked out of the building on to the huge asphalt area where the troops were assembled. He had just been conferring with state troopers and the local sheriff.

The troops continued to stand at attention, as it appeared Davis was going to address them. Instead, Davis looked up at the sky toward the north, taking down his Ray-Bans since the full sun wasn't over the horizon.

Within seconds, two helicopters appeared, one with the unmistakable Texas state seal and Texas flag on the tail, indicating it was the governor's chopper. Another chopper from the DPS flanked the governor's helicopter just to the north. The choppers landed on the asphalt close enough that many of the troops had to cover their eyes from the dust and particles being stirred up by the large choppers' blades.

Nobody exited the choppers for a few minutes. Most everyone expected to see the new governor step out. The blades and rotors slowed but had not quite stopped when the new commanding officer of the Texas State Guard stepped out.

The average Guardsman was ecstatic over the governor's choice to replace Gen. Barnes, who had been murdered at the Swingin' T. They knew their new commander was likely on the choppers.

Brig. Gen. Henry Sterling had barely touched the asphalt before guardsmen around the chopper started snapping off salutes. The six-foot four-inch tall commanding officer was a no-nonsense Marine, a Vietnam War veteran who had commanded patrol boats up the Nung River deep into North Vietnamese territory for years during the Vietnam War. Many believed that Sterling's experiences were used as the inspiration to fashion several of the characters in the dark war-time movie, Apocalypse Now.

Sterling was a crusty, tough son of a gun. His penchant for political incorrectness ended his career in the Marines, but Gov. Cooper had respected him and the new governor trusted him, realizing he might need Sterling's experience in dealing with the feds if the situation in Laredo came to that. Many in the Guard were anxious to see Brig. Gen. Sterling in the flesh. They knew that, if Sterling was making an appearance to directly address the Alamo Guard regiment, something big was up.

The next foot that came down off the chopper was clad in black alligator cowboy boots. A tall, lanky figure appeared, wearing a Stetson. There was no mistaking who this was. The assembled troops now had a pretty good idea of what their assignment was going to be and were already stoked. The sight of Brig. Gen. Sterling and Pops Younger only got them more hyped.

Younger stepped away from the chopper right behind Brig. Gen. Sterling, along with junior officers from the Texas Guard and four other Texas Rangers, heading toward the podium sitting on the asphalt in front of the troops. The energy and buzz on the asphalt was palpable. This was Texas royalty, and the men realized the significance of the moment.

Several officers addressed the Alamo Guard first. Then Pops Younger took the podium.

"I'm honored to be among true Texas heroes. I look forward to the success of this operation. God Bless Texas!" said Pops.

Pops was always short, direct and to the point. The excitement of the moment finally overtook the Guard. As Pops stepped off the podium, it only took one yell from the troops for them all to break into applause and yells of approval. Once the troops settled down, Brig. Gen. Sterling took the podium.

"Lone Star warriors, it's a glorious day today to be in your presence. I'll make this quick. We have an urgent operation before us. Your officers will be getting with each unit to explain your specific role in this operation. I am here to thank you in advance from the governor and the people of Texas. Godspeed. Dismissed!"

# CHAPTER 36

*"A majority of the people of the United States have lived all of their lives under emergency rule. For 40 years, freedoms and governmental procedures guaranteed by the Constitution have, in varying degrees, been abridged by laws brought into force by states of national emergency.... from, at least, the Civil War in important ways shaped the present phenomenon of a permanent state of national emergency."*

~ *U.S. Senate Report on Presidential Executive Orders 93rd Congress (1973-1975)*

L t. Col. Carranza received the call at 11:20 a.m. that federal government-friendly sources indicated two Apaches and one Blackhawk chopper had lifted off at Lackland Air Force Base in San Antonio and were following a southerly route parallel to I-35 toward Laredo. He calculated they could be hovering over the checkpoint within twenty-five minutes.

Carranza ordered his Border Patrol agents to take up pre-determined defensive positions. After notifying Washington that a conflict was imminent, he called the Mexican federales across the bridge to alert them. Both Carranza and the Mexicans closed the bridge, turning people away who had been streaming in from Nuevo Laredo since it opened. Carranza had instructed his agents to stand down at the border checkpoint. Since the border had been closed for weeks under the orders of DHS, the checkpoint was nothing more than an observation station. The agents hadn't bothered to verify the immigration status of a single entry since they took over the checkpoint from the Texans.

Advance notification of the border opening was spread by the administration to the Mexican embassy, which broadcast it to officials in Nuevo Laredo. Within an hour of the checkpoint takeover, there were hundreds of people lined up on the Mexican side waiting to file through the turnstiles at the Mexican checkpoint, cross the International Bridge and enter the United States. The opportunity to draw federal benefits and get in on the seemingly endless path to citizenship was a strong draw for thousands of Mexican nationals.

It wasn't lost on any Mexican in line that the U.S. Border Patrol was not checking status. Everyone who approached was let in, and the lines had gotten longer by the hour, easily reaching over a thousand in line. A steady stream of Mexican nationals were entering Texas unencumbered by their immigration status, courtesy of the United States government.

The federal government under several administrations kept at least a modicum of perception that border security was important, yet this administration made no attempt to hide its open border policy. This was especially true now that Texas was rebelling. The administration had an obvious policy to flood Texas with future Democratic voters sympathetic to the administration that was providing handouts to any illegal alien at unprecedented levels.

The Alamo Guard began surrounding the checkpoint while keeping their distance. After Carranza notified Washington, two U.S. carriers in the Gulf were put on high alert and F-15s were moved to launch-ready status on their decks. Fearing for the safety of the Mexicans crossing the bridge, the Mexican federales stopped the line on their side of the bridge, not allowing any further crossings. Within minutes, units of the Ejército Mexicano (Mexican Army) numbering over two hundred troops were readied just short of the Mexican checkpoint, including multiple armored personnel carriers mounted with 50-caliber machine guns.

The International Bridge spanned more than two hundred-fifty yards from checkpoint to checkpoint, with a center line drawn over the half-way point of the Rio Grande River. Painted on each side of the line was "Mexico" or "USA." Within a few minutes, the crowd on the bridge dissipated as they made their way through the U.S. checkpoint.

Carranza was on the phone with Director McDermott to get clarification for any possible engagement with the Texas Guard if they advanced on the checkpoint.

"Lieutenant colonel, the closest air support right now is in the Gulf of Mexico, likely thirty to forty minutes away. I am told by the Joint Chiefs that these resources are sitting on standby," said McDermott.

"Director, we have not ascertained their troop strength, but it wouldn't take much for them to outnumber us. I need orders, ma'am, if we are to engage."

"Lt. Col. Carranza, we are trying to reach the president and will call you right back," replied McDermott to a frustrated Carranza.

Carranza, contemplating the situation, was agitated that Washington didn't have an immediate back-up plan or immediate air support. How was he going to hold a checkpoint like this with a couple of dozen Border Patrol agents against militarily trained and outfitted Texas Guard troops? And what weapons did they possess?

While he was looking through binoculars at the growing number of Texas Guard troops within several hundred yards of the checkpoint in downtown Laredo, Carranza's phone rang. He fully expected it to be McDermott; however, he was surprised to get a call back so quickly.

"Lt. Col. Carranza, this is Atty. Gen. Jamail Tibbs."

Somewhat shocked, Carranza replied, "Yes, sir!"

"Under direct orders from the president, you are not to give up that checkpoint to the Texans! Do you understand me, Lt. Col. Carranza?"

Even Border Patrol agents are taught to follow the chain of command, and the attorney general wasn't in that command structure.

"Sir, I am waiting for orders from Director McDermott. She is in contact with the White House, or at least attempting to get orders."

"I'm telling you this is a direct order!"

Not sure what to call Tibbs, Carranza answered, "Sir, no disrespect, but I'm a career federal agent and my orders must come through my command."

Frustrated, Tibbs slammed the phone down on Carranza to call McDermott. Carranza continued to have no clear orders on how to proceed. Sensing he was running out of time, he instructed his men not to fire unless fired upon. His next call was to his Mexican counterpart on the other side of the bridge to keep him apprised of the situation.

Within minutes, the Texas Guard was upon the checkpoint, controlling every high point near the bridge and even on the roof of the customs building where Carranza's Border Patrol agents were stationed.

As the Mexicans observed the move on the U.S. Customs office checkpoint, the Mexican commandant ordered his troops to prepare to advance on the bridge to support the federal agents.

Carranza picked up his ringing phone, fully expecting it to be Washington with orders.

"Lt. Col. Carranza here."

"Sir, nice to speak to you again," said Col. Davis sarcastically.

Carranza was silent for a few moments.

"Sir, Texas would like to have its checkpoint back."

"Texas' checkpoint? Have you forgotten this is federal property?" asked Carranza indignantly.

"If it's on Texas soil, it belongs to Texas. My orders are to take this checkpoint by any means necessary. We will provide the same opportunity you provided my boys. If you do not want their blood on your hands, you are to vacate the premises within five minutes," said Davis.

"Colonel, I cannot agree until I receive my orders from Washington," replied Carranza.

Davis sensed weakness in Carranza's voice.

"Well, sir, my orders are to take this facility in five minutes. You will decide in the next five minutes if any of your men are to die."

"But..." started Carranza before being interrupted by Davis.

"When you vacate the facility, your people are to cross the bridge into Mexico. You and your men will not be permitted back into Texas. If we have to take the facility by force and, in the unlikely scenario that any of your men survive, they will be taken prisoner and indicted for crimes against Texas."

"You're a real piece of work, Davis!" Carranza responded.

"Carranza, you can jaw on the phone for the next five minutes, but I'm telling you right now that your men are going to die while you debate the issue."

Davis hung up the phone and radioed Brig. Gen Sterling and received the okay to advance on the facility by any means necessary. Sterling was hovering in his chopper three miles north of downtown Laredo monitoring the situation. The Texas Apaches were almost on the scene as the Blackhawk made a stop at the DPS facility just north of Laredo where Sterling and Pops Younger originally landed to muster the Alamo Guard.

Davis was just about to issue the order to advance when one set of double doors of the checkpoint facility opened onto the walking lane of the bridge. It appeared the Border Patrol agents were gathering to make the walk across the bridge over the Rio Grande.

Seeing the U.S. Border Patrol agents about to abandon the facility, the Mexican commandant ordered his troops to advance across the bridge, including the personnel carriers.

"Sir, the Mexicans are advancing on the bridge!" radioed Davis to Sterling.

"Pilot, let's go!" barked Sterling as he motioned to the bridge. "Shep, get your folks into the facility. I don't know what their intent is, but they aren't going to reinforce those agents or take the facility before we do!"

"Sir, we have a report that Mexican Falcons have been scrambled and are en route. They intend to provide air support!" radioed a junior officer to Sterling.

"Shep, things are heating up here. We have incoming Mexican Falcons. Take that facility now!" ordered Sterling.

The Alamo Guard troops entered the facility from every possible entry point other than where the border agents were assembling outside on the bridge. Apparently Carranza was confused on what to tell his agents to do, and Davis decided the Border Patrol had still not heard back from Washington.

The Alamo Guard took the facility quickly without a shot fired. The Border Patrol agents began filing toward Nuevo Laredo on the bridge walkway. Carranza was visibly agitated that he had to abandon the facility, hadn't heard from McDermott and had zero back-up support from the U.S. military. Looking toward the Mexican checkpoint, he was surprised to see the Mexicans advancing.

The Mexican force took up the entire width of the bridge with three armored personnel carriers, followed by a couple of hundred Mexican infantry.

Brig. Gen. Sterling was trying desperately to reach the Mexican commander, but fully expected the Mexicans to stop at the half-way line painted across the center of the bridge. If the Mexicans advanced all the way across the bridge before the Apaches arrived on the scene, Shep's Alamo Guard could be overwhelmed.

"Shep, the Mexicans are advancing across the bridge. Get your folks into defensive positions now!" Sterling yelled into the radio.

"We see 'em, General! They've got some firepower! Surely they will stop at the midway point."

"Shep, prepare for any scenario. This administration has gotten very cozy with the Mexican government, so anything is possible!" reasoned the general.

"And the Apaches?" asked Davis.

"En route. Will be over your facility in three minutes, I'm told."

"Roger that! Sir, what are my orders if the Mexicans cross the half-way mark? We have two .50-caliber guns that may be able to take out those armored personnel carriers. I don't think air support will be here before they cross, if their intent is to cross!"

"If they cross that mark, fire warning shots. If they continue, blow them the hell off the bridge. The Apaches will finish whatever you start. We've called in additional support from Lackland."

The Mexican force pulled up to the painted black line and stopped. The Border Patrol agents were swallowed in the mass of troops to the point that Davis couldn't separate them from the Mexicans.

Suddenly, the landline phone in the checkpoint facility rang.

"Sir, I have the Mexican commander on the phone," said one of the Guard.

Davis dashed back to the counter from the double-door area of the stark cinder block government facility and grabbed the phone.

"This is Col. Davis, Alamo Guard Regiment of the Texas Guard."

"Col. Davis, this is Generales Juan Ramon Soto," said the Mexican commander in broken English. "I am advising you to remove your troops from the customs facility on your side of the bridge. Your federal government has asked us to aid your Border Patrol to restore this facility to national control."

"Oh, is that so? Let me get this straight," Davis said as he intentionally stalled for the arrival of the Apaches. "The United States government has asked the Mexican military to intervene on Texas soil once again?"

"Col. Davis, on behalf of your government and your president, I am ordering you to abandon the customs facility. This border has been ordered to re-open at once."

Davis paused as he shook his head. "General Soto, Texans don't abandon their posts. This is a Texas facility, and you will not cross that center stripe and enter Texas. If you do, you will be fired upon," answered Davis without hesitation.

Word of the stand-off had spread through both towns, and citizens from both countries lined the Rio Grande, or sat with lawn chairs on rooftops and watched from their windows.

The Mexican commander gave the order and the armored personnel carriers rolled at slow speed across the midway point of the bridge into Texas.

"Fire! Fire now!" ordered Davis. The .50-caliber Barrett machine guns began strafing the three armored personnel carriers before they had gotten six feet over the line. The Mexicans returned fire from .30-caliber guns mounted in turrets on top of the carriers as glass, metal and mortar seemed to explode off the customs facility. Small arms fire from soldiers on either side echoed from both sides of the bridge as the late afternoon began to turn to dusk, and smoke began to rise from the bridge.

Suddenly, the three armored personnel carriers were hit with multiple rockets, seemingly out of nowhere. The two Texas Apaches had arrived and were on both sides of the bridge about one hundred yards away from the personnel carriers. Two of the vehicles stopped dead in their tracks as the rockets penetrated the carriers and exploded into fireballs.

The third was still rolling, but on fire. It veered hard to the right and hit the ten-foot tall iron link fence, eventually toppling a section of it. The carrier's wheels kept turning as the personnel carrier climbed the crumpled fence and, in a dramatic scene captured on local news cameras, crawled over the fence and then plunged one hundred fifty feet into the shallow Rio Grande River, exploding in a small, tight mushroom-shaped fireball that shot up to the bottom of the bridge.

The world was now seeing the live news coverage being broadcast from Laredo by local network affiliates. The Texas crisis was exploding again on television screens and streaming on the Internet for all to see, including the White House.

"Col. Davis, Mexican air support is inbound. We have to pull the Apaches!" yelled Sterling into his microphone. "Tell your men to take cover! I don't know if they will attempt to hit your facility!"

The Mexican Falcons' air-to-air missiles had a much longer target range than the Apaches, who were outfitted with air-to-surface rockets. Davis and his Texas Guard were sitting ducks for the Falcons if the Mexicans decided to hit the facility with their firepower.

Small arms and machine gun fire was still being traded heavily across the bridge. The Border Patrol agents who had crossed over into Mexico were now accompanying the Mexican troops shooting at the Alamo Guards.

The Falcons came in low, and began strafing the bridge and the customs facility on the Texas side of the bridge. Davis' troops hit the deck inside the facility, looking for any cover they could find.

Texas' first casualties of the conflict began mounting with the attack from the low-flying Falcons that strafed, circled and came back continuously. The Alamo Guards were hunkered down as Mexican troops began advancing slowly across the bridge and the small arms fire defense from the Texans became less and less with each strafing from the Falcons.

"General, we are taking casualties from the Falcons! The Mexicans are advancing on the bridge. We need air support, sir!" screamed Davis.

Sterling had already ordered F-16s at Lackland Air Force Base in San Antonio scrambled when he received word that Mexican Falcons were in the air. Two F-16s were scorching the Texas sky headed to Laredo, with afterburners aglow, even in the bright daylight. Leading the charge to protect the pinned-down Alamo Guard was Cmdr. "Tex" Parsons, who was famous for the destruction of the Mexican Falcons after the raid on the Swingin' T.

The Alamo Guard was under heavy fire, being attacked from the bridge and from the air.

"Col. Davis, hang tough, son. We have air support on the way!" yelled Sterling.

"We're giving them hell, sir! But we are almost out of rounds here!" pleaded Davis. "I've got six dead and eight that need medi-vac now!"

Dead Mexican troops littered the bridge, but more were slowly advancing and another armored personnel carrier was making its way through the Mexican checkpoint followed by four Russian-made light duty tanks.

"Davis, there are tanks approaching the bridge. If we don't get air cover soon I'm going to have you step back and retreat into downtown until we can recover the bridge!"

"No, sir! We can hold 'em!" responded Davis.

There was no way Davis' small regiment could hang onto the facility with the barrage coming from the air, infantry and now tanks.

"Eight minutes!" yelled a junior officer to Sterling.

"Shep, the F-16s are eight minutes out. Can you hold?"

"Yes, sir! We ain't budging!"

Sterling grabbed another headset as the chopper hovered five miles from the bridge.

"Laredo, this is Cmdr. Parsons. We are minus six minutes from the checkpoint. I need orders."

"Son, this is Brig. Gen. Sterling. The Alamo Guards are pinned down. Best we can tell, two Mexican Falcons are buzzing the checkpoint, causing our guys hell!"

Pops Younger had been monitoring the radio traffic from his jump seat on the Blackhawk with five other Texas Rangers he'd picked up at the state trooper regional headquarters. Under orders from Brig. Gen. Sterling, Younger's Blackhawk remained in a hovering pattern eight miles north of the bridge.

"General, I've got the two Mexican bandits on radar. Permission to take them out?" radioed Cmdr. Parsons.

"We've got a lot of civilians in the area watching the show, Commander. No air-to-air missiles unless you have a short-range shot that won't take them out over downtown or the bridge."

"We've got state troopers trying to clear the civilian areas, sir, but it's nowhere close to being clear," radioed Pops.

"Roger that. Laredo, we are closing in now," responded Parsons from his F-16.

The Mexican military radioed the Falcons circling to take one more run at the checkpoint facility and that the F-16s were closing fast.

"Take it out with missiles," was the command in Spanish from Matamoros military operations, referring to the Falcons' unused air-to-air missiles.

"Sir, the Mexicans just ordered the facility to be hit with rockets!" screamed a junior officer monitoring the Mexican radio traffic.

Cmdr. Parsons and the two F-16s were still two minutes out.

"Shep, get the hell out of there now!"

"Sir..." A sudden noise and then radio silence.

"Davis, are you there? Davis? Davis? Laredo checkpoint, do you copy?"

"Look, sir!" radioed the chopper pilot.

Sterling looked to the south and saw two separate columns of dark smoke climbing in the Texas sky.

"Damn it! Davis, are you there?"

"Sir, the Mexicans hit the checkpoint with either missiles or rockets from the Falcons!" radioed a ground coordinator. "The checkpoint is leveled, sir!"

"Davis? Davis?" repeated Sterling.

"Sir, the Mexican bogeys have bugged out. They are back across the river heading south!" said a junior radio officer.

Irritated that the F-16s hadn't arrived in time, Sterling barked, "Cmdr. Parsons, this is Brig. Gen. Sterling. Those Mexican bogeys took out the checkpoint and we likely have a high casualty count. Your orders are to take out that bridge. Do you understand?"

"Roger that, General, destroy the bridge."

"Get the governor on the radio now. I want permission for those birds to take out their entire damned customs office on the Mexican side of the bridge!" Sterling was fuming.

Two more Mexican personnel carriers were close to the rubble of the customs checkpoint on the Texas side of the bridge when "Tex" Parsons and the two F-16s banked hard south and low over downtown Laredo. The Russian-made tanks were now at the half-way point on the bridge, advancing slowly, followed by a couple of hundred infantry, including the U.S. Border Patrol unit.

"Fire! Fire! Fire! Missiles away!" came the excited voice of Cmdr. Parsons as he let go of the missiles.

The missiles from Parsons' F-16 struck the concrete bridge and sent fireballs into the sky, followed by the barrage from the second F-16. Large pieces of the bridge, steel fencing, tanks and bodies began falling into the Rio Grande River below in a surreal scene similar to a video game.

Parsons then banked and came back to the bridge with both F-16s strafing what was left on the Mexican side of the bridge.

"Permission to take out their facility, General?" yelled Parsons.

The action was happening so fast that the governor had no time to ponder the situation thrust on him, surprised that the event had escalated so quickly.

"Governor, they just killed a couple of dozen good men. They attacked our facility on our side of the river. Give me the order, Governor! Give me the order!" insisted Sterling.

Receiving the nod from the governor, Sterling replied to Parsons, "Take the damn Mexican customs office out. No mercy! Obliterate them!"

"Roger, General."

The next few minutes played out on worldwide television screens as the F-16s pummeled the bridge and the Mexican customs office. Dark smoke emanated from the bridge, the two destroyed customs offices, and the burning carcasses of the tanks and personnel carriers that weren't under water in the shallow Rio Grande. Bodies of dead Mexican troops were all over what was left on the bridge and on both banks of the river one hundred fifty feet below.

The Apaches and the F-16s continued to provide air support for recovery efforts in the destroyed Texas customs facility as fellow Texas Guardsmen looked for any Alamo Guard survivors.

The governor ordered two more regiments to the Texas-Mexico border just in case there were designs of the same kind on other Texas entry points by the federal government.

The president left the Oval Office during the stand-off to scurry down to the situation room, surrounded by his closest staff members and the Joint Chiefs.

"Mr. President, it appears that the Texans have killed the U.S. Border Patrol agents who were manning the Laredo checkpoint," said one general. "They hit the bridge with F-16s and Apaches from the air wing of the Texas Guard.

"Mexico is also saying our guys took out the Mexican customs facility on their side of the bridge. The bridge looks destroyed. There are literally dozens of Mexican casualties from the Mexicans attempting to aid the border agents."

"Well, general, this is true, but the Mexican air force also took out the Laredo-side customs facility and there are no doubt significant casualties of the Texas Guard," countered Avery Smith.

"Who controls the bridge and the checkpoints?" asked the president as he squinted to see the carnage being shown on the multiple LED screens in the room.

"Well, I guess nobody, sir," said the general. "Look! The bridge has been rendered inaccessible." The officer pointed to the screens showing gaping holes in the middle of the bridge and the wreckage of Mexican armored vehicles and tanks partially submerged in the Rio Grande River below. Looking back at Smith and McDermott, the president asked, "How are the networks spinning this so far?"

"They are playing up the fact that the Texans killed the U.S. Border

Patrol agents," answered a concerned Smith. "Only Fox is reporting the casualties in the Texas facility knocked out by the Mexicans."

"That will piss off America!" commented Tibbs, almost gleefully referring to the slanted mainstream media reporting.

"Yes, it will, but those agents weren't killed until the Laredo facility was hit. It's important we control the message here and the priority of events is that they struck the agents first," said Smith seriously.

"Mr. President, we are getting word that there is still some sporadic fighting on and near the bridge!" interrupted the general, pointing to the screen with one hand and holding a phone to his ear with the other hand. Everyone stopped talking and looked at the CNN screen.

CNN cameras were capturing the action on the bridge from a nearby outdoor market near the bridge that was normally frequented by Mexican nationals as they crossed over into Texas to shop.

The cameras captured a Blackhawk helicopter with Texas Guard insignia and Lone Star Flag as machine guns fired into the Mexican side of the bridge and the river. The Blackhawk circled the bridge, then banked as if to land.

"What the hell is he doing?" yelled Tibbs.

"The Texans are trying to get their wounded and dead out of the facility, but the Mexicans keep shooting at them from the bridge and off the river bank!" answered the general.

"Is someone in contact with the Mexican army? What the hell are they doing? Do they realize how this is playing out on TV?" asked an irritated Johnson as he stared at the Joint Chiefs.

At the bridge, Brig. Gen. Sterling radioed the Blackhawk. "We have reports of a Stinger shoulder-launched missile by the Mexicans near the river. Get the hell out of there, Pops!"

"Let us off on the bridge!" yelled Pops to the pilot.

"We have a Stinger missile somewhere. Got to bug out, sir!"

"Pilot, get me and my Rangers off this bird now or I swear we will jump off it!"

"But, sir…"

"Son, there are men dying down there! Get us down now, then git the hell outta here!"

"Pilot, this is Brig. Gen. Sterling. Change course immediately."

"Sir, the Ranger commander is demanding to be let off on the bridge!"

Sterling keyed the mic, but didn't say anything before releasing it. Then, talking under his breath to himself, he said, "Damn, Pops, you're gonna get yourself killed."

The Blackhawk lowered to the bridge among the rubble and set down unevenly as Pops and his five Rangers jumped off and scrambled to find cover among the toppled cinder blocks of the customs facility.

"It appears they let some troops off the chopper," said the general in the situation room. "They are probably providing cover so their people can get their wounded or dead out of that rubble."

As they watched, the Blackhawk rose upward quickly and banked hard to the north. The chopper swirled the smoke that was enveloping the entire bridge from the battle.

The CNN cameras made out an image in the smoke as the chopper got further away from the bridge. The outline of a familiar figure began to emerge from the smoke. He was easily recognizable to anyone who had been following the months'-old Texas crisis.

"What the hell?" shouted the general in the situation room.

"Not again..." said a disgusted Avery Smith as he plopped down in one of the leather chairs, unable to take his eyes off the screen.

"It's time to kill that son of a bitch once and for all! Maybe the Mexicans will do us a favor," said Tibbs hopefully.

Most in the room were fascinated by Pop Younger's audacity, yet it was hard for some to hide their fondness of this character who seemed misplaced in time.

The CNN cameras showed a tall, lean figure holding onto his cowboy hat to keep it from flying off his head in the chopper's blade wash while standing at the edge of the bridge where a giant hole existed from the rocket strikes.

Once the wind of the chopper was no longer a threat to his Stetson, Pops Younger pulled his two pearl-handled Colt .45s and began firing across the bridge at the Mexicans. Coming up to stand next to him were the five other Texas Rangers, all with rifles. They began shooting across and over the bridge into the Mexican side of the river bank.

"Cmdr. Parsons, change course to one-two-zero. Those Texas Rangers are trying to hold off the Mexicans so we can get our wounded out of the checkpoint. Light up the Mexican side of the river bank!" Sterling roared.

"Roger that! The cavalry is on the way!" radioed Parsons.

The F-16s came screaming along the river from the west, barely two hundred feet above its banks. Pops and the Rangers continued to unload on the Mexicans on the bridge as bullets whizzed by them. Reserve Guard troops and emergency personnel were making their way through the rubble as best they could, recovering bodies and looking for survivors. If anyone was still alive, Pops and the Rangers were laying down enough ground fire to back up several dozen Mexican troops on the bridge.

"*El Gringo Vaquero! El Gringo Vaquero!*" screamed the Mexicans as many rushed to get a better shot at Pops from their vantage point on the Mexican side of the bridge or in the brush up high on the river bank.

"Tell Mexico to stand down now!" screamed the president. "If they kill that damned cowboy, this crisis will never get settled."

Just as soon as the president issued that order, the CNN cameras captured "Tex" Parsons and the F-16s as they obliterated the Mexican side of the bridge still standing and the southern banks of the Rio Grande River bank with a combination of rockets and machine gun strafing.

Now all cameras from all the news outlets covering the event live were focused on Texas Ranger Cmdr. Pops Younger. Pops never flinched as the F-16s screamed by, but the lawman had to hang onto his hat again. In the meantime, the world saw the Texas Rangers calmly re-loading their rifles as Pops reloaded his six-shot Colt pistols.

Trying to make a name for themselves, two young Mexican infantrymen scrambled onto the bridge and began running straight toward Pops. The other Rangers were focused on the potshots that were coming from the raised river bank and didn't see the small charge coming toward them.

"Alto! Alto, you damn Mezcans!" yelled Pops.

The pair kept charging and began firing their weapons at Pops.

Pops calmly raised his Colt pistols and, with one shot each, dropped the two charging soldiers. One of them fell forward, rolled and plunged through the giant hole on the bridge, dropping one hundred fifty feet to splash dead into the Rio Grande. The other youngster dropped dead in his tracks. Pops calmly holstered his pistols and turned around to see how the recovery efforts were progressing, while sporadic covering fire was still coming from the Texas side of the river.

"Holy crap! Did you see that? Did we really just see that?" said the general in the situation room.

"Ladies and gentlemen, what you just witnessed was legendary Texas Ranger Pops Younger. I'm at a loss to describe what we all just witnessed live. The crisis in Texas is not over, ladies and gentlemen, and it appears to have just reached a new and even more dangerous level," said the CNN host from the studio.

# CHAPTER 37

*"The great object is that every man be armed. Everyone who is able may have a gun."*

~ *Patrick Henry*
*American Revolution Hero & Founding Father*
*Ardent Supporter of States' Rights (Federalism)*

A flood of news and TV reporters crowded the south steps of the Texas capitol. Satellite trucks from every conceivable worldwide news outlet clogged the blocks around the grounds. At the podium stood Gov. Brahman, flanked by every state official in his administration, including many state senators and state representatives.

"Texas is under siege by the federal government of the United States, and this administration has enlisted the help of Mexico to illegally invade a sovereign state." Brahman was clearly agitated. "Texans have had their governor and first lady murdered in the bedroom where they slept.

"They have killed our lieutenant governor, state troopers and Texas Rangers. As the world witnessed today, with the help of Mexico, they have killed thirteen Texas Guard troops who were simply manning a customs checkpoint at the border in Laredo." Brahman glared into the camera. "They have terrorized the citizens of Texas that have differing political opinions. They have had the ATF and the FBI raid the homes of our citizens without the due process guaranteed under the U.S. Constitution. They have shut down banking, shipping, and interstate commerce to and from Texas. Hell, they even blockaded our ports. Texans' constitutional rights have not only been trampled, but obliterated.

"I am here to tell the world, specifically the governors of our United States and specifically the United States Congress, enough is enough! If this criminal administration is not stopped, Texas cannot and will not subject itself to further tyranny.

"I call on Congress to immediately re-open emergency impeachment proceedings. I am convening a conference call with many fellow governors in two hours. I have asked our delegation to the United States Senate and the House to deliver an ultimatum. That ultimatum will be crystal clear. Either Congress brings this administration to justice or the Texas Legislature will put the future of Texas in this republic to the voters in a binding state referendum.

"Let me be clear to our fellow Americans. The injustices perpetrated on Americans here in Texas can and will be duplicated in every state. If they can get away with it in Texas, we have news for the rest of you. It can also happen to you, and I assure you it will. Liberty, as you know it, is over. Freedom, as you know it, is over. The United States Constitution has been rendered obsolete and irrelevant. The Bill of Rights is just a piece of paper. This government, and the duly elected representatives of the other forty-nine states have allowed this to happen. This government has violated the treaty under which Texas became a part of this Union.

"To the rest of America, you have largely been silent on the atrocities of this administration. You have continued to elect representatives who have steered this nation toward socialism, or worse. With each election over the last fifty years, this country moves another step from our founders' intent and the literal meaning of the Constitution. Texas will be silent no longer. You either help Texas by demanding impeachment, or you are part of the problem. Texans will stand for this no more."

Gov. Brahman took a deep breath, pausing as he turned to look at those in state leadership who flanked him. The governor had no notes and no teleprompters.

"With the help of the state leadership you see behind me, we are delivering a list of demands to this administration and to the United States Congress, including the leadership of both houses in both parties. Congress will have forty-eight hours to embark on new impeachment hearings against this president.

"We also demand the immediate resignations of various cabinet members including, but not limited to, the United States attorney general, the director of DHS, including the head of the U.S. Border Patrol, the Joint Chiefs of Staff, the directors of the FBI and ATF, and the head of the IRS. Upon their resignations, Texans demand an independent and bi-partisan prosecutor to be appointed by Congress within three days to open criminal investigations on these departments and cabinet members for their actions over the last several months of this crisis," stated Brahman flatly.

"We have also petitioned the United Nations Security Council, through various countries in which Texas has historical and economic ties, for an immediate hearing to address the escalating crisis. This crisis continues to impact global financial markets and I suspect that the rest of the world has been shocked at the illegal acts this administration has taken against one of its sovereign states," Brahman added.

Pausing again, Brahman looked directly into the nearest TV camera. "On February 24th, 1836, William Barrett Travis scratched out a letter from inside the walls of the Alamo while a simple tri-colored flag with the inscription "1824" flew from the crumbling mission. The tyrannical despot, Santa Anna, had invalidated the Mexican Constitution of 1824. Texians at the time simply wanted a return to constitutional rule and were willing to die for a return to liberty and freedom. I would like to read one small portion of Travis' letter as it is as appropriate today as it was then. I stand before you today in the same spirit and desperation as Travis," said Brahman as he unfolded a small piece of paper.

Even with hundreds of people on and around the steps of the capitol building, everything became instantly silent. Brahman took a set of reading glasses from his coat pocket and put them on.

"Then, I call on you in the name of Liberty, of Patriotism and everything dear to the American character, to come to our aid with all dispatch."

Taking the reading glasses off, Brahman looked up. "America, your fellow American brothers and sisters in Texas are under tyrannical assault from the jack-booted thugs of this administration. It's time for you to decide if this Constitution means anything to you. This is not politics as usual, and it's not about any political party. Now is the time to act. God Bless Texas."

# CHAPTER 38

*"If every person has the right to defend—even by force— his person, his liberty, and his property, then it follows that a group of men have the right to organize and support a common force to protect these rights constantly."*

~ Frederic Bastiat (1801-1850)
French Politician & Economist
Forefather of Libertarian Ideals
& Austrian Economics Theory of Thought

B reaking news from Austin, Texas: Gov. Brahman of Texas has just delivered an ultimatum to Washington, D.C. and to the rest of the country hours after the armed confrontation on the International Bridge in Laredo. His message? Impeach the president now, or else," said the MSNBC host.

"What do you make of it?" said the host to the group of three political pundits sitting on a brightly lit blue set.

"Well, the governor has just raised the stakes, essentially putting the rest of the country on the clock. I think this does nothing to quell the crisis. It was unfortunate that there were deaths in this latest incident on both sides, but his rant and demands will only inflame the situation," said an editor of the Huffington Post.

"The stakes are definitely raised. What if Texas votes to secede?" asked the host.

"It's unconstitutional, simply not doable," claimed a New York Times editor.

"What's the chance Congress acts?" asked the host.

"There will be a lot of gnashing of teeth by Republicans, especially southern Republicans. In the end, Congress is not going to impeach this popular president," stated the guest from the NAACP.

"His approval numbers are in the mid-thirties, sir. I'm not sure if his popularity is what it once was. He has been brutally criticized, even by members of his own party, for the handling of the Texas crisis. His approval ratings were at their all-time highest shortly after the assassination attempt, but those ratings have steadily declined, especially since the death of the Texas governor and his wife," returned the host.

"I think America will reject this ultimatum as extreme, and any further actions by this state government along the path of some type of twisted secession movement are treasonous. A governor of a state does not simply impose his or her demands on the federal government," claimed the NAACP guest.

"We do know Texans are mad as hell. How do you folks think the rest of America views these latest events, but especially how do you think they will view this speech by the new Texas governor?"

"I think his speech will resonate with those in other southern states or those that lean as a red state. Most of the nullification and Tenth Amendment wingnuts come from those states. The only folks that will view it favorably are the extremists in the Tea Party and other far right wing zealots, but his threats will ring hollow to the rest of and majority of America," responded the New York Times guest.

"Did the governor back his state into a corner? What happens in both scenarios? I mean, if Congress doesn't impeach and Texas puts secession to a vote and it doesn't pass, then what?" The host continued to query her panel.

"I just don't think there are as many crazies in Texas as we might think. I don't think a statewide referendum on secession would pass. I for one welcome it because of that reason. If it is defeated, as I predict, the governor will have no choice but to negotiate an end to this nonsense," snapped the Huffington Post contributor.

"So you think they will have the vote?" asked the host to the Huffington Post panelist.

"Well, I don't think there's a chance on God's green earth that Congress votes to impeach, so I take the governor at his word."

"So what if your scenario plays out and Texas votes to secede?" asked the host to the entire panel.

"I think at that point Texas invites further and more substantial U.S. military intervention," stated the NAACP guest.

"As much as I hate to say it, I think he's right about increased military intervention at that juncture. There is no way the United States allows a state to break away. For all their claims to the Constitution, they, meaning the Texas state leadership, forget that this issue was settled in 1860. If you want to change it, you do it through the ballot box," echoed the Huffington Post contributor.

"Well, if it goes that far, it will be over in a heartbeat. How does Texas stand up to the mighty USA and its military? The very minute this president wants to squash what amounts to an insidious little rebellion orchestrated by extremists, he will. I believe the president will send a very strongly worded message to Texas before any scheduled vote to let average Texans fully understand what the consequences of their votes will mean, and what will happen to them and their state leadership if they continue down this path. This is treason, plain and simple," said the NAACP contributor forcefully.

The host turned to the camera and, in a very serious tone, ended the segment saying, "There you have it, America. After months of this crisis, it would seem we are coming to an apex. How will the administration act now that the governor of Texas has put this administration on the clock? Will Texas vote to secede? Stayed tuned, folks. The next few days will be important to all Americans. Let's all hope this series of events doesn't culminate in more bloodshed."

# CHAPTER 39

*"Democracy is a form of government that cannot long survive, for as soon as the people learn that they have a voice in the fiscal policies of the government, they will move to vote for themselves all the money in the treasury, and bankrupt the nation."*

*~ Karl Marx (1818-1883)*
*Author of "The Communist Manifesto"*
*The Father of Modern Communism*

President Johnson was incensed, calling an immediate emergency cabinet meeting. No press was allowed to attend. He specifically called the Joint Chiefs of Staff, and instructed his press secretary to "leak" the fact that he'd summoned his top administration officials. This led to wild speculation in the media that the administration was exploring military options to end the months'-old crisis once and for all.

"Ladies and gentlemen, we need to make it crystal clear to Texans that any referendum for secession from these United States will not be recognized and will bring dire consequences to the people of Texas," the president said. It was clear Johnson had reached the pinnacle of his frustration with the Texas crisis.

"Mr. President, the question is, do we bring that message now or after the vote? What if the independence vote is defeated?" asked Sarah McDermott.

"Avery, what are the politics here? If they bring this vote, where does it likely fall?" asked the president.

"This is a hard one to gauge, Mr. President. The Swingin' T disaster and now the border bridge drama in Laredo are stoking Texas nationalism, if you will. Texans have a different mindset than the rest of the country, which is painfully obvious to all of us here."

"Can we stop the referendum?" asked Johnson.

"Short of a full military option, I don't think we can," answered Smith.

"Then let's do it!" blurted Tibbs, referring to a military option.

Ignoring Tibbs, Johnson asked, "Are we sure how this vote would turn out? I mean, if it was defeated, then it's an entirely different scenario, isn't it? A much easier one that just calls for removing the current state leadership and restoring the military bases?"

Hesitating slightly, Smith continued, "Mr. President, I think we need to face the more likely scenario that it passes. Also, you must remember that this type of election is not going to have any federal oversight, so we should expect the results the governor wants, one way or the other."

"Well, Avery, if you think this is going to pass, we need to ratchet up the pressure before the vote, don't you think?"

The rest of the cabinet sat riveted in the conversation that was essentially a conversation between the president and his most influential advisor who, interestingly enough, didn't hold an official cabinet position in the administration.

"Mr. President, it is a fine line. Depending on what those plans are, we could push a close vote over the top toward secession."

"I say we don't even let the vote go forward. It's time for a military occupation of Texas. How many opportunities to flout federal law and embarrass this administration are we going to let them have?" demanded Tibbs.

Smith sat in his chair next to the president, rubbing his balding head where he had combed over his few strands of hair, while the president sat with his chin in his left hand. Both these idiosyncrasies were tell-tale signs of the personalities of each man when in deep thought or extreme stress.

"I think the threat of military action at this point would drive a deeper wedge, Mr. President," offered Bartlett. "It would surely push the vote over to the independence-leaning faction."

"You mean the secessionists," replied Tibbs. "Let's not pretend these guys are Washington, Adams, and Madison. I think we need to make sure all references to these jokers are secessionists. Treasonous secessionists! We need to make sure that is the word used with the media and in all our talking points."

"I agree with that message. Secessionist is the word going forward," agreed Smith.

"So, do we launch a campaign to discredit any referendum, or do we wait? Do we issue warnings to Texans about the consequences?" asked the president, pressing for answers.

"Annabelle, you were the last person in this room to have any direct contact with their leadership. I would be interested in your take on this particular topic," said Smith.

Bartlett, dressed in a 1960s style blue dress of thick material with an out-of-date huge black bow on the front and a matching hair band, pondered for a moment, then said, "If I had to guess right now, even without any additional actions by the federal government, I would say the referendum would pass. The question is, how closely? I felt a very strong sense of Texas patriotism while I was there. You all saw what happened prior to the funeral on the Austin airport tarmac. The faction that is pro-independence—uh, excuse me, Jamail—pro-secessionist, is highly energized. If turnout is low, it will surely pass because that faction will turn out its base. This assessment is strictly subjective, Mr. President. What does your polling say?"

Smith took the opportunity to answer for the president.

"We are diligently trying to come up with polling numbers by this evening. Our polling before the Laredo bridge incident was running at the same percentage, plus or minus, as it was right after the governor's funeral. At that time, it probably peaked, but it was 68 percent with likely voters. I would suspect it has dropped some, but the Laredo incident may have shot the numbers upward again."

"Don't we still have control over elections there? I mean, I would think these guys would rig that vote, wouldn't you?" asked Tibbs.

"Only with Justice Department oversight. Any insertion of federal troops in relation to that vote will likely give them the impression of our validation of such a vote," reasoned the president.

"And send it the wrong direction," added Bartlett.

"We have people on the ground who can influence that vote, but it won't be Justice folks," said Smith. "If we are going to intervene, it should only be to stop or to avoid that vote completely; otherwise, we run the very high risk of throwing sentiment in the opposite direction we want."

"Are the sanctions we have in place having an effect on the everyday Texan?" asked McDermott.

"Yes, some. I just need to remind everyone here that Texans are fiercely independent by nature," said Smith. "Whatever sanctions, embargoes or blockades we put in place will take longer to work than most believe. Texas has a huge economy and they are very resourceful. They also have a trump card, and it's those damned oil and gas pipelines, and the refineries.

"Forty-one percent of all American gasoline is refined on the Texas Gulf Coast. We have allowed our allies to get tankers in and out but, if we really want to put the squeeze on them, then we have to tell our international friends their tankers will be turned back."

"We have a trump card, too. It's called the United States military," remarked Tibbs.

"If we think the referendum would succeed, it is my opinion that we need to put extreme consequences on such a vote in advance of it. Do you all agree?" asked the president.

"I do," affirmed Tibbs.

"What are you thinking, Mr. President?" asked Bartlett.

"We need to outline the consequences, and I suggest we do so in prime time," directed Smith.

"Whatever we outline, we need to make sure we will follow through. If we are going to point a gun at Texas, we sure as hell better have it loaded and be prepared to pull the trigger!" snarled Tibbs.

"I agree with Jamail," said Smith in one of the few situations where the two men agreed. "These cannot be empty threats or promises; therefore, these conditions must be carefully outlined, delivered and supported by Congress and the media. We need to isolate Texas and put them on an island. The Texas state leadership needs to be classified as extreme. Their motives need to be racist and terroristic."

"Let the propaganda fly?" questioned Bartlett.

"Technically, we are in a war, Annabelle. We need to use every means possible to prevent this vote, including controlling the message," answered Tibbs.

Smith stood up and began pacing, as if some light bulb just went off in his head. "We need to make a lot of references to Lincoln and position this president in the same light under similar circumstances. Done properly, sir, your approval ratings will rise."

"What if our warnings and cajoling don't work? What happens if the vote goes down anyway, and the vote turns out the way most of us think it will?" asked Bartlett, finally directly addressing the elephant in the room.

"Then we will have a break-away state, and they will have to be dealt with using the full force of the United States military. I don't see any other way. I don't see a diplomatic solution at this point. Like Lincoln, it would be my responsibility to save the Union," said the president proudly, almost relishing the idea that he could go down in history in the same light as Lincoln.

Avery Smith used the last few minutes before the president's live broadcast from the Oval Office to confer with the president over the style and substance of his delivery. It was not lost on either one of them that this was the most important message this president would deliver in his presidency to date.

Smith had already rejected the blue suit and yellow tie the president's staff had picked out for him to wear on the broadcast. His staff thought that this color combination would make him look compassionate and reasonable. Smith put Johnson in a dark suit with a red power tie. The speech was meant to be an authoritative message from the most powerful man in the world. This was all business, and Smith wanted Texans, Congress and the media to see Johnson at full strength as commander-in-chief.

While Johnson was normally calm, cool and collected when he was about to speak to live audiences, Smith could tell the president knew the gravity and importance of the message he was about to deliver. He watched nervously as the president uncharacteristically paced in the hallway outside the East Room, a small bead of perspiration showing above his eyebrows.

"Ladies and gentlemen, the President of the United States," came the introduction on every news channel imaginable to a world-wide audience. The scene instantly showed Johnson at his desk in the Oval Office, looking very presidential.

"Good evening, America. This administration and Congress have worked tirelessly with the governor and state leadership of Texas, our twenty-eighth state. This current crisis, which has grown over the last fourteen months, has included the deaths of federal agents, United States military and Texas law enforcement officials. Unfortunately, it also included the deaths of the Texas governor and his wife, as well as other state officials.

"All of these deaths and bloodshed were avoidable and this administration has taken every reasonable step with the state leadership in Texas to put an end to this crisis.

"This nation was founded on the principle that, if you don't like or agree with the current state of affairs, you change your elected officials at the ballot box. The acts that precipitated the governor's death were illegal, and his death, although extremely unfortunate, was the result of his own actions while federal arrest warrants were being served.

"It is time for those in Austin to come to the table with Washington, D.C. to put an end to this crisis. There are no differences that can't be worked out. This administration is poised to make reasonable compromises and to end the financial sanctions that have been levied on Texas. I call on the governor and the statehouse of Texas to sit down with my administration," Johnson said in an agreeable tone of voice.

The president paused, and changed the demeanor on his face as he changed the direction of his gaze to the teleprompter on his left.

"Let me be very clear. The demands recently put on Congress and this administration by the governor will not be heeded. The United States of America will not be bullied and will not be tethered by out-of-touch extremist demands of any kind from whatever source, even if it comes from a sitting state governor," Johnson said sternly.

"I have a message to this governor and all Texans. Any statewide, legislative referendum or vote of any kind to secede from these United States is unconstitutional, illegal and will not be tolerated. This administration will consider any such vote treasonous by any and all who organize the vote or maintain polling for such an illegal election." He pointed into the camera. "The Justice Department will consider these actions a violation of federal law and they will be prosecuted to the fullest extent of the law. Additionally, any citizen who casts a vote in favor of secession in such an illegal referendum will also be considered as committing an act of treason."

Johnson paused for a few seconds to let the effect of his last statement sink in.

"Over 600,000 American lives were lost the last time this issue was visited, and America is not going to revisit it. This issue was settled in 1865 once and for all by the Supreme Court.

"I am reminded of Abraham Lincoln and his struggle to maintain the

Union. Lincoln said, 'Stand with anybody that stands right, stand with him while he is right and part with him when he goes wrong'."

Johnson looked right into the camera. "Texas is wrong on this issue and it is my job as the president, as it was Abraham Lincoln's, to maintain and protect this Union and those in Texas who are proud to be Americans.

"To the average Texan, I say call your state legislator, state senator, your city leaders, and call your governor to demand that they settle this crisis."

Preparing for the most difficult part of his speech, the president hesitated to briefly clear his throat and appeared to gather his thoughts for the delivery he was about to read off the teleprompters.

"In the interest of all Americans, if the leadership in Austin does not recognize that the opportunity to end this crisis is at hand, my administration will do what is necessary to restore normalcy to Texas and to bring them in line with our laws and the Constitution. This means there are absolutely no options that will be taken off the table, and those include military options. This crisis has exceeded my patience and that of the rest of America," Johnson stated, furrowing his brow as if scolding a small child.

"Gov. Brahman, I call on you directly to lead a delegation to Washington to end this crisis now. Let Texans get back to the business of living their lives as productive Americans. If you do this, I can assure you America will welcome Texas back into the fraternity of states that make up this great country. There is no more important task for this administration and your leaders in Austin than to immediately come together in the spirit of compromise to end this crisis once and for all.

"Thank you. Good night, and God bless America."

The CNN host proclaimed, "The president may have just delivered one of the most important addresses in American history. Not only did he extend the olive branch to the Texas governor in a fully thought-out and reasoned attempt to end the crisis, but he just might have thrown down the gauntlet that would prevent Texas from even voting for secession by declaring the simple act of casting a ballot in such a vote as an act of treason. Simply brilliant!"

# CHAPTER 40

*"Revolution does not require a majority to prevail, but rather an irate, tireless minority keen to set brush fires in people's minds."*

~ *Samuel Adams (1722-1803)*
*Founding Father &*
*American Revolution Patriot*

"All the chips are on the table, folks. Are we all in?" asked Gov. Brahman to a close circle of advisors, business leaders, and elected and non-elected state government officials gathered at the governor's mansion.

"If the president is going to put all his chips on the table, then it's time for us to double-down," remarked Atty. Gen. Weaver. "It's just like him to twist the constitutional meaning of treason to fit his agenda. Unbelievable. Among the sad commentary on this entire crisis is that the average American doesn't know he's wrong. America's lack of constitutional knowledge works against us here, as my bet is public opinion for the most part outside of Texas will be against us."

"I think that's a given, Jeff, but this is a direct attempt to thwart the Independence referendum. I'm going to ask everyone here what they think. You are essentially in the same position as our country's founding fathers and the founders of the Texas Republic. Your freedom and your livelihoods are at stake here. Hell, based on what this administration is capable of, your lives and those of your families could be at risk as well," stated Gov. Brahman.

Weaver began walking through the process of how a vote like this would be constructed.

"The governor has to call a special session of the legislature, which will then vote on presenting a special statewide election on this referendum, absent a citizens' petition. No petition or signatures are required by state law unless the plan is to get this on a statewide ballot during a normal election cycle. This is totally up to the legislature and the governor to put to the voters of Texas," he stated matter-of-factly.

"So, anyone who casts a ballot for this referendum is betting the farm, or his life that, in the end, we will be successful; otherwise, and if it's not successful, we will likely be indicted for treason by the United States government?" asked one junior legislator.

"According to Johnson, yes. For what it's worth, I believe that if, in fact, we remained a state either because the vote failed or we reconciled later, that those tried for treason simply for voting for this referendum would eventually be overturned by the Supreme Court. But, of course, nothing is guaranteed," Weaver said. "However, those of us who have organized the referendum, and those who physically put the vote forward to the voters, will likely be targets of the Justice Department. It's also important to remember that, just because the vote passes, doesn't mean this administration will recognize the vote or the wishes of the people of Texas. Even if the vote were to pass, it is an entirely different task to officially *become* a Republic again."

"First steps first, Jeff," said the governor. "I have two questions for everyone here. First, will the legislature vote it forward and, secondly, will the referendum pass when presented statewide? Will Johnson's threats be enough to keep people home? I would like to get a sense of the average Texan's thinking. I know Gov. Cooper found Chuck Dixon to be a reliable barometer on issues facing those of us not tied to Austin in the state. Shelly, can you please see if you can track down Mr. Dixon? We should have had him here for this meeting, but I want to have a private conversation with him," the governor told one of his trusted staffers.

For the next two-and-a-half hours, the issue was hotly debated. At one point, the group was leaning heavily toward attempting one more shot at reconciliation. Tempers became heated. Each had a lot at stake and most felt incredible responsibility to their fellow Texans. Consensus between the high-powered and connected politicians and business leaders was hard to find.

Adding to the complexity of issues was guessing what the Johnson administration would actually do as a result of a vote, especially if it passed.

It was not lost on the group that the president left the door open to military intervention. Brig. Gen. Sterling had briefed the group on likely scenarios that could occur if Johnson let loose with a full military option.

Although Texas had fared well in the limited skirmishes with the feds and quasi-military units dispatched to Texas during the crisis, in no way did Texas have near the military resources to repel a full-out assault from combined U.S. military forces. It wasn't a pretty scenario.

There was some hope that Johnson would hold true to form as in other conflicts, backing down when challenged in other parts of the world.

Finally, Gov. Brahman, who had mostly been silent and had listened to many of the unilateral sidebar arguments being waged in the room, had heard enough. He stood up. What he was about to say would only be heard by a relative few but would be as significant as any speech or address that had been delivered on Texas soil in her rich and storied history.

The governor took another draw on one of the fine cigars given to him by the late Gov. Cooper and took a few paces, reversed and looked up at a portrait of the "Father of Texas," Stephen F. Austin. Brahman blew out a long billow of smoke that seemed to extend four feet by the time all the smoke had been expelled before reaching a ceiling fan and disseminating throughout the large Victorian-style room. The governor had their complete attention.

"I appreciate all the reasons many of you have laid out why we shouldn't put this issue to a vote. And ninety-nine percent of those reasons are valid ones. I also appreciate the fact that we would face incredible odds in following through with Texans' mandate if a vote for independence passed and, even more so, doing it without bloodshed," stated Brahman as he waved his cigar to make his point.

"If this *is* the desire of Texans, I mean to deliver it," Brahman said, looking straight at the group and pointing to them with the burning cigar.

"And it is *your* sworn duty to deliver it, if it is, in fact, the will of the people," Brahman declared defiantly to all present.

"We have the God-given right to put this to a vote. It is your duty to put this to a vote! We will simply have to prevail through political will." The governor paused to take another deep draw on the cigar.

"Now, we can all debate until the cows come home how independence would be accomplished if the vote carries. We can all guess what this president will do. What we do know is apparently the rest of America and Congress couldn't care less about the Constitution. Congress has proved it has neither the political courage nor the cojones to impeach a criminal president. Hell, they won't even follow through on the murder of a whistleblower! At what point do we tell our fellow Texans we give up? It's too hard. The odds are too great. We might be attacked. We have lost our governor and his beautiful wife. We have lost our lieutenant governor. We have lost Maj. Gen. Conroy. We have lost brave Texas Rangers, state troopers and everyday Texans. It is at least apparent to me the rest of this country simply doesn't give a damn. It is painfully obvious we are on our own."

The governor reached across a legislator sitting on a wing-back chair and flicked his cigar into a huge porcelain ashtray sitting on the end table to knock off the ashes, then drew another puff while everyone sat silently until he let out another huge billow of smoke.

"We won't win with bullets and Apache helicopters, ladies and gentlemen. What the rest of America and this damned president need to see is a unified and determined Texas. I say to ya'll, if they won't impeach this bastard and arrest the criminals in his administration, we have no choice. We have to be smart. We have to have a plan. And we have to execute it meticulously and with all dispatch. This president is indecisive and weak at the core. We need to act and we need to act now."

The people in the room broke into approving clapping, then the governor raised his hands to quell the applause.

"While I sat here listening to your arguments, my thoughts went to General Sam Houston attempting to keep his small army together in the rain and mud and belly-aching from his troops and volunteer militia. Half of them wanted to quit and go back to their families and farms, and the other half wanted to march on to the Alamo and Goliad to either save their countrymen or avenge their deaths at the hands of a tyrant. Houston had a plan and he stuck to his plan, even as his troops nearly mutinied.

"Imagine the men at Washington-on-the-Brazos as they met in a freezing cold barn and signed their fate to the Texas Declaration of Independence, essentially signing their death warrants, willing to risk it all.

"There is something glorious about this place we call Texas. Hell, I don't know, it must be in the water. Somehow, as overwhelming odds and pressures congregate over Texas like a spring storm, average men and women are transformed into icons of history.

"Ladies and gentlemen, everything you have done in your life, and I do mean EVERYTHING, has led you to this very place, this very time, and this very point in history. Make no mistake; the decisions we make tonight are generational and likely final.

"We will either decide to cower to a president and an administration that is destroying the very fabric of liberty, a Congress that no longer represents our values, and a country that has allowed a bloated, debt-ridden government to be the principal core authority of our daily lives, or we will embrace the values that have made Texas the very last bastion of free enterprise, liberty and self-determination."

The governor reached back over to the ashtray and smashed the cigar into it until the smoke stopped. Several in the group had tears streaming down their face.

"When you leave here tonight, I want you go to go home and look at your kids, your grandchildren and your loved ones and ask yourself if you are doing the right thing. Are you advancing the principles that endear you to your Maker? I say to you right here and now, this is *your* duty! Two generations from now, will your great grandchildren even know your name and the story of your life because you made some type of major difference in *their* lives and the lives of your fellow Texans? Will they know that you sat here this night, among modern-day Texas heroes who said to each other, no more tyranny and no more secular socialism! Will you make a difference to them and the future of Texas, or are you more interested in winning your next elections, maintaining your country club memberships, your private jets, and your social status among the so-called elite? What will *your* tombstone say? Will it say here lies a true Texas patriot? Will it say here lies a hero or heroine who took one last chance at freedom, against all odds?"

The governor took another long and uncomfortable pause. Tears were now running down his cheeks, too.

"Was it a long shot in 1836? Was it a long shot in 1776? Hell, yes, it was! I say to you right here and right now, no matter the odds, no matter the circumstances, if the dream of a truly free Texas is big enough in your hearts and the hearts of all Texans, the facts simply don't count!"

# CHAPTER 41

*"To compel a man to furnish funds for the propagation of ideas he disbelieves and abhors is sinful and tyrannical."*

~ *Thomas Jefferson (1743-1826)*
*Founding Father*
*American Revolution Hero*
*Author of the Declaration of Independence*
*3rd U.S. President*

Two days later, the Texas Legislature, called into a special session by Gov. Brahman, debated the passage of a bill that would present a statewide referendum for independence to the voters of Texas.

The bill was given an honorary designation as HB 1836, representing "house bill" with the date of Texas' original independence to a republic. The debates were televised live globally by CSPAN and nearly every major news organization in the world.

Following up on Johnson's last speech, the administration continued to claim any "yay" vote by a Texas state senator or legislator to put the referendum to a vote was an act of treason, and any elected official who voted affirmatively would be punished accordingly. This point was argued vigorously by constitutional experts on both sides, with those in the camp of the administration claiming such a move would initiate hostilities, including war and, therefore, should be considered aiding and abetting an enemy of the United States. Those on the side of independence claimed it is the right and duty of citizens to throw off a government they didn't want, and no such declaration of war was eminent or necessary by Texas to do so.

Johnson began to issue executive orders to increase the stakes. To mount pressure on Texas' elected officials and to attempt to terrify the average Texan, Johnson ordered the United States military to begin mobilizing ahead of the vote in the Texas Legislature. Johnson also announced that those in active military duty based in Texas report to several points in neighboring states within seven days or be considered AWOL, to be tried in military courts for high treason.

The administration continued all efforts to squeeze the average Texan in every possible scenario, halting all federal payments of any kind, including entitlements and even federal employee paychecks. This was a calculated move to elevate pressure on the governor, hoping Texans would rebel against their state leadership as day-to-day living for many Texans became increasingly difficult.

Under Avery Smith's direction, the most successful propaganda and disinformation machinery in the history of the U.S. presidency began an all-out blitz to sway public opinion both at home and abroad. The U.S. ambassador to the United Nations introduced a measure in the U.N. Security Council to denounce any passage of an Independence referendum but, surprisingly, it was not brought to a vote, held up by Russia. The Council indicated it might take up a vote if the referendum passed.

During the debate on the floor of the Texas Senate, several ranking Republicans in Congress attempted to re-ignite the impeachment process. The GOP knew that it was in serious trouble on two separate fronts. If the administration was successful in its propaganda war, the GOP would take another major hit in popularity because Texas was not only a red state, but possibly the reddest of the red. Damage to the GOP, labeled as extremist for years by the Democrats, could resonate even further as all Texas state elected leadership was Republican, Libertarian or Independent. The administration continued to link modern-day Texas pro-independence leaders to slavery from the Civil War by painting them with the secessionist label. Democratic and mainstream media were fawning over Johnson as the reincarnation of Lincoln.

And if, by a very long shot, the vote for independence was successful, the GOP would lose the cornerstone of its entire base by Texas detaching itself from the United States. There would no longer be a U.S. Republican Party in Texas or Texas Republicans in Congress.

Minority GOP leaders in both the House and Senate were now working overtime to broker a solution before a scheduled Texas Legislature vote, calling in favors and issuing dire warnings to those who did not follow the party line. Many in the GOP spoke vociferously against the referendum. Republicans everywhere were on defense and few were willing to speak out in favor, fearful of political reprisals in their own party but also wary of Tibbs' DOJ.

Before the Texas crisis, the most politically incorrect label one could be stained with was either being called a "racist" or a "terrorist." The administration and the willing mainstream media had been successfully labeling the pro-independence movement in Texas as both, just as it had done with the Tea Party.

The scene on the floors of the Texas Senate and House were surreal. Shouting matches. Name calling. Accusations of high treason nearly brought more than one argument to fisticuffs. If the same arguments were held back in Texas' early days, people would have witnessed challenges of duels to the death. Pro-independence legislators were free to speak their minds, protected by the First Amendment, but all bets were off when and if they cast a "yay" vote for an Independence referendum.

At the closing of the first day of debate, breaking news coverage showed four United States aircraft carriers just a few miles off the Texas Gulf Coast. Also, three full mechanized divisions were being mobilized on Texas' bordering states of New Mexico and Louisiana.

President Johnson was about to have another headache because Oklahoma state leaders were vociferously debating with the administration on the legality of placing a division in their state for a possible incursion into another state, and indicated that force would be turned back and federal forces would not allowed to mobilize near the Red River.

Texas legislators went home shortly after 10:00 p.m. CST, knowing they had but until the next morning to decide how to cast their votes. The House chaplain was brought in to dismiss the session at the conclusion of the debate on the floor. He sent the elected body home with a prayer.

"Almighty Father, bless these leaders as they travel home tonight. Bestow on them the wisdom to proceed in this endeavor with the will of the Father. May the Holy Spirit guide them in their conscious and subconscious to invoke Your almighty will. No matter the decision that comes out of this body tomorrow, Lord, guide them on the path that glorifies You. We also humbly ask that You protect this body and all Texans. May their decision tomorrow be Your will and may each accept that future that You have bestowed on each and every one of us. In Jesus Christ's name, Amen."

# CHAPTER 42

*"The Republic was not established by cowards; and cowards will not preserve it... This will remain the land of the free only so long as it is the home of the brave."*

> ~ *Elmer Davis (1890-1958)*
> *Director, War Information Office during WWII*
> *Author & Writer*

President Johnson made a brief appearance in the East Room of the White House at 8:30 a.m. the next morning. The media was told he would read a short statement, but would not take any questions.

"Today, the Texas Legislature is convening in a special session called by their governor to vote on presenting an illegal referendum for secession in a potential special election to the voters of Texas. This is quite simply a failure of state leadership. It is not only unconstitutional but is also anti-American. This administration has worked tirelessly to compromise with the former governor, and now the current governor, to avert the continuing crisis with the leadership of this state," stated the president smugly.

"Again, I will reiterate that a vote by any elected state official in favor of allowing this referendum to go to a statewide vote is an act of treason. Also, any action to carry forward an illegal referendum by the state elections commission and county administrators will also be considered an act of treason. I am confident, however, that the people of Texas will reject this extremism, as the majority are loyal and patriotic Americans."

From a media coverage standpoint, Austin had never seen anything like this. During the entire months'-long Texas crisis, TV and news coverage at the Austin capital was frenetic. But the magnitude, pace and sheer numbers were now off the chart pending the legislature's vote. The vote was scheduled to take place at approximately 10:30 a.m. CST.

Many legislators didn't sleep the night before. Some went as far as conference calls with constituents late into the night. More than two dozen traveled back to their districts across the state for late-night town halls. Most of these town hall events were surprisingly well-attended and followed almost the same script as the debates on the floor the previous morning. There was shouting, finger-pointing, and at least two broke into fisticuffs.

National and Texas GOP leadership made calls deep into the night, hoping to sway any undecided and freshman legislators with political bribes or threats. The national GOP was greedily trying to keep its fervent Texas base under its tent, not from any patriotic duty to save the Union, but because it was strictly concerned about self-preservation of the establishment. Texas Republicans were told the vote was a political death sentence at a minimum by national GOP leaders and that Johnson would make good on his threat to indict the co-conspirators who voted "yay."

In one of the best reports on the town hall meetings, the BBC reported that most of the acrimony was over a final vote, and not the right for Texans to decide themselves. A CNN poll among Texans reported the same phenomenon. Texans believed in large numbers that they had a right to decide, even if they disagreed with what the final decision would be. They overwhelming disapproved of the president's message that voting in favor of independence in itself was an act of treason; however, nearly half stated they would stay home and not vote at all for fear of treason charges for participating, no matter if they were for or against. Johnson's strategy appeared to be working.

At least two separate news organizations were reporting that Texas law enforcement officials who were loyal to the Johnson administration were against the vote, and were gathering in Austin to arrest those who voted for the referendum as they left the capitol building.

Johnson and his closest cabinet members were busily formulating plans in case the vote passed. Their internal polling indicated that a statewide vote would be very close, but they had no intention of taking a chance. If the referendum vote passed in the legislature, the administration was preparing to act swiftly and decisively.

The Speaker of the House hit the podium with his gavel at 10:36 a.m.

With the entire world watching, the legislature was preparing to vote on HB 1836. The gallery in the state capitol was standing room only. The tension was palpable.

It was not lost on a single legislator that this might be their final vote as elected officials. Although there were no administration-friendly law enforcement officers visible, word had spread that legislators who voted in favor of the motion to allow for a statewide Independence referendum could be arrested upon leaving the capitol building after the vote, or arrested at some later date for treason.

The debates over the last two twenty-four hour periods were epic. But now, the debating was over. The Speaker began, calling the historic roll himself. "On HB 1836, a motion for a statewide special election on the Independence referendum."

The roll call began.

"Mr. Aguilar."

"I vote for the preservation of this great country. I vote nay."

"Mr. Alvarez."

"Nay. Save the Union."

"Mrs. Amendola."

"No secession. Nay."

"Mr. Athens."

"Nay," said Athens, looking down at the floor.

"The referendum appears to be in trouble," said the MSNBC correspondent. "Athens is a Republican!" MSNBC had predicted the referendum would fail.

"Mr. Barborosa."

"I proudly vote the first yay for Texas sovereignty!"

Just as soon as the MSNBC reporter announced a Republican had voted against the referendum, a Hispanic Democrat broke ranks and voted for it. Soon, momentum began to build.

"Mr. Cortez."

"Texas first. Texas always. Yay," said another Democrat.

"Mr. Davidson."

"Remember the Alamo! Remember Gov. Cooper! Yay,"

"Mr. Derrickson."

"Remember Gov. Cooper! Yay."

"Mr. Donaldson."

"Yay. Remember Texas' first lady!"

"Mr. Edwards."

"Yay for Texas sovereignty!"

"Mr. Evans."

"Remember the Constitution. I vote yay."

"Mr. Frankel."

"I say no to this jack-booted administration. Yay."

"Mr. Georgeston."

"Don't Mess with Texas! Yay!"

Television hosts were taking advantage of the building drama.

"The vote started roughly for the pro-secession backers, but the momentum has clearly shifted. They're on a roll!" said the ABC news anchor.

Several news stations split the screen with breaking news.

"It appears legendary Texas Ranger Pops Younger has arrived at the capitol grounds with dozens of Texas Rangers and state troopers," said the Fox correspondent.

A local Austin television station managed to stick a microphone in Pops' face as he walked by with a look of serious intent in his eyes.

"Mr. Younger, why are you here? Mr. Younger? What are these Rangers for, Mr. Younger?"

"Ma'am, we are here to see that no legislator who votes today is arrested by any federal agent or law enforcement official working for the Johnson administration."

"You won't allow any who voted for the referendum today to be arrested?"

Pops thought about spitting out some of his chew before he answered as he paused, but decided against it. "No, ma'am. Not here. Not on my watch."

"Mr. Levy."

"Remember Gov. Cooper. Yay."

"Mr. Marquez."

"Viva Tejas! Yay!"

"Mr. McDaniels."

"The faith of the people of Texas stands pledged to the preservation of a republican form of government and, subject to this limitation only, they have at all times the inalienable right to alter, reform or abolish their government in such manner as they may think expedient. I vote yay for Texas, Mr. Speaker."

"Mr. Oswald."

"Give the people of Texas the right to decide themselves! Yay, Mr. Speaker!"

The roll call continued and, at one point, went through thirty-one straight voting for the referendum. Most expected the state senate would rubber-stamp the outcome of the vote, especially if it was in favor of the referendum. The Texas Senate was calmly waiting in its chamber to immediately take their vote if the referendum passed. If it passed both bodies, it would be fast-tracked and on the governor's desk to sign by early evening.

Any drama about the outcome began to fade as the pro-independence votes continued to dominate. Before the Speaker could confirm the outcome, the news had already spread like wildfire.

"The Texas House has voted to send a secession referendum by a vote of 112-38 to voters despite President Johnson's threat to indict them for treason!" read the headlines as they scrolled across the marquee in Times Square. "President Johnson has not issued a statement at this time," it continued. "The Texas Senate is taking up the measure in one hour. A total of seventeen Democrats voted in favor of the referendum."

The vote in the Texas Senate was quick. With the new lieutenant governor presiding, the referendum passed 21-10 with two Democrats voting in favor. All that was needed now was the governor's signature.

The governor's office was packed with news cameras and crews drawn randomly from the pool of reporters. He was flanked by Pops Younger and the leadership of the Texas Legislature. Also standing behind him were Chuck Dixon, Stan Mumford's widow and the sheriff from Llano County, home of the Swingin' T Ranch.

"Under the unlawful threat of arrest for trumped-up federal treason charges, this Texas Legislature has voted to send a referendum to the voters of Texas to which I will gladly affix my signature as the Governor of Texas," announced the governor.

"This referendum is a direct result of the same type of gestapo tactics this administration has used to continue its blatant flouting of the United States Constitution. Like in any democratic society, Texans should be allowed to vote their conscience and, if this is truly a government for the people and by the people, this administration should not have any quarrel with Texans' right of self-determination.

"I am so proud of the men and women in the Legislature who, despite these unlawful federal threats, found the duty to their fellow Texans and Texas freedom to be more important than the threats to their own personal freedom from the attorney general of the United States and this president.

"Our governor and first lady were murdered, as was our lieutenant governor, by this administration. This administration elicited help from a foreign government to invade Texas and kill Texans. This administration has enacted economic sanctions on our state by executive order. This administration has sought to do economic harm to Texas via banking, shipping and interstate commerce. It has halted federal payments for those who have earned those payments via contributions to Social Security or veterans' benefits from their military service. It has sanctioned the IRS to terrorize independent Texas businesses and those whose political beliefs differ from the administration. This president has violated our sacred Second Amendment rights and overstepped his constitutional authority," said the governor angrily.

"Meanwhile, this Congress has remained mostly silent and wholly inept. Despite clear indications of crimes within the administration, this Congress has done nothing to protect Americans but, more importantly, has allowed the federal government to run roughshod over their brethren in Texas.

"If this referendum is what it takes for the rest of America to wake up, so be it. My message to America is this: Texas is tired of waiting!" exclaimed the governor, pointing his finger forward as if lecturing the rest of America.

"To be clear, this referendum is a straight-up vote, yes or no, to be given the opportunity for the citizens of Texas to negotiate its independence from these United States. It is not a declaration of war as the media has portrayed. It simply allows those of us in state government to negotiate a peaceful separation if the people of Texas want independence. Once the terms of this separation are finalized, the citizens will once again have the right to vote it up or down. This is how a civilized society operates, folks.

"Before I sign this historic document, I would like to make an appeal to this president and his administration." He paused, then continued.

"Mr. President, we have heard your threats and your saber-rattling about what could happen should this vote pass. Throughout history, it has been proven over and over again that further bloodshed is only a temporary solution to the final will of a people who demand independence on their own terms.

"I have no prediction at this time how Texans will vote; however, as in any free society, we reserve the right to be governed by the people. If the people of Texas vote to seek independence, I implore you to listen."

Then the governor shocked everyone, including those standing beside him.

"Mr. President and my fellow Americans, I will delay signing this bill for twenty-four hours. During the next twenty-four hours, I will allow the rest of America and Congress to do the right thing." Again, the governor paused.

The looks on the faces behind the governor's desk said everything. They were shocked that the signature by the governor was not automatic, or that there were conditions on which he would sign.

"Congress has failed to act to preserve our sacred Constitution. I will veto this bill under one of two conditions. Either the president and his entire cabinet resign immediately, or Congress convenes in the next twenty-four hours and votes to impeach this president and assign a special independent prosecutor to investigate the attorney general, the Justice Department and Homeland Security for roles they played in the events over the last months in Texas that resulted in numerous deaths, including the deaths of Texas state officials."

The buzz in the room was growing, and it was evident the governor had a plan of his own. Was it something that just popped into his head, or was there an underlying strategy? Those who knew Brahman knew he rarely acted spontaneously.

The world would have to wait another twenty-four hours to see if a sitting governor could call for the resignation of a United States president, or force the United States Congress to begin impeachment proceedings against a sitting president. The odds were against it, and the governor was prepared to sign the bill that would call for a special election referendum where Texans, for the first time since 1860, would vote to leave or stay in the United States.

# CHAPTER 43

*"I hold it, that a little rebellion, now and then, is a good thing, and as necessary in the political world as storms in the physical. Unsuccessful rebellions, indeed, generally establish the encroachments on the rights of the people, which produced them. An observation of this truth should render honest republican governors so mild in their punishment of rebellions as not to discourage them too much. It is a medicine necessary for the sound health of government."*

*~ Thomas Jefferson (1743-1826)*
*Founding Father*
*American Revolution Hero*
*Author of the Declaration of Independence*
*3rd U.S. President*

Another damned cowboy! I'll give these Texans credit. They definitely have a flair for the dramatic. It's time to finally put our foot on their throats," said President Johnson as he sat alone in the Oval Office with Avery Smith, watching the events from Austin on live TV.

"The GOP has scheduled a news conference for first thing tomorrow, Mr. President."

"Any chance they have the votes this time?" Johnson asked Smith, referring to another run at impeachment.

"We are making calls, applying pressure. Right now, Mr. President, I would say they don't."

"Jamail wants arrests ahead of the referendum vote. What do you think?" asked the president.

"I think it would send a message, but we don't want some kind of armed confrontation again at this point. I think we take whatever opportunity we can to send a message to the rest of the voters in Texas that we are serious about the treason charges."

The president sat silently, thinking with his chin in his left hand. He loosened his tie, and propped his feet up on the famous desk. "Grab who we can and make a public spectacle out of them."

"That should be easy enough. Who do you want? A state senator, a state rep, or an election commission official?" asked Smith.

"Any of those folks would be easy enough, right? I mean those guys aren't going to have security details, correct?

"I doubt it. I'll send the word. I'm sure Tibbs will be happy to hear this."

Smith stood up from his chair facing the president's desk, running his fingers through his sparse hair strands to comb over his mostly bald head. As customary for him, he looked like he had slept in his suit and had a couple of stains on his plaid tie.

"Sir, we need to discuss what happens if the vote goes south on us. I think you should consider that it's conceivable that the vote passes, even though the polling is within the margin of error right now."

"I want to respond to the governor's demand first, Avery. Can we craft a statement to release?"

"Sure, Mr. President, but we need to determine what definitive actions we are going to recommend to your cabinet if the vote passes."

"We will do what Lincoln did," Johnson stated flatly.

"I agree, sir. They have gone too far. If the vote passes, it will be time to take the necessary steps. History will judge you positively for doing what you had to do to rein in a treasonous state and, like Lincoln, save the Union."

Within an hour of their meeting, the White House released a statement to the press:

"The governor of Texas believes he can dictate to this administration, to Congress and to the American people his narrow view of the future of Texas. America will not be held hostage by an outlaw extremist right-wing governor, a governor who holds his office by appointment of the legislature and not by an election by the people of Texas.

"If, in fact, the secession referendum is put to the voters of Texas, the Justice Department is prepared to act against those who perpetrate treasonous crimes against America. The results of this referendum will not be recognized by the United States or, for that matter, any civilized society.

"The president and this administration, as well as the American people, urge the state leaders of Texas to come to their senses and sit down to work through our differences.

"We are committed to the Union of States and any unlawful attempt to separate or secede will be met with the full capabilities and resources of the United States. It would be a mistake for the governor, state legislature and those sympathetic to their intent to secede, to underestimate our perseverance in this matter."

The national GOP leadership was in total disarray. They knew they could not muster the necessary votes for impeachment. Numerous establishment Republicans did not have the stomach for impeachment or the swing votes from the Democrats.

The Texas GOP caucuses in the House and Senate were formidable and were the backbone of the conservative movement, including Tea Party representation in Washington. If Texas was lost, the blow to the national GOP would be severe, and likely fatal for the party. The Democrats had cranked up their propaganda machine to link the Texans to the GOP "radical extreme right wing."

Time was running out on the governor's ultimatum. A pending referendum on Texas separation looked increasingly likely.

Less than twenty-four hours after the governor's statement, attempts by Texas congressional members to start a vote on impeachment, which would then be tried by the Senate, failed in two attempts from the floor.

The majority Speaker of the House took the podium in the House chamber: "There will be no impeachment vote on the floor of the House against this president. The motion fails."

Attempts to appoint a special prosecutor to investigate crimes by the administration also went nowhere.

When news of the failure on the House floor reached the governor, he didn't flinch. Knowing that another vote would not reach the floor and that the president had no intention of resigning, the governor offered zero hesitation. Without any fanfare, he signed HB 1836 calling for a statewide referendum to vote on Texas independence.

It was now up to the people of Texas. Would the administration wait for the outcome before acting further, or would they take immediate action?

Would Texans show up and vote despite the risks and, for that matter, would election officials defy the president's warning and actually conduct the special election?

At least three major news organizations were reporting the U.S. military was mobilizing in New Mexico, Louisiana, Arkansas and the Gulf of Mexico.

The mayor of San Antonio announced he would send city police officers to shut down any polling places in the city limits. He was followed by the same type of announcement from the Houston and Austin police chiefs.

CBS News reported from a rural Wal-Mart in East Texas as the segment was reporting that Texans had begun a run on food stock staples, generators, ammunition, and even guns.

The reporter stated, "It appears that Texans are preparing for some type of event. Other than the guns and ammunition, this is the same scene we see when there is a major hurricane in the Gulf threatening the Texas coast. The only difference is it seems ammunition and firearms appear to top their lists that would normally include bottled water, flashlights, batteries and toilet paper!"

*"The strength and power of despotism consists wholly in the fear of resistance."*

~ *Thomas Paine*
*Author & American Revolution Hero*
*Published "Common Sense,"*
*Sparking the American Revolution*

D allas-based federal FBI agents arrived at the home of Texas State Rep. Daniel Barborosa in Waxahachie, southwest of Dallas. Three black SUVs pulled up in front of the small brick home. Armed agents in full tactical gear poured out of every door of the vehicles. Once some of the agents were positioned in back of the house, the rest of the group began beating on the front door.

"Rep. Barborosa, this is James Henry of the FBI. We have a warrant for your arrest. Come out now with your hands up!"

A voice came from behind the door. "Who signed the warrant?"

"Federal Judge Belinda Mastert! Come out now, sir, or we will have to enter. I'm sure you don't want to put your family through this."

"What is the arrest warrant for?"

"Treason!"

"Mr. Barborosa, you..."

The same voice responded, "This is not Rep. Barborosa, sir. This is Bart Simmons, Texas Ranger. You are to vacate these premises immediately."

By orders of Gov. Brahman, each state senator and state representative who cast a vote for the statewide referendum was assigned a Texas Ranger, just in case Tibbs tried something exactly like this. Since there were only one-hundred forty-four Rangers in total, some representatives were staying in each other's homes to make sure they were all protected.

Surprised and taken aback, the lead FBI agent radioed back to headquarters in Dallas that the representative had a Texas Ranger in his house guarding him.

The orders from Justice were clear. They wanted a prop, a token or symbol to show they were serious about the treason charges ahead of the statewide ballot to discourage Texans from participating in the referendum.

"Mr. Texas Ranger, you are outnumbered. We have more than a dozen officers out here. Throw your weapons down now and send Barborosa out here with his hands up."

"Ain't happening, sir," said Simmons with authority.

"Like I said, there are more than a dozen of us out here. You're outnumbered. Surrender now."

"I'd say the odds are about even then."

The lead agent motioned for his men to bring up the tactical heavy black door ram shaped like a tube with handles used by two officers to batter a door off its hinges with one strike.

"Mr. FBI man, if you bring that thing any closer to this house, your people are going to die tonight."

Bam! The FBI hit the door once, then twice, knocking the door inward while those behind the ram trained their guns on the entrance.

A hail of bullets came out of the house, immediately dropping two federal agents in the doorway. Agents in the back yard broke a sliding glass door and entered from the rear.

"Agent down! Agent down!" came over the agents' radios.

Suddenly the quiet residential street became a war zone as the FBI agents used automatic weapons to unload their clips into the house from the front and back yards. Several concussion grenades were launched into the home, along with tear gas.

When all the smoke settled, two FBI agents lay dead. Inside the home, both the Texas Ranger and Rep. Barborosa were down in the small living room, riddled by multiple gunshot wounds each, soaking the carpet in blood.

"Headquarters, we have two agents down. Request backup and ambulance immediately!"

"Where is the state legislator? Did you get Barborosa?"

"Negative, sir, he received return fire and appears to be dead. So is the Ranger."

"The Ranger? What Ranger?"

"Sir, there was a Texas Ranger in here with him. They fired first, sir. We just returned fire. It does not appear there is anyone else in the house; we just cleared it."

"Does the politician have a gun? Are other law enforcement officers on the scene?"

"No, sir, not so far, but I imagine we will see them soon."

"Agent, walk outside and get on a secure line now!" commanded Regional FBI Deputy Director Lee Cabot.

The agent walked around the garage and out of sight from his fellow agents securing the crime scene.

"I want you to make sure that politician was armed. Do you understand me?"

"But, sir…"

"Agent! Did you hear my orders?" yelled the director.

"Well, yes, sir, but where…?"

"Damn it, son! I am ordering you to make sure both those men have weapons. Do you fully understand me or do you need me to spell this out?"

"Yes, sir. But I don't know where we will get…"

"Agent Henry, I can promise you a crap storm you won't survive if that politician doesn't have a weapon with his prints on it near his body before the local police show up. Now, do I make myself clear?"

"Crystal clear, sir."

Eight minutes later, sheriff's deputies and Waxahachie police were on the scene.

Lead Agent Henry began explaining to the sheriff's deputies what had happened.

"We were here to serve a federal arrest warrant. We fully identified ourselves and gave them the opportunity to exit the home. They wouldn't come out. They shot at us as we tried to enter. They took out two of our agents and we had no choice."

"Did they both fire at your men?" asked a skeptical sheriff's deputy.

"Yes, both of them. Looks like Barborosa had a .38 revolver." He pointed to a gun lying next to Barborosa's body.

"Breaking news!" came the interruption on the local Dallas Fox affiliate television station. "Federal agents have raided a home in Waxahachie belonging to State Rep. Daniel Barborosa. Initial reports indicate there are four fatalities on the scene, including Rep. Barborosa."

This bombshell began to spread worldwide. It was obvious to anyone with half a brain what had happened. The Johnson administration's threat to arrest Texas legislators for treason took another ugly turn.

The administration immediately made a statement that the deaths were unnecessary and were caused by Rep. Barborosa and Ranger Simmons, further proof of Texas officials' hostility to federal agents simply trying to do their jobs. Reports surfaced that Barborosa had a revolver in his hands at the scene.

That fact was argued vehemently by Barborosa's distraught wife on air, who claimed her husband never owned a gun, never a shot a gun in his life, and wouldn't know how to use one if he was handed one. The government did not say who the gun was registered to. The wife was believable and public sentiment against the administration began growing, even outside of Texas.

An enraged Gov. Brahman held a hastily called press conference. "Once again, this administration has murdered an elected state official and a Texas Ranger. Rep. Barborosa's crime? He cast a vote in his capacity as a freely elected state legislator to provide Texas voters a special election referendum. This president has determined that he is judge, jury and executioner, calling that most basic democratic right treason!" said a disgusted Brahman.

"America, it's time to wake up. You won't impeach this clown. You won't indict this criminal attorney general. I am embarrassed for America. I am sad but ticked off that Americans have let their country deteriorate to the point that the federal government can perpetrate these types of crimes and that people are more concerned over the score of Monday Night Football than the tyranny that exists," spat Brahman.

# CHAPTER 45

*"Congress has no power to disarm the militia. Their swords, and every other terrible implement of the soldier, are the birth-right of an American... the unlimited power of the sword is not in the hands of either the federal or state governments, but, where I trust in God it will ever remain, in the hands of the people."*

*~Tench Coxe (1755-1824)*
*Delegate to the Continental Congress*
*American Political Economist*
*Patriot*

Throughout a twenty-four hour period, various local law enforcement officials and federal agents made attempts to arrest more than two dozen state legislators. The result was zero successful arrests and four federal agents killed. President Johnson failed to get his symbolic treasonous *trophy* to present to the world ahead of the election.

Newfound outrage was beginning to be openly discussed on every level in the media, but was nothing compared to the rage in Texas that, already simmering, began to boil over. The administration now feared they were losing their grip on the entire narrative of the Texas crisis.

"What are our options, Avery?" asked the president to a small gathering of his most trusted cabinet members.

"Honestly, Mr. President, we are seeing the very beginning of a loss of our public relations advantage here. I apologize for recommending this course of action, but damn, we couldn't even get one of these jokers?" asked Smith, looking directly at Jamail Tibbs.

"Pops Younger," said Tibbs.

"What?" Smith asked.

"That damned old wily cowboy. He somehow knew *exactly* what we would do, and he put his people in place," said Tibbs.

"This seems to be a recurring theme," said Anna Bartlett sarcastically, never missing an opportunity to get a dig in on the attorney general.

"We have four days, Mr. President. It is going to require swift and extreme measures at this point. Those sons of bitches just don't get it," quipped Tibbs.

"I'm all ears, Jamail," said the president, resigned to the fact he needed a broad spectrum of ideas here. He was running out of time and all indications were this was going to be a close vote, even before the arrest attempts. It may have been just enough for Texans to dig in their heels and conduct the vote. Even worse, it increasingly looked like the referendum could pass.

"Well, let's suppose they have the vote and it passes. What would we do then?" Smith asked.

"We would have to intervene, militarily if necessary," answered Johnson.

"Exactly. So, if we think the vote would carry, then why wait?" asked Tibbs.

"He's got a point, sir," added Smith, nodding agreement.

"Gentlemen, we are talking about launching a military strike into one of our very own states, *against* fellow Americans. I can't imagine this is the corner we are backed into and that this would be our only solution," reasoned Bartlett.

"Anna, you have been to Texas during the crisis. What is your solution?" asked the president.

"Continue to negotiate."

"Negotiate?" yelled Tibbs. "They have a vote to secede from the United States in four days! If we *prevent* the vote from happening, nobody will *ever* know if the vote would have passed and we can make the argument until kingdom come that it would *never* have passed!"

The room was silent for more than twenty seconds as they all pondered Tibbs' reasoning.

"I think the debate takes a completely different turn if the vote is allowed to proceed. Jamail is right. The more I think about it, the more options his strategy gives us," said Smith.

"I just cannot believe this is our chosen course! Are we really talking about a full-scale military invasion of Texas?" asked Bartlett.

"Anna, do you want to excuse yourself for reasons of *plausible deniability?*" asked the president, referring to Bartlett's well-known intentions for the Democratic nomination for president during the next election cycle. She was the early frontrunner from either party.

Bartlett had to think for a minute. If this was successful, she should want to be part of it. Pausing for just a few moments, her political instincts kicked in. Everything Tibbs seemed to touch became an unmitigated disaster for one reason or another. She wasn't about to put what she felt was a shoe-in for being elected the first female president in the hands of Tibbs.

"Mr. President, I sincerely appreciate your concern. I believe I will take you up on your suggestion. Gentlemen, I wish you great success in your decision to end this crisis." She stood up, straightened her frumpy purple dress and calmly walked out of the Oval Office without hesitation.

As she closed the door behind her, Smith remarked, "That is one political warhorse, gentlemen. Mr. President, I'll never know how you beat her in the primary," he laughed.

"I had you, Avery. I simply had you and she didn't. Did I also mention I was black?" chuckled the president.

Tibbs wasn't much for small talk.

"The first thing we do is implement martial law."

"Jamail, you know we don't have enough sympathetic law enforcement presence there to make that very effective."

"It will serve its purpose. It will put common folks on notice and it will give us the legal authority to do what we need to do when our troops arrive," stated Tibbs.

"Jamail, you've obviously been thinking about this for a while," commented the president with a knowing grin.

"Sir, it would be the pinnacle of my career as your attorney general to rein in these treasonous bastards."

"Let's all be clear here. The strategy would be an all-in effort to take the State House in Austin, while controlling the message all along the way," said Johnson. "We simply cannot let the vote move forward. Avery, I want an immediate meeting with Homeland Security and the Joint Chiefs. How quickly can this be called?"

"Mr. President, we can have this convened in an hour, maybe two at the most," answered Smith.

"Mr. President, no disrespect regarding past decisions, but I am so happy to hear you say you are going to pursue this course of action," said Tibbs. "I personally think we should have done this quite a while ago, but I'm ecstatic that you both believe as I do that it's time to decimate the traitors in Austin."

Two-and-a-half hours later, the administration and the Joint Chiefs were in the situation room in the White House planning their strategy to prevent the Texas referendum from being rolled out to voters and to replace state government in Texas, *by any means necessary.*

# CHAPTER 46

*"I've heard over and over that people are afraid to tell their stories, but know this, my experience at the hands of this government the last five years have made me more determined than ever before to stand before you and all Americans and say, I will not retreat, I will not surrender, I will not be intimidated, I will not ask for permission to exercise my constitutional rights."*

~ Catherine Engelbrecht
*Founder of True the Vote & King Street Patriots*
*Testimony before House Committee on IRS*
*Targeting 2014*
*American Tea Party Hero*

In the months that preceded the American Revolution, the colonists could be generally described as belonging to three different political categories. They were either loyalists to King George III, completely indifferent, being pre-occupied with their responsibilities with their families, farms or shops; or they were adamantly in favor of independence. It has been estimated that less than two percent of the American colonists actually picked up a musket and participated in the American Revolution.

This was also true of the fight for Texas Independence in 1836. Texas historical record confirms roughly 2,100 Texas patriots actually took part in actual battles for independence that led to the Republic of Texas. Texas independence was forged from huge historical events that generally emanated from relatively small numbers of freedom fighters and patriots.

Less than one hundred fifty farmers and townspeople formed a militia, determined to keep their small cannon to ward off Indian attacks, openly defying Mexico's order to give up the cannon to Mexican dragoons. This action lit the fuse at the Battle of Gonzales, igniting the Texas revolution against Santa Anna. The first attempt at centralized government gun control in Texas failed miserably.

One hundred eighty-four courageous Texians were determined to buy time for Sam Houston. Time was needed for Houston to recruit and train troops and for the provisional government to be formed. Under twenty-six year-old Col. William Barrett Travis, these brave patriots bought thirteen precious days with their blood against more than four thousand Mexican troops and ultimately died heroically at the little mission in Bexar, forever known as the Alamo.

Three hundred three Texian volunteers captured at Fort Defiance were massacred on direct orders from Santa Anna in the Goliad Massacre.

Sam Houston led roughly 900 men in the Battle of San Jacinto and surprisingly defeated Santa Anna, his men yelling, "Remember the Alamo" and "Remember Goliad," and routing the Mexicans. This decisive twenty-minute victory is still studied in military academies worldwide and, to date, the results still represent the largest land mass transfer in world history as a result of a single battle, opening the door for eventual U.S. expansion in the southwest all the way to and including California.

There comes a time in all historic struggles for independence where a decision has to made at the individual level. Neighbors challenged neighbors on where they stood. If you stood on the side of independence and divulged that to a loyalist, you and your entire family could be hanged as treasonous traitors to King George III or Generalissimo Antonio Lopez de Santa Anna. On the other hand, if you were sympathetic to the redcoats, you were a "Tory." Many tried unsuccessfully to straddle the fence. That decision was not only life-changing, but life-threatening. Too many found out that to remain neutral, isolated, uninvolved or indifferent landed the conflict right at the doorstep of their homesteads.

As Santa Anna entered Texas with 6,000 battle-hardened Mexican Regulars determined to put down the rebellious Texians, colonists, farmers and merchants fled in the Runaway Scrape, in many cases leaving their evening supper still simmering in the kettle in the fireplace.

They knew the tyrannical Mexican ruler Santa Anna was ruthless. Who would stay and stand? Who would put their businesses, farms, ranches, and lives on the line for the principles of freedom, liberty and self-determination?

There was no hedging of your bets. If a Texian or American colonist chose freedom, it was win, or die.

With less than forty-eight hours before the election, the president was once again on prime time television from the Oval Office.

"Good evening, my fellow Americans," began the president. "I am sad to report to the country that the situation in Texas dictates further federal action from this administration. Under consultation with the United States Congress, I am hereby invoking my Constitutional authority and am announcing that, beginning at 6:00 a.m. Eastern Time tomorrow morning, the State of Texas will hereby be under martial law," he said grimly.

"The referendum authorized by the state legislature of Texas and signed by Texas Gov. Brahman to offer a vote on secession from the United States is unconstitutional and is, in fact, treasonous. Therefore, we are placing the state under martial law in order to prevent this unlawful act, and to replace state officials with federal government appointees until such a time where free and democratic elections can once again occur in Texas."

The president turned slightly to the left to read from the other teleprompter. "Local law enforcement officials will be assisted by the U.S. military in enforcing martial law. Under my authority, by executive order, I am officially declaring the scheduled secession referendum vote null and void. We have come too far in this country to allow a few extremists in state government to jeopardize this Union," said the president flatly.

"Let me assure the American people, especially those in Texas, that neither my administration, nor the congressional leaders we consulted, took the issue of declaring martial law lightly. The bloodshed, looting of federal buildings and occupation of military bases in Texas has tested my patience and that of fellow Americans, and it is simply time for it to end. And, let me assure you, it will end.

"Under martial law, I have signed the following executive orders to be implemented immediately by local law enforcement, various branches of the U.S. military and DHS, the FBI and ATF:

"First, there will be an eight o'clock curfew in all major Texas cities where residents will be required to be in their homes and off the streets and highways.

"Next, any persons in the act of organizing a polling place for the illegal referendum will be immediately arrested, as will any citizens who participate in the election for any polling places that manage to open illegally.

"Next, all firearms and ammunition sales in Texas are immediately halted and retail outlets are being instructed to remove any ammunition currently on store shelves. Selling, transferring, transporting or purchasing a firearm or ammunition while martial law is in effect will be treated as a felony.

"Federal employees are encouraged to show up for work as normal and are exempt from curfew with proper identification and if their jobs require them to be on the road past eight p.m.

"State officials who cast a vote in favor of the secession referendum will be required to turn themselves in to local law enforcement or federal officials.

"The governor of Texas, lieutenant governor, speaker of the house, attorney general, commander of the Texas Guard, commander of the Texas Department of Public Safety and commander of the Texas Rangers are hereby relieved of duty.

"Our objective during this period is to diffuse any potentially volatile situations and ensure public safety while we bring Texas back into the American community. To do this, some steps that may seem strict will be necessary to ensure public safety during this process.

"Under the authority of the National Defense Authorization Act and the Patriot Act, local law enforcement officials will work with reassigned federal workers and volunteers to assist those in Texas with temporarily turning in their firearms."

President Johnson furrowed his brow and now seemed even more serious as he stated, "Now, Americans know I am an avid Second Amendment supporter. We consider this an emergency situation and, in consulting with Congress, we believe this is a serious public safety issue. Citizens can voluntarily report to local law enforcement officials to turn in their firearms where they will be documented, recorded and stored with local law enforcement until the crisis is over and martial law has been rescinded. At that time, the firearms will be returned to their respective owners who have proper documentation."

Johnson continued. "During this time, I have dispatched U.S. Army and National Guard troops to be stationed at federal government buildings and installations including courthouses, IRS offices, post offices, VA hospitals, FBI offices and wherever local law enforcement asks us for assistance.

"While martial law is in effect, we ask that all citizens cooperate with federal authorities and local law enforcement. Right now, I cannot tell you how long martial law will remain in place, but you have my assurance it will not remain a single minute longer than necessary to return Texas to the community of American states. I am sure all Texans will be happy for their lives to return to normal as soon as possible."

Pausing again, the president attempted a reassuring tone as he continued. "The rest of America has watched this crisis over the last few months and has been saddened by your hardships. You deserve better from your leaders in Austin, and my administration and this Congress are committed to restoring state government in Texas to one dedicated to the interests of all Texans and not the extremist fringe it served in the past. Today is the first day in the restoration of an American Texas!"

# CHAPTER 47

*"Those who make peaceful revolution impossible will make violent revolution inevitable."*

~ *John F. Kennedy*
*35th President of the United States*

President Johnson's proclamation of martial law and the suspension of the referendum vote was a punch in the gut to many in the Texas Legislature, state, county and local government officials.

Johnson had clearly drawn the line. Decisions made forward by Texans statewide would be life-altering. During the next twelve hours, state politicians and election officials were in complete disarray. Although the threats by the administration were always hovering over Texas, this announcement was a clear threat that Johnson would use any and all means necessary to whip Texas into submission.

Christy Dixon sat in her small living room with her son watching President Johnson deliver his message to Texas and the country. The Dixons had literally been on the run since the events at Ellington Field, where the Texas Rangers rescued her husband, Chuck. The ATF had destroyed their home and the administration had an active federal arrest warrant out for Chuck.

Christy thought how much the life of her family had changed since Chuck became deeply involved in the Tea Party. They once lived in a comfortable home, Chuck had a very nice business and life was very much above average for the Dixons with many dreams for the future.

Christy sat on the edge of the couch with her hands clasped together, watching the president's message with a look of seriousness that didn't go unnoticed by Colton. He could see the instant fear and trepidation that came over her and the small tear that rolled down her cheek.

Chuck was away, meeting with fellow Tea Party members from across the state. He traveled away from his family now more than ever as the wheels of the Texas crisis had reached an accelerated level.

"Mom, what does this mean? Is dad in danger?" asked Colton.

Christy had to gather herself for a moment to wipe tears from her face. She knew she had to be strong for Colton.

"Colton, your dad is very strong. He is a hero to many people and he is a hero to you and me. Dad is doing what he thinks is the right thing for us as a family."

"But Mr. Mumford..."

"Colton, your dad is going to be fine. We are going to be fine," she repeated, trying to reassure Colton as he remembered all too well the friend of the family who was shot in the street in front of his family by federal agents.

Colton, traumatized by the Waco-style raid that destroyed their home while his dad was taken away in chains by the ATF, still had nightmares about that day.

After reassuring her son, she hugged him, kissed him on the forehead and sent him to bed.

Christy sat on a small chair in the bathroom in front of the mirror removing her make-up when she burst into tears while she held a hand towel to her nose and mouth, hoping Colton couldn't hear her.

She looked at her phone to see if Chuck had texted or tried to call her, but he hadn't since an hour before the president's address.

Christy was a strong woman. She had always unabashedly backed and supported her husband, but she remembered the words spoken to her husband early in the Tea Party days by a business associate of Chuck's that said he believed in the Tea Party principles but couldn't join.

"Don't think the federal government doesn't have an enemies list, Chuck," he told them both. "People in power will do whatever is necessary to keep their power. Do not underestimate the lengths people will go to when they try to maintain the status quo."

Their friend had politely declined to participate in any Tea Party event.

There was one quote in particular that had really stuck with her and, during some of the darkest hours of the Texas crisis, especially when Chuck was being held at an undetermined location, this quote had always come back to her.

"If you approach a traffic light that is green and you look to your left and a car is coming through their light that is red, do you continue through the green light or do you stop? You are in the right; your light is green. Do you continue on through the light, even though the driver to your left is obviously not going to stop and is going to ignore the law? Of course you don't. You avoid the accident, Chuck. What you and Christy are proposing is to drive through the green light anyway simply because you are right. The problem is, you may be right, but you will be dead right!"

Christy had never let the thoughts of questioning the principles in which their family stood enter her mind as she fought them back during Chuck's arrest. But now, they were back again.

The president's message terrified her. Chuck had become a symbolic and central figure in the entire saga of the crisis. Now, more than ever, it appeared her family was in serious danger. Then the phone rang. She picked it up with some apprehension and answered, "Hello?"

"Hey, baby," said Chuck.

"Hey, honey," she responded, trying to hide the fact that she had been literally sobbing in a towel as she wiped tears from her face and her dark blonde hair wet from tears.

"Did you see Johnson?" he asked.

"Yes, Chuck, and I've got to tell you, I'm really scared. Scared for you and scared for us."

"Christy, we have a plan, babe. Johnson has really shown his hand to the rest of the world. I have to believe God has a plan for us in this. Yes, it's serious, but we've come this far."

"Chuck, they're not messing around now."

"Honey, they never were. This is forcing Texans into a corner. If this doesn't unite us all, then it is really over and we will find another place to live. Have faith, babe."

"I'm trying, Chuck, I'm really trying."

"I know you are, and I love you for it," said Chuck, holding his own tears back now.

"What happens next?" she asked.

"Too much for the phone, babe. I'll tell you in person. I'll be home in about three hours."

"Chuck, please, please be safe," Christy pleaded.

"These are perilous but exciting times, babe. What we are going through now, other families during the American Revolution must have felt," answered Chuck, trying to lighten her burden.

"I'm glad you think this is fun," Christy said sarcastically, but with a smile on her face.

"If this doesn't wake people up, nothing will."

"God, I hope so," said Christy.

"How's my boy?"

"He watched Johnson tonight, too. He's pretty smart, Chuck. But he's scared, too."

"Stay strong, babe. Stay strong for him."

"I really need you, Chuck. Please come home."

"On my way, sweetheart. On my way!"

# CHAPTER 48

*"Violence, naked force, has settled more issues in history than has any other factor and the contrary opinion is wishful thinking at its worst. Nations and peoples who forget this basic truth have always paid for it with their lives and freedoms."*

~ *Robert E. Heinlein (1907-1988)*
*American Author*

Fox News began the day before the election with the report that sympathetic volunteer militia groups were pouring into Texas via unconventional routes not guarded by federal troops. Organized militia groups were reported from Missouri, Alabama, Georgia, South Carolina and Idaho. Fox interviewed a two-hundred member group that came in across the Red River from Missouri.

"We're sick and tired of this criminal administration, the federal overreach and especially the tyranny our friends in Texas are suffering. We are here to help in any way we can, including keeping those polls open."

The Fox reporter asked, "Will you raise arms against the feds?"

"Ma'am, we aren't here looking for a fight. But, at the same time, we aren't going to back down from the feds," answered one militia member.

"Will you use your weapons against the federal agents or the U.S. military?" she repeated.

"Let's just put it this way, the same way the president answered. All options are on the table," he said with a big grin.

In other U.S. cities, protesters critical of Texas and calling for an end to the crisis were taking to the streets in Los Angeles, Chicago, Detroit, Hartford and New York, mostly organized by far left wing organizations and unions aligned with the Democratic Party.

Gov. Brahman announced a news conference for 6:00 p.m. that was going to be broadcast worldwide on live television, seemingly to respond to the president's latest words and to tell the world whether Texas intended to go forward with an Independence referendum ballot despite threats from the administration.

Chuck Dixon desperately tried to get through to the governor's office all morning, finally speaking with the lieutenant governor at 11:00 a.m.

Chuck came out of the bedroom after the thirty-minute call and Christy could tell he was very deep in thought.

"Babe, it's time for us to implement the emergency plan we put in place. The governor is convinced the vote is still going forward. We are likely to have armed confrontation if Johnson makes good on his promises."

Christy measured her words carefully before responding. Again, the doubt began to creep in, but she fought it off.

"Okay, I'll pack now. When should Colton and I leave?"

"As soon as you're packed. We don't know when or how Johnson will move so we can't take any chances. I have just alerted the militia network and we will start implementing our plans in the next two hours. I need you to get out of Houston, babe," he said, referring to a pre-arranged rural safe house that was essentially off the grid.

Over the next two hours, those tied in with various Tea Party groups, volunteer militias, constitutional organizations and even some churches began mass migrations out of the major suburban areas.

By noon, reports were surfacing that a line of two hundred DHS armored vehicles, apparently poised to march into Texas, stopped at the checkpoint on Interstate 10 on the Texas-Louisiana border and the barricades had been removed. The checkpoint was less than two hours from Houston.

Chuck had gotten Christy and Colton off and on their way to a secluded spot in west Texas. Next he loaded prepared duffle bags and various other items into his truck from the garage and headed just west of Houston for the rendezvous point in the rice fields.

Chuck's heart dropped momentarily when he got within three miles of the chosen meeting place.

"What the hell are all these cars and trucks here for?" was his immediate thought, thinking their cover had been blown and the meeting spot was no longer a secret, until he started noticing the people in the vehicles.

Many had camouflage on. Many had Texas flags flying from windows and from the backs of their trucks. Many were brandishing weapons.

"So much for the element of surprise," Chuck thought to himself, as the plan devised in case of this type of emergency was to catch the feds off-guard. "If the feds have satellites focused on this area, they will definitely see that something is up."

Impatient as he was waiting for the line to filter through the narrow ranch gate, Chuck went off-road through a trail adjacent to a large irrigation ditch to avoid the delay. Several vehicles, seeing him take this route, decided to follow and, before long, the rice fields had two lines of cars and trucks traversing the mud to get to the designated GPS coordinates in the rice field. Those who had never seen a rice field were in trouble when they tried to navigate anywhere but on the ranch road or irrigation ditch. They found themselves quickly wallowed in mud up to the bottom of their doors. Not to be deterred from their chosen path, they quickly abandoned their vehicles and jumped onto other trucks.

Finally, Chuck reached the designated clearing and was shocked at the turn-out. He estimated eight hundred to a thousand people were congregated at the meeting site.

Chuck's long-time friend Mitch Lansford was already standing on a makeshift platform erected on the back of a Ford pick-up truck with a bullhorn in his hand. Standing next to him was Zach Turner, the president of the oldest Texas independence organization—Free Texas Now!

"Ladies and gentlemen, we need to move quickly and decisively. May I have your attention? Please help me welcome up here Texas hero Chuck Dixon!"

The crowd began cheering wildly and waving Texas flags. Lansford motioned with his hands for the crowd to go silent but, to many, the chance to see Dixon in real life on the eve of a monumental event in Texas had the crowd too giddy for reason.

Turner climbed down off the platform to make room for Chuck. As soon as Chuck was handed the bullhorn, the crowd spontaneously broke into "Texas, Our Texas," the Texas state song. The crowd was stoked and apparently ready for whatever President Johnson threw at them.

Dixon, dressed in blue jeans, cowboy boots and a polo pullover, waited for the crowd to finish each chorus. When the crowd finally quieted, all one could hear were dozens of flags popping in the brisk wind whipping across the prairie.

"Ladies and gentlemen, thank you for being here today. I guess our primitive communication system does in fact work for now." The crowd broke into cheers again.

"I spoke to the governor's office this morning. Meetings like we are having here are happening all over Texas today. We have one charter, ladies and gentlemen. Our single purpose is to assure that Texans have a right to cast a ballot in tomorrow's referendum. Period. We will all do what is absolutely necessary to ensure each and every Texan who desires to exercise the right to vote in a free election, no matter if they are for or against the referendum," stated Dixon as he pointed his finger in the air while the crowd cheered again.

"Now, let me be perfectly clear. To the rest of the nation, this crowd looks like some kind of lynch mob or anarchists gone wild." The crowd laughed and cheered simultaneously.

"Each of you have county coordinators to report to, with a plan of action approved by the governor's office and the DPS. I am going to ask you to please follow the plan and do not deviate. The entire world is going to be watching to see if we pull this off. They are also going to be watching how the Johnson administration reacts. We need to conduct ourselves in a manner in which future Texans, your kids and grandkids, can be proud of." He smiled as the crowd cheered again.

"Now, it is clear you don't need any motivational speeches from me. I mean hell, you drove out here to the middle of nowhere and you're about to put your necks on the line for your fellow citizens and for the idea of a free Texas, unencumbered by a tyrannical despot in D.C. So, let's get to it. God bless Texas and Godspeed," He finished to cheers once again.

The crowd broke into small groups across the fields based on portable numbered banners that dotted the landscape. Everyone there was assigned to a particular number ahead of time. Several dozen militia members from other states showed up and met with Dixon after he was finished.

"Listen, we sincerely appreciate your help. The governor's office has asked us to communicate to ya'll that you'll be used as poll watchers and possibly to assist our law enforcement if the need arises. However, we could lose all credibility if any militia groups initiate contact with protestors or the feds without due cause, especially those of you from out of state," reasoned Dixon to a mix of groups from various states.

"We have a special liaison who will make your assignments and go over what our plan is to make sure this election happens. I would like to introduce Sheriff Alvarez. He will be your liaison to the governor's office and the Texas Rangers. Again, we thank you for your help."

An hour later, the last pick-up truck pulled out of the ranch gate onto the farm-to-market road. All across Texas, similar gatherings were wrapping up.

An hour before Gov. Brahman's live press conference, reports were coming in that international poll watchers had been detained at various Texas border checkpoints by the feds. The feds had no intention of allowing the special election to move forward and was turning back any independent monitoring groups.

At 6:00 p.m., news channels from around the world focused on the south steps of the Texas capitol building.

Flanked by legislators, Texas Rangers, and other state government officials, Gov. Brahman stepped to the microphone. "The Texas Legislature, legally called into special session by the governor of Texas, passed a special election referendum that will go to the voters tomorrow as planned," said the governor matter-of-factly.

"Despite the president's claims, make no mistake; this scheduled election is correct under the Texas Constitution of 1876 and it is correct under the U.S. Constitution. This referendum is intended to voice the will of the people of Texas. If passed, it authorizes the state of Texas to begin dialogue with the United States for Texas independence. The terms of any such separation would then be voted on once again," stated Brahman.

"This administration has systematically rained tyranny and terror upon the people of Texas. President Johnson and his minions, especially with the complicit crimes of the Justice Department under Atty. Gen. Jamail Tibbs, have denied Texans due process and have violated the First, Second, Fourth and Tenth Amendments to the Constitution.

"The United States government, with very little protest from Congress, has launched paramilitary raids into Texas that have resulted in the death of our governor, first lady, lieutenant governor, the major general of the Texas Guard and many fine state troopers, Texas Rangers and everyday Texans.

To add insult to injury, this administration, with the knowledge of some in Congress, staged paramilitary raids into Texas with the help of a foreign country and dubbed the raids Operation Santa Anna! This is complete disrespect to the people of Texas," reported Brahman.

Taking his reading glasses off, it appeared the governor was about to break from his prepared statements.

"While this crisis in Texas has loomed, very few across the United States, in other states and in Congress have actively sought to halt the unprecedented power grab and, even after being presented with overwhelming evidence of the criminal behavior of the Justice Department and the White House, have simply cowered in a mire of gridlock, impotence and self-preservation," said Brahman with disgust.

"This is not the America Texas signed up for!" he said, looking into the cameras. "If this is the America the rest of you want, so be it. But I can tell you this. There are many in Texas who want no part of it. This referendum will provide them a voice and present a direction on how Texans want us to proceed."

There were already reporters trying to interrupt to ask questions. Brahman raised his hands for quiet, indicating he wasn't done.

"Now, this president and this administration have halted banking, quarantined our ports, set up roadblocks in and out of the state, halted air traffic in and out, and have stopped federal payments to those who have earned them while they protected their cronies and federal employees.

"This president has directed the IRS to inflict undue hardships on political enemies and the businesses of those who differ from the administration politically.

"This president has anointed himself judge, jury and executioner by declaring those who participated in the legislative process and those who will vote tomorrow in the special election as enemies of the state.

"I ask all fellow Americans: since when has voting in an election or participating in the tenets of a constitutional republic become an act of treason? Never, is the answer!" he stated emphatically.

"Now, on the eve of this special election, the administration has resorted to the attempted installation of martial law. This is the act of a desperate despot. Meanwhile, this Congress sits idle, more interested in self-preservation, fearful of the administration and focused on their next election cycle. The so-called free press and media have coddled this administration and are no longer the prideful watchdogs of a free nation, but instead have morphed into a lapdog for the Left, spreading socialist propaganda and becoming a willing tool of tyranny."

Brahman paused, took a deep breath and continued. "This nation has lost its identity. It has become a secular, socialistic cesspool of self-interests. I can tell you that most Texans believe this nation is a Christian nation, founded on Christian principles by Christian men and women. We should not be surprised by the acrid smell coming from the White House.

"In the effort to be tolerant to all, government has become least tolerant to Christians, has mocked our American heroes, has perverted the Constitution and vilified those who practice free enterprise, capitalism and a free market system. They have destroyed our education system, weaving it with socialist and communist ideologies to the point where most major universities are graduating little communists," said Brahman with great intensity.

"As the rest of the nation watches Texans go to the polls tomorrow to cast their ballots in a free election, we will be watching you," said Brahman, pointing to the throngs of reporters and cameras beneath him on the steps and out onto the lawn of the capitol.

"We will go to the polls tomorrow. I recommend all Americans call their congressmen and senators and demand that this administration allow Texans to cast their ballots as free individuals. Today, it's Texas; tomorrow, it could be you!" reasoned Brahman.

"And, finally, I have a message to all Texans. We are committed to conducting this special election in a peaceful and fair manner. To that end, I would like to introduce a few folks who have managed to find their way into Texas." The people standing behind Brahman moved so that approximately twenty people could make their way to stand behind him.

"Standing behind me here are fair election monitors from the countries of Scotland, Ireland, Ukraine, South Africa and Japan. We also have a human rights coalition from the United Nations. These folks have led delegations into Texas to monitor the election process and to witness and report on any irregularities or the suppression of votes by the federal government or anyone else," declared Brahman, disclosing a strategy that the administration did not calculate.

"Now, I would like all Texans to understand that it is their right as free Texans to show up to the polling places and cast their ballots, whether for or against the referendum. It is your God-given right!

"We will do everything in our power to make this a safe day at the polls. We hereby call on President Johnson to immediately reverse his declaration of martial law and to allow the vote to proceed. The state of Texas does not recognize his authority to declare martial law or to rescind a legal election," said Brahman.

"Please pay attention to your local newspapers, the state government website and your neighbors on where to report to the polls. Because of the federal government's threats to volunteer election workers, we will not have the normal number of polling places, so you may have to travel to a polling place that is different from places where you have cast ballots in the past," he announced.

"In order to vote, you will simply need to be a registered voter and present a picture ID issued from the State of Texas, whether it is a driver's license or some other form of state-recognized identification. You will be allowed to vote from any open polling place.

"Now, my fellow Texans," Brahman said as he peered off into the vast crowd, "it is your inherent God-given right to participate in this special election. No president, no governor, no military police, no federal agents can keep you from freely casting your ballot as a free Texan. The right to conduct a free election in this state is not an issue to be decided by a criminal administration or a do-nothing Congress. It is your God-given right, and I aim to provide you the means to cast your ballots in a safe, non-partisan manner." Brahman continually shoved his index finger down on the podium as he made each point.

"I will kindly remind all Texans of the words of the great Sam Houston, who said, 'Texas has yet to learn submission to any oppression, come from what source it may'."

As Brahman folded his paper to exit from the podium, an insistent reporter yelled, "What if the president launches a military strike into Texas to prevent the vote?"

"It would be the biggest mistake the president has made in his entire term of office, which has been full of criminal acts and mistakes," replied Brahman as he exited.

# CHAPTER 49

*"Terrorism is the best political weapon, for nothing drives people harder than a fear of sudden death."*

~ *Adolf Hitler (1889-1945)*

I t was dawn on election day in Texas.

The stock market gave early signs of worry, plunging three hundred points in pre-market trading. The United Nations Security Council was convening an emergency meeting called by France and Russia an hour after polls were slated to be open. World leaders called for calm and for the administration to exercise restraint. Many churches in Texas and elsewhere opened their parishes at six a.m. in the morning for those wishing to come in and pray for a safe election day.

The federal government had a plan in place to thwart the election. The Texas governor's office had a plan of its own, determined to bring the referendum to the people. Something had to give.

Chuck Dixon met with approximately fifty of his fellow Tea Party patriots. This was the first time he recalled meeting with his fellow organizers when they were all openly armed. As was the plan, all the volunteers displayed a yellow arm band on their left upper arms, emblazoned with the famous Gadsden Flag snake, which had been adopted by most Tea Party groups. This would be an indication to state lawmen that these were volunteers and pro-Texas supporters in the event there was any confrontation with administration-friendly police, federal agents or U.S. military officials.

Dixon and his followers were assigned to four polling places, including one location in downtown Houston, which would normally have up to six in a general election. This downtown hotspot, in addition to other statewide urban polling places, would be natural targets for the administration as the city police department and county sheriff were pro-administration. The governor's office, DPS and Texas Rangers felt like the big city polling places were likely the easiest for Johnson to target and shutter.

The two polling places that had volunteered to offer their facilities for the vote were a Jewish Community Center and a Catholic church. Regular polling places in city and county facilities were not made available, so state officials had to scramble in most areas of the state for places to vote. The polling place availability was reduced by almost fifty percent. Because of this, and the threats from Johnson and the declaration of martial law, most analysts were predicting a very tiny fraction of eligible voters to turn out.

At 5:00 a.m., Dixon had his volunteers at both downtown polling places. There were approximately fifty volunteers at each site, accompanied by two Texas Rangers and approximately ten DPS troopers each. There were also various constables and off-duty sheriffs' department officials, despite the fact that the Harris County sheriff condemned the vote and announced he would not support it.

"Chuck, there was an exchange of gunfire by Texas Guard and DHS troops in that armored column near Orange on the Texas-Louisiana border. The line broke through and approximately thirty vehicles are en route on I-10, presumably headed this way!" reported one of Dixon's men.

Dixon had just been notified by a Texas Ranger that all off-duty Houston police officers had been called in the night before, including SWAT and special unit officers. Also, the Service Employees Industry Union (SEIU) were gathering at the Mickey Leland Federal Building about ten blocks from the Jewish Community Center.

"Well, this is going to get interesting in a hurry, I'm sure," said Dixon to a DPS officer standing close to him.

Just then the loud sound of two fighter jets rocketing over downtown Houston rattled buildings and windows as Dixon's group strained to catch a glimpse in the breaking dawn.

More than one Tea Party volunteer turned militiaman was probably asking himself what he had gotten himself into.

"Look!" yelled someone near the southwest corner of the center.

"That's a very good sign!" said Dixon, as he saw a small line of people against the wall arriving early and seemingly ready to vote. The small group numbered less than fifteen but, to Dixon, it was a positive sign.

The media was already out in force. The local ABC affiliate was interviewing those already in line. Dixon was nervous about that. Because of Johnson's threats, he didn't want people to turn away, but none did.

"Ma'am, can you tell me why you are here this morning?" asked the reporter, with the camera light from the cameraman shining brightly on her face.

"I'm here to vote," she said.

"But, ma'am, the president of the United States said this vote is illegal and those that participated will be tried for treason!" retorted the reporter.

"That is exactly why I'm here to vote. I am against this referendum and, given the chance, will vote against it. However, nobody, not even the president himself, can tell me I can't vote in a free election!" she stated in a very cogent manner.

As the reporter went down the line of voters, most of them stated the same indignation with being told they couldn't vote.

"But aren't you afraid you will be arrested or indicted for treason?" the reporter asked them all.

"I don't like being told what to do," said one in a cowboy hat.

"This is Texas. We don't much like folks from Washington, D.C. telling us how to run things," said another.

"It's our constitutional right. Simple as that," said a man in a business suit.

"Me and my sister are here to vote in honor of our late governor and first lady. There was no reason for them to be shot down, murdered for no good reason," said one of the women.

"That's right," said the other one.

The scene in downtown Houston began to change rapidly. Houston Police arrived three blocks away and began barricading the area, surrounding both polling sites and diverting traffic. Even if this was just a traffic control issue, it was going to make it harder for people to vote because available parking was more than three city blocks away and now nobody had access to the Jewish Center's parking lot and adjacent garage.

"Chuck, here they come!" yelled someone in Dixon's direction.

Peering down Travis Street, Dixon could see Houston Police in full riot gear with Plexiglas shields and batons marching toward them. City workers were hastily erecting barricades to stop traffic in advance of their march. When the line of police got to the barricades, they stopped and held their position.

Others were reporting FBI and ATF personnel at various corners five to seven blocks away and behind the police lines. It was apparent the polling place was going to be surrounded and nobody was going to be let through to vote.

Two blocks away, the police let a large group of SEIU union members holding signs through the barricades and they were setting up right across the street from the center. They immediately began shouting at the volunteers and everyone who seemed to be involved in organizing the polling place. There were angry shouts back and forth between the union members and those in line to vote, which had now grown to nearly fifty people.

"Traitors!" a SIEU member yelled.

"Hang 'em high!" yelled another.

"Anti-American racists!" shouted an SEIU woman.

"Communists!" roared back one of the voters to the union members.

Several SEIU members came across the street to confront voters but were turned back by DPS troopers. The Houston Police made no efforts to calm the union. It was apparent that, if crowds on both sides grew, the polling place could quickly become chaotic. The SEIU crowd was especially insulting to the Tea Party volunteers. The fact that many of them were openly carrying firearms only stoked the rage of the union members.

"We need to make a hole!" yelled Dixon to his volunteers. "Voters can't get through the barricades!"

With zero hesitation, Dixon and approximately twenty of his volunteers, a Texas Ranger and three DPS officers strolled up Travis Street toward the police barricades.

Seeing a fully armed contingent heading their direction, the Houston Police started banging their batons against their Plexiglas shields, yelling for them to stop and turn around.

"Wait here!" Dixon yelled to his followers. "Ranger Schultz, let's go!" Dixon, the Ranger and the three DPS officers continued the last block until reaching the barricades. Even though Schultz was the ranking state official at the polling place, everyone recognized Dixon as the heart and soul of the movement.

"Who's in charge here?" yelled Ranger Schultz.

"Hold on for two minutes," answered an officer. "The Chief of Police is en route and will be here."

The Houston Police officers continued to beat their batons on their shields in cadence as an armored S.W.A.T. vehicle moved into place on the corner with no less than ten fully outfitted black paramilitary police hanging on from three sides.

Shortly thereafter, an SUV pulled up and several men in dark blue uniforms stepped out, including Houston Police Chief Cletus Henry.

"Gentlemen, good morning," he said as he greeted Dixon and the four others. "You will be dealing with me this morning, gentlemen. The Harris County Sheriff's department has been kind enough to attend your events at your other polling places around the county."

"Sir, your barricades are intimidating people and preventing them from getting to the polling place down the street. We kindly ask that you make a lane for them to be able to enter and exit freely."

"Your name, sir?" the police chief asked.

"John Q. Citizen," answered Dixon semi-sarcastically as he knew that a federal arrest warrant still remained for his capture.

Ranger Schultz, fully aware of the situation, stepped in front of Dixon and introduced himself to deflect from Dixon.

"I'm Texas Ranger Schultz. Now, sir, can we get that open lane established?" He glanced at his watch." The polls will open in fifteen minutes."

"I'm under orders to shut down this polling place, gentlemen. I also have orders in my hand from a federal judge that this vote will not be recognized or carried forward."

"Under whose authority?" asked Schultz.

"The mayor of Houston," Henry barked.

"Well, sir, I'm under orders from the Governor of Texas to keep this polling place open and, furthermore, I'm under orders to make sure that this polling place is free from intimidation and voter fraud. Now, I'll ask you kindly once more for your people to make a lane. I would also direct you to move those lunatic union members another two blocks east. They cannot be intimidating voters."

"We are not allowing this polling place to open. I have my orders. This vote is illegal," said Henry. "You will remove your people, dismiss those I see in line to vote, disperse and go about your day."

"Like hell we will, sir," said Ranger Schultz defiantly.

"Schultz is the name?"

"Yep."

"This doesn't have to be this way. You folks knew this was going to be the reaction. Surely you did not think this vote was going to occur in my jurisdiction?" boasted Henry.

Schultz turned away from the chief to the rank-and-file policemen behind the barricades.

"You men better be prepared to die today. The people you see behind you are willing to lay their lives down to allow those people you see in line to exercise their constitutional right to vote. This isn't a rock concert, and it sure the hell isn't the Occupy Wall Street people. These folks have been fully deputized by the governor. You need to know that you will also be moving on fellow career law enforcement officers."

"That's very cute and a little bit romantic, Schultz," Henry chided. "I'm sure by now you are aware that federal troops are en route. They won't be as sympathetic as we are..."

Suddenly, there was some commotion fifteen yards behind the chief. About a dozen Houston police were pushing and shoving to get to the front of the barricades and moved several aside and walked toward the group speaking with the chief, who suddenly looked very confused.

As they approached, the lead officer came directly to Dixon and turned to face the chief as if he was a friend of Dixon's or Ranger Schultz.

"My name is Officer Petersen. All of us are members of Keepers of the Oath. We are sworn to uphold the Constitution of the United States and we will not enforce any unconstitutional orders. The order to close this polling place is unconstitutional; therefore, we will assist these people in keeping this polling place open!" announced the officer.

"Officer, you are immediately relieved of duty and you men have just assured yourselves of a federal arrest warrant!" yelled an indignant Henry, the veins in his neck bulging conspicuously over his crisp dark blue starched collar. "I order you to surrender your weapons, now!"

Police officers behind the barricade started yelling at the policemen who crossed the line, reprimanding them as traitors.

"No, sir, we will not surrender our weapons unless you order these men to move back three blocks and create the clear opening for voters the Ranger is requesting. If you will do that, we will gladly surrender our service weapons and our badges to you right here."

Another commotion from behind the barricades was occurring on the corner opposite where the meeting with the chief was occurring. Four ordinary men with briefcases were brought to the group by a police officer.

"Sir, these men are stating that they are poll watchers from Scotland. They demand to be taken to the polling place."

"Geez, I have no clue how you got here but, gentlemen, there will be no vote today. I'm sorry you made this trip for nothing. Go back to Scotland."

"Aye, sir. We have heard this type of bull cocky throughout Scotland's history from Great Britain. We will just remain if it's all the same to ya."

Suddenly, police officers in the barricade were yelling at someone from Dixon's group to stay back. He was holding up a small piece of paper and was running fast towards them.

"He's bringing a message. Let him continue!" yelled Schultz at everyone within shouting distance.

"I have a message from the governor," whispered the volunteer into Dixon's ear as he gasped for breath.

"Gentlemen, excuse us for a second," Dixon said to the opposing group as the chief began to wonder aloud who this civilian really was. The message was given to Dixon instead of the Ranger or the DPS officers. Henry turned to his men to ask if anyone recognized him or knew who he was.

Dixon, dressed in blue jeans, tee shirt and tennis shoes, unfolded the note. It read:

*From Governor Brahman. The Texas Attorney General's petition to fast-track a hearing to overrule the federal judge's order to stay the special election is to be ruled on by 9:00 a.m. EST. Delay all polling places opening by one hour. Vote will proceed no matter the ruling. Open the polling places at 8:00 a.m. Supreme Court ruling could trump Johnson's orders and thus diminish any threat of violence.*

"This could possibly avoid any potential conflict, but it's going to be a real challenge to delay this opening. This is a highly charged environment. I'm sure we aren't the only ones going through it," whispered Schultz after reading the note.

The pro-vote Texans were in something of a quandary. Dixon wondered to himself that, if the Supreme Court ruled in favor of the stay, how they would react? What would be the perception? The Supreme Court was not infallible, making significant ruling errors in the past that needed eventual correcting, such as slavery. Chuck knew deep in his heart that no literal interpretation of the Constitution could deny their right to hold an election.

Dixon walked back to where the chief was standing.

"Sir, we have just received communications from the governor that the Supreme Court could rule on this election by 8:00 a.m. our time. It is entirely possible the Supreme Court could allow this vote to move forward," reasoned Dixon.

"You're Chuck Dixon, aren't you?" asked the chief after a fellow officer whispered in his ear.

"I'm once again asking you to open an area where people can get through to vote. We are going to delay opening the polling place until 8:00 a.m."

"My orders are that this polling place will not open at any time!" Henry roared.

"What if the Supreme Court rules otherwise?" asked Dixon, taking a huge chance that the high court would rule in their favor. He had no idea of what the chances of a favorable ruling were. The high court had been wrong on many issues of late, in his opinion.

"Well, what if it rules it's unconstitutional? Then what?"

"I'll follow the orders I receive from Austin," answered Dixon.

"And I will follow orders from the mayor and the president," countered the chief.

Dixon, Ranger Schultz, the DPS troopers, the poll watchers and the police officers that crossed over to Dixon's camp walked fifty yards away from the chief to talk in private. Chuck couldn't help looking over his shoulder to see if they were coming for him, but the chief didn't signal anyone to arrest him.

The chief had already figured out that he could kill two birds with one stone because his officers substantially outnumbered the small volunteer force at the center. He could shut down the polling place and arrest the infamous Chuck Dixon at the same time. He could hardly wait.

In the meantime, the DHS force that had been burning up the interstate to get to Houston from Louisiana arrived and began to set up in front of the barricades. Clearly, DHS was now taking over the operation. Meanwhile, two U.S. fighters continued to buzz the downtown skyline. If there was ever a time for Dixon and his Tea Party patriots to be intimidated by this show of force, it was now.

# CHAPTER 50

*"But, when a long train of abuses and usurpations, pursuing invariably the same object, evinces a design to reduce them under absolute despotism, it is their right, it is their duty, to throw off such government, and to provide new guards for their future security."*

~ *The United States Declaration of Independence, 1776*

A t 9:02 a.m. EST, the Chief Justice of the United States Supreme Court announced the Court had set aside the stay issued by the federal judge from Texas in a contentious and bitter 5-4 ruling.

It was a narrow ruling, only commenting on the facts of how the special election was called and structured. Texas had followed the letter of the law according to their state constitution and federal election laws in calling for a special election. The court, however, did not rule on the constitutionality of the referendum and stated that this particular referendum was not the "final" act or authority for the state to issue articles of secession or separation.

When the news hit the Jewish Community Center in downtown Houston, the volunteers and Tea Party faithful went up in cheers, as did the line now stretching around three city blocks, which was estimated at three hundred people waiting to cast their ballots. Frustrations began to show across the street with the SEIU, who began a new round of hurling slurs at those at the polling place.

"Well, I guess that's it," said Houston Police Chief Henry to his lieutenants. "I'm sure we will be getting orders to pull back or simply maintain."

Within minutes of the world news channels reporting the Supreme Court ruling, President Johnson issued a statement:

"Once again, the Supreme Court has missed an opportunity to clearly and correctly provide a concise interpretation of the Constitution. This ruling in no way changes the directives issued to the State of Texas by the federal government. Texas is under martial law and this referendum is illegal, and it will not go forward. I once again appeal to the governor of Texas to shut down this attempt at a sham vote and bring Texas in line with federal law and its fellow states."

Gov. Brahman's office immediately spread the word to each and every polling location, stating: "The Supreme Court has validated this free election. The election is ON! Open the polling places."

Cheers went up from the Jewish Community Center and polling places all over the state.

Chief Henry got off his cell phone with the mayor. The mayor instructed the chief to cooperate with DHS.

The DHS armored vehicles began slowly moving from three separate locations toward the center, followed by full paramilitary DHS forces, followed by Houston Police officers. TV news helicopters were instructed to move to an area five miles outside of downtown. U.S. military fighter jets were continuing to buzz the downtown area, and two more had arrived. The fighters had been launched eighty miles southeast of Galveston Island from a U.S. aircraft carrier.

Four Texas Guard Apache helicopters stationed in Conroe, Texas, approximately forty-five miles north of Houston, slowly lifted off the tarmac of the small regional airport, with two turning south toward downtown Houston, and one headed to Galveston and one to the Bay City Nuclear Power Plant. Two more Texas Air Guard F-16 fighter jets screamed down the runway at Ellington Field, where the Texas crisis was originally lit, afterburners aglow.

Reports from across the state were a mixed bag for the governor's office. Rural and smaller cities and communities were reporting no immediate problems, but major Texas cities were another issue altogether. Similar scenarios to Houston were beginning to play out in San Antonio and Dallas. Austin's polls were open, but seas of protestors were on hand. The

Democrats and the administration had been organizing the protests. Now that the polls were officially open, the drama began to unfold.

As the DHS forces began to slowly advance down Travis Street, Tea Party patriots, DPS officers and the two Texas Rangers formed a line across the entire width of the four-lane downtown street, weapons drawn. Unable to film from helicopters, news crews were in various buildings in the two blocks surrounding the center and had great vantage points from which to witness the escalating scene.

"Chuck, what the hell do we do?" screamed one volunteer as he knelt on one knee with an AR-15 pointed at a slowly moving armored vehicle plodding toward them.

"We hold this line until everyone in line votes! We do not give up this line!" yelled Dixon. He turned to other volunteers twenty yards behind him. "Keep 'em moving. Move that line! Get them in and get their votes!"

Many of the people who voted failed to leave despite the increasing tensions. Some joined the line on Travis Street, even though they had no weapons, and began to shout at the advancing federal agents, shaking their fists at them and at the SEIU on the opposite block.

Dixon became increasingly frustrated when he would turn to look back at the center.

"What the hell are they doing in there? There's only one item to vote for! How long does that take?" he yelled at everyone and nobody in particular.

"Chuck, the line isn't getting smaller… it's getting larger!"

"What? Why?"

"Chuck, look! People are streaming in!" Ranger Schultz pointed to people coming to the center from back alleys and any hole they could find in the barricades, but mostly from walking through buildings that had not been quarantined or locked shut.

"Chief, we have a problem!" shouted a police lieutenant on the radio. "We've got some out-of-state militia here behind us!"

"What? Militia? How many and from where?"

"Sir, there's about two hundred and they're from South Carolina and Missouri! They are on our flank, sir, and they are heavily armed. We have spotted at least two .50-calibers!"

CBS News went live and reported that the president gave orders to advance military units who were poised on the Texas borders in Arkansas, Louisiana and New Mexico. But, more importantly, the military was seeing mass confusion in regimental and battalion-level commands in the officer ranks that were refusing to march into Texas.

The minority leaders of both houses of Congress called emergency sessions. World leaders were already beginning to condemn the Johnson administration for its early actions to suppress the vote. The United Nations Security Council voted to condemn the United States for its heavy-handed actions in Texas, but was vetoed by permanent Security Council members, the United States and Great Britain.

Then, finally and inevitably, the Texas crisis hit its crescendo.

The DHS troops fired tear gas and concussion grenades at the line of volunteers and law enforcement officers on Travis Street. DHS agents began marching and firing their weapons. For the next few minutes, shots rang out from both sides as bodies dropped in the streets, buildings caught fire, glass broke and grenades continued to explode. Texas was in chaos, and it was happening live for the entire world to witness.

Dixon immediately became concerned for the unarmed voters.

"Hold the line! Hold this line! We've got to get those people outta here!" as he pointed to the stunned voters in line who began to frantically disperse.

No less than Atty. Gen. Jamail Tibbs issued the orders from the situation room at the White House to advance and to use any means necessary to take the center.

"No, no, no... this is not supposed to happen!" screamed Chief Henry into his radio. "Why the hell did they start shooting at them?" he said, referring to the DHS forces.

The chief ordered the police to stand down and maintain position. Many police officers were visibly upset and very angry that the feds were indiscriminately shooting at their fellow Houstonians and Texans. Some were even yelling and screaming at DHS to stand down.

Chief Henry was extremely nervous about his flank. Those heavily-armed militia were breathing down his neck, and he was sure they had no clue that his officers were not in the immediate battle being waged. He ordered staff to immediately go to them and tell them that they would not advance on the center.

Sudden breaking news announced that Texas Guard and Militia troops had stormed twelve Minuteman nuclear intercontinental ballistic missile sites near Abilene, Texas and had gained control of all twelve sites. Neither governor had concerned themselves with these sites during the crisis until now.

Gov. Brahman, seeing President Johnson make good on his threats, raised the stakes. Surprisingly, nobody in the administration considered this scenario for a single second.

News was coming in so fast, from so many different directions, that all the networks seemed to have their own exclusive stories breaking on the suppression of the Texas vote simultaneously.

The Missouri and South Carolina militia told the Houston Police liaison to clear Travis Street so that they could engage DHS forces immediately or suffer the consequences.

Chief Henry relented, as much because of the disgust of the rank-and-file police officers on the street as his fear of the trained and well-armed militia.

Both militia groups stormed through barricades unimpeded by the Houston Police and began to engage DHS agents. Many of the Tea Party volunteers and militia at the Jewish Center fled into buildings, positioning themselves in 2nd, 3rd and 4th story windows and were in serious firefights with DHS troops.

Gov. Brahman was operating his own "situation room" from Austin with Pops Younger and the Texas Guard generals. Houston, Dallas, Texarkana and San Antonio were in skirmishes with federal agents to some extent, but Houston's was the most intense at the moment.

As bullets, tear gas and concussion grenades whirled by him, Dixon's focus shifted to the safety of the voters and securing the precious votes that had been cast. The two blocks surrounding the Jewish Community Center were a war zone.

"Get those ballot boxes!" barked Dixon to volunteers to take the votes that had been cast to a pre-planned destination. Even though the voting booths had been open for less than an hour, Dixon was determined to have those votes counted.

The Missouri and South Carolina militia ripped into the DHS troops with a vengeance. Those agents had not been warned they were being flanked. The pompous attitude of the agents in charge didn't see the need to coordinate with the Houston police chief. Why should they, when they had a direct line to the attorney general! Chief Henry had no real method to warn them.

The chief watched in shock, stunned by the efficiency of the highly organized militia.

"Look, they have four .50s…" pointed out his assistant police chief. "Sir? Sir? Do we engage?"

"No, do NOT engage!"

The .50-calibers were making quick work of the armored vehicles. Many agents began running into nearby buildings or surrendering, throwing their weapons down to the advancing militia.

Two light battalions of the Texas Militia were advancing in parallel from Milam Street. DHS forces were suddenly outnumbered and outmatched.

The two fighter jets launched from Ellington were making a beeline to the U.S. aircraft carrier and its support ships in the Gulf. The fighters that were buzzing downtown had bugged out to engage the Texas fighters before they could launch their deadly missiles on the carrier. The two Texas Apaches were now moving in and out of sight of the Jewish Community Center.

The scene on the ground was so hectic that the Apaches had no clear shot on DHS troops. Even the exposed armored vehicles were too close to Texas Guard militia and Tea Party volunteers to use any weaponry. The choppers continued to scour the outskirts of downtown for any DHS reinforcements or U.S. military troops.

The Texas Guard generals were outflanking Washington and the Joint Chiefs. Brahman's plan all along was to take the offensive and hit Johnson with surprises he never expected. He needed enough distractions to allow the vote to go forward. So far, Johnson and Tibbs definitely had unplanned contingencies to deal with.

Chuck was still herding people out of the area as skirmishes continued to break out within a four-block area. He had successfully gotten most of the voters out of the center and had helped load the electronic ballot boxes into a van, which screamed out of the alley, cut across a concrete basketball court, clipping a fence but managing to escape with the votes that had been cast before the violence broke out.

The number of shots being heard was rapidly decreasing. As Chuck ran through the first floor of the Jewish Center, he rounded a corner next to an escalator and came to an immediate and painful stop.

Lying on the floor was a young woman with two gaping bullet wounds and lying in a pool of blood. She was gasping for air, but was still alive. She had a flag attached to a homemade flag pole that looked as if it was made from a broom handle.

"I need a doctor! We need a doctor here! Somebody call 9-1-1!" Nobody was listening, as the scene was still too hot. The woman, who he guessed to be nineteen or twenty years old, grasped Chuck's hand with her left hand, but would not let go of the crude flag pole.

"Damn it! I need a doctor!" he continued to scream as he tried to apply pressure to the wounds.

She was dying—quickly.

"Sweetheart, what is your name? You're going to be okay," he lied.

The young woman tried to speak, but was aspirating badly. Blood was also streaming from her mouth. She was desperately trying to tell Chuck something.

"Hang on, sweetheart. We'll get someone here to help you soon," Chuck said to her as he tried to hold back his tears.

She continued to try to speak. Chuck thought maybe she was trying to tell him her name. He lowered himself to get very close to her face to try to hear her over the noise of the chaos that was still intermittent on Travis Street.

"Yes, honey?"

She let go of the tight grip she had on his hand and tried to lift her arm. At first, Chuck wasn't sure what she was trying to communicate. Her arm and hand were blood-soaked. But, underneath the blood, on the back of her hand, Chuck saw it. Covered with blood but still stuck to her hand was a little white sticker that read: "I voted."

"I'm so proud of you, honey! You're going to be okay," said Chuck. He could no longer hold back his tears, as he tried to move her dark chestnut hair out of her face.

She was still trying to speak. Chuck again lowered his head to her face to try to hear her name.

"I… I.. I love… love Texas," she managed in a barely audible whisper. Then she gasped, and her arms shook slightly as she died.

"Oh, God, no… Oh, God. You poor thing. Oh, God! Noooo!" he sobbed.

Gunshots were still ringing in the street and occasionally still in the building. A round that hit the escalator barely ten feet above his head startled Chuck back to reality.

He rose up and looked at the young woman once more, then reached over and closed her eyelids. Then he noticed she still gripped the flagpole lying in the blood.

He picked up the improvised flagpole and saw the Texas flag, mostly drenched in blood. On the white bar, stitched boldly in red letters, was the number "1789."

The young girl had taken it upon herself to make her own statement. She had defied the order not to vote and, in protest, stitched "1789" on the Lone Star Flag, the year the United States Constitution was ratified. This young girl had simply wanted her government to follow her Constitution and allow her to cast a vote. Like the heroes at the Alamo, she was making her own personal statement to return to the Constitution. And, like those heroes, she was killed for it.

It took just ten seconds for this to set in for Chuck.

Chuck set down his rifle, and used both hands to carry the blood-slippery handle. He began walking to the Travis Street entrance, then he slowly began to run. The glass doors had already been completely shattered. He ran out of the building, onto the plaza in front of the building, his clothes soaked in the young girl's blood. He began waving the flag and screaming to anyone who would listen.

"YOU KILLED A GIRL FOR VOTING! DO YOU HEAR ME, YOU SONS OF BITCHES? I SAID YOU KILLED A YOUNG GIRL WHO SIMPLY VOTED! THIS IS HER BLOOD! DO YOU HEAR ME? YOU— UGH..."

Suddenly Chuck's chest exploded, ripped by bullets from the corner building. Chuck looked briefly confused, but tried to wave the flag higher. Then he was again hit by another round in his right thigh.

Chuck stumbled forward onto his knees, landing face first against one of the six large concrete planters in front of the building. The planter held Chuck in an awkward position, but the broom-handle flagpole was wedged between him and the planter. The flag furled and covered most of Chuck's body.

Modern-day Texas hero Chuck Dixon died within seconds, holding the young girl's blood-soaked flag. Within minutes, the entire world witnessed this heroic but disturbing image of Election Day in Texas.

# CHAPTER 51

*"We view ourselves on the eve of battle. We are nerved for the contest, and must conquer or perish. It is vain to look for present aid: none is at hand. We must now act or abandon all hope! Rally to the standard, and be no longer the scoff of mercenary tongues! Be men, be free men, that your children may bless their father's name. But, when a long train of abuses and usurpations, pursuing invariably the same object, evinces a design to reduce them under absolute despotism, it is their right, it is their duty, to throw off such government, and to provide new guards for their future security."*

*~ General Sam Houston (1793-1863)*
*Hero of the Battle of San Jacinto*
*First President of the Republic of Texas*

Images of Chuck Dixon began hitting the world news by 10:45 a.m. Most of the violence being broadcast was located in Houston, Dallas, San Antonio and Austin.

In Austin, Gov. Brahman became physically ill upon seeing the video of Chuck Dixon being shot; it had been captured live by CNN cameras. Before excusing himself to the rest room to throw up, the governor barked out orders to a staffer to immediately reach the safe house where Christy Dixon was moved before she and her son could see the pictures or video streaming from almost every news site.

When the governor came back into the large room, he seemed to have a new level of intensity, which was saying something since he was commonly known to be intense anyway. The room, proud and defiant a few minutes before, had the wind knocked out of it as staff and state officials watched the very likeable and popular Dixon gunned down, his body wrapped in a bloody Texas flag and propped up by a concrete planter.

"Jeff, what are these scenes in Houston and elsewhere doing to us throughout the state?" asked the governor, wondering aloud if the carnage was keeping voters away.

"I won't have the new numbers until the top of the hour, but this can't be good," said Weaver.

"Why hasn't the military moved? What is his next move?" asked the governor.

"Sir, we are getting reports that there is serious dissension in the troops. We are being told there are conflicting orders. Some aren't willing to move on another state or fellow Americans. There is a slight crack in the chain of command, it appears!" yelled Brig. Gen. Sterling, smiling wryly.

"Where's our fighters in the Gulf?"

"They've peeled off from the route to the carrier as planned, but the Navy jets are on their tails. At least we pulled them out of Houston," answered Sterling.

What the governor and his staff couldn't know was that the live images being carried on television and the Internet were having an effect on Texans, but not the effect Gov. Brahman expected and certainly not the effect the administration intended.

Texans were outraged. They were leaving their work, homes and schools and migrating to polling places en masse.

In College Station, Texas, the home of Texas A&M University, the school cancelled classes so those eligible to vote could. The nearest polling place, in Bryan just a few miles away, was moved to the A&M campus by 11:00 a.m. to accommodate more voters. Schools and businesses around the state followed, but the mainstream media was reporting school closings because of the isolated cases of violence in the major cities.

"Governor!" screamed a staffer. "I've got various polling places calling in saying they're overwhelmed with lines stretching around their polling places and some saying they have a two- or more-hour wait!" she said proudly.

Cheers went up in the governor's makeshift situation room.

"Thank God!" exclaimed Brahman.

The joy was short-lived as casualty reports began coming in, especially from Dallas and Houston.

"Governor, sir, we have unconfirmed reports of at least eighty dead in Dallas and some number that will eclipse two hundred in Houston. I have no idea at this point if they are voters, feds or Texas Guard troops," Brig. Gen. Sterling reported somberly.

"I hope Texas remembers," said Texas Atty. Gen. Weaver.

"Texans never forget. That's either our curse or one of our best attributes, I'm not really sure which," replied the governor.

Meanwhile, the president and key members of his cabinet were in the situation room, which was adorned with snacks, drinks and party favors as if they were sitting down to watch the Super Bowl. However, it was clear their team was being outscored. What began as an apparent victory for President Johnson in shutting down the Texas election suddenly started to show that momentum was shifting.

The Joint Chiefs were all in attendance and suddenly all eyes turned to Chairman Herrera.

"General, why are our military troops not moved from the checkpoints? Where the hell are they? Houston needs them NOW!" yelled Tibbs.

The members of the Joint Chiefs from each branch of the military sat in chairs against the wall behind Herrera. They looked down toward the floor as Herrera was berated in front of all.

"Mr. President, what we had not guessed or planned for was the resistance of our troops to initiate hostilities against another state. We have widespread acts of conscience hurting our ability to maneuver and operate. Even in the officers' ranks, it has disrupted our chain of command," Herrera admitted.

Both Johnson and Tibbs were incensed. Neither had served in the military and neither had much regard for the military. To both, the military was a tool to advance their political agenda.

"Fix it! I mean fix it now! Are you telling me that troops are going AWOL, that they are committing treason and are refusing to obey orders?" asked the president.

"Mr. President, if I may?" said the Marine Corps Commandant, which irritated Herrera as he considered this speaking out of turn.

"Texans represent the highest percentage of enlisted Marines and it's not even close, sir. Regardless of any plan to invoke hostilities on a sovereign state and the constitutionality of such an action, this plan was flawed from the standpoint that Texans are simply not going to fire on fellow Texans, much less whether Americans will fire upon fellow Americans," said the commandant stiffly.

Tibbs turned to glare at Herrera, with a look for the ages.

"Why the hell wasn't this considered?" demanded Tibbs.

"Mr. President, this concern was raised in various meetings with some of you present but, as events transpired, we simply did not have the time or resources to cull out every Texan from the units without either tipping our hand or maintaining combat readiness," replied Herrera.

"Sir, the Keepers of the Oath are also playing a large part," continued the commandant, to the visible dismay of Herrera.

"What the hell are you talking about?" demanded the president.

"Sir, many have taken an additional oath not to obey or follow orders that one considers unconstitutional," answered the commandant.

"They will be shot by firing squad!" roared Tibbs.

"Mr. President, in light of the fact that I have also taken this oath, I hereby tender my resignation."

"Resignation? You are refusing to obey a direct order to launch troops into Texas? That is treason, commandant. We will have you shot, too!" screamed Tibbs, veins popping out on his neck as he jumped up from his chair.

"Mr. President, I also offer my resignation," said the vice admiral flatly.

One by one, each member of the Joint Chiefs offered their resignations, turned and saluted Herrera and the president, and walked out of the situation room.

"Arrest them!" yelled Tibbs to his staff members as the Joint Chiefs left the room. The staff scurried with Secret Service agents and senior FBI officials as they met the military professionals on the first floor and placed them under arrest.

"General, you better get your act together and get these plans back on track in a heartbeat!" said the president ominously.

"Yes, sir," said Herrera as he left the room with his staff to try to re-establish some semblance of chain of command to re-implement the game plan.

"Mr. President, reports are coming in that voter turn-out in rural and small towns in Texas began with light turnout, but are now very heavy," said an astonished Avery Smith.

"Damn, Avery. I know we couldn't shut down every polling place. It sure would have helped to have the military rolling by now, but it's not too late. Hell, it's not even noon there yet, is it?"

"No, sir. Let's hope Herrera can get the plan back on track. We do have one contingency, sir, and I'll be happy to go over that with you now," said Smith as he began to lay out the back-up plan.

By mid-day, world leaders were expressing a wide range of responses to the escalation of violence resulting from the United States federal government's attempt to suppress the special election vote being held in Texas.

Responses ranged from outrage to regret. Even some of the United States' allies were issuing strongly worded condemnations of the Johnson administration. There simply was not a country or ally wherein the U.S. had a better relationship since Johnson took office than the U.S. had before his election, with the possible exception of Mexico. Johnson's amnesty orders and refusal to deport Mexican nationals had endeared him to Mexico City, which favor was returned by the Mexicans' cooperation in *Operation Santa Anna*.

Fox News was the first to report that the Joint Chiefs had been arrested in the White House. The White House would neither confirm nor deny the reports. When Johnson learned of the report, he was incensed; there had to be a leak in the West Wing. Even the Navy recalled its fighters to the carriers positioned in the Gulf.

Fox also reported that Johnson was planning a large-scale military invasion of Texas. Even some of Johnson's most ardent supporters in Congress began to waver and openly question the end game and the violence. Top Democratic leadership in Congress had been assured that the administration could shut down the election without such a drastic measure. Only the most liberal wing of the Party was open to such a strategy, and many couldn't wait to punish Texas and the fundamental Conservative ideology deeply rooted in Texas culture.

By 3:00 p.m. CST, the state had beaten back attempts to shut down polling places. Even where the administration had been successful in closing a polling place, another would pop up within an hour near where the first had closed. Tibbs referred to the mobility of the polling places as "cockroaches." Some of the polling places were simply large RVs that could be moved quickly. Volunteers using two-way radios coordinated their movements and many were assigned to educate voters where to go once administration-friendly police departments or sheriffs dispersed them.

News reports were picking up a trend at polling places all over Texas. Voters were showing up with Texas flags with "1789" written on the white bar in red letters to honor the young unnamed girl and Chuck Dixon.

Gen. Herrera reported back to the president that the original plan was not possible in the original time frame. His officer corps was fractured and the news of the arrest of the Joint Chiefs had alarmed senior officers, who already did not trust this president.

Casualty reports continued to scroll across every news broadcast on the bottom of the screen, updated like a ticker symbol from Wall Street. Governors, especially in the south and mountain west regions, were outraged and began again calling for Johnson's impeachment.

The White House received the news that Austin, San Antonio, Houston and Dallas polling places were secured for the governor. DHS, the FBI, ATF and various other agencies that had seen weaponry build-up in the Johnson administration had been turned back or defeated at the hands of the Texas Guard, Texas Militia, volunteer militia from out of state, and Tea Party volunteers.

Without military intervention, Johnson's strategy was failing. Even the police departments in Texas friendly to the administration were neutered simply by overwhelming numbers or the lack of fortitude.

Now, Texans who had no plans to vote in the special election were either inspired or compelled to cast their ballots by the actions of the Johnson administration. By late afternoon, Texans were overwhelming polling places wherever they could find them.

The wheels were coming off for Johnson, Smith and Tibbs. Johnson and his minions had doubled-down on their bet that they could scare the people of Texas away from the polls. Their strategy was backfiring.

But they had one last option...

# CHAPTER 52

*"... and by Authority of the good People of these Colonies, solemnly publish and declare, That these United Colonies are, and of Right ought to be Free and Independent States; that they are Absolved from all Allegiance to the British Crown, and that all political connection between them and the State of Great Britain, is and ought to be totally dissolved; and that as Free and Independent States, they have full Power to levy War, conclude Peace, contract Alliances, establish Commerce, and to do all other Acts and Things which Independent States may of right do."*

*~ The United States Declaration of Independence, 1776*

The finger-pointing in the situation room over the apparent failure to stop the election in Texas was brutal, as blame was being dished out to everyone by the president. He suddenly realized the debacle that had become the Texas crisis was a very real and present danger for his presidency.

"Ladies and gentlemen, whatever your contingency plan was, it better be implemented now. Despite all of your plans, these yahoos just had an election!" said the president sarcastically.

"Mr. President, we have our people in place," answered Gen. Herrera.

"Is this Seal Team Six?" asked the president.

"No, sir. This is a crack team of U.S. Army Special Forces that is fully capable," answered Herrera.

DHS Director McDermott cringed. She knew Johnson's next question was coming.

"Why not Seal Team Six? They have been successful at every mission we have given them," he asked.

"Sir, Seal Team Six has a very high concentration of native Texans," Herrera answered quickly.

"Does everyone understand this is our last shot to shut down and take control of this illegal election?" snapped Johnson, who looked like he had aged ten years in the span of one day.

"Failure is not an option here. Everyone better fully understand that," said Avery Smith who, more than anyone, knew the political damage the president was suffering today. He knew the failure to stop Texas' election after this much effort could be a failure the president could not survive politically.

"Pops, General, what are your thoughts here?" asked the governor. "It's been several hours since we have seen any new developments from them. Surely this morning's failures aren't sitting well in the White House!"

"It would appear the military options are gone. Reports are surfacing everywhere that the Joint Chiefs were arrested. Johnson's military leadership is in revolt. The word I'm getting from my contacts who are career military is there is a total breakdown in the chain of command, morale is low and there is some paralysis regarding which orders to follow," said Brig. Gen. Sterling.

"Are we safe then from that threat?" asked Brahman.

"We need to remain on guard, but I'm optimistic," answered the general.

"Pops, you are standing over there with something on your mind. What do you think?" asked the governor.

"I think those damned folks are evil. I just believe he's got one more ace somewhere," announced Younger.

"What do you think it is?"

"Well, he obviously can't stop the election. The polls close in two hours. That bird flew the coop about one today." Pops spit some chew into a paper cup, then rubbed his large, bushy handlebar mustache with his sleeve.

"What would he do now?" asked Weaver with a curious look on his face.

"If the sum' bitch can't stop it, he'll probably try to steal it," suggested Pops.

Nobody knew exactly what Pops meant at first.

"How would someone go about stealing this election?" asked the governor.

"It's too late to alter the outcome. The votes will all be cast in less than two hours," Sterling remarked.

Everyone turned back to Pops, who seemed to be enjoying everyone's puzzled look.

"Well, if'n it were me, I'd just steal the damn thing," Pops said again.

"Okay, Pops, how's he going to do this?" repeated the governor.

"He can't stop it. So my bet is he tries to steal the results," answered Pops, followed by another spit of tobacco into his cup.

Still, not everyone in the situation room got it for a few seconds.

"Holy crap, Governor. He's right!" shrieked Weaver as he jumped to his feet.

"Somebody please share with us how he would do this. I still don't get it," said Brahman, who was becoming slightly anxious.

"Where is the central collection point to tally all votes from the precincts? It's on Brazos Street two blocks from here at the secretary of state's offices!" answered Weaver.

"They're gonna steal the ballots? Most of the voting is with electronic machines? I don't get it," pressed the governor.

"They'll either take the systems or destroy them onsite," said Weaver.

"What good will that do them? The results are still stored at the precinct level," said the governor.

"It will either be covert, through the NSA, or they will attempt to physically take down the systems onsite," said Sterling.

It didn't take too much explanation for the governor to react. He immediately turned to his staff. "Do not have the precincts report as normal. We need to come up with another reporting method. We need to assume the NSA has hacked the secretary of state's systems. We don't have much time. The central repository for votes needs to be changed. Does everyone understand what I am stating here? Pops, what else do we need to do?"

"Well, sir, knowing that Tibbs is a vindictive little sum' bitch, I would say he is either going to take one last run at you, or us in here, or he's going to think the election results will be counted there on Brazos," surmised Younger.

Sixteen U.S. Army Rangers and four CIA operatives had made their way into Texas dressed as oilfield workers, with heavy trucks and equipment that appeared to be headed to the south Texas oilfields.

Poised forty-five minutes northeast of Austin near Taylor, Texas, the elite unit had been onsite for three days and were being hosted by a small rancher friendly to the administration. At 6:00 p.m., four heavy trucks were headed down the caliche ranch road to the gate, throwing up a large column of white dust, and headed for Austin.

The polls closed as planned at 7:00 p.m. Texas had its election, but at a price. Casualty reports were still fluid and the non-stop coverage of the special election by worldwide news organizations was entering a new stage.

The day's events brought new concerns to America. The fact that Texas had apparently succeeded in having an election despite the administration's efforts to prevent it made the president look weak and foolish. Now, reports of his Joint Chiefs being arrested created all kinds of potential problems. Intense speculation ran the gamut of: Was there an attempted coup? Why would the executive branch arrest its sitting Joint Chiefs? It was looking more and more like Washington was operating like a Banana Republic.

World leaders were denouncing the day's events and more than one expressed deep concern that Texas now possessed the Minuteman nuclear silos near Abilene.

In D.C., the political rats began jumping ship mid-day. There were new calls for impeachment by Republicans. Many Democrats were disavowing the strategy to bring Texas in line publicly, but behind the scenes had been solidly behind the president.

Poll watchers from the United Nations and other countries were quick to point out that the only anomalies in the election were caused by the administration and that Texas carried out the election fairly but crudely, due to the circumstances it was put in.

Throughout the day, media outlets continued to show the video or picture of Chuck Dixon propped against the concrete planter with the bloody Lone Star Flag stitched with "1789."

Of the countless interviews across the state by the media, it was apparent that this single event may have turned the tide in the election turn-out. Many Texans claimed to be concerned about the president's edicts, but the attempt to forcefully prevent the vote clearly angered them. If that wasn't enough to get them to risk voting, the death of Chuck Dixon enraged them.

The world anxiously awaited voting results. By 8:00 p.m., a full hour after the polls had closed everywhere in Texas except El Paso, neither the governor's office nor the secretary of state's office had released any vote tabulations.

★   ★   ★

Four large oilfield service trucks were parked within two blocks of the five-story Texas Secretary of State building on Brazos Street in Austin, which was two blocks from the capitol building.

The offices were fully lit, with a hub of activity inside, and DPS troopers stood guard at each of the three entrances. But there was nothing that looked daunting to the Special Forces unit. Their mission was simple. Enter the building and destroy all the voting records, computers, communications lines, servers and turn the building to rubble.

Much like other scandals of this administration, Tibbs, Smith and the president believed they were fully capable of controlling any resulting message through the media and that message would be that the Texans destroyed its own records to cover up the fact that the referendum vote had failed. There was a follow-up plan by the administration to deal with each county and precinct votes, and it was diabolical.

Suddenly, gunfire erupted just north of the capitol grounds. As DPS and Rangers rushed to the scene, Texas Guard troops were celebrating and high-fiving each other. In the street lay a large drone about the size of a riding lawn mower, with a DHS emblem barely legible in the twisted metal. The drone had been shot down by Guard troops from a nearby rooftop.

The burnt orange sunset to the west of Austin had finally sunk into darkness as the Special Forces unit readied themselves and got into their gear in the large trucks. The navigation officer indicated he had lost communication with the drone for some reason. They checked their weapons, communications systems, night vision and ammo supplies. They had received word from Langley. The president was concerned election results would begin being broadcast. Drone or no drone, it was go time.

The plan was for the trucks to circle the block, each truck to stop at one of the four corners on the block and take out any DPS or Texas Guard, then enter the building, move employees to a central area out of the building, then take out the systems, set the charges and evacuate. This was supposed to take all of eighteen minutes.

The lead truck started his diesel engine, confirmed the other three trucks were ready, and turned his headlights on.

The Army captain who was driving the truck looked through the front windshield as he was about to put the truck in gear.

"What the h..." he muttered as the rest looked forward.

"Who the hell is that?" said another in a loud whisper.

Standing in the headlights was a figure right out of a Larry McMurtry novel.

Illuminated by dim street lamps and the headlights of the truck was a tall, lean man with a cowboy hat, cowboy boots, twin holsters with a western blazer pulled back to reveal two Colt .45s with pearl handles.

Pops Younger was standing in front of the truck, less than twenty yards away, smoking a huge cigar!

Pops drew a large intake from the cigar and let out a large billow of smoke as he spread his feet apart shoulder width as if ready to drop his cigar and draw down on the truck in a heartbeat with both revolvers.

"Is that that damn cowboy from the Laredo bridge?" asked a lieutenant.

"Arrow One, what's the delay?" came the radio message in the ears of the front truck.

"We have a problem," said the captain.

In the same instant, the four trucks became bathed in spotlights coming from all directions, including the roof tops of other buildings as Texas Guard troops, appearing out of nowhere, rushed in and surrounded the trucks at gun point..

"We've been made. Radio Langley. Mission aborted," snarled the captain.

Pops continued to stay at the same spot, determined to finish his cigar, as he was being fully entertained by the scene in front of him. The Guard emptied the trucks as the Army Rangers and CIA operatives surrendered.

Finally, Pops walked over to the men who were shackled and lined up against the trucks.

"Which one of you Yankee boys is the communications officer?"

"I am," said the shortest one in the unit, who was barely 5'6."

"Well, you're a little sawed-off sum' bitch, ain't ya?" laughed Pops. "Who ya'll reportin' to, son?" he asked.

"Langley, sir," came the reply.

"Well, son, git them boys on the line for me," Pops instructed.

A Guardsman brought out his headset, and released the prisoner's handcuffs. The officer connected with Langley and handed the headset to Pops. Pops looked at the headset, not sure what to do with it. He wasn't about to take his cowboy hat off to use it.

"Does this contraption have a speaker?" he asked.

The officer reached over and flipped a switch to a speaker position.

"Hello, Arrow One, do you copy? This is Langley," said the voice from the speaker.

"Howdy, up there in Langley. This is Pops Younger with the Texas Rangers. We've got your boys here. They seem to be involved in some type of malfeasance. We need some type of forwarding address so we can send their personal effects," said Pops.

For a brief moment, there was no response.

"This is the Assistant Director of the CIA. What is your intent with these men?" he asked.

"Well, sir, in Texas, we used to hang people for stealing horses or cattle. I can't say I'm quite up to speed on the law for someone trying to steal an election, but I'm sure they'll git what's comin' to 'em," Pops said in his unmistakable Texas drawl.

"Sir…"

"Son, can you git a message to the president?" asked Pops.

"Well, yes, I can…"

"Can you get these instructions exact, by God?"

"Yes, I'm writing this down."

"Tell him this," said Pops. "Tell him this exactly."

"Tell him what?"

"Don't mess with Texas, ever!"

At ten minutes before midnight, Gov. Brahman walked to a crowded podium in the historic rotunda of the Texas State Capitol.

"Today is a historic day for Texas. Despite cowardly federal military incursions by the federal government of the United States, orchestrated by the president and attorney general, Texas held a free election.

"It is also a sad day for America. Today the world witnessed modern-day tyranny by a government that no longer considers the Constitution the sacred document it is and a general populace that has lost the sense of who they are as a country."

Brahman now appeared to be fighting back tears.

"I am also sad to report that Texans lost their lives today simply trying to conduct a free election or by simply standing in line to cast their ballots.

"Today, 189 fellow Texans lost their lives. Despite the threats from this president, they risked everything simply to exercise their God-given right to cast a ballot in a free election in what is supposed to be a Constitutional Republic," decried Brahman as he struggled, tears rolling down his cheeks.

A small murmur went through the huge throng of supporters crammed into the rotunda.

"And, yes, that number is significant and should not be lost on anyone. That is the same number attributed to the brave Texians who died that March day in 1836 at the Alamo. We shall never forget either sacrifice.

"Before I disclose the vote totals, I want to reiterate that poll watchers from the U.N. and numerous countries participated in this election when they weren't being shot at by federal agents. None reported, let me repeat, none reported any irregularities. They also participated in the tabulation of the ballots," claimed the governor.

Taking a deep breath, Brahman built up the drama. "With one hundred percent of the precincts reporting and all votes tabulated, the referendum passed with a vote of 78 percent to 22 percent," he announced proudly.

The rotunda erupted in chaos. Cheers went up as reporters tried to exit the rotunda to get the news out to the world. Brahman tried to continue, but the next four minutes made it impossible.

Finally, the governor continued. "This vote is a resounding message to me and the Texas Legislature. Tomorrow, I will call another special session of the Legislature to formulate and draft terms of separation with the United States. The people of Texas will have one more opportunity to vote and approve these final terms of separation," explained Brahman.

Again, the governor was interrupted by cheers, reporters asking questions, and noise in the rotunda.

"This vote should also be a resounding message to the rest of the United States. This is simply the will of the people of Texas. We will not succumb to outdated and incorrect interpretations of law regarding the right of Texans to abolish their current form of government and establish what works for them. I would encourage Americans everywhere to work to fix Washington and not to fixate on Texas," Braymer said defiantly.

"God bless the re-born Republic of Texas!"

By 9:00 a.m. the next morning, Scotland had announced it was recognizing the Republic of Texas' sovereignty and welcomed them as a nation. Scotland was soon followed by Ukraine and France.

Pressed hard by their constituents, formal impeachment proceedings were gaining popularity, with the GOP announcing it had the votes for impeachment.

The state legislatures in South Carolina, Oklahoma, Georgia, Missouri and Alabama signaled that they were drafting legislation that mirrored the Texas referendum.

Jamail Tibbs was arrested leaving the White House by Alexandria, Virginia police after the local district attorney issued a warrant for his arrest relating to the "whistleblower" Spilner couple's deaths. For all his efforts to see the governor of Texas do the "perp" walk, Tibbs did his own for the entire world to see.

The girl who died at the bottom of the escalators in Chuck Dixon's arms was a nineteen-year-old student at the University of Houston named Amanda Flores. Her stitched "1789" flag sits among the most famous flags in Texas history.

Gov. Brahman and Pops Younger traveled to the suburbs of Austin the next morning to pay their respects to Christy and Colton Dixon.

Sitting in the living room with the little family, the governor turned to Colton. "Son, your dad was a true Texas patriot. He was as brave as Travis, Crockett, Houston or Bowie. His name will be forever linked with freedom, liberty and justice. I want you to know that Pops and I had the greatest respect for him. Without your dad, Texas would never have had this election and we wouldn't be free today."

"I've seen TV programs that say Texans committed treason. Is that true?" asked young Colton.

"Son, one man's treason is another man's patriot," answered Pops, not fully sure if Colton understood.

"They say Texas is A State of Treason," said Colton.

Pops adjusted his cowboy hat, smoothed over his handlebar mustache and pondered Colton's comment for a few seconds, then smiled.

"Son, Texans wouldn't have it any other way!"

*"I have said that Texas is a state of mind, but I think it is more than that. It is a mystique closely approximating a religion. And this is true to the extent that people either passionately love Texas or passionately hate it and, as in other religions, few people dare to inspect it for fear of losing their bearings in mystery or paradox. But I think there will be little quarrel with my feeling that Texas is one thing. For all its enormous range of space, climate, and physical appearance, and for all the internal squabbles, contentions, and strivings, Texas has a tight cohesiveness perhaps stronger than any other section of America. Rich, poor, Panhandle, Gulf, city, country, Texas is the obsession, the proper study, and the passionate possession of all Texans."*

*~ John Steinbeck (1902-1968)*
*Pulitzer Prize Winning Author*
*Author of "The Grapes of Wrath"*

# About the Author

Early in his life growing up in San Antonio, Texas, David Thomas Roberts made regular trips to The Alamo with visiting family, friends, and schoolmates. The story of The Alamo, the spirit of all its Texian Heroes, and the fight for Texas independence left an indelible impression on him that has endured a lifetime. As a "naturalized" Texan, Roberts has become a staunch defender and admirer of all things Texas, including the Republic's rich history of fierce independence, self-reliance, liberty, unique history, culture and people. Roberts is a serial entrepreneur and CEO of a technology firm he founded and owns several businesses. He is active in politics and is an accomplished public speaker. Roberts lives in Montgomery, Texas—the birthplace of the Lone Star flag—with his wife of thirty-plus years. Together, they have four grown children and one grandchild, all of whom have been blessed to have been born "Native Texans."